THE
DROWNING
PLACE

SW KANE

THOMAS & MERCER

Text copyright © 2023 by S W Kane

Published by Thomas & Mercer, Seattle

www.apub.com

Amazon, the Amazon logo, and Thomas & Mercer are trademarks of Amazon.com, Inc., or its affiliates.

ISBN-13: 9781542020060
eISBN: 9781542020053

Cover design by Dominic Forbes
Cover image: © CreativeZone / Shutterstock;
© Guy Corbishley / Alamy Stock Photo

Printed in the United States of America

*In memory of Pancho Villa,
my brindle bandit*

CHAPTER 1

Jason Roye, who had disappeared from the Grasmere Housing Estate several decades ago – and who some thought had killed his best friend, Kevin Shires – was currently asleep in Vernon Reid's spare room. Reid was creeping around his own council flat in the hope he wouldn't wake his guest, who'd appeared like a ghost from the past the previous night. At first, Reid had thought he was hallucinating. His flashbacks had been getting worse recently – brought on by the demolition of the flats adjacent to his block – and for a moment or two Reid had genuinely thought the figure on his doorstep had been another manifestation of his increasingly fragile mental state. But Jason was real. As real as he had been all those years ago on the day he and Kevin disappeared.

In the dim hallway, Reid put on his coat and as quietly as he could, which was difficult with the multiple locks, opened his front door and slipped out on to the communal balcony, gently pulling the door shut behind him. He began walking to the main stairwell, passing through the polytunnel he'd erected over the walkway. The early morning sun had warmed the makeshift greenhouse, and he looked over his plants distractedly as he went, not stopping to check the young seedlings as he usually would. He'd told Jason he could stay one night, two at the most, but he wanted him gone by the end of the weekend. Reid wasn't good with other people in confined spaces. It wasn't that he didn't want Jason there – he didn't want anyone there.

Reaching the stairwell, he began the ten-storey descent to ground level on foot. The lift still worked, although the word 'worked' was being generous; it went up and down. It didn't always stop, and if it did the doors didn't always open. For as long as he'd lived on Grasmere the lifts had had a mind of their own, fuelling the urban legends that abounded about the estate. Before Reid had even left primary school he was aware of the rumour that the erratic lifts were a result of the dead trying to push their way up from below, losing momentum and sinking back down – the daisy pushers, as they'd become known after a spate of fatal falls. Reid clearly recalled, as a child, adults whispering in corners as he went to school: *the daisy pushers have been at work again*. What they meant was some poor devil had thrown themselves off one of the communal balconies, or one of the many walkways that connected the labyrinthine housing development. Not all the falls were suicide; some people had actually been pushed off on purpose. It was that kind of place. Drug deals gone wrong. Domestic disputes. Gang rivalry. All often ended in violence, and the geography of the estate proved an efficient weapon.

The stairwell felt cold and damp after the warmth of the polytunnel and Reid upped his pace. There had been no heating on since February – it was now April – and the building had become a vast cold-storage unit. In the past, when the estate was still functioning, the heating had always been on, even in summer. It was little wonder it used to see a spike in domestic violence during the hottest months; the residents were roasting alive, fractious and deprived. Now their numbers were almost down to single figures the council deemed it a waste to heat an entire estate for the sake of the last few tenants, so had turned it off completely.

Reaching the ground floor, he exited the block of flats just as a huge piece of masonry came crashing down on the adjacent building site, and he felt his stomach clench and sweat break out on his face. He fought back the images that threatened to flood his mind and watched as dust rose up from behind the hoardings like a mushroom cloud of bad memories. He could see the top of an excavator pick at a piece of stubborn concrete that was still clinging on. It made him feel nauseous to watch, like a wound being constantly picked at, so shoving his hands deep in his pockets, he hurried across the cracked tarmac of what had once been the children's playground and towards the trees that lay at the heart of the estate.

The trees formed what everyone referred to as 'the woods'. The development had been built around the two-acre plot, and under the shelter of the broad branches Reid felt himself relax a little. He often came here when he felt he was drowning. The estate frequently had that effect – not just on him, but on other residents too – the feeling of being dragged down, unable to surface. Life on Grasmere was like existing in a living thing that could swallow you up at a moment's notice. As he walked deeper into the greenery he contemplated his conversation with Jason the previous night.

He was so lost in thought he hadn't realised he'd veered off his usual route and on to one of the smaller paths that criss-crossed the woods. Something caught his eye to the left and he stopped to peer through the branches. A rudimentary tent had been erected with an old piece of tarpaulin hung across the lower boughs. This must be where Jason had spent the night before he'd come knocking at his door. He moved nearer for a closer look. Inside, the foliage was trampled down; an empty can of soup and a bag of mouldy white bread lay discarded next to a damp copy of the *Evening Standard*. Cigarette butts were scattered on the ground. He moved forward, drawn by the front page of the newspaper. A woman's face stared out. The headline read FIND MY BOY BEFORE I GO, and beneath that was a photograph of a teenage boy. Some innate sense of respect born out of sympathy and guilt made him pick up the paper and take it with him as he went on his way.

Emerging from the trees he looked to the sky, which had turned slate grey, the sun hidden behind thick, threatening clouds. He pulled his jacket a little closer as he crossed the road and passed All Hallows Church, the newspaper tucked under his arm. He could smell rain in the air now and quickened his pace. Leaving the estate by the pedestrian exit on Grayshott Road, he crossed the busy main road that ran to the north. It effectively cut the estate off from its neighbouring area, Pinder Hill, which was far more affluent and where Reid was heading. After fifteen minutes or so he arrived at his destination, a large house at the top of Pinder Hill, where he unlocked the side gate, bypassing the main building, and made his way through the garden to the far end. He'd looped back on himself and from this higher vantage point could see the estate in the distance like some lost city. He let himself into a small structure that was in a particularly overgrown part of the garden, which doubled as a shed, and closed the door behind him.

He heard the first drops of rain hit the tin roof as he sat down, carefully unrolling the wet newspaper on his lap. Sally Shires' ravaged face stared back at him. He read the article slowly, carefully turning the pages, which were threatening to disintegrate in his hands. When he'd finished reading he remained seated for several minutes, deep in thought. The rain became heavier, as though someone were throwing rocks at the roof, and he thought about Sally Shires in hospital, dying of cancer, pleading for information about the disappearance of her son, Kevin. About how she wanted the truth before she died. As the rain battered the shed roof he also thought about Jason, asleep in his flat, and whether, between them, they might be able to give it to her.

CHAPTER 2

Connie Darke banged on the door of flat 16, Ullswater House and waited. She'd been reliably informed that this was where Brian Kaplinsky lived, a man who she'd been trying to trace for a little over a year now. She'd also been reliably informed that Kaplinsky had been with her sister, Sarah, when she'd fallen to her death from a disused water tower six years before. An inquest recorded a verdict of death by misadventure and the case closed. It had never been closed for Connie, and until she spoke to the man who'd been with her sister it never would be. Because after calling the emergency services Brian Kaplinsky had done a runner.

While she waited, she crossed the communal balcony that ran the length of the block and looked out across the derelict Grasmere Estate. The view wasn't bad – a small forest of trees formed the central part of the south London estate, softening its harsh edges and giving life to its bleak surroundings. Since the flats had been emptied – apart from a handful of residents who had clung on to the bitter end in the hope of negotiating a better deal with the council – the woods appeared to have expanded, encroaching on the concrete blocks around them. Saplings had sprung up everywhere and, left alone, nature would soon take over this once bustling, if not feared, council estate. A flock of parakeets squawked overhead and dived into the canopy of leaves where they instantly disappeared. On the other side of the estate – in stark contrast – was Windermere House, the mirror image of Ullswater House. Its facade had been ripped off, revealing a patchwork of small boxes. It seemed the developers couldn't wait for the remaining few residents of Grasmere to leave so had started work in spite of them. Connie could see the exposed remnants of the stairwell that ran up the side of the building. What had once been people's homes now resembled a giant doll's house with the front removed. Neglected paintwork and wallpaper covered what looked like impossibly thin dividing walls. The twisted rods of steel mesh that once strengthened the structure reached out like tentacles in search of something to grasp in a last-ditch effort to save itself. It was like looking at a giant beast in the midst of its death throes, and Connie felt a sadness she couldn't quite explain.

Despite the desolation and its undeniable faults, the Grasmere Estate wasn't without architectural merit. The architectural archive where she worked, the Repository of Architectural Drawings and Ephemera, or RADE for short, held the original drawings. On paper, at least, the project had worked. The flats were bordering on generous, the wood at the estate's centre a place where people could stroll and children could play, the walkways linking the three main blocks with one another and leading to the smaller maisonette blocks easy to navigate, providing additional space for neighbours to congregate. And yet it had all gone terribly wrong, as it had on so many council estates of the sixties and seventies.

She turned back to flat 16 and stooped to lift the letterbox. 'Brian, are you in there? It's Sarah's sister, Connie. I need to talk to you.' Anger tinged her words as she squinted into the flat.

Through the window of the letterbox she could see into the hallway and was surprised she'd never done this before. The living room was devoid of furniture, and apart from a few carrier bags in the hallway the flat emanated neglect and emptiness. No one was going to open the door, least of all Brian Kaplinsky. She let the metal flap of the letterbox snap shut. From her bag she took out a short note she'd written earlier, which included her mobile number and email, and posted it through the letterbox. Deep down, she knew Kaplinsky wasn't coming back. Soon Ullswater House, and the rest of the estate, would be torn apart like its counterpart and whatever secrets it once held would be reduced to a pile of rubble.

Turning to leave, she watched the arm of the excavator prodding at the carcass of Windermere, eventually sending a piece of concrete crashing to the ground, a plume of dust thrown up in its wake. Distance muffled the noise to a degree, but the parakeets took flight, startled by the sudden sound. She began walking along the deserted walkway back towards the stairs. All the other flats on this floor were boarded up. Over the past month she'd seen a few of the remaining residents – there were literally only a handful left from what she'd read in the papers – scurrying across the cracked playground carrying shopping, or letting themselves back into their flats, casting a glance over their shoulders as though they were being watched. There was a sense of that here, of being observed. The wind whistled around the empty walkways and corridors making sounds she'd never heard before, like a creature from another planet. Light cast strange shadows around the angular corners and gaps in the walkways, tricking the eye into seeing things that weren't there. It was little wonder the estate had a reputation for strange goings-on.

A figure emerged from the woods below and Connie stopped to watch as they crossed the road by the church. It was the first sign of life she'd seen that morning. Her steps echoed in the graffitied concrete stairwell as she made her way down. She didn't dare use the lift. It went up and down as if operated by a demented puppet master, and she'd never seen anyone get in or out of it. By the time she reached ground level the sky overhead had taken on the hues of Grasmere's concrete; pewter patches of grey hung heavy as a hangover and the light had acquired an odd green quality that usually preceded a heavy downpour. She began walking towards the nearest block of maisonettes, disappointment coursing through her veins. Kaplinsky was gone. She'd missed him. Now she'd have to start her search all over again. The bleakness of her surroundings did nothing to elevate her mood. Skirting around the maisonettes, she stopped to look into their overgrown gardens, the green-tinged light lending a surreal air to the scene. Mundane objects took on a sculptural quality; discarded garden furniture anchored to the ground by bindweed and grass that had threaded its way through cracks and slats. Some objects were so consumed by nature it was impossible to tell what they were. Other gardens weren't as overrun, as if poisoned, only managing to produce thin, straggling weeds on coarse, pale soil. The disparity was stark. She took a few photos on her phone before moving on.

From the maisonettes, she cut through the uppermost corner of the woods and emerged where she'd seen the figure earlier. On leaving the shelter of the trees the sky had darkened considerably and a heavy splat of rain landed on her face. London had been having regular showers, some so heavy as to cause flash flooding; another portent that climate change was really happening. She felt another drop hit her face, this one bigger. Dark spots appeared on the ground as the large, fat drops started to fall faster and faster. Before she knew it, she was running towards the porch of the old church.

By the time she reached the boarded-up building the rain was torrential and streaming down her face, her hair plastered to her head. A lightning flash divided the sky, followed by an enormous crack of thunder overhead. The sound was deafening even over the pounding rain, and she could have sworn the ground vibrated. The rain, which had been coming down like stair rods, was now being buffeted by a wind that had come from nowhere, and it danced across the ground in sheets. A sudden gust blew it towards her, and she shrank back further against the building. It was then she noticed the door to the church was slightly open and, seizing the opportunity as would any urban explorer worth their salt, she slipped inside.

◆ ◆ ◆

A lot of urban exploration came down to luck and timing; finding that elusive point of entry, the day the security patrol were off sick or feeling lazy, finding a building before it had been properly secured or just finding an interesting place so off radar it had no security at all. All this was going through Connie's head as she went into the old church, the familiar frisson of excitement that came with gaining entry to a new 'explore' running through her body.

The church was dark inside, the windows boarded up with metal shutters – like most of the estate – the only light coming from the open door. Another loud crack of thunder shook the building and a burst of wind blew the door shut and she was plunged into darkness. She patted down her pockets, searching for her phone. She'd only had it out a few minutes ago, *damn it*. The rain was now pounding against the outside of the building as the wind changed direction yet again. It was as if the church were under attack from every side, creaking and groaning from the onslaught. The wind whistled ferociously, looking for a way in, for any crack or crevice it could slither through. She'd just felt the hard outline of the iPhone in an inside zipped pocket and had slid it half out when something touched the back of her head.

Letting out a yelp she instinctively ducked, dropping the phone, which clattered to the floor where it disappeared into the blackness, screen side down. The wind changed direction yet again, sucking the front door open briefly before blowing it shut. Rain began hammering at the opposite side of the church and in the gloom Connie felt her heart thumping in her chest. She moved in the direction she thought the phone had fallen and felt something tap her forehead. She groped blindly into the darkness but there was nothing there. Then another gentle tap, this time to the side of her head and she wheeled around, her hands briefly colliding with something before it was gone. She sensed the air above her move before another tap to the back of her head sent her lurching sideways. The wind rattled the door again, affording a brief burst of light into the church interior, and she glimpsed her phone. As she stooped to pick it up the wind suddenly dropped, the rain abating just enough for her to hear a gentle creaking. It was rhythmical, and for a split second she saw the swing her father had made for her and her sister when they were small. He'd made it out of an old wooden pallet and had hung it over the bough of a tree. It had a peculiar creak as it swung back and forth. Grabbing the phone, she swiped the home screen and switched on the torch, shining it in an arc in front of her. There was nothing there. A slight tickle on the top of her head caused her to spin around and she came face to face with a pair of shoes.

For a split second she thought it was some kind of sick joke – a bonfire effigy strung up by kids pratting about. Except this wasn't an effigy. This was real. A man was hanging from the ceiling by his neck, gently swaying. The rope tied around his neck quietly groaned as it rubbed rhythmically on the scaffold pole from which he was hanging. Connie backed away and for a few seconds was unable to tear her eyes away from the grotesque swinging man, the harsh white light of her phone emphasising the horror. Then the fear and revulsion hit her and she ran outside as fast as she could into the pelting rain.

CHAPTER 3

The toasted panini Lew Kirby had had for breakfast at Verona Airport that morning was threatening to make a cameo appearance in what felt like a scene from a disaster movie. It was one of the worst flights he'd ever experienced, the turbulence so bad over London that the pilot had tried several times to land only to abort and circle the airport again. Below, the city had looked its usual grey, wet self but the storm raging outside was the most dramatic he'd seen. Several passengers had actually been sick, while others were so terrified they'd frozen in their seats. As a rule he enjoyed flying. There was something relaxing about being thousands of miles above the earth, because no matter what horrors were happening below there wasn't a damn thing he could do about it. The freedom was almost spiritual.

Eventually the plane had landed, bumping along Gatwick's runway like a bouncing rubber ball, coming to a juddering halt that forced everyone forward in their seats. A few people at the back of the plane had clapped, and the pilot's voice had come over the tannoy with a joke. *It's a good job he became a pilot and not a comedian*, thought Kirby. God, he felt knackered. After his first flight had been cancelled, he'd spent several uncomfortable hours at the airport waiting for the next available one. He yawned and checked his watch. He should have been heading into the office now after a decent night's sleep, but after the cancelled flight it meant he'd only have time to drop off his bag at the boat and take a quick shower before heading in – and that depended on the traffic being on his side. As the plane taxied towards the airport, he switched on his phone. There was a message from his girlfriend, Isabel, and a missed call from his partner, Pete Anderson, in MIT29, the murder team where he worked. He hit redial.

'Pete,' he said, unbuckling his seatbelt as other passengers stood up and began the impatient wait to leave the plane. The woman next to him was still plugged into whatever she was listening to, and gave him a shrug and a smile that told him she was in no hurry to stand up pointlessly for the next ten minutes.

'Where are you?' asked Anderson.

'Just landed. My flight was held up.'

'Sorry to have to break it to you but you need to get your arse in gear. We've got a swinger. And not the key-swapping kind.'

Kirby smiled. He'd missed his partner's humour. 'Where?'

'Grasmere Estate.'

Kirby had had cause to visit the estate on numerous occasions over the years, none of which had been pleasant. It was now abandoned, awaiting demolition and the inevitable gentrification. 'Whereabouts?' he asked Anderson.

'The church, All Hallows. And do you want the punchline?'

'Go on,' said Kirby, feeling his stomach tighten.

'Connie Darke found the body. Welcome back, Lew.'

◆ ◆ ◆

Ironically, Kirby cleared Gatwick faster than he could remember and within an hour was coming off the M23 and on to the A23 into south-west London. Here the traffic began to slow, surface water from the on-off rain showers reducing it to a crawl. Eventually

12

he turned into the Grasmere Estate via the entrance on Marshall Street – the only vehicular access to the estate still in use – where a uniformed officer stopped him. Kirby wound down his window and showed the constable his identification. 'Didn't think you were supposed to drive personal vehicles at work,' said the officer, eyeing the green Citroën SM that was Kirby's pride and joy and increasingly a drain on his finances.

'It's an emergency,' said Kirby, driving off before the officer could say anything else. The last thing he needed was a bloody lecture about driving the Citroën to work – he'd get that from his boss, DCI Idris Hamer, no doubt. The uniform had been right, of course: he shouldn't be driving it. He should have driven home then got a bus, or a cab, but he hadn't wanted to waste any more time – he was late enough as it was. His usual police car, a Corsa – generally known as the Fucking Corsa – was at the carpool where hopefully something terrible had befallen it while he was away. To say that he disliked it was an understatement. Even Livia, his mother, had called it a 'student car' which had only made matters worse.

The Grasmere Estate was built on an awkward dip, a triangular piece of land that was bordered by the A3 to the north and the railway line to the south. On the far side of the estate Kirby could see some of the large houses on Pinder Hill. They overlooked both the estate and the A3 – the latter near enough to be useful, far enough away not to be a nuisance. For the former occupants of the estate – especially those in the northern block – the A3 had been a constant presence, while those on the south side had had the incessant noise of the trains to contend with. Three slab-built concrete blocks formed the perimeter of Grasmere with clusters of maisonettes within. It would have been quicker to reach the church by driving straight on, but the road had been blocked off due to the first phase of demolition so he had little choice but to turn right and drive the long way round. He'd been here a few times when he was in uniform – before they'd started to move residents out of their homes – usually to check out reports of domestic violence, drugs and antisocial behaviour. He still had a vivid memory of chasing a suspect along the maze of concrete walkways while wearing a stab vest during the height of summer. Even as a fit officer in his twenties it had still damn near killed him. Now, only a handful of residents remained. It was like driving through a ghost town and he wondered which was worse: living in the nightmare that it had been, or rattling around in the concrete coffin it had become.

As the Citroën bumped along the potholed road, he could feel the neglect and decay seeping from every inch of concrete. The empty walkways and bridges that linked the various buildings were a photographer's dream of perspectives and vanishing points. A series of bridges connected the perimeter blocks to his right with clusters of maisonettes on the left. Detritus scattered the ground in these damp and cavernous areas, and as he drove under the bridges he saw the junk of lives past: fridges, mattresses, a burnt-out car, the ubiquitous shopping trolley and other pieces of garbage that had been left to rot. It was a relief when he emerged into the sunlight.

He followed the road around to the left and saw All Hallows Church up ahead with a wide cordon around it. It had been easy to rope off as it stood alone, unanchored to the rest of the estate, as though its mooring had come loose and was slowly floating away. A group of people stood outside the cordon near two patrol cars, an ambulance and a Forensic Services van. He recognised Anderson's Astra and pulled up next to it. A black BMW was also parked nearby, which signified the presence of DCI Idris Hamer, alongside a blue Subaru that belonged to Carter Jenks, the forensic pathologist.

As he got out of the car, a figure clad in a white crime scene suit emerged from the church and waved. Kirby recognised the bulk of his partner and raised his hand. He looked around for any sign of Connie and breathed a small sigh of relief when he couldn't see her. He hadn't told Anderson she'd moved into his mother's old place in Ealing yet. Anderson's jokes were bad enough without him knowing Connie was now his tenant. Kirby had developed an unlikely friendship with Connie after a case last year – urban explorers and police were odd bedfellows – so when he'd discovered she'd been turfed out of the pub she'd been renting he'd offered her his mother's place. Livia had been dead a couple of months by then and he was still in two minds about what to do with the house. He'd far rather someone live in it than it stand empty, so it had been a win-win situation.

'You want to come and take a look?' Anderson asked, coming over. 'They've just taken the body down. Male, Caucasian. Late sixties, possibly older.'

Kirby nodded and went over to the SOCO van where he got suited up in protective clothing. After the scene guard had noted down his name and the time, he ducked under the police tape and followed his partner towards the church.

'How was Italy?' asked Anderson, against the rustle of their white PPE jumpsuits.

'Italian.'

'You don't say. Bet the whole fucking village turned out then. Did you scatter Livia's ashes by the lake, like she wanted?'

Kirby nodded. 'It was beautiful there. Peaceful.'

'Sounds like the perfect place to say goodbye.'

Kirby remembered what their actual goodbye had been like at his mother's house in Ealing. The pills. The silent understanding that had passed between them as he'd left the house feigning a cheery goodbye for the neighbours' benefit. When they reached the church door, Kirby paused to pull on plastic bootees to cover his shoes. 'Where's Connie?'

'Kobrak took her to the station to make a statement. She was pretty shaken.'

That was hardly surprising. It wasn't every day you stumbled upon a dead body and Kirby made a mental note to call in at his mother's place later. As he followed his partner into the church he began to wish he had thrown up on the plane. Inside, he saw Carter Jenks crouching down in the glare of the arc lights that had been set up over the body, Idris Hamer standing close by watching his every move. A scaffolding rig, the type used by decorators, ran across the church roof. At one end was a rope pulley, the area below it scattered with evidence markers. Metal tread plates had been placed on the floor and he and Anderson followed them over to the body.

Idris Hamer looked up as they approached, a solemn look on his face. 'Sorry, Lew, we weren't sure how long it would take you to get here.' His gaze drifted up towards the scaffolding and pulley. 'He was hung from up there.'

'I take it this isn't what it looks like then,' said Kirby, looking up at the pulley. 'Otherwise we wouldn't be here.'

'Hi Lew,' said Jenks, cheerily. 'And no, this isn't suicide. But it's possibly what someone wanted us to think.'

'What makes you say that?' Kirby let his eyes drift down to the body. He took in the clothes first – pressed jeans, a blue workwear jacket that was more Paul Smith than Amazon, and canvas trainers that again had a designer look to them. The nails were manicured but blood tipped the fingers of the right hand. He spotted what looked like an Apple watch on the left wrist and a gold signet ring on the left hand. As his eyes made their way up the body towards the head his first thought was, what was someone like this doing here? The estate was almost derelict, only a handful of residents left. Yet this man clearly had money.

'There are drag marks on the floor over there,' said Jenks, pointing to the evidence markers. 'Also, there's no ladder near the scaffolding. There's one over there, by the font. He could have climbed up, but it's odd not to use the ladder.'

Kirby looked at the scaffolding. The first proper footholds were at shoulder height.

'There's a swelling on the back of his head,' said Jenks. 'But this is the giveaway.' He pulled the collar of the jacket away from the neck and Kirby could see the ligature mark left by the rope. But there were other bruises present too, bruises he was all too familiar with from past cases.

'Someone strangled him?'

'These definitely look like thumb prints, but I'll know more when I get him back to the mortuary.'

Kirby looked across at the evidence markers. 'Where was he dragged from?'

'Only a few feet away,' answered Hamer. 'It looks as though he was attacked, dragged here so that he was beneath the rope pulley and then hoisted up.'

'Is there anything in his pockets – any ID?' asked Kirby, noticing a bulge in the front pocket of the dead man's jeans consistent with a bunch of keys.

With his gloved hand, Jenks pulled the object out and it was indeed a set of house keys. He handed it to Anderson who had an evidence bag waiting. 'There's something in his back pocket too,' he said, sliding his hand under the victim's body. 'Feels like a wallet. Can you help me turn him?' he asked one of the SOCOs. While the SOCO held the body on its side, Jenks removed a black wallet from the back of the man's jeans and passed it to Kirby.

Flipping the wallet open he saw several bank cards. Sliding one out, he read the name: 'William Stark.'

'I'm sure I know that name,' said Hamer.

Kirby went through the rest of the wallet's contents. Twenty pounds in cash, receipts – several from a taxi firm – various loyalty cards and a membership card for the British Library.

'I thought so,' said Hamer, who'd taken out his phone and was scrolling through what looked like Google search results. 'He's an architect.'

Something nudged at Kirby's memory as his boss spoke. Something he'd read in the paper? A petition? He looked at the man lying on the ground. A web of spit covered his chin like spun sugar, the protruding tongue dark in contrast. Short, cropped grey hair. Then it came to him. The steps of Wandsworth Town Hall a few years ago. A group of residents being photographed by the local paper. The dead man at their centre.

'Has he built anything famous?' asked Anderson.

'In a manner of speaking,' replied Hamer. 'He designed this place.'

Anderson looked puzzled for a moment. 'The church?'

'Not just the church,' said Kirby, tearing his eyes away from the dead architect, remembering the man's impassioned words to the small crowd outside the Town Hall. 'He designed the whole estate. This man created Grasmere.'

CHAPTER 4

Because it was Sunday the council offices were shut, which meant they wouldn't get an official list of who was living on the estate until the following day. As Kirby and Anderson peeled off their white crime scene suits, Kirby spotted a man outside the cordon looking on with interest. 'Maybe he can help,' he said to Anderson, nodding towards him. The man looked to be in his early fifties, bald, with a slight paunch but otherwise fairly fit. He was wearing jeans with a navy hoodie. Once divested of the white PPE they headed over.

'Surely Stark wasn't still living here?' said Anderson as they walked. 'It's a dump.'

'He was a year or so ago – he was still battling the council. Whether he'd moved on or not I don't know.'

The man's name was Tobias Hoffmann and he lived in one of the maisonette blocks. When Kirby had seen William Stark on the steps of Wandsworth Town Hall, he'd been leading a group of residents from the Grasmere Estate in their quest for appropriate remuneration for selling their flats back to the council. He wondered whether Hoffmann had been among them.

'Were you at home last night?' Anderson was asking.

'Yes. With my wife, Mary.'

'Did you see or hear anything unusual?'

'Um, no. I don't think so. What's happened?' He kept peering behind them towards the church.

'Is the church usually kept locked?' Anderson asked, politely ignoring Hoffmann's question.

'Always. The council used it for storage at one point. But everything is locked or boarded up now, as you can see.'

'Would any of the residents have a key?' asked Kirby.

Hoffmann shook his head. 'I doubt it. Just the council.'

'Do you know if a man called William Stark lives on the estate?' Kirby saw immediate recognition on Hoffmann's face at the mention of Stark's name.

'Yes, he does. Why? What's happened to him?'

Kirby and Anderson exchanged looks. 'Does he have family here?'

'A daughter, Alma. They don't live together though.'

'No one else? No Mrs Stark?'

Hoffmann paused, then shook his head. 'No, just the daughter.'

Kirby made a note of William's and Alma Stark's addresses. Alma lived on the first floor of Ullswater House and her father on the top floor.

'Has something happened to Will?' Hoffmann asked again.

'A body was discovered in the church earlier today, who we believe to be Mr Stark,' said Kirby. 'Can you think of any reason why he might have been in there?'

'None,' said Hoffmann, a look of shock on his face. 'I can't believe it. Alma will be devastated. And Mary – we were close to Will and his daughter. This is terrible news.'

'Did Mr Stark have any enemies that you know of?'

'What? No! Everyone here liked Will.'

'How many of you are there?' asked Anderson, looking around.

'There are ten of us left. You've got the Falkes and the Carmodys in Ullswater House – they're both on the ninth floor. Elliott Falke ran the church when it was still functioning – he lives with his wife, Kay – Michaela. Mrs Carmody lives with her son, Ralph, who has something to do with the railway. Dan Scribbs lives in Woodcroft, near us.' He pointed to the block of maisonettes behind him but offered no information as to Scribbs' occupation. 'And then there's Vernon Reid. He lives alone in Coniston House.' Hoffmann turned and pointed across the estate towards the first block Kirby had passed when he arrived. Only the top was visible from where they were standing. 'He's a gardener. Among other things.'

What 'other things'? Kirby wondered. 'Do you have flat numbers?'

Hoffmann shook his head. 'I've long forgotten those. You'll be able to tell which flats are occupied because they're the only ones that aren't boarded up. Floor numbers are all you need.'

'Mr Reid's floor is . . . ?'

'Top. He doesn't take too kindly to the police though.'

'Why would that be?' asked Kirby.

'You'd have to ask him,' said Hoffmann, suddenly checking the time on his phone. 'Sorry, I need to go. You'll be going to see Alma?'

Kirby nodded. 'And you'll get a visit from a uniformed officer who will take a statement.'

'But I thought this—'

'This is just a chat. But you've been very helpful, Mr Hoffmann.'

Kirby relayed the information Hoffmann had given them to uniformed officers who would conduct the door-to-door – or floor-to-floor – enquiries.

'The daughter?' asked Anderson, when he'd finished.

Kirby nodded. 'Let's go via Stark's flat. Just to make sure he's not tucked up in bed watching something on Netflix.'

The view from outside Stark's flat on the top floor was nothing short of stunning. The wooded area at the centre of the estate spread out before them like a giant quilt of greenery. The leaves shone brightly – new and fresh after the recent rain – and the air felt clearer. There was no answer from the flat, and when they tried the keys found on the victim the front door opened easily. The flat was a surprise – it was large and open plan and Kirby quickly worked out that the architect had knocked through to the flat next door, making one huge living space. He wouldn't have minded living there himself, had it not been on one of London's most notorious estates. After a quick look around it was clear Stark wasn't at home, and judging by the food in the kitchen hadn't been home since the previous night. His mobile was on the kitchen table and to all intents and purposes it looked as though he'd just popped out. There was little doubt in Kirby's mind that the body in the church belonged to William Stark.

He left Anderson to secure Stark's flat and went to see Stark's daughter on his own. On the way, he arranged for a family liaison officer to come over and meet him there. When he reached the first floor where Alma's flat was, he felt his feet get heavier. Despite seeing many horrific crime scenes in his career, telling someone a loved one had died was the worst part of the job and something he'd never got used to.

The view from the first-floor gangway was significantly different from that at the top. It still overlooked the central wooded area, but from here Kirby also had a bird's eye view of the uneven road below where weeds had forced their way through the cracked tarmac, as well as the brutal concrete walkway that joined this block with one of the maisonette blocks. Hoffmann had been right – every door and window he'd passed had been boarded up with faceless metal screens. Alma's door was painted bright green and sat at the end of the communal balcony where it met the external concrete stairway on the corner.

'Alma Stark?' Kirby asked the woman who'd opened the door.

'Yes, what is it?'

'My name's DI Kirby.' He showed her his ID. 'Is it possible to come in for a moment?'

'Yes, I suppose so,' she said hesitantly. 'What's this about?'

Kirby followed her into the flat, closing the door after him. The hall was dimly lit and Alma Stark led him into a room off to the left. It wasn't what he'd been expecting at all. The walls were covered in murals and it took him a moment to recognise the River Thames as it snaked itself around the entire room. Every bit of wall space was covered in a hand-drawn, densely illustrated map of London.

'Take a seat,' said Alma Stark, pointing to a plain white leather sofa. She appeared unaware of the effect the room had on her guest as she took a seat on a matching chair and looked at Kirby expectantly.

Kirby tore his eyes away from the walls and focused on the woman seated in front of him. He guessed her to be in her early forties. Attractive – what Anderson would have called 'Bohemian'.

'Ms Stark, I'm—'

'Alma, please,' she interrupted.

'Alma. I'm afraid I have some bad news. You may have seen the police presence this morning by the old church.'

She shook her head. 'No, I've been in all morning and I can't see it from here. Has something happened?'

'A body was found in the church and we recovered a wallet belonging to a Mr William Stark, who I believe is your father?'

'Yes, he is. I can't imagine what his wallet was doing in the church, although he can be absent-minded.'

Kirby could see her frowning, trying to work out what it meant. 'I'm very sorry, but the wallet was found on the victim. We think it might be your father.'

Alma stared at him, incomprehension written over her face. 'You've made a mistake. You must have done.'

'I'm afraid not. He was found hanging from a decorator's scaf-folding rig.'

Alma's hand went to her mouth. Her face had gone white and her breathing was coming in short, sharp bursts.

'I'm sorry Alma. Take your time,' said Kirby. 'Can I get you anything?'

Alma raised her hand. 'I'm fine, I'll be okay.'

Kirby waited for a few moments before continuing. 'We don't know yet exactly how he died but there is some evidence to suggest that a third party was involved.'

'Third party?' She looked confused. 'You mean someone helped him? My God . . .' The penny dropped.

'We don't know anything for certain at the moment, but I'm very sorry, there will have to be a post-mortem on your father's body. We need to find out how this happened.'

'Who found him?' Her breathing was now back to normal and a veneer of control settled over her features.

'A young woman sheltering from the storm – no one who lives here. Do you have a recent photograph of your father I could have?'

'Yes, of course.' She fished her phone out of her pocket and scrolled through some photographs, eventually settling on one. 'Will this do?' She held out the phone with a shaking hand.

It was hard to align the man in the picture with the man he'd seen in the church but Kirby felt fairly certain they were one and the same. 'May I?' Kirby indicated his own phone and when Alma nodded he quickly forwarded the image and passed her phone back. 'When did you last see your father?'

'Um . . . yesterday morning. And I spoke to him in the evening, around seven. He was fine, absolutely fine.'

'And you haven't spoken to him since then?'

'No . . . I did call this morning but there was no reply. I assumed he was in the shower. Or had gone for a walk.'

'Did he usually carry his mobile phone with him?'

'Most of the time, but he wasn't obsessive. Wrong generation. Look, are you sure you haven't made a mistake? Maybe his wallet had been stolen and he didn't realise. He's probably at home now—'

'He's not, Alma,' Kirby said gently. 'A colleague is at his flat now and he's not there.'

'Then he must be out.' Kirby could hear the edge of hysteria creeping into her voice. He needed to keep her on track as much as possible.

'Was your father retired?'

Alma nodded. 'He was an architect. He designed the estate – did you know that?'

Kirby nodded. 'How long had he lived here?'

'Since it was built in 1973.'

Kirby hoped the surprise didn't show on his face and wondered what on earth had possessed Stark to stay. 'Can you think of any reason why he might have been in the church – did he have a key?'

'No,' said Alma. Kirby detected a slight hesitation. 'Even if he did have a key, I don't see why he would be in there. I can't believe this is happening—'

A knock on the door interrupted them and Kirby stood up. 'It's okay, I'll get that.' He went into the hall and opened the door, relieved to see PC Catherine Wren outside. She was a family liaison officer who Kirby had worked with on several occasions. He showed her into the front room and introduced her to Alma, who was staring at the wall as if searching for something on the map that covered it.

'PC Wren will stay with you for a while, but there are a few more questions I'd like to ask you before I go. Can you think of anyone who might have wanted to harm your father? Did he have any enemies on the estate?'

'No one,' she answered, her voice finally breaking.

'I'll get some water,' said Wren, slipping out of the room.

'When you spoke to him last night was he alone?'

'As far as I know.' Tears were now running down her face and she took out a tissue.

'Do you know if he had any plans to go out after you spoke? Maybe he was meeting a friend?'

Alma shook her head and sniffed. 'He wasn't going out. He rarely went anywhere at night.'

Wren appeared with a glass of water and handed it to her. 'Who would do something like this? And why the church?' Alma gulped down the water.

'Was he religious? Perhaps he'd gone there to pray if he had a key.'

'No. Absolutely not.' The water glass fell from her hand and rolled on to the carpet as the strength seemed to drain out of her. 'I knew this would happen.' Her voice quavered. 'I knew the estate would take him in the end.'

'What do you mean?'

'My father spent his life doing the best he could for Grasmere but it wasn't enough and now it's taken him.' She buried her head in her hands and began to sob.

Kirby stood up to leave. After offering his condolences he left Alma and Wren alone. As he closed the front door and stepped on to the walkway he heard a scream from inside as Alma finally went to pieces.

CHAPTER 5

When Reid got back to the estate it was almost dark. He'd worked in the garden all day, apart from when the heavens opened and he'd taken shelter in the shed, and had stayed until the light had begun to fade. The soil had been satisfyingly easy to dig after all the recent rain, like slicing through a rich, dark chocolate cake, and by the time he left he'd come to a decision; he would let Jason stay. He'd spoken to God, and to his spiritual mentor, David, and they'd both urged him to put his own issues to one side, so that together he and Jason could find out what had happened to Kevin. It was a tall order, as the police hadn't managed it in almost three decades. Yet, somehow, with Grasmere on the verge of destruction, coupled with his own belief that the End of Days was imminent, it felt entirely possible, and Reid entered the estate with a sense of hope he hadn't experienced for years. The feeling was short-lived. There was police activity near the church. Anxiety prickled his body, and he felt the scars on his hand begin to itch. The urge to run was overwhelming, but he knew that would only draw attention so he skirted around the church and as calmly as he could made his way to the rear of Ullswater House. He prayed he wouldn't run into any patrols on the way and wondered what had happened to warrant such a large police presence. Something serious.

As well as no heating, there was no outdoor lighting on the estate, not even along the walkways or communal areas, so he picked his way carefully, not wanting to use his torch until he was hidden by the block of flats. It was still a risk switching the torch on there, but he was fairly certain no one would see him, and he kept the beam as low as possible. The path that ran along the back of the block was overgrown and strewn with discarded bits of machinery and even the odd car. Garages took up the entire ground floor of each of the three perimeter blocks but for some reason those at the rear of Ullswater House had all – with the exception of Alma's – had their doors removed. They stood like dark yawning caverns, some with uncovered inspection pits, dangerous and deadly for the unsuspecting intruder.

Ullswater House was connected to his own block of flats, Coniston House, by a series of zigzagging concrete stairs in poor repair, so he decided to take his chances and walk to the front of his block and use the main entrance. The last time he'd used the stairs had been at Christmas. He'd dislodged a small piece of concrete, which, had anyone been beneath when it fell, would have caused more than a headache. It was only a matter of time before someone died due to the council's wilful neglect of the place.

He could see no sign of the police anywhere, and Coniston was shrouded in darkness as usual. Just as he was about to enter the main entrance, the beams of a car's headlights swept over the children's playground opposite. He quickly ducked inside the building, hoping he hadn't been spotted, only to see a light coming down the stairs towards him. It was a uniformed police officer.

'Mr Reid?' said the officer.

He nodded. The car had stopped outside. He heard a door open and the sound of a police radio.

'I've just been to your flat looking for you,' said the officer on the stairwell. 'Must keep you fit going up and down here all day.'

He was smiling but clearly out of breath. 'Just wanted to ask you a few questions about last night.'

'Last night?' Reid asked, aware he was sweating.

'A body was found in the old church this morning. We think it belongs to William Stark. Did you know him?'

The name sent what felt like a gut punch to his stomach. 'William Stark?' he repeated.

'Yes.' The officer was watching him closely.

Reid nodded; it was all he could manage. *Amen. Amen.*

'We're talking to all the residents to see if anyone saw or heard anything unusual yesterday evening. Were you at home?'

'Yes,' said Reid, pulling himself together. 'I was here all evening. Alone.' He thought about Jason. *Forgive me Father for the lie. Amen.*

'You can see the church from the balcony outside your flat,' the officer went on. 'You didn't happen to go out, maybe for a cigarette, and see a light or anything like that at the church?'

'I don't smoke.' *Amen.* 'I didn't go out at all.' He was aware of the officer outside, who'd got out of the patrol car, approaching the main door, and started to feel trapped, like he had at the compound all those years ago. *Look down upon me, Lord, and cast your strength over me. Amen.*

'Have you been past the church today?' the officer asked.

'This morning, on my way to work. It was around ten.'

'And where is it that you work, Mr Reid?' The policeman was looking at him very strangely and Reid's throat felt impossibly dry.

'Big house up on The Drive. I do the garden.'

'What number?'

'Forty-six,' said Reid, clearing his throat.

The police officer made a note. 'Did you see anyone when you went past the church? Mr Stark, maybe?'

Reid shook his head. 'No.'

'Did you notice if the door was open?' The policeman was really staring at him now.

Reid shook his head. 'It was about to rain. I didn't hang about.' *Rain washes away the sin.*

'So you haven't seen anyone hanging around the estate, any strangers?'

'No. Is there anything else?' He turned to the other officer who was now in the doorway, waiting for his colleague.

'I'll need a number for you in case we need to contact you again. It's just routine,' said the policeman who'd come down the stairs.

Reid gave him his details – he didn't have much choice – he just wanted to get away from the two officers as fast as he could.

'That's all for now, Mr Reid. If you think of anything, give us a call.' The officer gave him a card. 'Have a good night.'

He watched the police officers leave and started up the stairs, his legs weak from the shock. He let himself into the flat where he leant against the front door and prayed in the darkness, *You are among us, Lord, and we bear your name; do not forsake us!* All he could hear was his heart thumping in his chest and felt the drowning coming over him. It was like a magnetic force pulling him down and he compelled himself to stay upright. Will Stark was dead. The man who'd befriended him as a teenager, who'd got him the job up at the big house on The Drive. The only person to help him when he'd returned from America. He had been an ex-con and religious nutter to boot, or that's how most people had viewed him, but Stark hadn't cared. *May the Lord bless you and keep you; may the Lord make his face shine on you and be gracious to you; may the Lord turn his face toward you and give you peace. Amen.* Eventually his breathing, which had been fast and erratic, began to settle.

The flat was silent. Jason must be out, but he switched on the lights and checked all the rooms in any case before double-locking the front door and sliding the safety chain in place. In the kitchen he began to peel off his clothes – damp from rain and sweat – pushing them into the washing machine as he went. No wonder the policeman had been staring at him; his clothes were filthy with mud from the garden. He was now chilled to the bone, his jeans clammy against his legs, and he had to sit down on a kitchen chair to wrestle them off. The vinyl seat was cold on his damp thighs and stung as he stood up, like ripping a sticking plaster off too quickly. Momentarily, he was reminded of the stifling heat of Texas and the interior of the pickup, its seats too hot to sit on in shorts.

He stood in the shower until he was warmer and then put on some clean, dry clothes. After checking the front door was still secure, he went back to the kitchen where he boiled the kettle and put the radio on. He wasn't sure what radio station he was listening to, but they were playing a Johnny Cash number from the *At San Quentin* album. He tried to imagine what would have happened if someone had organised a concert at the prison he had been held in. A riot, probably. As the song ended he thought he heard something outside. He went to the front door and peered through the spy hole but couldn't see anything. He picked up the cricket bat that he kept by the door and slid back the bolts. Keeping the safety chain on, he eased the door open. He saw nothing through the small gap afforded him between the door frame and the door, and slid the chain off.

He swung his torch along the balcony. There was a fox at the far end. It turned and stared at him before running off. There were more foxes on the estate than people, the overgrown gardens and the woods ideal for their dens. That, and the piles of uncollected refuse by the entrance. He switched the torch off and stood for a moment looking out across the estate. The demolition site to the left lay quiet and desolate. Across the woods he saw lights still on at the old church. The police were working late. He scanned the

31

rest of the estate and saw a dim glow from Alma Stark's place. He wondered whether he should go over and see how she was doing but decided against it. They'd never got on particularly well; she didn't have her father's kindness.

He was about to go back inside when another light source caught his attention. It was very faint, a thin line, and he almost missed it, blinking a few times just to be sure. It was coming from one of the front garages beneath Ullswater House. Unlike the ones he'd passed earlier to the rear of the block, these had been sealed or, in some cases, simply locked. Over the years they'd been graffitied over so many times that they'd provide a social history of the estate should anyone care enough to preserve them. But among the tags one door stood out. Its graffiti remained intact, whether by accident or design. Not that he could see it from up here, he was too far away, but he was sure this was where the light was coming from. He went back inside and reinstated the bolts and chain. Jason wouldn't be back tonight, but Reid knew exactly where he was. He was down there, in the garage that had once belonged to the Shires family.

CHAPTER 6

A corner of the open-plan office at MIT29's headquarters – known to everyone as Mount Pleasant for reasons no one could remember – had been allocated to the Grasmere murder case. The building had once been an abattoir – a fact Anderson never let anyone forget when Halloween came around. Photographs of the victim and crime scene had been pinned up on a whiteboard, along with a list of names – mainly residents of the Grasmere Estate. Hamer had called a briefing to be appraised of what they'd learned so far that day, and after grabbing a cup of water Kirby went and joined the small group congregated in the corner. He was now operating on adrenaline, his earlier tiredness pushed to one side. After talking to Alma Stark, he'd joined Anderson in William Stark's flat and between them they'd gone over it. First appearances indicated that Stark had been preparing his supper when he left. The table was laid for one and a fish pie was on the countertop next to the oven waiting to be heated. Green beans lay topped and tailed on a chopping board, a small saucepan of water on the hob. The cooker was off. Stark had either planned to get everything ready in advance, with the intention of eating on his return, or he'd been interrupted by something, or someone, that caused him to leave before he had a chance to cook. Either way there was no sign of a struggle and nothing looked out of place. Stark's mobile phone was on the kitchen table.

Hamer emerged from his office – the only part of the room partitioned off – and joined the assembled group. Along with Kirby and Anderson, there was DS Mark Drayton, DS Steve Kobrak, the newest member of the section DS Hiromi Masters – whom everyone called Romy – and a civilian, Vicki Ash, the case recorder.

'Okay,' said Hamer. 'Let's take a look at what we have so far. Let's start with the victim. Lew?'

'We think the deceased is William Brendan Stark, age seventy-four. His daughter hasn't seen him since yesterday and the victim was wearing a ring very like one Stark wears and was also carrying his ID. They're about the same age and build. We're hoping for a positive ID tomorrow.'

'Good,' said Hamer.

'The body was found by Connie Darke,' Kirby went on, staring at her name on the whiteboard.

'The same Connie Darke?' asked Hamer, looking at Kirby.

'Yes, the same Connie Darke who was involved with the Blackwater case last year. Archivist and urban explorer.'

'Blackwater case?' Masters frowned.

'A woman was murdered in the grounds of the abandoned Blackwater Asylum and a friend of Connie's was implicated,' replied Kirby.

'What on earth was she doing at Grasmere though?' Hamer asked.

'Visiting an old friend, only he wasn't in, according to her,' cut in Kobrak, who'd taken her statement.

'A resident?'

'He had been, but he moved out a few weeks ago. That's according to the other residents in the block at any rate. The council haven't even boarded up his flat yet.' Kobrak referred to his notes. 'He lived in Ullswater House, flat sixteen.'

Hamer looked at the list of residents' names on the whiteboard. 'Is his name up here?'

'Oh, er, no,' said Kobrak. 'I'll add it now.'

Kirby watched as Kobrak wrote the name in block letters under the list of current tenants and felt his stomach flip. BRIAN KAPLINSKY. Kaplinsky had also been involved in the Blackwater case the previous year and had worked for Patricey Developments, the company who had planned to redevelop the old Blackwater Asylum. But that wasn't all – Connie was convinced he'd had some involvement in her sister's accident at the asylum and had been on a mission to find him ever since. 'If it's the same person, then he was site manager at Blackwater,' said Kirby.

Hamer raised an eyebrow. 'Please don't tell me there's a connection between that and Stark's murder.'

'There isn't,' said Kirby, quickly. 'Ms Darke is convinced it was Kaplinsky who was with her sister when she had her fatal accident – he being the one who called the emergency services and then fled the scene. My guess is she wanted to talk to him about that. That's if it's the same person.'

'Get him checked out,' said Hamer. 'What is it with these explorers?'

Apart from Kirby, no one in the office had any sympathy for urban explorers. They were viewed as irresponsible meddlers not worthy of police time, unless of course they happened to stray into sensitive areas, so Kirby kept his own opinion that they were actually rather interesting, and in some cases quite useful, to himself. 'Miss Darke discovered the body at ten twenty this morning in the disused church on the estate and immediately called 999. The victim had been hung by the neck from a decorator's scaffold. Estimated time of death based on body temperature is some time last night. The victim was wearing a gold wedding band, an Apple watch and his wallet was found on him, so robbery doesn't appear to be a motive.'

'The perp could have been disturbed,' Drayton commented.

'That's a possibility, obviously,' said Kirby. 'But by who? If one of the residents had disturbed a mugging they would have reported it.'

'People don't want to get involved these days,' said Drayton. 'And in a place like Grasmere it's easier to turn the other way.'

Kirby didn't subscribe to that. 'I don't think that's the case any more. According to the witness statements the residents all know each other. It's likely that if they saw someone being attacked they'd call 999 – even if they didn't physically intervene.'

'I agree with Lew: it's unlikely they were interrupted,' said Hamer. 'The first question we need to answer is why was Stark in the church?'

'He might have seen something suspicious and gone to investigate. The perp panicked and then ran,' said Drayton, refusing to give up.

'Nothing's ruled out, Mark,' said Hamer. 'Did the daughter have any explanation as to why her father might have been in the church?'

'None.'

'Are there any other relatives?'

'Not that we know of at the moment,' said Anderson. 'Mrs Stark died in the late eighties when Alma was a child.'

'What happened to her?' asked Masters.

'She threw herself off the top of Windermere House. That's the block currently being demolished. Alma was eleven.'

'Jesus. And he stayed there?' Masters looked shocked.

'Since the estate was built,' said Kirby, who was also having a hard time getting his head around it.

'Did Stark remarry?' asked Hamer.

'No.'

'Any enemies that we know of? We need something.'

'None.'

'Okay, well, we need to find out more about Mr Stark – friends, any family lurking in the background, anyone he'd had an altercation with recently. And look at the daughter. In cases like this it's usually someone the victim knows. And he'd have trusted his daughter. Is she set to inherit? We need all that. Now,' Hamer checked his watch, 'moving on to the residents.'

Kirby nodded at Kobrak who'd been gathering their data from the uniforms' door-to-door statements. 'We don't have an official list yet – and we won't until the council offices open tomorrow morning,' began Kobrak. 'But Tobias Hoffmann, who lives in one of the maisonettes, gave us a list of who's left and uniform managed to speak to all of them and a couple of interesting things came up. First off, I ran them all through the PNC and got one hit for a Daniel Scribbs, aged forty-nine. He's unemployed and has a record for petty stuff like shoplifting, benefit fraud and stealing cars, but nothing violent. The others are all clean – there's a retired clergyman and his wife, Elliott and Michaela Falke, Mrs Pat Carmody and her son, Ralph – they all live in Ullswater House, the same block as William and Alma Stark. Hoffmann and Scribbs both live in Woodcroft, one of the maisonette blocks. And lastly, there's Vernon Reid who lives alone in Coniston House. That's the second interesting thing. According to Mrs Carmody, Reid's been in trouble with the FBI.'

'The FBI?' said Hamer. 'Did she say what for?'

'No,' said Kobrak. 'The officer thought she might have been having him on. Quite a character from what I can gather.'

'Is Reid American?' asked Anderson.

'There's nothing here about him being American,' said Kobrak.

'What else?' asked Kirby.

'Mrs Carmody and her son saw a light in the woods last night at around ten, half ten,' said Kobrak.

'That in itself isn't suspicious. It could have been anyone,' said Anderson. 'There's no outside lighting at night. All the residents carry torches or use the one on their phone.'

'No lighting?' said Hamer, incredulous.

'The council turned it off. The only lighting left is in the occupied flats,' said Anderson. 'Oh, and in the lifts. Which no one dares use.'

'Bloody hell,' muttered Drayton. 'What a shithole.'

'Did anyone admit to being out last night?' asked Masters.

'All of them said they were at home,' said Kobrak. 'Apart from Dan Scribbs, who was in the pub until eleven. He then got a lift home with a friend who dropped him at the Grayshott Road entrance.'

'That's the pedestrian entrance nearest the church,' said Kirby. 'He didn't hear or see anything?'

'No. But the officer who spoke to him got the impression he'd had a skinful.'

'We need to talk to the friend,' said Hamer. 'And establish the exact time. Could Mrs Carmody have been mistaken and seen Scribbs arrive home?'

'I can't see how,' said Kirby. 'Scribbs lives in the maisonette block. He wouldn't have to go anywhere near the woods. We should ask Hoffmann if he heard Scribbs come home. They live near one another.'

'There's something else,' said Kobrak. 'That wasn't all Mrs Carmody saw. She also said she saw Vernon Reid on the roof of Coniston House at about half ten.'

'What the hell was he doing up there at that time of night?' asked Hamer.

'He keeps pigeons, apparently,' said Kobrak. 'Reid said he didn't leave his flat all evening though. The officer who spoke to him made a point of asking, because from his balcony you can see across to the church. He specifically said he was indoors all evening.'

'Hang on,' said Kirby. 'How the hell did Mrs Carmody know it was Reid from that distance?'

'Binoculars,' said Kobrak. 'She goes out on clear nights and scopes out the estate. She recognised Reid's jacket. It's got a reflective strip on it.'

'Okay,' said Hamer. 'Take a closer look at Reid, see if there's anything in Mrs Carmody's claim he's been involved with the FBI and whether that links to William Stark in any way. Like I said, what we really need to know is what Stark was doing in that church. Why did he leave his flat? Was he going to meet someone? If so, who?'

'What about CCTV?' asked Masters. 'If he was going to meet someone and it wasn't a fellow resident then we should be able to pick them up entering the estate.'

Kobrak was generally regarded as the CCTV expert. 'Expert' meaning that he had patience and eyes like a hawk to sift through hours and hours of grainy footage. It was a job no one relished, except, it seemed, Kobrak. Anything on a screen and he was hooked, which Kirby, perhaps unfairly, put down to age. He was twenty-five.

'There is no CCTV inside the estate,' said Kobrak. 'There were cameras but they've long since been out of action. There's only one at the main entrance but we won't get that until tomorrow when the council offices reopen. I'm in the process of pulling footage from the surrounding area.'

'What about cameras on the demolition site?' asked Kirby. 'They should cover the entrance on Grayshott Road, the one Scribbs said he used.'

Kobrak nodded. 'I'll get on to them.'

'Forensics will be searching the wooded area first thing tomorrow. We need to pinpoint exactly where Mrs Carmody saw the light,' said Hamer, standing up. 'Right, I'll go and brief the chief super and then I've got to prepare for tomorrow's budget meeting.'

Kirby sent a silent prayer of thanks that the department's budget wasn't his responsibility. Or briefing the chief superintendent. It was bad enough answering to Hamer on a daily basis. He often thought about how the police was like a giant pyramid made up of people reporting to the people above them and so on until the buck stopped at the top, and what a terrible place that must be.

'Steve, can you stick with the CCTV tomorrow and comb all the surrounding streets for anyone walking in the direction of the estate,' said Kirby to Kobrak. He then turned to Drayton. 'Mark, can you make a start on Stark's past? Find out what you can about him. He was involved with the campaign to save the estate so perhaps he had enemies on the council. See if he's had any run-ins on the estate itself. And double-check for any more family. Same with the daughter.'

'Sure,' said Drayton, standing up and stretching. 'I'll take a look at his finances while—'

'No, Romy can do that,' said Kirby, nodding to Masters. 'Bank and credit card statements. Anything unusual, put a flag next to it.'

Drayton opened his mouth to protest then shut it again. 'What about his computer and phone?' he asked flatly.

'I doubt we'll get those back by tomorrow but feel free to give them a nudge.' Kirby turned to Anderson. 'We need to speak to the daughter again. She's identifying the body in the morning. Can you go with her? I want to talk to the other residents myself.'

'Sure. I have to talk to Carter about the Tyler case anyway. I need him to walk me through the blood spatter.' The Tylers had been a typical family living in a typical cul de sac. Except there was nothing typical about the way Mr Tyler had stabbed all three members of his own family and then slit his own throat. Kirby was glad he'd been away when it happened and hadn't had to witness the bloodbath that greeted the first responders when they'd arrived. The crime scene photos had been bad enough.

'What's up with him?' mouthed Anderson, as Drayton sloped off.

Kirby shrugged. 'No idea.'

'Fancy a pint later? You can tell me all about Italy. Bet you ate like a king.'

'Sorry, Pete, not tonight.' He decided not to mention his intention to check in on Connie at his mother's place – that bombshell could wait. 'I'm seeing Isabel then having an early one.'

Anderson raised his eyebrows. 'Lucky you. Eleanor's away visiting her sister so it looks like I'll be having a lonely takeaway.' He pulled a sad face. Eleanor was Anderson's wife, and Kirby knew full well that when she was away his partner's diet consisted of either take-outs or pub food.

'You'll live.'

Kirby would have given anything to be going back to the boat after a few pints with his partner and eating a takeaway by himself, but he had to talk to Isabel. The trip to Italy to scatter Livia's ashes had given him time to think, and to reflect on the secret he'd been carrying with him this past year. He'd been putting off telling her, worried how she'd react, but now he was back he had no excuse. Not even a pint with Anderson was going to get him out of this.

CHAPTER 7

After giving her statement, which seemed to have taken an age, Connie had wandered aimlessly around Soho, which was bustling even on a Sunday. She'd drifted in and out of shops in a bid to distract herself for a few hours, afraid of going home and being alone with the memory of the hanging man. Eventually, she'd tired of town and the weekend crowds and had sat on the bus home in a daze. Home these days was an Edwardian semi-detached three-bedder on a quiet, leafy road in Ealing. Her tenure at the Four Sails pub, where she'd lived for several years, had come to an abrupt end a few months ago. As a property guardian she'd paid a modest rent for the old pub, which had been an unusual but charming place to live. The downside – there was *always* a downside – was the fourteen-day notice period should the owners sell or begin building work, which was exactly what they'd done. When the company who managed the property had called to tell her she had two weeks to find a new home she'd gone into a tailspin. She'd been offered another property nearby, but that had been an old office building with a portable bathroom pod and was depressing beyond words. Then she'd bumped into Kirby who'd come up with the perfect solution: would she like to rent his mother's old house? At first she'd hesitated. Livia had died in the bedroom upstairs – not just died, but killed herself – plus, there was no way Connie would be able to afford a three-bedroom house all by herself. As it turned out, Kirby wasn't bothered about getting the full rent; he simply wanted the house occupied by someone he trusted while he decided what to do with it. After he'd shown her around, Connie had been smitten and said yes immediately.

Livia had had the kitchen at the rear of the property opened up, so the ground floor consisted of a living room at the front and then a large kitchen diner at the back. In the few months since she'd been there, Connie had spent most of her time at the back of the house, rarely venturing into the living room, which seemed dark and depressing by comparison. It was also the one room, apart from Livia's bedroom – which she'd never been in – that Connie most felt the presence of this woman who she'd never met. On one or two occasions she'd tried to watch a film from the large squishy sofa in the front room, but it had somehow felt wrong and she'd retreated back to the kitchen. It was hardly a sacrifice; the kitchen was as big as some flats she'd lived in and looked out on to the long, skinny garden, which was just starting to come to life after winter.

As well as a good-sized dining table where Connie had set up her laptop, and a smaller kitchen table, the kitchen had a battered old sofa covered in sheepskin rugs. After a long, hot shower she collapsed on to it and closed her eyes. The events of earlier that day kept buzzing around her mind like an annoying fly. She tried to think about something else – even Brian Kaplinsky – but it was no use. All she could think about was the disused church with its door ajar. How it had seemed like too good an opportunity to miss. She'd gone in without a second thought and remembered the feeling of something scraping her hair, tapping her head. Then the sensation that something was hovering above her and the shock she'd felt when she'd seen the gently swaying hanging body. Small details were coming back to her she hadn't remembered in her blind panic to exit the church. The man's short hair full of dust and blood, his blue jacket, the crease in his jeans. But it was the dangling feet that haunted her the most, and the untied shoelaces that had danced across the top of her head like a ghost.

She'd been sick on the way to the station to make her statement, much to her embarrassment, and suddenly realized she was ravenous. She made herself some toast and a cup of coffee and sat at the kitchen table. Terror, her cat, appeared and jumped up next to her. He watched with barely concealed annoyance as she ate the whole lot without even offering a finger to lick. 'Bad luck, buddy. You'll get yours in a minute.'

Whoever the hanging man was, he wasn't Brian Kaplinsky, which for some reason had been her first thought. Once the police had arrived and the shock of what happened had started to wear off a little, she'd realised that the dead man was too old to be Kaplinsky. She'd felt relief, then guilt. If it wasn't Kaplinsky, then she still had a chance to find him. Not that it would be easy – this was the closest she'd come in nearly a year. He never stayed anywhere for long, moving about the city like a shadow. It was one of the reasons she was so sure he had something to hide. Or he could just be an old-fashioned coward.

She returned to the sofa and the soft sheepskin rugs, where Terror curled up next to her. Soon her eyes were closed and the next thing she was aware of was a ringing sound. It slowly insinuated itself into a dream where she was walking through the crumbling remains of Windermere House, the phone ringing somewhere in the ruins, but she couldn't find it to answer. When she woke, the phone was still ringing, and it took her a moment to realise it was her mobile, which had slipped down the side of the sofa.

'Hello?' she answered groggily without noticing who had been calling.

'It's me,' said a male voice. 'I'm on the doorstep. You at home?'

It was Kirby. Connie groaned and stood up too fast, feeling light-headed. How long had she been asleep? Darkness had crept over the garden, tripping the outdoor lights, and Terror was nowhere to be seen.

'I must have fallen asleep,' she said, letting Kirby in. It was the first time she'd admitted him into his own mother's house – and she suddenly felt awkward. 'What are you doing here?'

'Came to see that you were okay. I heard about earlier. Kitchen?' He nodded in its direction.

'It was awful,' said Connie, sinking on to one of the kitchen chairs. 'He was just . . . hanging there. His feet touched the top of my head.' She shuddered again at the thought.

'I read your statement,' said Kirby, sitting down opposite. 'Pete and I are working the case. It wasn't a pretty sight.'

'So it's not suicide then, if you're involved?'

'No.'

'Who was he?' she asked, as the implication of what Kirby had just said settled in. Not suicide. That meant murder. It also meant that if he'd read her statement he knew about Kaplinsky.

'A retired architect called William Stark.'

'What?' Connie sat up. 'William Stark? But he designed the estate.'

'And lived there. Did you know him?'

Connie shook her head. 'No, but we have the drawings for the estate at work – and some of his other buildings – that's how I know who he is. Bloody hell.'

'He has a daughter, Alma, who also lives on the estate.'

Something nagged at her connected to William Stark, but she couldn't remember what it was. Or was it about his wife? She looked up to see Kirby rubbing his eyes and for the first time noticed how tired he looked.

'Shit, sorry,' she said, suddenly remembering. 'How was your trip?' Perhaps if she steered the conversation away from the case then she could avoid the inevitable question about why she'd been there.

'It was fine. Closure. All that bollocks. I got delayed coming back and haven't had much sleep.'

All Kirby had told her about his mother's suicide was that Livia had killed herself rather than become seriously ill with an unspecified disease. When Connie had asked if it was cancer, he'd muttered 'something like that' and changed the subject. There was definitely more to it, but she was his tenant, not confidante, so she'd left it.

'It has helped,' he went on. 'And it's a beautiful part of the world. I needed a change to be honest.'

'I'm surprised you didn't take Isabel with you,' said Connie.

'She couldn't get time off work. In any case, I needed to be on my own for a bit. Working with Pete you learn to enjoy moments of solitude.'

'He does rather fill every room going.' Connie smiled.

'Going back to today. You said in your statement you were visiting an old friend.'

Connie had been on the receiving end of Kirby's piercing green eyes before and reminded herself she'd done nothing wrong. 'Well, the "old friend" bit was a lie, but yes, I'd been told Brian Kaplinsky was living there. I could hardly say, oh, I was visiting the bloke I think might have been involved in my sister's death, could I?'

'You could have done, yes, but that's beside the point. I'm more interested in whether you were planning on telling me you'd found him.'

'I would have done but you were away.' That was actually a lie; she probably wouldn't have told him. 'You'd have only said not to go.'

'Not necessarily, but I would have told you not to go alone.'

46

'Okay, maybe that was a bit stupid. But he wasn't there, so it doesn't matter. He's gone. I was too late.' She stood up and went to get a glass of water. Tears were pricking at the corners of her eyes, and she didn't want Kirby to see. The shock of what had happened in the church meant that she hadn't fully processed the disappointment of not finding Kaplinsky and it suddenly hit her that she might never find him.

'We'll have to trace him,' said Kirby. 'Now he's part of the investigation I'll need to speak to him.'

'Really?' Connie could feel hope re-emerging. 'If you do find him can you—'

'I'll see what I can do. But I have no authority to question him about Sarah's death, you do understand that?'

'I know . . . but what if he was involved?'

'It was an accident, Connie. I know you want answers but perhaps there aren't any. Anyhow, you should see Victim Support.'

'It's a bit late for that.'

'No, I mean about today.'

'Nuh-uh,' she said, shaking her head. She'd seen Victim Support after the Blackwater case and although it had helped a bit, she couldn't face going through it all again.

'Think about it.' He pulled a leaflet out of his jacket and placed it on the table.

'What about you? Are you seeing anyone after Livia's death?'

'You are allowed to say the word, you know. Suicide.'

'Sorry.'

'But in answer to your question, I was but no longer am.'

'Oh?'

'It wasn't helping. I only did it to keep the DCI off my back.'

Connie wasn't sure she entirely believed that, but it was none of her business what Kirby did or didn't do.

'Going back to Grasmere and the church,' said Kirby. 'Did you notice anything unusual? Apart from the body, obviously.'

'Nothing. The only person I saw was the figure coming out of the wood before I made my way down to the ground floor. A man.'

'Vernon Reid. And he didn't go into the church?'

'Nope. I'd say he was heading for the Grayshott Road exit.'

Kirby nodded. 'What about the church – anything special about it?'

'Not really. I saw an opportunity and took it. You know me.' She smiled. 'Ever the urbex. Why, you think it's relevant?'

Kirby shrugged: 'Maybe. Or perhaps it was just an easy place to meet. Someone had a key. It hadn't been broken in to.'

'Surely that narrows down your list of suspects,' said Connie. 'Find the key, find your killer.'

'If only it were that simple,' said Kirby, standing up, getting ready to leave. 'I just wanted to make sure you were okay. Think about it.' He tapped the Victim Support leaflet on the table.

'I will.' Connie knew she wouldn't but didn't want to argue.

It had started raining again when Kirby opened the door to leave. 'It goes without saying, if you remember anything—'

'I'll call you. Yada, yada, yada.'

After locking the front door, Connie went back to the kitchen and picked up the Victim Support leaflet. She skim-read it and then threw it in the bin.

CHAPTER 8

Back at his houseboat, Kirby rummaged through the freezer where he found a tub of Livia's Bolognese sauce. It was the final one and he'd been saving it. It would be the last time he'd eat his mother's food and it seemed like as good a day as any. Isabel wasn't due for another half an hour and so he took a moment to sit down while the pasta sauce slowly thawed on the hob. He hadn't quite been truthful when Connie asked about counselling in the wake of Livia's suicide. Yes, he had done it to appease Hamer, and to a certain extent, his father, but the reason he'd quit wasn't as simple as he'd made out. The reality was he'd found the sessions difficult because he couldn't tell the truth. He'd sat there as the therapist had talked about guilt, about how we process the horror of a loved one taking their own life, unable to fathom why we hadn't seen any of the signs, the feeling that we should have done something, that we might have been able to stop them. But that wasn't Kirby's problem; he'd known exactly why his mother had taken her own life. How? Because he'd been complicit.

Yes, he'd tried to talk her out of it, that was only natural, but that had been before he'd been in full possession of the facts. Once possessed of those his stance changed drastically. It hadn't been an immediate transformation. His grief and anger had been thrown into conflict, but he'd eventually realised his reactions were based on his own selfishness, the bottom line being that he didn't want to lose his mother. Then the reality hit – who was he to dictate whether she should continue to live with this terrible disease? It was her life. There was no cure. More to the point, he'd then put himself in her shoes and realised with sudden clarity that he would want to do the same. So he'd abandoned the therapy sessions. And now, somehow, he needed to tell Isabel about the whole damn thing.

He got up to stir the sauce before opening a bottle of wine. He'd just poured himself a glass when he felt the boat rock. Isabel. It wasn't that he didn't want to see her – he did – but he wasn't looking forward to the conversation he knew was coming. She didn't know about Livia's illness, the fatal familial insomnia. Isabel thought it had been an aggressive cancer. How she'd come to this conclusion he wasn't sure and even wondered whether it was Livia's doing. Regardless of how Isabel had come under the misapprehension, he'd made no attempt to correct her, and the longer it went on the harder it became. It was now eating away at him day and night. The stupid thing was that he didn't know what he was afraid of – that Isabel would drop him like a hot potato? Unlikely. Would it hang over their relationship like a cloud of doom? Possibly. Would he feel pressured into taking the test that would tell him if he'd inherited the fatal gene, something he was adamant he didn't want to do? That would depend on Isabel's reaction. What he wanted more than anything was to continue their relationship as it had been until Livia's illness, a perfect balance of casual and yet serious. Their relationship was also – and this was the unusual part – blissfully uncomplicated. Except now it wasn't, and he bloody hated it. He also knew how upset she'd be, possibly angry, too, that he hadn't confided in her.

'Lew!' Isabel threw her arms around him and he smelt roses and geraniums in her hair. 'I've missed you. How are you? You look tired. No sleep?'

'Not much, no. The seats at Verona Airport are spectacularly uncomfortable and I had to go straight to work from Gatwick.'

'What, in the Citroën? I bet Idris Hamer had a fit.' Isabel laughed.

'It's not his fault,' said Kirby, hardly believing he was defending his boss. 'The rules about using civilian cars are there for a reason. Anyhow, he didn't say a word.'

'Maybe he and Andrea are getting on better.'

'Maybe.' Kirby wasn't convinced about Hamer's marital situation improving. He'd uncovered an affair his boss had had the previous year.

'Something smells good. Is that Livia's sauce?' asked Isabel, shrugging off her jacket and throwing it over a chair.

'It is.'

'I'm honoured.' Isabel helped herself to a glass of water and leant on the kitchen counter, smiling.

'What?'

'It's just good to see you, that's all.'

'Same. Glass of wine? Or some bottled water?'

'No wine for me. Early start in the morning. And tap's fine.' She raised her glass.

'Come on, let's sit down for a bit,' said Kirby, heading to the sofa. Isabel followed and they both made themselves comfortable. 'God, I'm glad to be home,' he said.

'Was it tough then?' asked Isabel.

'I don't mean that – Italy was fine. Cathartic. It's what Livia wanted. Being stuck in an airport for ten hours then going straight to a murder scene isn't the best welcome back I've had.'

'But you're here now, with me, and that's what matters.' She kissed him on the cheek. 'It'd be nice if we could go away somewhere together. You need more than a week.'

'I know, but it's difficult.' He rubbed his eyes, trying to think of the best way to start what he needed to say.

'Policemen are entitled to holidays you know. And you need to look after yourself.'

'I do look after myself,' he said. 'I'm careful what I eat and get lots of exercise. I'm not following in Pete's footsteps.'

'Still being naughty then?'

Kirby rolled his eyes. 'Eleanor's away, up in Scotland visiting her sister. Pete will probably eat his own bodyweight in carbs and sugar while she's gone. He's having a takeaway this evening and I can tell you now it won't be sushi.'

'How's their daughter – where is she, America?'

'Yeah, Boston, I think.'

'Must be weird having a daughter so far away.'

'As far as I can see Pete's glad of the peace and quiet. He's finally got somewhere to store all his taxidermy stuff. Mind you, when she comes back to visit she'll be sharing a room with God-knows-what.' Kirby's eyes fell on the three-legged stuffed fox standing in the corner – a present from his partner a few Christmases ago – and tried to focus on what he needed to say. 'Isabel, while I was away I did a lot of thinking. About us.'

'Me too,' said Isabel, shifting around to face him.

'Oh?'

'Don't look so worried, Lew. Nothing bad. At least I hope not . . .' She suddenly looked serious.

'Well, I wasn't thinking anything bad either. Quite the opposite in fact.'

'Good, because I need to tell you something.' She reached out and took his hand and in that moment he felt the fear. Livia had said almost the exact same thing just before telling him she was dying of an incurable disease that he had a fifty-fifty chance of inheriting.

'Please don't tell me you've got Bob Dylan tickets,' he said in a bid to deflect the fear.

'Stop it! I'm trying to be serious.' Isabel was a fully paid-up member of the Bob Dylan fan club, whereas Kirby was most definitely not. She had managed to educate him enough to appreciate Dylan's writing and composing skills, but he couldn't get past the voice. He'd tried – oh *God*, had he tried – but it just irritated the hell out of him.

'Sorry. Go on. I'm all ears.'

'Well . . .' She was playing with his fingers now, always a bad sign as far as Kirby was concerned.

'Can you stop doing that and just tell me?' He pulled his hand away.

'I had a bit of a shock while you were away. I missed my period and . . . I'm pregnant.'

The word hung in the air between them. Kirby was speechless, his brain thinking a million things at once. Then he remembered the pasta sauce. 'Shit!' He leapt off the sofa and slid the pan away from the heat just in time. 'Shit,' he said again, this time turning to look at Isabel. 'You're really pregnant? Are you sure?'

'As sure as I can be. The tests are pretty accurate.'

'Christ,' he said, returning to the sofa where he pulled Isabel close. 'Bloody hell. I mean, Christ.'

'That's how I felt when I found out,' said Isabel. 'I don't know how it happened, but it has. Contraceptives aren't as infallible as we think.'

'Why didn't you call me?'

'I didn't want to disturb you – the trip to Italy was important.'

'So's this,' said Kirby.

'I know, I know . . . but I wanted to tell you face to face.'

'I need a drink,' said Kirby, letting go of Isabel and standing up.

'Have one for me.'

'Oh . . .' He stopped and turned. 'You don't mind if I do?'

'Course not. Go ahead.'

Kirby went back to the kitchen where he retrieved his glass and tried to untangle his thoughts. He and Isabel had talked about children, briefly, neither of them particularly bothered one way or the other. He hadn't not wanted kids; he just never actively wanted them. The FFI had changed that. If he had inherited the faulty gene then he'd have a fifty-fifty chance of passing it on, so in his mind the whole issue of kids had been closed down. Until now. He had to tell her about the FFI. He took a long swig of wine, topped up the glass and went back to the sofa.

'How do you feel about this, Lew?' Isabel asked. 'I know it's a shock. It was for me too.'

'If I'm honest, I don't really know . . .'

Isabel raised her eyebrows in a look that said, *careful, Lew.*

'What I mean is . . . before we get into this, I mean *really* get into this, there's something you need to know. I've been meaning to tell you for a while, but I kept putting it off.'

'Don't tell me – you listened to an entire Dylan album without throwing something.'

'Touché,' said Kirby, raising his glass. 'But no, seriously, it's about Livia.'

'What about her?'

'Livia didn't have cancer, it was something else. A disease called fatal familial insomnia.' He saw the incomprehension on Isabel's face followed by the hurt that he hadn't told her. But there was worse news to come. 'It's a hereditary disease and so there's a fifty-fifty chance I've got it too and if I do . . .' He trailed off, not wanting to say the words.

Isabel stared at him. 'The baby as well?'

He nodded. 'And as things currently stand, there's no cure.'

'Why didn't you tell me any of this?' Isabel looked crestfallen.

'I was going to but . . .' He shrugged. 'I couldn't find the right time.'

'Well, you sure as hell found it tonight. Christ, Lew.'

'I'm sorry,' he said. And he was. Desperately.

CHAPTER 9

Reid had slept badly on Sunday night, plagued by dreams that were all too familiar. He'd eventually fallen into a fitful sleep after his alarm went off and was shocked to see it was gone seven when he woke up. Without even bothering to shower he got dressed and went outside. He had no idea how long the police had worked at the old church the previous night, or whether they'd be back today, but he wanted to speak to Jason before they did. He locked up and quickly made his way through the polytunnel to the main stairwell and down to ground level. A fine drizzle greeted him as he stepped outside. The demolition site sat still and quiet, the workmen yet to start. Without delay, he headed towards Ullswater House, his head bent down against the fine rain. The recent deluges had invigorated the weeds which sprang up with enthusiasm in any crack or crevice they could. The paving stones along this part of the path had buckled badly and he thought of the daisy pushers. Left to their own devices they'd demolish Grasmere from below with no need for machinery. When the End came – and it would soon, Reid could feel it – all of this, the estate, Pinder Hill, London – the world as he knew it – would be gone.

After a few minutes, he reached Ullswater House and the garages that lined the ground floor. There was no chance of missing the Shires'. The graffiti was faded now, but the image was still clear: hands clasped as though in prayer. It had appeared in the weeks following Kevin and Jason's disappearance and had remained ever since. Reid stopped by the metal door and gently knocked.

'Jaye?' He waited and then knocked again harder. 'Jaye, it's me. I need to talk to you.' He checked his surroundings to make sure no one was around – it was a little early, although the Falkes were early risers, probably up but not out. He heard a noise on the other side of the metal door and watched as it swung up a few inches. Reid then pulled the door up himself, just enough so that he could slip inside. It slid shut with a metallic clang.

Jason was sitting on a battered old sofa, another relic of the eighties that wouldn't have looked out of place in Reid's flat, where he'd presumably slept. He was rolling a cigarette, a crumpled blanket next to him. 'What are you doing here?' he asked Reid without looking up.

'Will Stark's been found dead in the old church,' Reid replied, without preamble. 'Remember him?'

A flicker of recognition passed over Jason's face. 'Vaguely.'

'The police were here all day yesterday, didn't you see them?'

'Nope. I wasn't here. I went to the hospital and got the key to this place. Got back late.'

'You could have stayed at mine,' said Reid. 'I came back to tell you but you'd gone.'

'Yeah, well, made my own arrangements, didn't I? I've stayed in worse.'

So had Reid, far worse. 'How was she?' he asked.

'Sally? Dying.' Jason lit his cigarette and inhaled deeply. 'She knows I had nothing to do with it, Vern. She just wants the truth.' He blew out the smoke and picked a piece of tobacco from his lower lip. 'She wants to know what happened to Kev.'

Reid nodded. 'Why'd she give you the key to this place?' he asked, looking around the garage properly for the first time and realising with a shock that it was full of Kevin's things.

'Thought I might want something of his. Told me to take as I want. Otherwise it's landfill.'

The thought appalled Reid. He'd had no idea Sally Shires had kept her son's things locked up in here for all these years.

'She also hopes I might find something the police missed,' said Jason. 'Not like I ever had the chance to look back then, is it?'

Jason was right. He knew Kevin better than anyone and yet it would have been strangers who'd searched through his stuff looking for clues as to what might have happened to him.

'I'll help,' said Reid.

Jason smiled. 'In that case a cup of tea would be a good start.'

Reid nodded. He was gasping for a cup too, having left the flat without even a glass of water. He hoped he wouldn't run into any police on the way out or coming back. He was about to reach down to pull the door open when Jason spoke.

'This man, Stark. What happened to him?'

Reid turned. 'I don't know, I'll see what I can find out. He had a daughter, Alma.' At the mention of Alma's name Reid saw unmistakeable recognition on Jason's face. She was a similar age to both men but hadn't attended the same school. 'She still lives here.'

'More fool her,' said Jason. 'Hey, you'll never guess who I saw yesterday on my way back. Toby Hoffmann.'

Reid nodded. 'Someone else who never left.'

'Remember the time we caught The Hoff in the church?'

Reid smiled. 'I'd forgotten about that,' he said. 'Him and Michaela Falke. The Falkes never left either.'

'I reckon they're still at it. He looked like he'd seen a ghost when he saw me – like he knew we'd seen them.'

'He hasn't seen you for nearly thirty years, Jaye, no wonder he looked as though he'd seen a ghost.'

'Reckon it was more to do with me asking how the preacher's wife was,' said Jason, snorting with laughter.

'Adultery's no laughing matter, my friend, and he'll pay for it when the Day of Reckoning comes.' Despite his words a smile crossed Reid's face. He'd never liked Toby Hoffmann, nor Elliott and Michaela Falke for that matter. They looked down on him, he knew, and told everyone he'd been in a cult. They were ignorant, too. 'By the way, the cops asked me where I was on Saturday night. If I was alone. I lied.'

Jason nodded his thanks. 'It's not like you to lie, Vern, so I appreciate it.'

'It's true, I don't like to lie. But I like the cops even less.'

CHAPTER 10

Monday morning was usually a real slog, fuelled by coffee and the occasional fried breakfast depending on how much she'd drunk over the weekend, but today Connie was glad to be back at work. It would help take her mind off Kaplinsky and William Stark's dead body hanging from the scaffolding. She was in the main reading room at RADE where she was currently acting curator while her boss, Richard Bonaro, was on sabbatical. A long table with angle-poise reading lamps along its centre dominated the room and she'd managed to cover the entire thing with William Stark's drawings of the Grasmere Estate. Windermere House, which was currently being demolished, had been identical in almost every respect to Ullswater House apart from one thing. Ullswater House had one flat on the top floor that was bigger than any of the other flats on the estate. After a bit of digging, she'd surmised this was where Stark had lived. From the plans, it looked like two flats had been knocked together. Architectural journals of the time – which she had access to online – showed a stunning open-plan space with views over the woodland at the centre of the estate. One photo-graph showed what looked like a party in the flat that couldn't have been taken long after the estate opened, judging by the 1970s clothes and haircuts, with Stark and his wife posing for the camera.

At her computer she typed 'All Hallows Church Grasmere' into Google. A suspected arson attack from 2005 was the first story to come up, after which there was nothing about the current church at all. What there was, however, was a lot about the previous church that had once stood on the land where the estate was built, a tin tabernacle called Saint Agatha's. There were only two tin tabernacles – the smaller tin churches were often referred to as tabernacles – left in London that she was aware of. One in Hackney – currently up for sale – and another in Kilburn connected to the Sea Cadets. She clicked on a link dedicated to the history of tin churches within the UK, which covered both existing and demolished buildings, and scrolling down to the entries for London she found Saint Agatha's and read the short piece of text.

'Made by William Cooper Ltd, the Church of Saint Agatha was purchased for £150 and erected on Chalfont Street in 1901 to serve the local community. Erected over a natural spring the church soon became very popular as the water was deemed to have healing properties. It escaped two wars with minor damage and had been in constant use as a place of worship until 1965 when it fell into disrepair. It was dismantled in 1971 to make way for Grasmere Housing Estate.'

As she lingered on the word 'dismantled', she heard the large oak front door downstairs slam shut and a few moments later footsteps echoed on the stone staircase that led up to the reading room. There were only four people, including Connie, who had keys: her boss, Richard Bonaro; Ty, the cleaner, who only came in on Fridays; and her overall boss, Art Blunt, whose family had set up the archive in the late 1800s. She heard the footsteps reach the top of the stairs followed by a familiar sneeze. Being April the tree pollen was high and even Connie had felt the odd twinge in her eyes, but her boss Art had always suffered badly.

'Art!' she said, cheerfully. 'How are you?'

'Not so bad. This damned hay fever is killing me though.' He took off a pair of wraparound sunglasses that made him look like he'd stepped out of a 1990s pop video. 'What's all this in aid of?' he asked, peering at the drawings laid out on the table. 'This is the Grasmere Estate.'

'Yes . . .' She wasn't sure whether Art would have heard the news. 'Did you hear about William Stark? He was found dead on Sunday morning. Actually, it was me that found him.'

'Good God,' said Art. 'Are you alright? Do you need time off? Just say the word if you—'

'It's fine, Art, really. It was a shock, obviously, but I'm okay. I found him in the estate's church.' She paused. 'I've just found out about the tin church that used to be there. I was hoping we might have something on it.'

'I doubt it,' said Art. 'But you might find an old photograph pre-construction. I believe we have quite a few images of the site before it was flattened to make way for the new build. They should be here somewhere.'

'What happened to the church? I read that it was dismantled, which isn't quite the same as being demolished.'

'Correct. I think Will Stark saved it, but I have no idea why, or what happened to it. I used to know him, you know,' said Art, waving his hand. 'Long time ago now. Before you were born. Strange man. You know that he lived at Grasmere?'

Connie nodded.

'He and his wife held parties in his flat – Jean and I even went to one. Ironic that he should die in the place he not only built but spent a lifetime defending. Anyhow.' Art paused and a serious look settled on his face. 'Forget that for the moment. I need to talk to you about something more pressing. Shall we go to the kitchen and have some coffee?'

It clearly wasn't a question – the tin church would have to wait.

They made small talk as Connie prepared coffee in the small kitchen at the rear of the building, but the atmosphere had changed. Art definitely had something he wanted to get off his chest. They sat at a well-worn wooden table that had once belonged to some architect whose name Connie could never remember.

'Do we have any biscuits?' Art asked.

'Oh, somewhere, I think. Hang on.' Connie got up and rummaged about in the cupboard. 'Plain digestives. That's all.'

'That'll do,' said Art, grabbing two from the packet and dipping them simultaneously into his coffee before continuing. 'Jean's got me on some weird old people's diet. She won't allow biscuits in the house now. Bloody stupid.'

Art was stalling, she could tell. 'What is it you wanted to talk to me about?' Perhaps Bonaro was coming back. His sabbatical seemed never-ending.

'I've been going through the finances,' Art began, slowly. Connie didn't like the sound of this – anything to do with money always signalled trouble.

'There's no easy way to say this,' he said. 'I'm afraid that unless we can raise some funds we might have to close the archive.'

This had not been what Connie was expecting. As far as she knew Art and his wife, Jean, were rolling in it.

'*Might* have to close?' she said. *What the fuck is that supposed to mean?*

'*Will* have to close. I'm so terribly sorry.' He looked at her with his red, hay-fevery eyes and for a moment Connie wondered whether there were tears too. She sat in stunned silence as the information sank in.

'This must be an awful shock for you, and I'm really very sorry. I thought that I should give you some warning in case you wanted to look for another job.'

'But won't Richard be coming back? He's brilliant at fundraising.' It was all she could think of to say.

'That was the other thing I wanted to talk to you about. Richard's not coming back. He's taken another post. Far more money than I could ever offer him and with a research fellowship attached.' By the look on Art's face he was none too pleased.

'How long do we have?' asked Connie, trying to think practically and to quell the panic she felt rising. Fundraising couldn't be that difficult, could it? The last thing she wanted was to have to look for another job. Plus, she liked it here. In fact the more she thought about it the more she wanted to stay.

'Three months,' said Art.

Connie nearly spat out her coffee. '*Three months?* I don't understand, how long's this been going on? Why didn't you say anything?' Connie did the accounts for the day-to-day running of the archive and knew everything was in order. There had to be another reason.

'It's Ethan,' said Art. Ethan was Art's son. He worked in the City and drove a flash car. Connie had only met him once but that was enough: he had 'wanker' stamped all over him. 'One of his business investments has gone sour,' Art went on. 'There's every chance I'll have to bail him out.'

Connie bit her tongue. Art's family affairs were none of her business. Then again, this was her job they were talking about. 'But RADE is part of your family, Art. It's your history. This building, the collection, it's the Blunt family archive as much as it is a resource for the public. You can't let that go just because—'

Art held up his hand to stop her. 'Believe me, Connie, this is the last thing I want, but Ethan's family – my flesh and blood.' Connie fully expected him to start banging his chest. She'd never understood why lovely, caring parents such as Art and Jean stuck by their dickhead children. Perhaps she was missing a gene. 'I have a duty to him as well,' Art finished.

They fell silent, Connie's brain processing the ramifications of what Art had just told her. RADE would probably be closed. She'd lose her job. Ethan's fucked-up business venture was going to cost the family its history. The red mist began to descend and Connie made herself take a deep breath.

'I'll do everything that I can to avoid this but . . .' Art shook his head. 'I'm not getting any younger and Ethan has no interest in the archive.'

He would if it made shitloads of money, thought Connie.

'I'd make sure the collection went to a good home,' Art went on. 'Perhaps the V&A might take it. Integrate it with the RIBA collection. I don't know.'

'You sound like you've already made up your mind,' said Connie, unable to keep the irritation from her voice. 'There must be someone out there who'd be willing to invest with us. Heritage is big business these days. What about Richard, can't he help as a favour? A swan song?'

'He won't have time. Although you could talk to him.'

'Me?'

'I'm afraid that I was a little short with him when we spoke. A plea for help might be better coming from you.'

Connie couldn't imagine why Bonaro would give her advice if it was for Art's benefit. Still, it was worth a try. But she wanted something in return.

'I'll speak to him,' she said. 'On one condition. I've been running this place single-handed now for over a year. With no help and for no extra money. If you want me to save your family archive I need to know my job is secure and that this won't happen again. What if something happened to you and Jean and Ethan was left in charge? Where would that leave me?' There was no way that she was going to waste her time saving the archive only for Ethan to sell it in a year's time.

'Message received, loud and clear,' said Art, contritely. 'I'll speak to Jean. I'm sure there's a solution to keep us all happy.'

Connie hoped so. Because if there wasn't she was out of a job.

CHAPTER 11

Kirby had just finished interviewing the Carmodys on the ninth floor of Ullswater House when he received a text from one of the search teams on the estate. A makeshift camp had been found in the wooded area at its centre. He was glad to leave the block of flats, as he was finding its bleak concrete gangways inordinately depressing that morning, and he headed into the woodland which felt more of a tropical paradise the longer he spent on the estate. The earlier drizzle had given way to sun and the trees shone bright in the spring light, the smell of fresh foliage and new life totally at odds with its impoverished surroundings. Anderson was at Westminster Mortuary with Alma Stark for the formal identification of her father, so Kirby was alone.

The primitive camp was in one of the densest parts of the wood and he followed the sound of voices until he came to an area cordoned off under a broad oak tree. He could see that someone had draped an old tarpaulin across the tree's lower branches to make a shelter. Various bits of detritus lay scattered in the surrounding grass. A SOCO was carefully picking up cigarette butts from the trampled ground and dropping them into evidence bags, while another was bagging various items of food packaging. There was no sign of any personal effects and Kirby felt vaguely disappointed. The camp could have been there for weeks, if not months. The recent storms – not to mention the foxes – redistributed litter on the estate like confetti.

The camp had been well sheltered and he doubted anyone would have noticed it from the flats during the day. But a light at night – especially if it was moving – would have been visible had anyone been watching. If someone had been camping there on the night Stark was killed then it might account for the light the Carmodys had told him about. It had been moving, according to Mrs Carmody, from the woods towards the church, or the pedestrian exit on Grayshott Road behind it. There was also access to the demolition site on Grayshott Road, but that was secure and he had trouble envisaging anyone gaining access to the rest of the estate from there. From the walkway outside the Carmodys' flat Kirby had been able to clearly see Reid's pigeon coop, but he doubted Mrs Carmody would have been able to say for certain that the figure she'd seen was Vernon Reid, something she confirmed when he asked, even with her binoculars. She'd *assumed* it was Reid.

He walked the area around the camp and spoke to one of the SOCOs before deciding there was nothing much else to see. He was enjoying being outside under the trees and decided to walk through the woods to Vernon Reid's flat in Coniston House. As he walked, his mind inevitably wandered to his conversation with Isabel the previous night. She'd been hurt that he hadn't told her about the FFI, lying about the cancer. He'd tried to explain that he hadn't meant to, that it had just happened. They'd talked into the early hours until they found themselves going round in circles. Central to their discussion – along with whether they were ready to become parents – was whether Kirby should take the gene test to determine whether or not he'd inherited his mother's FFI. He was adamantly against taking it, whereas Isabel had argued he should on the grounds that if the gene had been passed to him then there was also a chance the baby might have it. Until now it had been his decision only to make and he wasn't sure he liked the idea of having to be accountable to anyone else. Having a kid would change everything. His refusal to take the FFI gene test would become indefensible and he couldn't inflict that on Isabel. Eventually, they'd agreed to give it a few days – they both needed time to process what was happening. Luckily, it was early in the pregnancy so they had some time, at least, to think things through. So much for an uncomplicated relationship.

Emerging from the shelter of the trees into the children's playground on the opposite side of the estate, Kirby was met with a blast of icy spring wind. He pulled his jacket tighter and tried to visualise the play area as it must have been when the estate was new; small, happy children playing safely while their parents looked on. In later years, as the estate fell into disrepair, the children's swings and see-saws had become home to more malign activities drug dealing, prostitution and loan sharking. He crossed the now derelict play area with its sun-bleached, chipped dinosaurs until he came to the main entrance of Reid's block, where he paused for a moment. A sea of satellite dishes clung to the facade – hundreds of them, like limpets, with nothing to transmit and no one to transmit to. The overhead walkways to the left cast dark, cold shadows that seemed to constantly shift. Large puddles of water from yesterday's downpours reflected the surrounding decay with crystal-clear clarity in the bright light.

An initial search on Reid after last night's briefing had thrown up a few interesting facts. That morning, unable to sleep, Kirby had slipped out of bed at 5 a.m. and sat on the deck of the boat with his iPad and a cup of coffee, and done some more digging. Reid and his mother, Frances, had left the Grasmere Estate in 1992 for a new life in Waco, Texas, where they'd joined a group of almost a hundred Branch Davidians living at a compound called Mount Carmel. The compound had been run by a charismatic preacher called David

Koresh, who professed to be an incarnation of Christ, blessed with the gift of prophecy. Reid's mother had initially heard Koresh talk at Newbold College in the late eighties, when he'd come to the UK on a recruitment drive, and had immediately fallen under his spell.

The year after arriving at Mount Carmel, Reid and his mother were caught up in the Waco siege that had gripped the world. Seventy-six men, women and children – twenty-four of whom were from the UK – died after a botched raid by the FBI and the Bureau of Alcohol, Tobacco, Firearms and Explosives. Reid had survived the stand-off, unlike his mother who had been one of the unlucky twenty-four, but had been charged with firearms offences and sentenced to fourteen years in the American penal system. Upon his release, in 2008, he'd been deported back to the UK, where he returned to his childhood home, the Grasmere Estate. To say he'd been in trouble with the FBI was an understatement. Small wonder he disliked the police.

Texas must have seemed like an exotic world by comparison, thought Kirby, as he gazed up at Reid's block. The nineties had been a particularly low point for the estate with murders, drug-related deaths and the disappearance of two teenage boys dominating the London press. On the top floor Kirby saw what looked like plastic sheeting covering part of the walkway. He'd first spotted it through Mrs Carmody's binoculars and wondered whether Reid was growing cannabis. There had been no mention of it in the uniformed officer's report.

In the block's main hallway he bypassed the lift, which was miraculously still working, and took the stairs. Nothing felt safe in this decaying skeleton of an estate and he certainly didn't trust anything mechanical. The concrete stairwell was strewn with rubbish – carrier bags, cigarette packets, leaves, flyers – and when he reached Reid's floor and turned on to the walkway he was hit by a strong gust of wind driving grit into his eyes. When they began to clear he saw a figure standing at the entrance to what looked like a makeshift polytunnel. The man was as still as a marksman's practice target, holding what looked like a thermos flask, but something about the way he carried himself suggested it could have been a shotgun.

'Vernon Reid?' Kirby called.

'Who's asking?'

'Police.' Kirby held up his ID and began walking towards the man past more boarded-up doors and windows. He sensed a simmering hostility from Reid, who looked to be in his late forties. A scar ran down one side of his face, the crow's feet around the eye disjointed like a re-routed path. Reid scanned his badge intently and only when he appeared satisfied did he look up. Kirby noticed what looked like burns on his left hand and wondered whether they were a relic of Waco or something more recent.

'What do you want?' asked Reid.

Now he was up close, Kirby could see behind Reid into the home-made greenhouse. Seed trays were neatly lined up against one side and a trellis had been tacked to the facade of the building that some kind of plant had crawled up. Hoffmann had said he was a gardener.

'I'd like to ask you a few questions. Can we go inside?' said Kirby.

Reid regarded him for a moment and with a barely perceptible nod of the head turned and led him through the polytunnel and to his flat, which was the only dwelling on the entire floor that wasn't boarded up.

'Is this about Will Stark?' Reid asked once they were inside. He put the thermos down and gestured to a couple of wooden chairs in the sparse kitchen, their padded vinyl seats a leftover from the 1970s. Looking around the room it was clear nothing had been updated for decades. Despite that, it was clean and tidy with a cross hung over the doorway and photographs Blu-Tacked to the fridge door. They, too, had been there for decades, judging by their curled edges and yellowing paper.

'Yes,' said Kirby. 'Did you know him?'

'Everyone did,' said Reid.

'I'll take that as a "yes", then. Did you like him?'

'What kind of question is that?'

'Did you?'

'Yes, I liked him.'

'Did he have any enemies that you know of? Perhaps he'd fallen out with someone here on the estate?'

'Not that I know of.' Reid shrugged.

'Can you tell me again where you were on Saturday night?'

Reid sighed. 'I was here. I told the officer that yesterday.'

'Did you leave the flat at all for any reason? To water the plants? Smoke?'

'I don't smoke,' came the quick reply. 'And no, I didn't.' Reid was leaning against the sink with his arms tightly folded. Kirby could sense his nerves and would have bet his hands were shaking had they been visible.

'We have a witness who saw you – or someone who looked like you – on the roof that night.'

'They're mistaken. I didn't leave the flat.'

'Any idea who it might have been then? Only we're under the impression there's no one else in this block apart from you.'

'There isn't. But anyone could have walked in, gone up there.'

It was a good point; Kirby had walked straight in, the main entrance unlocked. 'Do you leave the door to the roof open too?'

'Sometimes. I keep pigeons up there. I probably forgot to lock up.'

'What do the council make of that?'

'They don't care,' said Reid, simply.

'Do you get many visitors to the estate? People wandering in, hanging about in the woods? Only it looks as though someone's been sleeping rough there recently.'

Reid's eyes flickered towards the window then back to the interior of the kitchen. 'No one comes here any more. It's a ghost town. Are we nearly done? I need to water my plants.'

Kirby followed Reid back out on to the walkway where it was blindingly bright after the interior of the kitchen.

'I'm curious,' said Kirby. 'What's it like living up here all alone?'

'It suits me,' said Reid. 'And I'm not alone, I have the pigeons. They're all the company I need. Them and God.'

CHAPTER 12

'Man, what took you so long?' said Jason, when Reid returned to the garage.

Reid eased the door down as quietly as he could. 'The police came looking for me. They wanted to know about Stark. I had to wait until they'd gone.'

Jason eagerly took the flask Reid proffered and set about pouring two cups of tea. It was lucky that he'd used the thermos. Explaining why he was carrying two mugs of tea would have been awkward. Reid had watched the detective leave the block of flats and walk towards Ullswater House where he'd disappeared under one of the walkways. He'd said he was going to talk to the Falkes, but Reid didn't trust him and had waited until he was well out of sight before slipping out of the flat and sneaking back to the garage where Jason was waiting.

'They're all over the estate?'

'No. This one was on his own. They're in the wood and around the church mostly. I reckon now they've spoken to me they'll be concentrated up the other end. What are we looking for, anyhow?' Reid asked, keeping his voice low as he looked around the garage.

'Dunno. Probably nothing. Thanks for the brew.' Jason raised his cup.

Reid sat down on the sofa and began opening a stack of brown envelopes addressed to Kevin. From the postmarks he could see they'd arrived after Kevin's disappearance. 'Do you miss him?' he asked Jason.

'Yeah. At first I was pissed off with him, you know? Then when I realised something must've happened to him it kind of hit me. So yeah, I miss him.'

Since Jason's arrival Reid's emotions had been thrown into confusion. He'd never mourned the loss of his gentle friend, believing that one day they'd pick up where they left off and that Kev's dirty laugh would once more have him bent double. But from the little he now knew, this was never going to happen and rather than grieving, he felt anger. How could he grieve until he knew the truth? 'So tell me again what happened that day?' he said, looking up at Jason. He wanted it straight in his head. He'd known about their plan to run away but Reid had been busy with his mother that day, packing for Texas, sorting the flat out.

'Thursday, after school, we went and hung out in the woods by the old tyre. Remember that?'

Reid nodded. He remembered it well – someone had strung up the tyre from one of the trees, as well as some other odd bits of rope, and they'd spend hours there, smoking and climbing on to the tyre, swinging back and forth. One of the men from the estate, Joe Rickman, came with his Staffie sometimes. He'd trained it to catch hold of the rope with its jaws and it would just hang there in some kind of canine trance as Joe swung the rope in circles. 'I still see Joe Rickman,' he said. 'Remember him?'

Jason looked up. 'Yeah. Decent bloke.'

'He and his missus were moved somewhere, I don't know, but he still comes back to walk his dog sometimes.'

'Another Staffie?' asked Jason.

'How'd you guess?' Reid flicked through the fanzine he'd just pulled from one of the envelopes before tossing it aside. It was called *High Rize*, a fanzine Kevin had subscribed to, and was typical of the nineties, a mixture of graphic stories and rambling text on anything from the arts to politics. 'You were saying,' he said, opening another envelope. 'You met Kev by the tyre.'

'Yeah, we met in the woods. Went over our plan. I'd even booked the train tickets to Glasgow. Gave Kev his. Didn't think anyone would find us up there. It may as well have been Timbuktu to us back then.'

'Or Texas,' said Reid.

'Yeah, well, we'd've come with you if we could.'

'Lucky you didn't,' said Reid, dryly. He pulled out another copy of *High Rize*.

'I'm not sure Glasgow was much better,' said Jason, shaking his head. 'Those first few months were tough. Anyhow, on that Thursday, me and Kev arranged to meet up later, as planned. He seemed a bit, you know, jumpy. I wondered if he'd taken something.'

'Not Kev's style.'

'Maybe not. Anyroad, I gave him his ticket and we went our separate ways. Kev mentioned about how he had to do something before we went. I stopped and asked what, told him he mustn't draw attention to himself. He said not to worry, that he wouldn't. That was the last time I saw him.'

Reid had now opened six editions of *High Rize*. 'Did you argue?'

'Man, I told you on Saturday night. We never argued. Whoever said that was talking bullshit. They were doing that to make me look bad.'

'You were quite bad,' said Reid, smiling. 'Although a lot of folk here seemed to think it was that Flynn character. The one who turned out to be a paedophile.'

'I read about that. Burned him to death didn't they? Poor bastard.'

'Perhaps he got what he deserved.'

'Maybe,' said Jason. 'But not for anything he did to Kev.'

Reid looked over at his friend and wondered why he was so sure. 'And Kev never said what it was he had to do before you left?'

'No. But he'd been acting funny for a bit, like he was hiding something. I dunno.'

'We were all hiding something,' said Reid.

'Yeah?'

'If my mum had ever found out I was hanging with you lot she'd have killed me. Told me I'd burn in hell.'

'Man, not that again. I can't be doing with your End of Days shit. At least, not until we find out what happened to Kev.' He laughed.

It was fair enough. Jason didn't believe like he did and Reid wasn't in the conversion business. They'd talked about it on Saturday night and like most people who knew, Jason couldn't get his head around Reid's faith, especially after what had happened to him. But that was part of it, Reid reasoned. You didn't just walk out of a situation like Waco and stop believing. If anything, it had made his faith stronger.

They worked in silence for a while. Reid stacked the fanzines in a pile and made a start on the rest of the stuff in the box he'd found them in. More fanzines – these opened and read judging by the worn pages – Kevin's Super Mario, an old, deflated football, birthday cards, badges – all the crap a sixteen-year-old kept. He went through the cards and saw one that looked familiar. He opened it and saw his own handwriting, feeling a lump in his throat. He'd missed Kevin and Jason when he arrived in Texas but had comforted himself with the knowledge that they were having their own adventure, and that one day they'd see each other again. The card brought the sickening reality that this would never happen and he quickly put it aside and looked at the next card. A slip of paper fluttered out.

'What's that?' asked Jason.

'Drawing of some kind,' said Reid, bending down to pick it up. It was a comic strip-style drawing of a teenage boy – an accomplished one too. The boy was wearing a band T-shirt with a plaid shirt over the top that kids wore in the early nineties. But it wasn't this that had caught his eye so much as the boy's face. The crooked nose, broken in a fight one evening with boys from the Sunny View Estate, the floppy hair, hands shoved deep in baggy jeans.

Jason had come closer for a better look. 'That's our Kev,' he said. 'Give it here.' Jason studied the drawing closely. 'Who did we know who could draw like this?'

'No one,' said Reid.

'Well someone did it. What about the card?'

Reid opened the birthday card it had been slipped into. It had been signed with a crude peace symbol. 'Could be anyone,' he said, passing the card over. Graffitied peace signs had cropped up on the estate all the time, especially in the eighties when the Greenham Common protest was in full force. Often they'd been painted over the old anarchy signs that had sprung up in the late seventies when the punk wave had gripped the UK.

'We've learned something, then,' said Jason, pocketing the card and the drawing. 'Our Kev had a secret.'

CHAPTER 13

When you're trying to move house the last thing you want is a police-man in your face. Or that's the impression Dan Scribbs had given when Kirby had tried to interview him. With a cigarette jammed between his chapped lips, Scribbs had answered his questions using as few words as possible while loading his belongings into a van parked outside the Woodcroft maisonettes. The cigarette had been more expressive, waggling up and down as Scribbs spoke, like an accusing finger. According to him he knew nothing and had seen nothing. In other words: *fuck off and leave me alone*. After taking down Scribbs' new address – a scuzzy estate about a mile away – Kirby headed to the Hoffmanns' place, six doors along, hoping they would be more amenable. It wouldn't be difficult.

A woman with blonde streaks in her hair opened the door. 'Mrs Mary Hoffmann?'

The woman nodded. 'You with the police?'

'DI Kirby. May I come in? I have a few more questions.'

Mary Hoffmann showed him in and led him into the living room. 'Excuse the mess. We're leaving. It's chaos.'

The room was indeed chaotic. Piles of clothes and books lay in one corner with a box of cooking paraphernalia balanced on the top.

'We're trying to sort out stuff for the charity shop,' she said, following Kirby's eyes. 'The new place is smaller. I'm not sure how we'll manage.'

'Who was that at the—' Tobias Hoffmann appeared in the doorway and stopped mid-sentence. 'Detective . . .' He clearly recognised Kirby but couldn't remember his name.

'It's DI Kirby,' said Kirby, putting him out of his misery. 'We met outside the church. You kindly provided us with a list of remaining tenants.'

'Of course, yes. Have you found everyone?'

'We've managed to contact everyone, yes. I have a few more questions. I can see that you're busy, but this won't take long.'

'Well, yes, okay,' said Tobias, looking at his wife. 'Sit down if you can find a space.'

Kirby preferred to stand. 'I'm fine. Perhaps we could start with the night of the murder. You said that you were both at home. You can see the woods from here – did either of you see a light there?'

'A light?' Mary repeated, looking at her husband. 'No.'

'We'd've mentioned it if we had,' said Tobias, shaking his head.

'I'm told everyone here uses torches at night, so a light wouldn't be necessarily suspicious,' said Kirby.

'Well, no, but no one walks through the woods after dark, it's not safe. In any case, we have an outside light on a timer which we keep on all night so we probably wouldn't have been able to see a light in the woods. Why, did someone see something?'

'Mrs Carmody and her son saw a light at approximately ten thirty. Moving in this direction. And there's evidence someone's been sleeping rough.'

'That rules all us out then,' said Mary.

'You mean residents?' asked Kirby.

'Who else?' said Tobias. 'My goodness, to think a murderer's been sleeping there all this time.'

'Let's not jump to any conclusions,' said Kirby. 'We don't know how long the camp has been there – it could be months old.'

'Surely you can't think one of us killed Will?' Mary looked affronted at the idea. 'Someone who lives here?'

'At the moment we're exploring every possibility. You'd be surprised what people will do, Mrs Hoffmann. At the moment the camp is unexplained but if anyone's been there recently we'll find out. What I really wanted to ask you about was William Stark. How well did you know him?'

The Hoffmanns looked at each other and it was Mary who spoke first. 'He was like family. We've known him for nearly thirty years.'

'From living here?' asked Kirby. 'Or did you know him before you moved here?'

'Oh, no, we met him here,' replied Tobias.

'Were you here when his wife died?'

'That was a few years before we arrived,' said Mary. 'We moved here in 1990 and it was obvious Will was really struggling. Alma was a teenager by then – a difficult age in any case but without her mother . . .'

'We liked him,' Tobias picked up. 'We hit it off and Alma got on with one of our foster children. She spent a lot of time with us, so did Will. Up to that point I don't think he'd had much help. People here didn't know what to do. Most of the local kids avoided Alma, like she was damaged goods because of what happened to her mother. She also went to a different school to a lot of the kids around here, so she didn't have many friends.'

'Why did Mr Stark stay here?' asked Kirby. It had been bothering him.

'He never really spoke about it,' said Tobias. 'I suppose he felt he was close to Louisa – that was his wife – here. The estate seemed to have a hold over him which he could never quite shake off. Personally, I never really understood.'

'Creative integrity, maybe?'

'I wouldn't know about that,' said Tobias. 'I'm more of a hands-on man. Practical.'

'What is it that you do, Mr Hoffmann?'

'Retired electrician, although I still do the odd job.'

'Useful skill to have living here, I imagine,' said Kirby, thinking of the lack of lighting.

'Nothing can fix this place. The electrics have been buggered for decades. Pardon me.' He glanced at his wife. 'My time is mainly devoted to our church these days.'

'Going back to Will Stark – what was he like? Was he outgoing? Private? He must have been quite a cause célèbre when the estate first went up.'

'What do you mean?'

'Being the architect of the estate and then moving in. Not many architects do that.'

'I wouldn't know,' said Mary. 'He was a private man. In fact I'd say most people living here didn't even know who he was – or they didn't by the time we'd moved in.'

'Did he ever fall out with any of the tenants? Maybe he didn't approve of how they treated the place?'

'He wasn't confrontational if that's what you're getting at,' said Tobias. 'Will didn't want to dictate to people how to live their lives. It was all about respect in his eyes. If the council had looked after the buildings and the grounds and demonstrated respect for the tenants, they, in return, would respect their surroundings and fellow neighbours. Or at least, that's how Will saw it. But of course the council didn't upkeep the buildings – the reverse – and things ended up the way they did.'

'That must have been difficult for him. Did he complain to the council?'

'He did what he could,' said Mary. 'But they weren't interested. He was old news. I think they just saw him as a nuisance. One council official even told him that if he didn't like it then he should move out.'

Kirby felt sorry for Stark and again wondered why he'd stayed. That he was a man of principle seemed indisputable and yet someone had had reason strong enough to kill him. 'I know you've been asked this before, but can you think of any reason why Mr Stark would have been in the church?'

The Hoffmanns shook their heads in unison. 'None at all. We've racked our brains, haven't we, love?' said Tobias, looking at his wife.

'There was absolutely no reason for him to be in the church,' said Mary, adamantly. 'Whoever lured him there is sick and depraved. Poor Alma is in bits.'

Anderson had said something similar after their visit to the mortuary earlier. 'Thanks for your time. I'll leave you to your packing. When do you actually go?'

'Day after tomorrow,' said Mary. 'To be honest it'll be a relief after what's happened. Even though it was dangerous here at times, what with the gangs and the drugs, you knew what you were up against. Now . . . now it feels like the estate wants us gone, it even feels structurally unsafe at times, too. Like it's trying to get rid of us.'

Kirby made a note of the couple's new address and they headed into the hall where he paused by a framed photograph. 'Are these some of your foster kids?'

'Yes,' said Tobias. The picture showed the Hoffmanns and three children, two boys and a girl. 'Tall lad,' said Kirby, pointing to a lanky teenager who had to be pushing six feet.

83

'That's Steve,' said Mary, pride in her voice. 'He joined the Navy.'

'And the others?'

'We lost touch with Marek,' said Tobias, pointing to the other boy. His finger moved to the girl and lingered for a second before he let his arm drop by his side. 'That's Angela. She died.'

Silence descended into the small hallway and Kirby felt as though he'd intruded into a subject that was off limits. 'I'm sorry. That must have been difficult.'

'Our faith kept us going,' said Tobias, opening the front door. 'Without God Grasmere would have destroyed us years ago.'

◆ ◆ ◆

Michaela Falke, a retired schoolteacher, was a vivacious woman in her late sixties. Her husband had been minister of All Hallows – up until its closure – where William Stark's body had been found. He looked of a similar age but was more reserved with a quiet power about him. Kirby could imagine Elliott Falke at the pulpit, credible and strong, his outwardly gentle charisma a mask for something altogether more powerful underneath. He was not a man you'd want to cross.

'To think this happened in our old church makes it even more shocking,' said Michaela, sitting down. Elliott remained standing behind his wife, sentinel-like.

A crucifix bore down over the fireplace, antimacassars adorned the chairs and photographs of family past and present lined the mantelpiece. A box of unframed photos sat on the floor as though someone had been sorting through them. A pile of flat-pack boxes was stacked in the corner, the only indication that change was afoot.

'I presume that you knew William Stark?' Kirby asked.

'Of course we did,' replied Elliott, as though it was a stupid question. 'We all know each other here.'

'Can you tell me where you were on Saturday night?'

'You must already know that, surely? I don't know why you're wasting your time with us, Detective.' Vernon Reid wasn't the only tenant who didn't like the police, then.

'But I'd like to hear it from you, Mr Falke,' said Kirby. He half-wished Anderson was with him as he had a strong suspicion that if his partner flicked a Tic Tac into his mouth, as he was wont to do when people irritated him, it would really piss Elliott Falke off.

Elliott sighed dramatically as if it was all a huge effort. 'We'd been to visit our church in Earlsfield. When they closed All Hallows here on the estate we had to find new premises.'

'When was that?'

'All Hallows was decommissioned over a decade ago. It was used for storage and estate meetings before being boarded up several years after.'

'That must have hurt,' said Kirby. 'Seeing your church sitting empty.'

Elliott shrugged. 'The decommissioning was inevitable, so I'd started looking for alternative premises long before it happened. I'd heard about the old meeting house on Elm Grove and as soon as I walked in I knew it was for us.' He spread his arms. 'The Church of Fulfilment was born. We'll be celebrating ten years in a few months' time.'

Kirby recognised the name. He'd driven past the red-brick building a million times with its 'Jesus Loves You' banner strung across the facade. 'So you were there on Saturday?'

'Correct. I'll be retiring after the ten-year anniversary.' Elliott glanced at his wife. 'There's a lot of paperwork to sort out in the meantime. It's only a fifteen-minute drive from here but on the way back we got stuck in traffic and didn't get back until around 5.30 p.m.'

'We didn't go out again – we watched a repeat of *Inspector Morse* on TV,' added Michaela. From the look on Elliott's face, Michaela had watched Morse alone. Of course she had; Elliott wouldn't waste his time watching a detective show.

'Did you see anything unusual when you got back? Anyone hanging around?'

'Nothing,' said Michaela. 'We saw no one.'

'That's not strictly true,' said Elliott. 'We saw that man going into Coniston House.' He looked at his wife pointedly.

'Oh, yes, I suppose we did. I don't know his name.'

'What time was this?' No one else had mentioned seeing anyone going into Coniston House.

'As I said before, we got back around half past five,' said Elliott.

'Could it have been Brian Kaplinsky? He used to live in Ullswater House,' ventured Kirby.

'Oh,' said Michaela. 'It might have been, I suppose. But we didn't really know him.'

'Or Mr Reid?'

'No. This man was a different build,' said Elliott, emphatically.

'But he had a big coat on, Elliott. It might have been Vernon.'

'It wasn't,' Elliott snapped back at his wife. 'You didn't get as good a look as I did.' He turned to Kirby. 'He was on the driver's side and I was driving so I had the better view.'

'Could you describe him?'

Elliott shook his head. 'He had his back to me and was wearing a black woolly hat and a padded jacket. But his legs were thin and he did not carry himself like Vernon. Or that other man, Kaplinsky, for that matter. Not that I knew him.'

'Taller?'

Elliott thought for a moment. 'Shorter. Vernon's my height, this man looked shorter.'

From what Kirby remembered of Kaplinsky he was about the same height as Reid. 'Okay, well thank you, Mr Falke, that's very useful. Tell me, how well did you know William Stark?'

'Fairly well,' said Elliott, reclaiming the conversation on known territory. 'We moved in when the estate was first built. He was keen the church should be a success even though he wasn't a worshipper himself. There used to be a church in the area before the estate was built and he made it his business to see another went up in its place.'

'Can you think of a reason why he was in the church on Saturday night?'

'None.'

'Do you still have a key?'

'Why, yes, I do. But I didn't go to the church on Saturday night if that's what you're implying.'

'Can you show me the key, please?'

Elliott got up reluctantly and went into the hall, returning with a bunch of keys on a key ring. 'This is it.' He held up the bunch by one key.

'Why didn't you tell the officer yesterday that you had this?'

'He didn't ask,' Elliott said, simply.

Fucking idiot, thought Kirby to himself, if, in fact, that was the case. 'Does anyone else have a key besides you?'

'Not that I know of.'

'And these keys would have been with you on Saturday night? You didn't lend them to anyone?'

'Why on earth would I do that? My house keys are on here.'

'So as far as you're aware, Mr Stark didn't have a key,' said Kirby.

They both shook their heads.

'Do you know if he'd had a falling-out with anyone recently – either here on the estate or elsewhere?'

'No.'

Kirby got up and went over to the window and looked out over the woods. 'You have quite a view from here. You didn't happen to see a light on Saturday night did you, in the woods?'

'Why do you ask?'

Kirby told them about the makeshift camp and the light the Carmodys had seen, and they echoed what the Hoffmanns had said, that no one walked through there at night.

'It must be recent though,' said Michaela. 'I like to walk in the woods sometimes – during the day,' she quickly added. 'And I haven't noticed anything.'

'You know I don't like you walking in the woods alone,' said Elliott to his wife. 'It's not safe.'

'I wasn't alone. Mary was with me.'

'Mary Hoffmann?' asked Kirby.

'Yes. We're close friends.'

'I gather they helped Mr Stark with his daughter after his wife died,' said Kirby.

'They did,' said Elliott, not elaborating. Kirby sensed disapproval in his voice.

'How do all the residents get on?' he asked, as they showed him to the door.

'We are united by circumstance,' said Elliott. 'We get along just fine.'

Pausing by the door, Kirby asked, 'I'm curious: why are you all still here?'

It was Elliott who answered. 'This used to be a thriving community – a church, a crèche for the children, a youth centre for the youngsters. Then they took all that away, slowly, bit by bit, chipping away at the threads that bound us together. This community has been unravelled, people sent far and wide, to places where they know no one, have no family. God does not look kindly on such things. Someone had to stand up for what's right.'

Kirby said goodbye, still unsure as to why the Falkes were still on the estate, and realised neither Elliott nor his wife had asked how Alma was coping. Something else that God wouldn't look too kindly on, either.

CHAPTER 14

After her conversation with Art the previous day, Connie felt no desire to rush into work early the next morning. Instead, she got off the bus several stops before her regular one and made a detour to the Grasmere Estate. The compulsion to go and visit William Stark's daughter had been growing ever since she'd learned who he was. When Kirby had mentioned her and that she also lived on the estate, Connie found she couldn't get her out of her mind. Finding Stark's hanging body had given her a connection to his daughter in a way she couldn't fully comprehend. All Connie knew was she had to see her. While there had been nothing she could have done for William Stark – she'd known he was dead as soon as she'd seen him – she somehow felt responsible for him in death. It was stupid really. Except that it wasn't. Brian Kaplinsky had had that responsibility with her sister and had abused it. Connie had no way of knowing whether her sister had been dead or alive when Kaplinsky had called the emergency services and scarpered, but to think he might have left her at Blackwater alone to die was inconceivable. Connie was Alma's last link with her father and needed to know there was nothing she could have done. Because that's what she wanted from Kaplinsky: just to *know*.

There was also another, more selfish, reason for wanting to see Stark's daughter, which Connie didn't really want to admit to, and that was Stark's archive. What would happen to all his drawings now he was dead? They'd be a good acquisition for RADE – that's if Art didn't sell it off as a result of his son's disastrous business dealings.

Alma's flat wasn't difficult to find. She'd known it was on the first floor so it had been a case of looking for a flat that wasn't boarded up. As it turned out, there was only one on the first floor and Connie rang the bell feeling nervous. After a minute or so, the door was opened by a tall, slender woman with blonde-streaked hair.

'Alma Stark?' asked Connie.

'No, I'm Mary, one of her neighbours. She's inside. Who are you?' asked the woman brusquely.

Connie explained and the woman appeared to soften a little before disappearing inside, reappearing a few moments later. 'Come in, Alma's through there, in the front room.' The woman was wearing a coat now. 'I'm just leaving. I'm sorry if I was rude, but Alma's very upset. I can't just let anyone in.'

'It's okay, I understand,' said Connie.

The woman lingered for a moment. 'It must have been awful for you finding Will hanging like that. I'm very sorry.' The woman reached out and touched Connie's arm before letting herself out of the flat.

Connie knocked gently on the living room door, which was half open, and went in. Alma Stark was seated on the sofa; a magazine lay discarded on the seat next to her. She looked at Connie and seemed at a loss for what to say. 'Take a seat. It's good of you to come.' Alma was in her forties, salt and pepper hair piled on top of her head and held in place with two chopsticks. Her clothes looked like they'd come from Toast – simple and utilitarian but expensive – dungarees, a poplin shirt, chunky cardigan. The look suited her, which was no mean feat.

'I just wanted to offer my condolences,' said Connie, sitting down.

'That's kind of you. I'm sorry that you had to find him. It must have been shocking.'

'Yes.' Connie cleared her throat. 'It was. I, um . . . I also just wanted you to know that there was nothing I could have done.'

'Done? Oh, I see. What on earth were you doing there anyway?'

'Sheltering from the storm. The door was open so I went in.'

'I bet you wish you hadn't,' said Alma.

Connie didn't know how to respond because she was right, she did wish she hadn't gone in and yet didn't feel she could admit it. 'It's nothing compared to what you must be going through. How are you coping?'

'I'll be a lot happier when whoever did this is caught. Have the police said anything to you?'

'Nothing. But they wouldn't.' She wasn't going to mention her friendship with Kirby. 'I lost my sister six years ago – not in the same circumstances as this, but suspicious – so I understand a little of what you're experiencing.'

'What happened?'

'She fell from a derelict building. It was an accident but the person she was with fled the scene. It left a lot of questions unanswered.'

Alma stared at her for a moment before speaking. 'I lost my mother the same way. From that building over there.' She pointed towards the window. 'The one that's being pulled down.'

Now Connie remembered what it was about Will Stark that had eluded her yesterday when Kirby had told her his name, and felt her face redden. 'I'm so sorry. I seem to be making this worse, not better.'

'You weren't to know. In fact, it's refreshing that you didn't know. Makes a change from being known as the girl whose mother jumped. Now I'll be known as the woman whose father was found murdered. Double whammy.'

'I knew of your father,' said Connie, trying to steer the conversation away from the morbid subject. 'I work in an architectural archive. We have some of his drawings. Including Grasmere.'

'Really? Where did you get them?' Alma looked surprised.

'They were donated by someone clearing out their parents' attic.'

'What's this archive called?'

'RADE. It's a large collection, some big names. He's in good company.'

'Even stranger you found the body then.'

'I suppose so. I didn't know he lived here though – or that he'd lived here for so long. It sounds like he was very committed to the estate and all it stood for. You must have been very proud of him.'

'Immensely. He was a very loyal and devoted father and the estate was a huge part of his life, but I did worry that one day it would kill him and now it has.'

'How do you mean?'

'It consumed our lives – not just ours but everyone who ever lived here. He wouldn't leave though, and I wouldn't leave him.' She shrugged helplessly. 'He designed so many other wonderful buildings and yet this will be his legacy.' Alma wiped away a tear with her hand.

'I'm sorry. What will happen to his drawings now? Did he keep very much?'

'Why, are you angling to have them for your archive?'

Connie couldn't tell by her tone whether Alma was upset, annoyed or merely curious, and she wished she'd never asked. 'I only meant that if you needed help knowing what to keep and what to throw away then I could advise you. I'm sorry, I shouldn't have mentioned it.' Connie stood up. 'I'd better be going. I only came to offer my condolences. Oh.' She rummaged in her bag and pulled out a card. 'My details,' she said, handing the card to Alma.

Alma stood up and rather formally they shook hands.

'I'll see myself out,' said Connie, just as the doorbell rang. Alma physically flinched at the shrill sound. 'Would you like me to get rid of them?' Connie asked.

'Please.'

Connie slipped out of the front room, closing the door behind her. On the surface, Alma was holding it together remarkably well, but beneath it all Connie sensed a woman on the edge. She opened the door ready to give whoever it was a polite 'get lost' only to find Kirby and his partner Pete Anderson standing on the doorstep. Inexplicably, she felt as if she'd been caught doing something she shouldn't. 'I was just leaving. I came to offer my condolences to Alma.'

'How is she?' asked Anderson. Kirby said nothing, just stared at her, his face unreadable.

'Um . . . she wanted me to get rid of you. I mean, whoever was at the door, not you personally. She's in the living room.'

Anderson nodded. 'And how about you? Did someone give you details of Victim Support?'

'Yes, they did, thanks,' replied Connie, glancing at Kirby. 'I'll be off then. I need to get to work.'

'Take care of yourself, Miss Darke,' said Anderson.

'I will. Bye.' Connie slipped past the two detectives and headed for the stairwell. Kirby hadn't said a word.

CHAPTER 15

'Oh . . . it's you,' said Alma distractedly. 'The woman who found my father was just here . . .'

'She let us in,' said Anderson. 'How are you doing today, Alma?'

'Oh, you know.' She shrugged. 'Do you have any news?'

'I'm afraid not. But we'd like to ask you a few more questions if we may. Are you up to it?'

Alma nodded. 'Actually, before we get started – when will I be able to get into my father's flat?'

'Most likely tomorrow, once Forensics have finished,' said Kirby. 'We need to be sure nothing took place while your father was at home, although so far there's nothing to indicate that this is the case.'

'The flat was neat and tidy and it looks like your father was preparing supper when he left. We need to establish why he left – the obvious reason was that he was going to meet someone, or someone called at the flat and lured him to the church. You said yesterday you couldn't think who that might be.' Anderson paused. 'Has anyone come to mind since then?'

'No one. Are you sure he was murdered?'

'We're still waiting for the official report but I'm afraid there's little doubt that someone killed your father and then hung him from the scaffolding to make it look like suicide.' Anderson was using his gentlest tone. Kirby knew he'd got little of use from Alma after officially identifying her father's body the previous day.

'Did your father have many visitors?' Kirby asked, watching her closely. She appeared tense. Her manner was brusque, not the distraught family member he often encountered. He sensed it was about control, that if she let her guard down the flood waters would pour out uncontrollably.

'Not recently. We were about to leave. It's not exactly the kind of place you hold dinner parties at the moment.'

'How about people on the estate? Was there anyone he was particularly friendly with?'

'You could talk to Toby Hoffmann, he probably knew him best. He was caretaker here at one point. But none of us are close.'

This contradicted what the Hoffmanns had told him yesterday – unless they'd had a falling-out. 'How about you and your father, what was your relationship with him like – were you close?'

'Meaning?'

'You lived near to him,' said Kirby. 'Which would suggest a close relationship, or at least a supportive one. You also stayed here when most people left.'

'The estate means a lot to both of us. The start of his career, our family history. I couldn't leave him.'

'Going back to Mr Hoffmann – when was he caretaker here?'

'Oh God, I don't know,' said Alma, sounding irritated. 'Fifteen years ago? Ten?'

'As caretaker would he have had a key to the church?'

'Probably. Ask him.'

'We will,' said Anderson. 'Was the church of any special interest to your father?'

'What do you mean?' Alma was actually rather difficult, Kirby decided.

'Did it have any special meaning to him – he designed the estate and I wondered whether the church was significant in any way?'

'No,' said Alma, after a slight hesitation. 'The church wasn't.'

'Had anything happened recently to upset him?'

'What do you think?' Anger blazed in her eyes. 'The place is about to be bulldozed. Of course he was upset.'

'You said that your father lived here from the beginning?'

'Yes. He moved in with the first families. He wanted to put into practice what he preached. People who design places like this aren't usually the ones to live in them. My father wanted to be different.' There was pride in her voice for the first time.

'It must had affected him badly when the estate went downhill,' said Anderson.

Alma didn't say anything at first and stared out of the window. 'It did,' she said, finally. 'It wasn't his fault though – it was the council's. They didn't invest in the long term and failed to maintain the buildings. It's scandalous, really. And people like my father got the blame.' The anger flared again.

'Did your father have any enemies?' asked Kirby. 'People who may have held him responsible for what happened here, for example?'

'Like what?' she asked.

'There have been a number of high-profile incidents here over the years. Things that have made the news. I'm not suggesting any of them are linked to your father's death but we need to explore every possibility.'

'Nothing that happened here in the past was my father's fault. None of the suicides, the stabbings, the—' She stopped short. 'The other things. But to answer your question, no, there's no one I can think of who would hold a grudge like that.'

'What about the campaign to restore rather than demolish and rebuild the estate – did your father get on the wrong side of anyone in connection to that?'

'Not badly enough for them to kill him.'

Kirby felt as though they were going around in circles and decided they needed to take a more practical approach. Anderson appeared to have the same idea. 'We need to build up a picture of your father's movements over the past week – people he saw, where he went, that kind of thing.'

For the next few minutes, Alma gave them a rundown of what her father's last week on earth had been like. There were no surprises and nothing stood out as unusual.

'Did he have any health issues?'

'None. He was remarkably fit.'

'Where was he working before he retired?' Anderson asked.

'SFG Architecture. Stark, Finch and Gould. Now it's F&G Architects.'

'Did your father keep in touch with his old colleagues?'

'Yes. He'd visit the office regularly. He liked to see what new projects they were taking on.' Anderson made a note of the practice details.

'Have you seen anyone hanging around the woods recently? Only it looks as though someone's been sleeping rough there.'

Alarm spread over Alma's face. 'No, I haven't. You mean someone was watching him and planned this?'

'It could be unconnected but we want to find whoever it was to rule them out. Whoever killed your father must have had a key to the church – unless he had one, but you said he didn't.'

Alma shook her head as though she had no answer to anything any more. 'I simply don't know.'

'We'll leave you in peace then,' said Kirby. 'When do you move out?'

'In a couple of days,' said Alma.

'Where are you going?'

'I . . . I don't actually know. My father had bought a house and was sorting everything out, I left it all to him.' A panicked look crossed her face.

'You were moving in together?'

'There's no need to sound like that,' she snapped.

Kirby wasn't aware he'd sounded like anything but the set-up struck him as a slightly odd one. 'Do you have any relatives who you could stay with, until this is sorted out?'

'I have a godmother, but . . . I don't think that's an option.'

'We'll need her details,' said Anderson. 'Is she local?'

Alma nodded. 'Not far.'

Anderson made a note of the godmother's name and address. 'I'm sure your solicitor will be able to advise you about the house your father had bought.'

'I'll ask,' said Alma, as they moved into the hall.

'The map in there,' asked Kirby. 'Is that your work?'

'Yes, why do you ask?'

'I like it a lot. It's a shame you can't take it with you.'

'Believe me, far more important things will be lost when this place comes down than my mural.'

Once they were outside, Anderson popped a Tic Tac into his mouth. 'What do you think she meant by that?'

'I don't know,' said Kirby, just as his phone began ringing. 'Steve, what you got?'

'I've found Brian Kaplinsky,' said Kobrak. 'I finally spoke to the right person at the council and a company called Archer Holdings have been renting flat sixteen Ullswater House for their employees for the past ten years. For the last eight months Brian Kaplinsky has been the sole occupant. He's officially due to vacate this week but they think he's probably already gone.'

'Damn,' said Kirby. 'Did he leave a forwarding address?'

'No. But I know where he works.'

'Where?'

'He's currently working on the demolition of Windermere House.'

'Windermere House?' The name was familiar and it took a few seconds for Kirby to realise what Kobrak was saying. 'You mean Windermere House on the Grasmere Estate?'

'The very same. In fact, he should be there now.'

Kirby thanked Kobrak and hung up.

Anderson raised his eyebrows. 'Kaplinsky?'

Kirby nodded. 'He's only working over there.' He pointed across the estate, towards the demolition site.

'You going to talk to him now?'

'No time like the present.'

Anderson waggled his lucky paw key ring. 'In that case, I'll pay F&G Architects a visit. Leave you and Kaplinsky to have a cosy little chat. What are you going to tell Connie?'

Kirby had been mulling this over ever since he knew he'd have to speak to him. He couldn't pass Kaplinsky's details on to her; that was out of the question. But he could ask Kaplinsky about Sarah Darke's accident. 'I'll think of something.'

CHAPTER 16

There was considerably less of Windermere House left than there had been the last time Kirby had seen it two days ago. On Sunday when he'd been at the estate the front had been ripped off and the side staircases were in the process of being demolished. It was now Tuesday and half the flats had disappeared. It wouldn't be long until there was nothing left. After being given a hardhat, Kirby had been escorted on to the demolition site and was now waiting in the office of the site foreman, a man called George Allegra. Allegra had gone to fetch Kaplinsky, who was operating one of the site excavators. After ten minutes or so the door to the office opened and Kaplinsky walked in. He registered surprise on seeing Kirby.

'I thought the Blackwater thing was all over,' he said, pouring himself a cup of water from a machine and sitting down.

'That's not why I'm here,' said Kirby, distaste in his mouth as he tried not to picture Kaplinsky abandoning a dead or dying Sarah Darke at Blackwater. 'I'm here about the flat in Ullswater House. You've been living there recently, I understand?'

'Yes, why?'

'Are you still living there?'

'No, I left a few weeks ago. Still got a bit of stuff that I need to collect but . . .' Kaplinsky shrugged. 'Why do you want to know?'

'There was a murder on the estate on Saturday night and we're talking to all the tenants in case anyone saw anything.'

'A murder?' Kaplinsky looked alarmed. 'Nothing to do with me.'

'Can you tell me where you were?'

'Like I said, I've moved out. Living over in Tooting now and my wife can vouch for me.'

Kirby hadn't known Kaplinsky was married and didn't know why he was surprised. 'So it wasn't you who was seen entering Coniston House at approximately 5.30 p.m. on Saturday evening then?'

Kaplinsky looked genuinely surprised. 'No. I've never set foot in Coniston House. At 5.30 p.m. I was in the bloody cash and carry. It was heaving. You'll find me on camera if you have to.'

Kirby made a note of the time and the name of the cash and carry. 'Where did you go after?'

'Home. Wife was annoyed I'd taken so long. Ask her.'

'I'll need her name, address and phone number, please.'

'Sure,' said Kaplinsky, and scribbled the information down for Kirby. 'We've been going through a rough patch,' he said. 'I moved out for a bit – lived over there.' He jerked his thumb towards the rest of the estate. 'Company flat. No one minded.'

'So when was the last time you were there?'

'A few weeks ago. I'll actually enjoy knocking that place down,' said Kaplinsky, smiling. 'Depressing isn't the word.'

'I thought you liked derelict places,' said Kirby, not smiling.

Kaplinsky frowned. 'It's how I make my living, so yeah, I suppose I do.'

'You must have spent a lot of time at Blackwater on and off.'

'All part of the job. Or was until all that trouble. Not much happening there for the foreseeable.'

'Yes, it was a nasty business,' said Kirby. 'But you must be used to things like that.'

'I had nothing to do with what went on there, you know that.'

'Oh, yes, I know you had nothing to do with the murder of Ena Massey last year. I'm talking about what took place at Blackwater six years ago. Sarah Darke's death.'

It was as though the small office had suddenly shrunk. Kaplinsky's bulk shifted uncomfortably in the plastic chair and he blinked rapidly. A pause in the work outside and the ensuing quiet made the space even more uncomfortable. A siren wailed nearby.

'I don't know what you're talking about,' said Kaplinsky, finishing his water. He hadn't expected this turn in the conversation and looked nervous.

'I think you do,' said Kirby, quietly. 'What happened that night, Brian? You were there, weren't you?'

'Nothing happened.' He raised his cup before realising it was empty. 'I don't know who you've been talking to but you've got it all wrong. I wasn't there.' He stood up and went over to the water dispenser and poured another.

'Does your wife know?' asked Kirby.

'What?' A look of panic crossed his face as he turned.

'I'll have to speak to her to corroborate your whereabouts on Saturday evening. It might crop up in conversation.'

'You can't—' Before he could get any further the door to the cabin opened and a man wearing a hardhat walked in. 'Oh,' he said, when he saw the two men. 'Sorry to interrupt, but there's a problem with one of the diggers, Brian. Can't do anything until you come and take a look.'

'I'll be right there,' said Kaplinsky. The man in the hardhat left, not bothering to close the door. 'I need to get on with my work.'

'Far be it from me to stop you,' said Kirby, standing up. 'By the way, do you have a key to the church on the estate?'

'The church?' Kaplinsky looked confused. 'Why on earth would I have a key to the church? Ask Toby Hoffmann. He's got keys to all the communal areas.' Kaplinsky downed the water he'd poured in one and threw the crumpled water cup into the bin. 'Look, about the accident at Blackwater.' He leaned in close to Kirby. 'I don't know anything about it. I wasn't there and you can't prove that I was.'

George Allegra appeared in the open doorway. 'I assumed you'd finished,' he said, looking at the two men.

'We have,' said Kaplinsky, staring at Kirby for a second before leaving the Portakabin without another word.

'This about the murder over there?' asked Allegra, tilting his head in the general direction of the rest of the estate.

Kirby nodded. 'We're speaking to all tenants as a matter of course. Was Mr Kaplinsky working here on Saturday?'

'He was,' said Allegra. 'We clocked off at two. One of your lot's been on the phone to me already asking for our security footage. I sent it over.'

Good, Kobrak's doing his job, thought Kirby. After donning his hardhat the foreman escorted him off the demolition site. Back at the car Kirby saw he'd had several missed calls from Hamer. Something significant must have happened for his boss to call that many times. He pressed Hamer's number and waited. His boss picked up on the first ring and Kirby knew immediately something was up by his tone of voice.

'Pete's been in an accident,' said Hamer, dispensing with any pleasantries.

'What kind of accident? Is he alright?' asked Kirby, imaging a small prang in Anderson's Astra. As much as he dreamt of writing the Corsa off, the paperwork would be a nightmare.

'I'm afraid not. He was hit by a piece of falling masonry from one of the walkways at Grasmere.'

'Where is he now?'

'On the way to St George's Hospital.' Hamer paused. 'You'd better get over there now. It's serious.'

CHAPTER 17

Kirby had driven to the hospital as fast as he could, making judicious use of the blue light. St George's Hospital was a large, sprawling set of buildings near Lambeth Cemetery in Tooting that also happened to be a major trauma centre. On arrival he'd been directed to the Atkinson Morley Wing where he was now waiting for news about Anderson's condition, his stomach a tight knot. He hated hospitals with a passion only second to his hatred of the Corsa.

'Is there a Mrs Anderson here?' said a doctor who suddenly materialised. She glanced at Kirby and then along the corridor at the few people who were there. They all looked at her blankly.

'She's away. She'll be back later tonight,' said Kirby, standing up.

'You're Mr Anderson's colleague, then?' said the doctor.

'Yes, I'm his partner, DI Kirby. How is he?'

'He's stable for the moment,' said the doctor. 'But the CT scan reveals subdural haemorrhaging – that's bleeding due to the impact he sustained when he was hit by the masonry. Due to his age, his brain is more likely to swivel inside his cranium resulting in a tear to a vein and so a slow leak. At the moment this is small, but it needs careful monitoring. He's also fractured a vertebra.' She tapped the back of her neck. 'He's going to need physio at the very least. You might want to think about a new partner for the next few months.'

Kirby felt sick. 'Is he awake? Can I see him?'

She shook her head. 'He's still unconscious. Call us in a few hours and we'll update you. Do you know what time his wife will be back?'

'Late tonight. She's on a train from Scotland.'

'Good. The sooner she can get here the better.'

'Meaning?'

The doctor looked at him. 'Meaning things could change.'

Kirby swallowed down the nausea that was rising in his stomach. 'Can you call me if it does? It doesn't matter when.'

The doctor smiled. 'I'll make a note.'

'His personal effects,' began Kirby. 'There's something I need.'

The doctor frowned. 'We only release those to next of kin.'

'It's his car keys. I need to drive his police vehicle back to the station.'

'Wait here,' said the doctor, and disappeared.

Kirby sat down again and rested his head in his hands. He studied a black scuff-mark on the polished floor and remembered how it had squeaked under his feet when he'd arrived. He zoned out for a few moments trying to block out the general hubbub of hospital life in the background. He didn't know how long he'd been sitting like that when a rabbit's paw appeared in his sights. The doctor had returned and was dangling Anderson's car keys in front of him on the lucky paw key ring. He grabbed them and thanked the doctor, hurrying out of the hospital as fast as he could.

He'd just reached the Corsa when his phone rang. It was Eleanor. 'Lew, how is he?' She sounded breathless.

Kirby relayed what the doctor had told him. 'He's a strong man, Eleanor, there's every chance he'll pull through.' He said it with more conviction than he felt. They chatted a bit more, Eleanor asking questions Kirby couldn't answer until he gently said he needed to go.

He drove back to Grasmere in a daze, his brain trying to comprehend what had taken place and to piece together the facts as he knew them. Anderson had been under one of the overhead walkways when a large piece of masonry had fallen from above. It couldn't have happened that long after Kirby had left him outside Alma's flat. Tobias Hoffmann had found him unconscious with a serious head wound and called an ambulance. Kirby wondered whether that was the siren he'd heard from the foreman's office. The council was going to have some serious questions to answer about safety on the estate. At the moment the prevailing thought was that the rain and wind must have dislodged what had already been an unstable structure. The other scenario was too dreadful to contemplate – that someone had deliberately targeted Anderson – but it had to be explored and to this end the area had been cordoned off and was now a crime scene.

When Kirby arrived at what he was now beginning to think of as a concrete mausoleum, the cordoned-off area near the walkway was bustling with activity. Scenes-of-crime officers and structural engineers from the council were all focused on one area of the walkway. It was clear to see where the masonry had fallen from – one of the concrete slabs forming a ridge along the walkway had sheared off. The rusted metal pins inside were clear enough to see. The immediate point of concern was how safe the rest of the structure was. Until that had been decided, no one was allowed near. Kirby spotted Hamer talking to an official-looking man wearing a high-vis jacket over a suit and carrying a clipboard. Kirby managed to catch his eye and waited for his boss to finish talking before the two of them moved away from the huddles of people.

'How's Pete?' asked Hamer. He looked pale and worn and Kirby realised it had hit his boss as hard as it had him.

Kirby told him what the doctor had said.

'We can only pray the bleeding doesn't worsen,' said Hamer. 'Pete's as strong as an ox.'

'Yeah,' said Kirby, trying to shake the dread that was building. 'You're right. It could have been a lot worse.'

Hamer nodded grimly. 'The concrete that fell only clipped his head. If it had hit him full-on we'd be in a very different place right now.'

'What are the structural engineers saying?' said Kirby, keen to get off the subject of what might have happened. 'Is the whole thing unstable?' He had a sudden image of Sarah Darke falling to her death from the structurally unsafe water tower.

'They think not. It appears the concrete that fell was just on the facia. If that's the case then they can easily remove the rest without compromising the actual walkway. Hoffmann said it's not the first time pieces have fallen off.'

'Why was it left to get this bad?' Kirby asked, suddenly feeling anger well up.

'Probably a combination of factors – the hard winter we had last year with all that snow and ice followed by the deluges we've had this year would have accelerated deterioration. That, and out and out neglect.'

The snow last year had brought London to a virtual standstill. How could Kirby forget? He'd been up to his eyes in the Blackwater case. 'Someone needs to drive Pete's car back,' he suddenly remembered, taking the keys out of his pocket.

'I'll see to it,' said Hamer.

Kirby handed the keys to his boss, which he'd removed from the lucky paw key ring, and felt his phone vibrate in his pocket and saw that Anish Morton from the forensic team had sent him a text. 'Forensics have something.'

'Good,' said Hamer. 'That should keep you occupied. And Lew? Look after yourself. I don't need another man down.'

CHAPTER 18

Strictly speaking, Kirby could have spoken to Anish over the phone, but he didn't feel ready to head back to the office just yet, so he drove to the Met Police Forensic Science Laboratory in Lambeth where Anish had her office. The building, like Grasmere, was Brutalist in style but had recently undergone total refurbishment and now housed specialist state-of-the-art forensic labs. There was no logo or sign on the building; the only clue as to what went on there was the odd white-coated lab technician having a cigarette and a few marked police cars outside.

After clearing security and parking the Corsa, Kirby made his way to Anish's office in the bowels of the building, which was also where the secure firing range for firearm investigation and ballistic analysis was located. He found her office and knocked gently on the door before going in.

'Lew, nice to see you in person. I got us both a coffee.' She held up a takeaway cup from a local coffee shop, which he took gratefully. 'I was sorry to hear about Pete.' She gestured for Kirby to take a seat. 'How's Eleanor holding up?'

'I haven't seen her yet. She was in Scotland visiting family and is on her way back now.'

'Send her my best won't you? Right, let me see if I can cheer you up a bit.' Anish put on a pair of reading glasses and turned to her computer. Kirby could see the document reflected in the lenses as she scrolled to the part she wanted. 'Have you had Carter's report yet?' she asked while she searched.

'Should be in later today. Fingers crossed.'

'Good. Right, here we are. This is what we found in the church. As you'd expect, the place is covered in latent print evidence – fingerprints, footprints and so on, so it was a nightmare to process. However, something's been stored there recently, near the rear door. You can see where the dirt on the floor has been disturbed and what look like drag marks – as if someone's slid a box along the floor. I also found *Aesculus hippocastanum* scales – that's horse chestnut – on the floor by the rear and front doors, the kitchen and below the scaffolding where your victim was hung. I also found them on the victim's shoes and on the back of his jacket, which is consistent with him being in contact with the floor. The buds are made up of scales which are extremely sticky. There are several horse chestnuts on the estate so anyone who walks near one will probably pick these scales up on their shoes. The ones I found in the church were in various states of freshness, which suggests activity over the last week or so.'

'So someone's been there recently to remove something as there weren't any boxes there on Sunday morning. That means they must have had a key. Any shoe prints?'

'Nothing outside – the rain washed everything away. Inside there are hundreds and all too smudged to get anything clear. I found a set of very clear fingerprints on the rear door and the door-frame, so I ran them through the system and got a hit.'

'Who?'

'Daniel Scribbs.'

'He's one of the residents. Petty criminal. Nothing violent – that we know of. Did you find his prints anywhere else? On the scaffolding or the pulley?'

'On a chair by the back door but nowhere else. It looks like his activity was confined to the rear of the building.'

'Is there anything to put Scribbs near the victim?' asked Kirby, hopefully.

'I'm afraid not. But there are a couple of other things you might be interested in; although whether they relate to your murder I can't say. First off, someone's been using the church for sex – we found signs of sexual activity on and around the altar and in the kitchen area.'

'The altar?' said Kirby, wondering what Elliott Falke would have to say if he knew. Not the most comfortable of places but it would be private.

'Yes, and a good set of prints.'

'Can you tell if this is recent?' asked Kirby.

'Not specifically, but both areas look as though they've been wiped clean within the past few months. But that could be last week or last month.'

Kirby sighed. 'I presume neither of the prints matched Scribbs'?'

'No. He might have been watching but he wasn't participating.'

'Christ,' said Kirby massaging his face. It wasn't much to go on – having a quick shag in the church wasn't illegal – but he would need to talk to Scribbs again. The joy. 'What about the front or rear doors of the church?'

'Whoever the amorous couple were, they used the rear door, like Scribbs, or at least one of them did. I was able to match a thumb print from the kitchen to the rear door handle. As you can imagine the doors were like the rest of the building – covered in prints. I found Miss Darke's prints on the front door, as you'd expect, and also on an area of the floor near the body.'

'She dropped her phone,' said Kirby.

'I also found partial prints belonging to the victim on the front door. His and the hundreds of other people who would have touched the handle and door over the years. Interestingly, there was a very clear fingerprint on the door latch. Like someone had hooked a finger round the latch to open the door. Look.' Anish swung the screen round so Kirby could see. He recognised the door handle of the church. The entrance was a set of double oak-framed doors with glass inserts, the right-hand door of which was used most frequently. A close-up of the lock showed a clear print on the latch.

'It would have to have been ajar to do that.'

'It would. It's the kind of thing you might do when you're being cautious, or trying to enter a room quietly.'

'And it didn't belong to Scribbs or the love birds?'

'No. But I did find it somewhere else – on the soup can and the plastic bread wrapper taken from the camp. And that, Lew, is all I can give you at the moment.' Anish glanced at the time. 'I've really got to go. Sorry.'

Kirby finished the last of his coffee and stood up. 'Were the victim's prints on the rear door?'

'No,' said Anish, tying her dark hair back and grabbing her keys.

'Could one person have hoisted the body up alone or would they have needed help?' Kirby asked, as they began walking towards the lift.

'Depends on how strong they are. Someone Pete's size probably wouldn't have had a problem. Someone smaller, or not physically strong, would have struggled.'

In the lift Anish pressed level 1 for Kirby and level 4 for herself. Within seconds of the doors closing they were opening again at ground level.

'Thanks for the coffee,' said Kirby, exiting the lift.

'Your turn next time. Let me know if there's any news on Pete.' The doors closed and Anish was gone.

Kirby was glad to get outside into daylight and fresh air – or as fresh as it ever got in Lambeth – and made his way to the car park where he'd left the Fucking Corsa. He checked his phone in case the hospital had been in touch but there was nothing. He thought about Elliott Falke as he unlocked the car. He was the only person who had admitted to still having a key to the church. How had Scribbs got hold of a key and what had he been doing there? He didn't strike Kirby as a church-goer. He thought back to the church's interior. There wasn't much worth stealing – some pots of paint, scaffolding, old chairs – and the council hadn't bothered boarding up the doors, only the windows, so it was hardly Fort Knox. They could really do with getting prints from the Falkes and the Hoffmanns for elimination purposes but so far there was no evidence to suggest any of them had killed William Stark.

As Kirby started the engine it occurred to him that just because Stark had arrived by the front entrance didn't mean his killer – or killers – had. It also might explain why the front door had been left ajar. If the killer entered and exited by the back door they might not have realised the front entrance was open. Did that mean Stark had a key or had someone let him in and forgotten to secure the door? Whatever had happened, it was fortuitous the door had been left open because had it not been, the body probably wouldn't have been found until much later. Not that it had been fortuitous for Connie. For her it had been downright unfortunate.

CHAPTER 19

The mood at Mount Pleasant was subdued when Kirby got back; news of Anderson's condition had knocked everyone's spirits. On the plus side, Carter Jenks' pathologist report was back and after skimming over it Kirby headed to Hamer's office.

'Carter's report is in. Stark was definitely strangled. He thinks the blow to the back of the head is consistent with him hitting it on the scaffolding as he fell. It may have dazed him but he died of asphyxiation. Carter found a fracture of the hyoid bone; conjunctival and petechial haemorrhages around the eyes; contusions on the neck. Everything you'd expect as a result of being throttled.'

'Any drugs or alcohol in his system?' asked Hamer.

'None.'

'Time of death?'

'Between 8 p.m. and 10 p.m. on Saturday.'

'Okay. And what did Forensics have to say?'

Kirby leant on the doorframe feeling drained – he thought if he sat down that he might not get up again. He told Hamer about the church being used for sex and the print on the door latch matching those found in the camp.

'So whoever was sleeping rough could have witnessed the murder,' said Hamer. 'They saw the door ajar and thought they could sleep inside for a night. Only they heard someone inside and that's why they opened the door cautiously.'

'That could account for the light Mrs Carmody saw in the woods. Or perhaps they found the body much later on and scarpered.'

'Stark was wearing an expensive watch and a wedding band – they'd pay for more than a few nights in a hostel but they weren't taken.'

'Not everyone sleeping rough is a criminal,' said Kirby. 'I also spoke to Brian Kaplinsky earlier. He swears he wasn't on the estate on Saturday night.' He'd also called his wife after leaving Anish and she'd corroborated his story. 'If the person the Falkes saw entering Coniston House wasn't Kaplinsky then perhaps it was our mystery camper.'

'What were they doing in Coniston House?' asked Hamer. 'Vernon Reid is the only tenant in that block. Ask him about it.'

'I also need to speak to Dan Scribbs. If he's been sneaking in and out of the church then he might have seen or heard something.'

'Or, if Scribbs was up to something illegal Stark might have disturbed him and Scribbs killed him.'

'It's possible,' said Kirby. 'It's also possible that Stark walked in on someone having sex. Or knew what was going on.'

'You mean blackmail? In that case it would have to be someone he knew – presumably someone from the estate as I can't imagine anyone else travelling there for sex on a regular basis, can you?'

'Not unless they were paying for it, or had a kink for derelict places.' Was that even a thing, sex in derelict buildings? 'There's nothing in Stark's bank account to suggest he was blackmailing anyone. No large deposits.'

Hamer looked thoughtful. 'Do we know if he had any other accounts? Most people of his status have a savings account or investments of some kind.'

'I'll get Romy on to it,' said Kirby. In his mind he went through the residents on the estate trying to work out the most likely to be involved in an affair. There wasn't a great deal of choice. He pushed himself off the wall and straightened up. He had a pounding headache and was hungry. He needed to eat something despite having no appetite.

'When's Eleanor back?' asked Hamer.

'Tonight. I'll drop in at the hospital on my way home.'

'He's in good hands, Lew.'

'That's what Anish said. Did Scenes of Crime find anything suspicious at the walkway?'

Hamer shook his head. 'It would have been very difficult for someone to engineer an accident like that – easier to aim for a car windscreen if you were intent on causing injury. I think we'll find Pete was incredibly unlucky. As I said, it's not the first time debris has fallen on the estate. But we'll know more by the end of the day.'

While some of the residents had been stand-offish, none had been openly hostile, not even Reid who had very good reason to hate the police. Kirby left Hamer's office and grabbed his coat. On his way out he stopped by Masters' desk and asked her to find out if Stark held any other accounts. 'Go through his personal papers – Pete had them boxed up and brought over; they should be here by now. See if there are any unusual transactions – regular sums being paid in, for example. Someone had been having sex in the church.'

'You think Stark might have been blackmailing them?'

'He could have been. Scribbs has also been up to something in the church, so I'm off to talk to him now. Where's Mark?'

'He's gone to talk to a friend of Stark's. They were at school together, met up every other week apparently.'

'Good, let's hope they can tell us a bit more about him.'

'Any news from the hospital?' asked Masters.

'Not yet,' replied Kirby. 'I'll see you later.' He made a dash for the lift before Masters could ask anything else. In the lift he sagged against the handrail, glad to be alone for a moment. Everyone he'd seen on the way in earlier had asked about Anderson. He'd been patted on the back, asked if he was okay, a few people had even joked about the Astra in a bid to lighten the mood. All Kirby wanted to do was cover his ears and get on with his job. They meant well, he knew, their concern born not just out of anxiety for his partner but for him, recently bereaved and not just bereaved, bereaved through suicide. He knew what they were all thinking – *What if Pete dies? How will Lew take it?* He didn't want to think about it. Instead, he focused on Stark as the lift doors opened and he made his way to the carpool where, instead of the Fucking Corsa, he took Anderson's Astra.

CHAPTER 20

Ethan Blunt was far more of a problem than Connie had anticipated. She'd finally managed to reach her now ex-boss, Richard
Bonaro, on the phone and they'd had a long and rather illuminat-
ing conversation about the archive. It turned out Bonaro had had
several run-ins with Art because of his son over the years. This was
all news to Connie – Bonaro had never bored her with the day-
to-day politics of running the archive while he'd been there – and
when she'd asked him about fundraising, he'd flatly refused to help,
even as a favour to her. The conversation had left her feeling flat
and she stared out of the window at the square below. Perhaps she
should look for another job. Art would give her a good reference,
and so would Bonaro, but where would she find something that
gave her the same flexibility as RADE did? She'd expected more
from Bonaro, too. The world of academia had frequently struck her
as one of fragile egos, where allegiances could change at the drop of
a hat, often dependent on where the next grant was coming from.
And so it seemed with Bonaro. He'd been offered a great job with
a hefty wage attached. The petty politics of a small archive such as
RADE were no longer his problem. It felt like betrayal.

Bonaro hadn't been the bearer of entirely grim news, though.
He was fairly certain there was information surrounding the
original tin church – and the current church – somewhere in the

archive, and that if Connie looked in the large plan chest in his office – surely now her office, technically? – she'd find a folder of drawings pertaining to the estate. They'd come in separate to the bulk of the drawings and had yet to be catalogued. Not just that, he hadn't even noted them in the catalogue entry as 'unsorted'. Connie sighed, wondering what else was languishing in Bonaro's office she didn't know about. He was turning out not to be the loyal and efficient boss that she'd thought he was.

At least the folder was exactly where Bonaro said it would be and she carried it from his old office into the main reading room. Flipping it open, Connie saw it contained yet more plans of the estate. With groups of drawings such as these there were often duplicates, sometimes blueprints, not all of which were worth keeping. As she went through the pile of uncatalogued drawings she came across a plan of the church. She put the drawing to one side as she went through the rest of the material. At the bottom was a smaller folder containing photographs, which she also set to one side. The rest of the drawings were unremarkable or duplicates of those that had been catalogued.

Outside, the sky suddenly darkened – it looked like another storm was on its way – and despite two sets of large French windows that opened on to a small balcony, the reading room was gloomy. Connie switched on the nearest Anglepoise lamp and settled down to study the church drawing and the folder of photographs. She began with the church drawing. It was an original, not a copy, and consisted of a front elevation of the church and a floor plan. The porch under which she'd sought shelter during the storm on Saturday looked sleek and modern, albeit 1970s modern, on the drawing, the copper cross at its corner boasting simplicity and practicality. The church building itself was rectangular with storage space and a small kitchen to the left. To the right lay the vestry. It was pretty ordinary. The font was marked to the left of the entrance with the altar straight ahead at the far end. What she'd been expecting she didn't know and stifled a yawn. Perhaps some revelation about why Stark had been killed there rather than anywhere else on the estate. Why not just kill him in his flat?

She then moved on to the photographs as rain began pattering on the small balcony outside. A couple showed demolition of the Victorian back-to-backs that had once been there and which had been badly damaged during the war, but most were of the cleared site, the wooded area an island at its centre. One photo, however, held her attention; it showed the vast triangular plot completely cleared of property, its past obliterated, apart from one building – a small tin church. Connie flipped the photograph over and saw the date was 21 September 1971. She went back to the images of the cleared estate where work could be seen commencing on the foundations for the three main blocks: 30 September 1971. Somewhere between 21 and 30 September the tin church had disappeared or been dismantled. Putting the photo aside, she gathered up the rest and returned them to the envelope, where she saw she'd missed a piece of folded paper. It was an invoice from a haulage firm, Wellard & Son, for the 'removal of a dismantled iron structure' from the Grasmere building site, and was addressed to 1 Traps Lane, SW18 and dated 23 September 1971. There was a phone number with the old London 01 dialling code but no name. Could the iron structure be the church? The date fitted, and looking back at the photographs she couldn't see what else it might refer to.

If the number listed on the invoice, 01-646 8871, referred to the address at Traps Lane then it would have fallen into the 081 dialling code when 01 was abandoned in the early nineties and then the 0181 code that came in a few years later. Those had then been replaced with the 020 prefix in 1998, making the number, if it was still in use, 020 8646 8871. She picked up the phone and dialled, hardly believing her luck when she heard a ringtone. She waited expectantly as it rang and rang in the hope an answerphone would kick in, but it didn't and she hung up, disappointed.

Outside, the rain had stopped and the sky was clear. It looked like it was going to be a nice evening. The clocks had gone forward a few weeks ago and the extra hour of light had given people a new lease of life after the unrelenting grey of winter. Connie had certainly felt her spirits lift, but after her conversations with Art yesterday and then Bonaro today they'd dipped. Looking around the magnificent reading room with its old wooden plan chests, busts of architects, models of churches, framed paintings and drawings, Connie felt a sudden overwhelming sense of sadness. Ethan Blunt was more than likely going to destroy all of it – or destroy it in its current form – and the thought made her feel sick. Why Art was prepared to allow this to happen she couldn't understand. All at once, she was overcome by the urge to clear her head. It wasn't locking-up time but she had no visitors booked in, so she decided to close the archive early. Walking had helped with difficult decisions in the past and she needed to think clearly about her future at the archive. As much as the Blunts might like her, at the end of the day they'd make their decision based on family priorities. Connie was a mere employee, and a young one at that, who had plenty of time to find work elsewhere. That Art was even contemplating relinquishing his family archive to an outside party made Connie uneasy. The seed was sown.

Not bothering to put the Grasmere drawings away, she shut down her computer and pulled down the blinds in the reading room before setting the alarm and securing the building. It was cold out, but the air smelt fresh after the recent downpour and she instantly felt the brain fog lift a little. On her phone she opened Google Maps and tapped in Traps Lane. It was an unassuming road that connected the wealthy enclave of Pinder Hill to the nitty-gritty of the A3. In fact, it ran in a straight line from the top of

Pinder Hill down to where it joined the A3, a stone's throw from the Grasmere Estate. Only one building was marked, a rectangular outline sitting alone, so she entered '1 Traps Lane SW18' and watched as the red pin appeared next to it. Online maps weren't always accurate when it came to building numbers so she switched to street view for a better look. The building appeared to be some kind of electrical substation. It was set back from the road behind a chain link fence covered in 'Keep Out' signs. It was a strange place to send an invoice. Tucking the phone in her pocket she set off, a familiar flutter of anticipation in her stomach. 'Keep Out' signs had the same effect on urban explorers that light had on moths. They were irresistible.

CHAPTER 21

Dan Scribbs had been rehoused in a small one-bedroom flat on the Sunny View Estate. Unlike Grasmere, there was no wood to stroll through; just patches of bleak communal space with notices telling people not to walk their dogs on the grass. Judging by the state of the grass no one took any notice. Kirby felt eyes watching him as he walked up the path that led to the squat block where Scribbs was now living. So much had happened in the twenty-four hours since he'd spoken to Scribbs outside his flat at Grasmere it seemed a lifetime ago. It was still only Tuesday and already Kirby felt exhausted. He had yet to catch up on his much-needed sleep.

A group of twenty-something males sat on a wall and he heard them spit as he walked past. Scribbs would probably be in his element here – as he no doubt had been on the Grasmere Estate back in the day. Kirby wouldn't be surprised if he was nicked within months of moving in. He rapped on Scribbs' door and waited. Scribbs answered in his vest top and jeans. It wasn't a pretty sight, although he was more muscular than Kirby had realised beneath his baggy clothes. More than capable of winching a dead William Stark off the ground.

'Mr Scribbs, I need a word,' said Kirby, stepping inside before Scribbs had time to argue.

'What is it now?' Scribbs sounded irritated. The front door led directly into the living room, which looked like a bomb had hit it. There were boxes everywhere.

'I'd like to know what it was you were storing in the church at Grasmere and when you were last there.' Kirby looked around the room. He flipped open the lid of the box nearest to him and saw it was full of cigarettes.

'I don't know what you're talking about. Mate brought those back last month,' said Scribbs, looking at the box of cigarettes.

'Mr Scribbs, we have your fingerprints on the back entrance of the church, and inside. We know you were there recently. Were you there on Saturday night? Was William Stark threatening to report you?'

'Report me? Wait, you think I killed him?'

'I might unless you tell me what you were up to. What's in all these other boxes?' Kirby picked one at random and began pulling the tape off.

'Wait,' said Scribbs, holding his hands up. 'Okay, I did use the church for keeping a few things in.'

The box Kirby had been opening was full of DVDs. He took one out, *Pussy Galorgeous*. The cover left nothing to the imagination. 'There's still a market for this?' he asked.

'Some people prefer it to digital. It's easier to hide. Anyhow, I just look after them for a mate. They're not mine.'

'The same mate who pays you in fags? Or don't they belong to you either?'

'I didn't know what was in the boxes. I just stored them.'

'Right, so when you moved house you brought them all with you without checking?'

Scribbs nodded. Maybe he was as stupid as his record suggested. Who sold DVDs in this day and age?

'Look, Mr Scribbs, I don't really give a fuck how many dirty videos you have, although I would be interested to know if the people having sex in the church knew they were there. Perhaps they borrowed a few before getting down to business.'

'What are you talking about? What people?'

'Did you film them? Is that what all this is? You sat on the chair in the church, were you watching them?'

'Course not.'

'Did William Stark find out you were storing them in the church?'

'I don't know, maybe, but I never saw him or anyone inside. I went early in the morning before most people were up. My mate would come over with a van. We were quick, in and out.'

'Where did you get the key from?' Scribbs was now looking very worried. His little storage business had suddenly landed him in the shit.

'I . . . I was given a key.'

'When?'

He thought for a moment. 'Fifteen years ago?'

'*Fifteen?*'

Scribbs nodded. 'I had keys to loads of places at Grasmere. When I did odd jobs people sometimes gave me their keys.'

'And you didn't return them?'

Scribbs shrugged. 'You never know, do you? There was a fire one night, poor bastard nearly died, but we only got him out because I had a key. I'd fixed his shower the month before.'

'How many keys did you have?'

'Fifteen, twenty? Maybe more,' he answered sheepishly.

Jesus Christ, thought Kirby. How many burglaries on the estate were probably Scribbs simply letting himself in? 'What about Stark's flat, did you have a key for that?'

Scribbs shook his head. 'Never. He always got someone in from outside to do anything in his place.'

'And where are all these keys now?'

'I threw them away. Not much good to me here, are they?'

'So when were you last in the church?'

'A week ago? I never saw anyone. It was before Stark was killed. I was pissed that night – ask Tobias Hoffmann. He saw me coming home.'

'I beg your pardon? You saw Tobias Hoffmann on Saturday night? You didn't mention that before.'

'I . . . I forgot. The drink, it affects my memory.'

'What time did you see Mr Hoffmann and where was this?'

'Um, when I got home. Eleven? He was outside his flat, he couldn't get the key in the lock – his outside light was bust. He pretended not to see me, but I know he did.'

'Did you see him before he reached his flat and tried to unlock the door?'

Scribbs scratched his head. 'No, he was just there, on his doorstep.'

'And you didn't speak to him?'

'Nope.'

Kirby left Scribbs sitting on a box of porn films, ripping open a carton of cigarettes with shaking hands. He drove straight to Grasmere where he pulled up outside Woodcroft. He knocked on the Hoffmanns' door and waited. Scribbs was an unreliable witness, but if he had seen Hoffmann then where had Hoffmann been? He'd told Kirby he'd been in all night – something his wife had backed up. While he waited he noticed the Hoffmanns' outside light fitting. It looked quite new, not one of the old ones the other maisonettes in Woodcroft had. Kirby figured Hoffmann must have fitted it himself. He rang the bell a second time and peered in through the window. The flat was dark inside and he could see no sign of life, so he decided to pay Vernon Reid a visit and come back to the Hoffmanns' later. Instead of driving round to Coniston House he decided to walk through the woods – he was beginning to feel drawn to them every time he visited the estate. Anderson's accident had left him feeling hollow and he was still churning over his conversation with Isabel.

The sun was low in the sky and what little warmth it had imparted earlier in the day was fading fast. In the shadow of the trees it was actually quite dark, and he didn't see Michaela Falke at first. She certainly hadn't seen him. She was standing by the remains of the camp talking quietly into her mobile phone. Kirby cleared his throat so he didn't startle her too much. Even so, she swung around, and he could have sworn a look of relief washed over her face on recognising him. She quickly cut her conversation short and slipped her phone into her coat pocket. She hugged herself and Kirby wondered how long she'd been out there; she looked frozen.

'Mrs Falke,' he said, as he approached. 'Sorry, I didn't mean to startle you.'

'You did rather.'

'What are you doing out here? I didn't think you came here alone.'

'I don't, usually. Elliott doesn't like it. But I wanted a last walk before we leave tomorrow.'

'Is there a specific reason he doesn't want you walking here alone, even during the day?'

'Oh, um, no, not really. He's protective, I suppose. He's a good husband.'

'I'm sure he is. I'm glad I've bumped into you actually,' said Kirby. 'There's something I wanted to ask you.'

Without discussing it they began slowly walking and Kirby wondered what Elliott Falke would say if he saw his wife with another man in the woods, even if it was a policeman. 'Did you know someone's been using the church for sexual encounters?'

'What?' Michaela glanced at him, shocked. 'No, I didn't. Who?'

'We don't know. It might not be relevant to the case, but it would be useful to eliminate whoever it is.'

'I'm not sure what made you think that I'd know.' She seemed embarrassed by the thought.

'You have a key to the building; you might have walked in on them. Or seen someone leaving.' When she didn't say anything, he went on. 'We also found out Dan Scribbs had been storing illicit material in there.'

'Now that I can believe,' said Michaela. 'Dan's harmless but he's not very trustworthy.'

'Tell me again about the man you saw entering Coniston House on Saturday evening,' said Kirby.

'Now I think about it, I'm sure it must have been Mr Kaplin,' she said.

'Kaplinsky,' corrected Kirby. 'You said you didn't know him well?'

'Hardly at all. I mean, I'd seen him around. He wasn't particularly friendly.'

'You seem very sure it was him and yet your husband was adamant that it wasn't.'

'Elliott's not very perceptive. When he gets an idea in his head there's no changing it. I should know, I've been married to him for long enough. Talking of which, he'll be home soon, I really must go.'

Kirby watched her walk back the way they'd come. The light was now fading fast under the trees, but there was still just enough for him to see her join another figure near the camp and embrace. Kirby couldn't see who was with the pastor's wife, but something told him it wasn't her husband.

CHAPTER 22

The 'Danger of Death High Voltage' sign left no doubt in Connie's mind that she'd arrived at the electricity substation on Traps Lane. It was the first building she'd come to after turning left off The Drive, a wide, highly desirable street that marked the top of the Pinder Hill enclave. She'd gawped at the houses as she'd passed – they had to run into millions. Pinder Hill wasn't really a hill, or not a steep one, but the views from the top floors of The Drive must have been quite magnificent once – still good now, no doubt, despite overlooking the A3 and the Grasmere Estate, although the latter was partially obscured by greenery. Tearing her eyes away from the view, Connie turned her attention to the substation.

Made of red brick with large wooden doors, the building was covered in a variety of signs all designed to scare the crap out of anyone even thinking of breaking in. Which was fine, because on this particular occasion she wasn't. It was the land next to it she was interested in. Adjacent to the substation was a gate, which she at first assumed led into its grounds. Closer inspection revealed that the substation was fenced off and the gate actually led to an over-grown pathway that ran alongside it. A battered 'Keep Out' sign was chained to the gate. This had to be 1 Traps Lane.

Another look at Google Maps informed her the substation was most likely 3 Traps Lane. The red marker for number 1 was bang next door. Switching to satellite view, the map showed a dark, rectangular shape that was the substation, behind which was a large overgrown area where the path seemed to lead. Connie zoomed in as much as she could. The land looked derelict – it was a decent-sized plot that would have accommodated two or three houses comfortably, more if you were a greedy developer. Apart from a few sparse patches the whole area showed up as dense green foliage. Connie had discovered a lot of derelict places to explore in the countryside with the help of Google Earth. Solid blocks of dark colour, a vague outline of a roof – anything that looked out of place – were often a giveaway to some hidden structure and there was something about the patch of land behind the substation that made her want to know more. A particularly solid patch of colour caught her eye. The kind a small building would make.

Traps Lane wasn't a lane in the country sense, but it was a fairly narrow road with a regular flow of light traffic. It was rush hour now, the A3 at the bottom of Pinder Hill busy with commuters. Connie pressed her phone to her ear and began an imaginary conversation with herself. To passing traffic she was idly chatting on her phone. As she talked rubbish into the handset, she casually checked out the gate with the 'Keep Out' sign. There was a gap at one side, narrow but manageable. She stopped and pretended to laugh at something as a taxi and four cars swept past. As the last vehicle pulled away and the road was momentarily empty she took her chance and squeezed through the gap between the gate post and a concrete pillar. There was just enough room – any smaller and she wouldn't have got through. Once she was on the path she walked quickly without looking back, the imaginary phone conversation over.

The path led down the side of the substation, which was cordoned off by a chain link fence. It was overgrown with weeds and became more overrun the further she went. Despite that, it looked as though someone had been there fairly recently. The grass had been trampled in a few places and a newish-looking empty pouch of tobacco had been discarded. An apple tree ahead marked the place where the land opened up behind the substation. Looking to her left, she could see the top floor of the house on the corner of The Drive, where it joined Traps Lane. The house – which Connie had noted was in the seemingly random numbering system on The Drive – stood out like a beacon. Unlike its exclusive neighbours, it had an unkempt air and could even be uninhabited, despite a dim light that seemed to emanate from nowhere in particular. Pushing on through the undergrowth towards the densest area of the plot she saw it bordered what had to be the garden of number 46. A wooden pillar and post fence separated the two bits of land and was well maintained.

Connie veered off the path she'd been on towards the centre of the overrun plot. Here, ivy had grown up the trees and Connie spotted a clematis and a rose, too, running rampant through the branches forming a canopy of entwined stems and leaves. In summer it would be amazing, and it crossed her mind that at one stage it might have been part of number 46's garden. Or perhaps it still was, and she was trespassing on someone's private land. The thought made her hesitate just as a flash of orange caught her eye. She peered through the trees and in the rapidly dimming light saw something up ahead: a dark mass of corrugated metal and tangled foliage.

The exact shape of the small building was impossible to see as it was so overgrown, but Connie felt the thrill of finding what had to be the old tin chapel tingle through her limbs. The sun was now kissing the horizon and the deep orange and red sky was reflecting off one of the building's windows. It gave the impression the church was glowing from the inside like some alien spaceship that had just landed. As Connie pushed on towards the small chapel she felt something tug at her ankle. Creeping vine as strong as wire had caught on her boot buckle and she fell, her ankle twisting as she went down. She lay on the ground for a few minutes, listening to her own breathing, before sitting up and disentangling her buckle. As she tried to stand, pain shot through her ankle – not the excruciating pain of a sprain, probably more of a twist, but painful nonetheless.

Ignoring it, she limped on to the small building in front of her. A patch of green-covered corrugated iron was just visible through the leaves, and she tugged at a piece of ivy that came away with a popping sound as its aerial roots were torn off the metal. Hobbling her way around it she came to a small arched window, its wooden frame remarkably intact. The sky behind her was now a blaze of mango and reflected off the glass, turning her surroundings an eerie pink.

Mindful of finding her way back to Traps Lane in the dimming light she hurriedly searched for the entrance and soon found a simple wooden doorway. A cross set in an inverted triangle had been carved into it and just as she'd taken a photo she heard a noise. A fox? Or maybe a cat? The sun had nearly sunk below the horizon, taking the temperature with it. The traffic volume which had been a constant hum was now also diminished and an unnatural quiet settled over the area. Then she heard it again. It was coming from behind the church door, which she now noticed was ever so slightly ajar. Remembering what she'd found when she'd entered the last church with its door open, she instinctively stepped back. Then, in what seemed like an out-of-body moment, Connie watched as her hand gently nudged the church door open. What was she thinking?

'Is someone there?' she asked, peering in.

What was left of the setting sun filtered into the small church as the smell of tobacco wafted out. Connie stood on the threshold, like a vertigo sufferer caught midway across a rope bridge, unable to move, as a figure stepped out of the shadows. The man's face flashed briefly in the dimming light as he pushed past her with a hard shove. Staggering back on her painful ankle, Connie felt herself falling for a second time. Her hands grasped at the ivy as she went down, the *pop, pop, pop* of it being pulled from the corrugated metal the last thing she heard before she hit the ground.

CHAPTER 23

Vernon Reid had either been out or not answering the door when Kirby had tried his flat, so he decided to head back to the car. He'd had enough of today, it could go and do one as far as he was concerned. He walked back along the bleak, rutted path that skirted the trees, which, although nearly dark, wasn't quite as black as the woods that had taken on a menacing impenetrability as the sun had sunk. After a few minutes he found himself passing the walkway that had been the scene of Anderson's accident. Where earlier it had been swarming with SOCOs and structural engineers from the council, it now stood quiet and taped off. A 'Danger' sign stood to one side like an afterthought. A lone van was parked with its headlights on and door open, a man in a high-vis vest reading something on his phone. Kirby went over and introduced himself. The man was from the council and had been part of the team assessing the safety of the walkway. There was nothing he could tell Kirby other than it wasn't deemed a risk and it appeared Anderson had been in the wrong place at the wrong time. Despite that, they didn't want to encourage anyone to walk near it. It would be demolished in a few weeks so they'd seen fit to leave it as it was.

Kirby left feeling angry and frustrated. Even though the council wanted the tenants off the estate as soon as possible, they still had a duty of care. He walked back to the car, keeping his eyes peeled. It was dusk, when shadows morphed into solid things and objects you thought you knew turned out to be something entirely different. A fox trotted along to his left, unfazed by Kirby's presence, until it darted off into the woods. By the time he reached the car it was completely dark, and he noticed the light on outside the Hoffmanns' flat. Tobias Hoffmann answered the door almost immediately. He had his coat on and looked startled to see Kirby.

'Off out?' asked Kirby.

'What? Oh, no. I'm just back,' said Hoffmann. 'I went for a walk. In the woods.'

So that was who he'd seen Michaela Falke embracing in the woods. Were they having an affair or was it an innocent greeting of two friends?

'What do you want – is there any news?' Hoffmann asked.

'No news, I'm afraid. I just need to ask you a few more questions. Can I come in?'

Hoffmann looked nervously behind him. 'It's Mary, she's not feeling well,' he said, lowering his voice. 'It's this business with Will, it's been a huge shock. Can we talk out here?' He pulled the door closed before Kirby could argue and stepped outside. The flat's outdoor light was bright and harsh, highlighting the bags under Hoffmann's eyes and accentuating his bald head. Kirby probably looked equally as bad. 'What is it you want to ask me?' Hoffmann asked.

'The keys to the church. Are you sure you don't have a set?'

'Um, yes, I think so.' He didn't sound very sure.

'You were caretaker here. You didn't mention that when we spoke. Caretakers often have keys to communal areas and someone we've spoken to said you had keys to all of them. Did that include the church?'

'Well, yes, it did. But I'm fairly sure I don't still have the key. I can check for you, if you like. Not now though' – he waved behind him, indicating the flat – 'I don't want to disturb Mary.'

'Tomorrow will do.'

He nodded. 'If that's all?' He turned back to the flat and had his hand on the door handle when Kirby spoke.

'We have a witness who says they saw you on Saturday night letting yourself back into the flat around 11 p.m.'

Hoffmann stopped. 'Who?'

'It doesn't matter who. Where had you been?'

'Nowhere. I told you, I didn't go out.' Hoffmann paused. 'It was Dan Scribbs, wasn't it?' He laughed an unamused laugh. 'I'm sorry, Detective, but the man is a drunk. He's about as reliable as a blind dentist.'

'So you didn't see him coming back from the pub? He's certain he saw you and that you saw him.'

'He's lying. Or mistaken,' he quickly added. 'He doesn't like us because we go to church. He thinks we don't understand the world; that we look down on him. It's people like him we try to help but he won't listen. He's a bigot.'

There was obviously no love lost between the two men and it occurred to Kirby that Scribbs could have made the entire thing up just to annoy Hoffmann. 'I see you've fixed your light,' he said, looking up at the modern fitting next to the Hoffmanns' door.

'Fixed?' Hoffmann frowned.

'Dan Scribbs said the light was off – that you couldn't get your key in the door.'

'But that's ludicrous. It's on a timer. It's always on at night. I told you that yesterday. It's why we didn't see any light in the wood. If there was one.'

'Yes, of course. I remember now. Well, thanks for your time, Mr Hoffmann. If you could look for that key I'd appreciate it.'

◆ ◆ ◆

Kirby had just slammed the car door shut when his phone rang. It was Hamer. 'Sir?' he answered, putting his seatbelt on. All he wanted was a long shower and to lie down but he'd promised Eleanor he'd meet her at the hospital on his way back and give her a lift home. She'd texted an hour ago to say she'd arrived.

'Have you seen the news?' barked his boss.

'No, why?' He started the engine.

'The *Daily Mail* have run a story about Sally Shires. It's online now and will be front page in the morning. You do know who she is, don't you?'

'Of course I do,' said Kirby, wondering what the fuss was about. The *Evening Standard* had run an interview with her recently. Same stable, different horse.

'According to their source, she had a visit from Jason Roye on Saturday, who told her he'd come back to find out what had happened to Kevin.'

'As in Jason Roye who went missing at the same time as Sally's son, Kevin? From Grasmere?'

'The very same.'

Jason Roye had disappeared, along with his friend Kevin Shires, from the Grasmere Estate in 1992. The story went that Jason was a tearaway and often led Kevin astray. On the day they disappeared a witness had seen them arguing, which led many to speculate that Jason had done away with his best mate – accidentally or otherwise – and run away. Not that there had been any evidence to support this as far as Kirby could remember. It was before his time. 'When you say come back, do you mean—'

'Yes,' said Hamer, irritably. 'Back to the Grasmere Estate. Jason Roye, who's been missing for decades, has arrived back at the very

139

estate he disappeared from at precisely the same time the body of William Stark is found.'

'We have nothing connecting Jason Roye to Stark,' said Kirby. 'Who is this source anyhow?'

'It has to be someone at the hospital.'

'Do you want me to talk to Sally Shires?'

'Yes. We need to verify whether this visit actually took place, and if it did whether or not she knows where Jason is. It could have been his camp in the woods and his light our witness saw. Ask Sally about Stark, too, while you're at it.'

'Which hospital's she in?'

'Same as Pete, St George's.'

Kirby groaned inwardly. 'I'm on my way there now to see Eleanor. I said I'd meet her there then take her home. I doubt they'll let me in to see Sally this late though.'

'Get up there first thing tomorrow. Give Eleanor my best, won't you?'

When Kirby arrived at the hospital he sat in the car park and pulled up the *Daily Mail* story on his phone. 'BOY TURNS UP AFTER MISSING FOR DECADES' was the headline.

'Jason Roye, who went missing as a teen from the notorious Grasmere Estate, turns up at London hospital to visit missing pal's dying mother. Sally Shires, whose son, Kevin, went missing at the same time as Jason, is dying of cancer. She recently spoke about her dying wish that Kevin's disappearance be solved before she passes away. In what sounded like a confession, Roye was heard to say to the dying mum that he was sorry and that it was time she knew the truth. Police were stumped in 1992 when the two lads went missing and despite several appeals no trace was ever found. The Grasmere Estate is currently in the headlines after a gruesome discovery on Sunday morning in the boarded-up church where a body was found.'

Kirby skimmed the rest of the article. There were no new quotes from Sally, only rehashed ones from the *Evening Standard* piece. He shut down his phone and got out of the car. If Jason Roye was really back then the press would have a field day. Whether it connected in any way to the current case was something he didn't know yet, but as he went to find Eleanor he had a nasty feeling that it might.

CHAPTER 24

It took Connie what felt like an age to disentangle herself from the undergrowth she'd fallen into when the man had pushed past her. Goose grass stuck to her like Velcro, its tangled mass refusing to relinquish its grip. Brambles had caught her hair, along with her jacket sleeves, and the more she tried to escape the worse it got. Finally, she was free, and gingerly stood up, wincing as she put weight on her twisted ankle. Her ears strained for any unusual noises but all she could hear was the distant rumble of traffic. The man – whoever he was – had gone, but that didn't mean he wouldn't be back.

With shaking hands, she switched on the torch on her phone and shone it over the church. The door was closed – not that she had any intention of going in now – and the surrounding foliage looked impenetrable in the dwindling light. Using the silhouette of the house on her right and the sound of traffic to her left to guide her, she slowly navigated her way back towards Traps Lane. Panic threatened to take over at intervals and she fought the urge to charge blindly through the undergrowth. It would achieve nothing – except, perhaps, another fall – so she concentrated on moving carefully back to where she thought she'd come from. Veering too far left, as she found herself at the back of the electricity substation but on the wrong side. An eerie humming sound emanated from the rectangular building and a movement on its flat roof made her pause. It was large enough for a fox. Following the fence she eventually found the pathway leading back to the gate where she'd entered and felt relief flood through her. Wriggling through the gap between the pillar and the fence she felt her coat snag on the wire and swore under her breath as she stumbled on to the lane.

She hadn't seen the man with the dog standing in the shadows. He was picking up dog crap from the pavement, and for a moment they stared at each other as the dog made a low rumbling sound.

'Evening,' said Connie, brushing herself down. What must she look like?

'Evening,' said the man. 'Bit dark for poking about in there, isn't it?' He nodded to the area behind the substation. 'Buster got in there one day through that gap. Had the devil's own job getting him out. His collar broke. That's why he's growling – it's not you, it's because he wants to get back in.'

'There must be something in there he really wants,' said Connie. *Or someone.*

The man chuckled. 'You can't be angry with 'em for long though. Only doing what they're bred for. Probably smelt a fox.'

'I've just seen one on the roof,' said Connie. The man looked to be in his seventies, maybe older. He had a kind face and didn't seem in the least bit perturbed at seeing someone making an exit from what was clearly private property. The dog, a Staffie, tried to lick her hand.

'Stop it, boy,' said the man, pulling the dog away. 'Sorry.'

'It's fine,' said Connie. 'He can probably smell my cat. I don't suppose you know who owns that land, do you? I'm doing some research.' It sounded lame, even though it was the truth.

'Research, eh?' The old man smiled, as if to say, *Yeah, right.* 'No idea who owns it. Been derelict for as long as I can remember. Must be worth a packet too.'

'Do you know anything about the church that's there?'

'The tin chapel?' The man nodded. 'Used to be down there.' He pointed at Traps Lane and towards Grasmere. 'It disappeared overnight. Word was the minister there had it moved. I only knew it came here because one of my mates drove the lorry.'

'Do you remember the minister's name?'

'Sorry. I'm not religious myself, and I didn't live here back then. People do strange things, don't they?'

'What about that house?' asked Connie, pointing to the rear of the property whose garden backed on to the derelict land. 'Is it occupied?'

'I've seen a light on sometimes,' said the man.

That didn't mean anything. The light could be on a timer. There may even be a property guardian in situ – not that Connie had seen any signs at the front of the building. Buildings occupied by property guardians usually had warning notices outside to deter burglars – she should know, after all.

'An actress used to live there,' said the man. 'Whether she still does, I don't know. She'd be getting on a bit now. Probably as old as me, although I dare say she has more hair.' He rubbed the bald patch on the top of his head and shivered. 'Brrr, I must get on. Standing still isn't doing my arthritis any good.'

'No, of course not. And sorry if I startled you. I'm Connie, by the way.' She held out her hand.

'Joe,' said the man, and they shook. 'Lovely meeting you, Connie. Goodnight. And be careful,' he shouted over his shoulder as he ambled off in the direction of the main road, whistling something Connie didn't recognise. She turned back to look at the house when something occurred to her.

'Joe! Wait!' she called, limping after him. Her ankle was beginning to throb.

'What is it?' asked Joe, turning around.

'You didn't see anyone come out by the fence? Before me?'

'No, why do you ask?'

'Oh, nothing. I just got the feeling there was someone else in there, that's all.'

'No one went in or out while I was there.' The old man pottered off leaving Connie alone on Traps Lane. The traffic was now non-existent and a couple were walking up the road on the other side, holding hands, laughing at something. As their laughter faded, Connie was left with the hum from the substation and the faint drone of the A3. At the top of Traps Lane, the house on the corner appeared to blink as two upstairs lights flicked on simultaneously. A black cab turned off The Drive and came towards her, its light on, so Connie stuck out her hand. Even hobbling to the nearest bus stop would be difficult and she climbed into the back of the cab with a sense of relief. She gave the driver Livia's address and as he took off down Traps Lane she turned and looked back at the house. A figure was standing in one of the lit upper windows. Connie kept her eye on it until they reached the bottom of Pinder Hill and it was too far away to see, but the image stayed with her all the way home.

CHAPTER 25

The next morning, Kirby was greeted by a beautifully clear blue sky. The air was cool and crisp and he wished he had time to sit and drink a coffee on deck instead of driving back to the hospital to interview Sally Shires. Last night's visit to see Anderson had been depressing, although he was at least now conscious. His partner had seemed confused. He kept repeating himself and saying things that didn't make sense. The doctors had reassured Kirby and Eleanor the confusion was to be expected and that it should eventually wear off. Their main concern was monitoring the subdural haemorrhaging. Eleanor had clung to Kirby when he'd arrived. She was a practical, sharp-witted woman, used to taking charge of situations – she frequently had to take charge of Anderson – but Kirby knew she'd been badly shaken by seeing her usually ebullient husband wired up to machines in a hospital bed. He'd driven her home, where she'd insisted on making some food and so he'd stayed longer than he'd intended, not getting back to the boat until nearly midnight. He'd fallen asleep as soon as his head hit the pillow and had an uncharacteristically dreamless night. His reflection in the mirror was an improvement on the previous day so he took that as a good omen as he locked up.

Jumping on to the walkway that linked the small cluster of houseboats, he glanced over to Isabel's. She lived on a red painted

Dutch barge. The spring bulbs she'd planted last winter were now coming into bloom, the early tulips bright in the sun. Another month and the deck would be a florist's dream. They hadn't seen each other since Monday morning, when Isabel had found him huddled in a blanket on the deck of the boat. She'd come to join him, smothered by one of his old ski jackets, and they'd sat in silence watching the early morning boats go by. When it had been time for Kirby to leave for work, they'd parted awkwardly, the previous night's conversation left unmentioned – an unspoken agreement between them that they both needed some time. There was another reason Kirby hadn't wanted to talk about it that morning, and that was because he hadn't quite told Isabel everything. He hadn't told her about his involvement in Livia's suicide. The news about the baby and the FFI was enough, never mind throwing in that he'd assisted his own mother in taking her life by helping her plan the deed and would face criminal prosecution if anyone ever found out. No, that was one secret he intended to keep to himself.

He walked to the car deep in thought. He tried to imagine how he would have felt on hearing the news of Isabel's pregnancy if the FFI didn't exist. Would he feel differently? Maybe not ecstatic, but certainly more open to the possibility of having kids. Or was he just lying to himself? Perhaps he didn't want kids and the FFI gave him the perfect excuse not to? Isabel would make a great mother but what about her career? She was a successful radio producer and loved her job. And what about their living arrangements? Neither of their boats was particularly large and certainly not big enough for two adults and a baby. He loved Isabel and more than anything he wanted her to be happy, but not at the cost of sacrificing their freedom, which, he realised, played a huge part in the success of their relationship. Also, if he took the gene test, as per Isabel's wish, and it came back positive, then he'd be living his life as a dead man walking. And what about the baby? Would

Isabel want a termination? Livia had decided to end her life when the symptoms of the FFI had started to become more pronounced and she'd felt herself degenerating day by day. If Kirby found himself in the same position he'd also want to end things before he became bedridden – bedridden by a disease that kills you through lack of sleep! You couldn't fucking make it up.

His mood plummeted even further when he set eyes on the Fucking Corsa. He lived for the day some bastard set it on fire or stole it. But no, there it still was, sparkling in the sunlight, flicking the Vs at him. To add insult to injury the traffic was relentless and the drive to the hospital took him well over an hour. The first thing he did when he arrived was go straight to the Pret concession and order a double espresso. He wondered whether he should see Anderson while he was there and checked his phone again for any update from Eleanor, but there was nothing. Feeling marginally better after the coffee he went in search of Sally Shires' ward, where he was greeted by a stern nurse who showed him to Sally's bed. The nurse drew the curtain and left them to it.

Sally Shires looked like a woman who didn't have long left. Her eyes were sunken with dark shadows beneath, her short hair harsh and unforgiving, leaving her features with nowhere to hide. Kirby wished he were anywhere else but here at that moment; even the shabby interior of the Corsa seemed preferable.

'I'm very sorry to disturb you,' he began. 'I won't take up much of your time. I'm here about the story in the *Daily Mail*. I take it you've seen it?'

Sally Shires nodded. 'The nurse showed me,' she croaked. 'It was a private conversation.'

'So Jason Roye did come and visit you?'

Sally nodded. 'Yes.' She closed her eyes as if talking was effort enough. 'I never for one moment thought he hurt my Kev. And he wanted me to know that.'

'Is that why he came to see you, to tell you that?'

Her head moved in a slow nod. 'He'd seen all the press about Grasmere being pulled down. Then he read the *Evening Standard* interview I did and that was what clinched it.' She opened her eyes. 'He wanted to find out what happened to Kev before it was too late. That estate . . .' She began to sit up. Kirby helped by moving her pillows into a more comfortable position before passing her the glass of water she'd pointed to on the bedside table. 'That's better,' she said, taking a sip.

'You were saying about the estate,' prompted Kirby.

'Oh, yes. Have you been there?'

'Yes, a few times.' It occurred to Kirby she didn't know the real reason he was there.

Sally nodded again, as if his answer confirmed something to her. 'So you'll know then. It's a place full of secrets. I'll never see my boy again, but that doesn't mean I don't want to know what happened to him. I left a tealight in a jar outside the front door every night since he went – did you know that?'

Kirby hadn't and felt an overwhelming sense of desperation.

'So if he came back he'd know I was waiting for him. When I became ill and had to move out, Will Stark said he'd do it for me.' Sally appeared to drift off and Kirby wondered how much longer he could stay.

'Did Jason say where he was staying?' he asked gently. 'We need to speak to him quite urgently.'

'Why? He had nothing to do with whatever happened to Kev – he swore to me. He was just a silly lad who ran away.'

'He told you that he ran away?' This was news to Kirby.

Sally nodded weakly. 'I believed him. His home life was terrible. Who could blame him?'

If what she was telling him was true, that Jason had run away, it changed everything about the missing boys' case. 'And he has no idea what happened to your son?'

'No . . . it's haunted him all these years. Like it has me.'

Someone from the cold-case review team would have to question Sally about her conversation with Jason Roye – as well as Roye himself when they found him. Kirby needed to concentrate on his own case, the murder of Will Stark. 'There's something else we need to speak to Jason about. You heard about the death on the estate over the weekend?' He presumed she did if someone had shown her the *Mail* story.

'Will Stark,' she said. 'Awful news. You can't think he's involved with that, though – why would Jason kill Will Stark?'

'We're talking to everyone who's been on the estate over the last few days, and if Jason was there then that includes him, too. He's not a suspect.'

This seemed to satisfy her and after a few moments she said, 'He stayed with Vern Reid, on Saturday night. I don't know where he was going after that. Vern wasn't keen on him staying – he's funny about people after what happened at Waco. You know about that I suppose?'

Kirby nodded.

'Poor sod.' She took another sip of water and stared at the glass in her hand as though the answers were there in the clear liquid. 'They were dark days – first Kev and Jason went missing, then the following year there was little James Bulger and then we all watched Waco burn on the telly, knowing Vern and his mum, Frances, were in there. Vern got out but his mother wasn't so lucky.' She shook her head at the senselessness of it all.

They talked for a few more minutes, Sally barely able to keep her eyes open. Kirby stood up to leave feeling suddenly drained. The raw pain of Sally's loss hit him harder than he'd anticipated. How would he cope if something happened to the child Isabel was carrying, should they decide to keep it? How would Isabel cope? Would they survive it together or would it tear them apart? The answers were too awful to contemplate and the desire to get as far away from the hospital as possible was overpowering. He pulled the curtain back just as a nurse was picking something up from the floor outside the cubicle. She was young and pretty and gave Kirby a flirtatious smile. 'Dropped this. Clumsy me.'

Kirby bade Sally goodbye, but whether she even heard him he couldn't tell as her eyes were now closed. He beckoned to the nurse to follow him out of the ward, where he pumped her for information about Sally – had she had any visitors, if so when and so forth. By the time he left to go and look in on Anderson, he was fairly sure he'd found the source of the *Daily Mail* story.

CHAPTER 26

Reid was on edge today, more so than usual. It was Wednesday and Jason's return last week had shifted the very fabric of the estate; he'd felt the tension from the other residents as he'd seen them go past. The lift in Coniston House had got stuck on Reid's floor the previous night, its doors opening and closing with a clatter he could hear from his flat. Then there had been the incident with the police officer the day before, hit by a piece of concrete as it fell from one of the walkways. Toby Hoffmann had found him unconscious and called an ambulance. Police and council officials had then swarmed the area, heightening the feeling of unease. In a panic, Reid had managed to sneak Jason off the estate – the police were bound to see him sooner or later and then the questions would begin.

The only place Reid had been able to think of where Jason wouldn't be found was the old church up on Traps Lane. It was adjacent to the garden he worked in on The Drive and belonged to the same owner. The key to the gate was on the same bunch as those to the garden. Invisible from the road, it was the perfect temporary hiding place, and he'd taken Jason up there yesterday as soon as the coast had been clear. He was glad he had, because this morning he'd woken to the *Daily Mail* story about Jason's visit to Sally Shires. It would only be a matter of time before the police spoke to Sally and then came calling on Reid. He had to hope Jason had the sense to stay put in the old church until things calmed down. But in the end, he wasn't Jason's keeper and Jason would do as he pleased, like he always had.

It was a clear day with a light breeze and Reid made his way up to the roof to begin the task of cleaning out the pigeon coop. Today, he fixed pigeon whistles to a few of the birds – small devices fitted to their tail feathers that made a noise when the birds flew. He'd learnt about them from a fellow inmate in prison, a seemingly gentle man, originally from Beijing, who used to make his own. The man had become embroiled in a rooftop altercation over birds and killed a fellow pigeon fancier. Pigeon racing was big in NYC and the rooftop lofts became the inspiration for Reid's own. He'd learned a lot from the pigeon man, and as soon as he'd returned to the UK and settled at Grasmere he'd set up his own coop and started making whistles. His first attempts were dismal; it was a definite skill, and it had taken him years to perfect the design, but the effort had been worth it.

With the last whistles attached, he set the birds free and watched them fly off making their own music as they went. As they circled overhead, something made Reid go to the edge of the roof, where he saw a car parked below. He recognised it as belonging to the policeman and felt the tension that had momentarily left him when he set the birds free return in an instant. The policeman must be here to see him, there was no one else, but it had happened faster than he'd anticipated and he felt the drowning wash over him. He quickly retreated behind the air vent where he kept his box of gear for the birds. He opened it and took out the blow torch he used to clean the trays in the pigeon coop. The policeman was bound to ask some awkward questions and it would feel good to know he had a weapon. Not that he intended to use it; that would be a last resort. *It's just for security*, he told himself, slipping the lighter into his pocket.

CHAPTER 27

A strange whistling sound, almost ethereal, made Kirby look around. He was on the balcony outside Vernon Reid's flat. He'd rung the doorbell several times but had got no answer. The concrete walkway to his left was empty. The strange noise returned and, looking up, he saw a small flock of pigeons fly over. The whistling seemed to eddy on the wind before fading, replaced by a sudden rumble from the demolition site which had started work again.

Kirby went back through the polytunnel to the main staircase and up another floor where he found the fire door on to the roof propped open with a fire extinguisher. He called Reid's name as he stepped out. The flats' roof was like a landing strip, narrow and long, the air vents at either end much bigger than he'd expected and covered in graffiti. Reid's pigeon coop had been erected in the shadow of the vent nearest to him. He approached the wooded structure, which was open, the birds gone.

'What do you want?' said Reid, who'd appeared from behind him and now stood by the doorway to the stairwell, blocking Kirby's exit.

'I need to ask you a few more questions. Can we go down to your flat and talk there?'

Kirby saw that Reid was holding something in his right hand – a blow torch – and wished Anderson had been with him. Kirby could look after himself in a fight, but no one was a match for a blow torch.

'I have nothing to add to what I told you the other day,' said Reid. Another rumble, followed by a crash from the demolition site momentarily distracted him as his eyes flitted across to what little was left of the block of flats.

'I've been to see Sally Shires.'

'What's that got to do with me?' If Reid was surprised, he didn't show it, striding past Kirby and into the pigeon coop, where he put the blow torch down and began pulling out the trays from beneath the perches.

'She had a visit from Jason Roye on Sunday. He told her he was staying with you.'

Reid said nothing and began scraping the bird droppings from the trays out into a bucket.

'If you'd rather talk at the station I can call them and let them know we're coming.' Kirby took out his phone and pulled up the number.

Reid stopped what he was doing for a second. 'There's no need for that.'

Kirby slid his phone back into his pocket. 'Then talk to me.'

Reid was rigorously scraping the pigeon shit off but it wasn't enough to hide that his hands were shaking. 'Jason did come and stay. Just the one night – Saturday. What of it?'

'That's the night Will Stark was murdered. You told us you were here alone that night.'

'Jason didn't want people knowing he was back.'

'He went to see Sally Shires, which is hardly keeping a low profile.'

155

Reid didn't respond. He finished scraping the tray before spraying it with disinfectant and dropping it on the ground. He pulled out another and started the process over.

'So to be clear, you and Mr Roye were here, together, on Saturday night. Is that correct?'

'Yes.'

'And which one of you came up here?'

Reid looked up and frowned. 'I don't understand.'

'You were seen up here – or someone wearing your jacket was.'

'Jason came out for a smoke. I lent him my jacket. He must have come up here.' He paused. 'I didn't know.'

Kirby cast his eyes around looking for cigarette butts and saw one by the fire door. 'How long was he gone for? Long enough to get to the church and kill Mr Stark?'

Reid stopped what he was doing. A crash echoed across the open space from Windermere House and Reid flinched. A line of sweat marked his upper lip. 'I don't know how long he was gone for. But he had no reason to kill Will Stark.' He resumed the scraping more vigorously than ever, only stopping to wipe his brow every now and then.

'Did they know each other? You must have talked about his murder to Jason.'

'A bit.' He shrugged. 'I think he remembered the name but they had no reason to know each other.'

'What about you?'

'He was a good man,' said Reid. 'I can't think why anyone would want to kill him.'

'Did you know him growing up or only when you returned from America?'

'I knew him before I left. He got me a weekend gardening job. Then when I came back he was the only person who tried to help me. Got me my old job back.'

'At the same place?'

Reid nodded. 'House up on Pinder Hill.' Another boom echoed across from the demolition site and Reid's eyes darted towards the source of the noise. He wiped the sweat from his upper lip with the back of his hand.

'What time did Jason go out?' Reid was becoming more agitated and Kirby regretted not insisting they go to his flat to talk.

'I don't know!' It was an innocent enough question but Reid stopped the scraping and pushed the heel of his hand to his temple as though he had a headache, his eyes still flitting to and fro towards the skeleton that had once been Windermere House. 'I don't know,' he repeated, more quietly. 'But it was after ten. Maybe half past.'

'And where is Jason now? Is he at your flat? I need to speak to him, if only to rule him out.' Reid shot him a look Kirby was all too familiar with, which roughly translated as, *Yeah, right.* 'Mr Reid, giving false information to the police is a serious offence. Do yourself a favour and tell me where he is.' The demolition site suddenly fell silent and Reid visibly relaxed.

'I don't know. He was freaked out by all you lot being here over the weekend. When I got back from work on Sunday he was gone.'

'So the last time you saw him was on Sunday morning?'

Reid nodded. 'He was asleep. I didn't want to wake him so I slipped out.'

'I see. What did you talk about on Saturday night? You must have had a lot to catch up on.'

'I don't remember.' Reid extracted another tray and began scraping the pigeon shit off that.

'Don't take me for a fool, Mr Reid. One of your close friends who disappeared several decades ago suddenly appears at your door one day and you don't remember what you talked about? Did he tell you where he'd been all those years?'

'Scotland. Glasgow, I think . . .' mumbled Reid. 'I didn't take much notice. It was a shock seeing him again.'

'And what about Kevin Shires? Did you talk about him? Only, like I said, he'd been to visit Kevin's mum in hospital, or didn't he tell you that?'

'Look, he saw the interview Sally did with the *Standard* and knew the estate was about to be pulled down. He *had* to come back.'

'Why? What happened to them, Mr Reid? Tell me – the case is still open so if you have any information on the whereabouts of Kevin Shires, or what happened to him, you need to let me know. Sally deserves to know.'

'I know she does.' His hand went to his forehead again and he ground the heel of his palm into it so hard that he left a red mark. 'I don't know what happened to Kevin. And Jason didn't know either. He just disappeared.'

'What do you mean "just disappeared"? In Glasgow?'

'No—' Reid stopped as if weighing up whether or not to answer. 'I guess it doesn't make any difference now but they'd planned to run away. They'd bought tickets to Glasgow – the overnight train – only Kevin didn't show up as arranged. In the end Jason had to leave without him. He assumed Kevin had chickened out.'

'And you knew about this plan?'

Reid nodded.

'Why the hell didn't you say anything at the time?'

'I wasn't here!' Reid yelled. 'I was leaving for America the following morning. I had no idea things had gone wrong.' He picked up the blow torch and took a lighter from his pocket. 'And neither did Jason – he left thinking Kev had bailed. It was only months later he found out Kev never made it home.' Reid flicked the lighter and ignited the torch, sending a large flame in Kirby's direction causing him to step back. 'Damn thing,' said Reid, adjusting it to a more manageable size before running it over the disinfected trays. 'Truth is, first I knew about any of this was when Jason turned up on my doorstep.'

CHAPTER 28

Dan Quatremaine was a man Connie had longed to punch in the face for some time. That morning, after a restless night's sleep, the urge was even stronger. She'd lain awake for half the night churning over the events of the previous evening. She'd spent a large part of that time debating whether or not she should tell Kirby about the encounter. She hadn't been attacked, per se, just knocked over. And she had been trespassing – which she assumed the other person had been too. Eventually, she'd dropped off to sleep around five only for her alarm to wake her at seven. The alarm had also woken Terror, who then proceeded to walk all over her, yowling loudly. She'd forgotten to feed him last night so, feeling guilty, she'd eventually got up. It hadn't been the best start to the day and now Quatremaine was clearing his throat in that irritating way he had as he sat hunched over drawings of Hunstanton Manor, an estate he was writing an article about for *Country Life* magazine. As much as she disliked him, she couldn't fault his research.

Quatremaine was a corpulent man in his early fifties who smelled of mothballs – although judging by his clothes that horse had already bolted. His hair was grey, thick and wavy, with a nicotine skid mark that sometimes flopped over his forehead. He was the type of man whom her ex-boss, Bonaro, got on with effortlessly. Connie struggled to find anything to say to him beyond pleasantries and even those evaded her on occasion, because Quatremaine was a misogynist. He had barely acknowledged her when Bonaro had been curator and only did so now because he had no choice. To Quatremaine – and he wasn't alone, unfortunately – RADE was the preserve of scholars, and therefore men. She wouldn't be surprised if he was a member of a gentlemen's club somewhere.

With Quatremaine engrossed in his work, Connie went on to the Land Registry website and put in a search for 1 Traps Lane. A free search would tell her when the property was last sold and for how much, but for £3 she could get the title deeds that would give her the name of the owner and she considered it would be £3 well spent. What she hadn't bargained for was the *No information held* notice that came up on screen.

'*Damn it*,' she said under her breath, causing Quatremaine to briefly look up. There could be several reasons why there were no records, but the most likely – given the land was derelict – was that it hadn't changed hands in decades and its records weren't held digitally, which meant she'd have to make a postal enquiry if she wanted to pursue the matter. She also tried a few local history websites but again, she found nothing. She sat back, frustrated. As she did so her mobile phone pinged, indicating a text message. She grabbed it quickly, switching it to silent mode, but it was too late. Quatremaine gave her one of his disapproving looks and then made a big show of getting comfortable in his chair again, sighing loudly. True, mobile phones were banned from the main reading room, but anyone would think Quatremaine had been blasted by a loudhailer from his body language.

The text that had come through was short and to the point: *will be at the grasmere flat @ 1.30 BK*. Connie stared at it for a few moments in disbelief. Brian Kaplinsky had messaged her. She'd completely forgotten about leaving her details in his flat. He was going to be there that lunchtime – the man she'd been chasing for over a year. The man she was sure had been with her sister when she fell from the water tower six years ago. Who'd called an ambulance and then fled. She stood up suddenly, banging the chair against the leg of her desk.

'Are you alright, Connie?' said Quatremaine. 'Only you seem a little on edge.'

'Sorry, Dan. I need to make a call, that's all.' She left the reading room and headed for Bonaro's office where she locked the door behind her. She reread the message over and over just to make sure she wasn't imagining it. Quatremaine would probably go for lunch quite soon and she prayed he wouldn't want to come back in the afternoon. If he did, she'd have to make an excuse. She wasn't going to miss the opportunity of meeting Kaplinsky for anything. Feeling a little calmer, she unlocked the office door and went back to the reading room. As she passed Quatremaine her eye caught the headline of the *Daily Mail* he'd brought with him.

'May I?' she asked, pointing to the paper.

'Be my guest. I don't usually read the *Mail* but someone left it on the train.'

Connie took the paper back to her desk and stared at the front page. 'BOY TURNS UP AFTER MISSING FOR DECADES' screamed the headline. But it wasn't that which had caught her eye so much as the photograph at the bottom of the page with the caption: *The hellhole Grasmere Estate where the two boys lived.* The image showed one of the walkways on the estate with a group of skinheads pulling faces at the camera.

'You heard about Will Stark, I take it?' said Quatremaine, who had been watching her. Among other things, he was a terrible gossip.

'Yes,' said Connie, quickly skimming the article about the two missing boys, Jason Roye and Kevin Shires. Apparently Jason Roye had shown up at the hospital where Kevin's mother was currently being treated for cancer.

'Such a dramatic exit.'

'Pardon?' said Connie, looking up. 'What was?'

'Will getting himself killed like that. In his own condemned church no less. There's a certain irony in the situation, don't you think?'

'It was me who found him, and irony wasn't the first thing that sprang to mind.'

Quatremaine's mouth was now hanging open. This had to be the best gossip he'd had in decades. '*You* found the body?'

'I did,' she said, folding the paper and returning it to the table next to Quatremaine. 'I'm sorry I disturbed you.' She went back to her computer and began furiously typing with a deeply concentrated look on her face. She could feel Quatremaine's curiosity coming off him in waves and was enjoying his discomfort.

After a few minutes he couldn't contain himself any longer. 'I knew him, you know. Will Stark.'

'Really?' said Connie, looking up from her typing. 'I'm sorry.'

'Lovely man, although why he dedicated his life to that monstrosity we'll probably never know. Rumour has it he only got the job because—' Before he could finish the sentence the doorbell rang. It was rigged up so it rang upstairs as well as down.

'Excuse me,' said Connie. 'I need to get that.'

'I'm about done here anyhow,' said Quatremaine. 'I'm giving a lunchtime talk at the Wallace Collection.'

Connie breathed a sigh of relief at that news. 'I really am sorry about the disruption today. I'm a bit jumpy, that's all.' The bell rang a second time and she hurried out of the reading room, leaving Quatremaine nodding sympathetically.

At the front door she greeted a courier and remembered she'd ordered a new kettle for the kitchen. After signing for the package she went back upstairs and met Quatremaine on his way down.

'You must forgive my comments earlier about dear old Will Stark,' he said. 'Totally inappropriate. I hope you won't repeat them to anyone.'

'Of course not,' replied Connie, mentally filing them away for future use. 'You were about to say something about how he got the Grasmere contract when the bell went. I'd be interested to know.'

'Oh, that.' He looked at his watch and shook his head. 'I'll be late for my lecture. Next time I visit. I've finished the Hunstanton research so I'm not sure when that will be, but you know me, there's always something on the horizon. Cheerio.'

As he left, it occurred to her Quatremaine had fingers in many pies and could possibly be of use when it came to fundraising. The crushing reality that it was people like him who could help her deepened her sense of frustration and she felt despondent as she went to the kitchen to unpack the kettle. Will Stark's murder and her subsequent discovery of the tin church were easy distractions, but the spectre of a nine-to-five office job or stacking supermarket shelves stalked her mind like a bad dream. She had to come up with some kind of plan to secure the archive. But right now, with her meeting with Kaplinsky, she had bigger fish to fry.

CHAPTER 29

A glazed brick structure with a framework of pipes overhead was all that was left of the former bakery in which F&G Architects was housed, just off a trendy street in Shoreditch. Anderson had been on his way there when he'd had his accident and, much to Kirby's frustration, no one in the team had followed it up, so he'd detoured to the architectural practice after his conversation with Vernon Reid. He'd filled Hamer in on his interviews with Sally Shires and Vernon Reid by phone as he'd driven across London, his boss still irked they'd had to learn of Jason Roye's return through a tabloid newspaper. Finding Roye was a number one priority, but Stark's colleagues were also important – so far they had little insight into the man Stark had been and more often than not this was where the answers lay. Kirby didn't think Stark's murder had been random so there had to be something in the architect's life that had driven someone to kill him. All he had to do was find it.

The glazed brick structure had once been one of the ovens, the overhead pipework carrying steam heated by atomised oil fires that regulated the heat distribution and made for the perfect loaf. Kirby had been told all this by an elegant young man called Radar de Souza, who had greeted him at the practice reception when he'd arrived. Without being asked, de Souza had explained his parents had been fans of the TV series *M.A.S.H.* and that he'd been named after the character played by Gary Burghoff. De Souza told him senior architect Dan Gould wasn't in the office so Kirby waited for Thadeus Finch, whose father had set up the practice with William Stark in the mid-seventies.

From reception, Kirby could see through to the main office, a large open-plan space with generous white workstations. The tall roof was supported by industrial metal beams that had been painted white. He could see right through to the other end of the building to an outside space with lush leafy plants. It was all very light and airy, and Kirby wondered what life would be like working in a space like that every day, rather than the dull interior of the cramped MIT29 office where the only view was of the carpool and the bastard Corsa. While he waited, his phone buzzed. Eleanor Anderson's name flashed on screen and Kirby felt his stomach lurch.

'Eleanor,' he answered. 'Is everything okay?' Eleanor didn't answer immediately and Kirby knew something was wrong. 'What is it? What's happened?'

'They've taken Pete into surgery. The bleed got worse overnight. Lew, I'm so worried.'

Kirby watched a tall man with close-cropped silver hair and a neatly trimmed goatee making his way through the office towards him. Kirby recognised him from the company website from his trademark chunky blue acetate glasses. 'Eleanor, I've got to go, but hang in there – I'll be there as soon as I can. Any news you call me immediately, got that?'

'Okay,' she whispered and was then gone. Kirby stared at the phone in his hand as if it were somehow personally responsible for the bad news. The thought of losing Anderson was something he couldn't bear to contemplate. He *wouldn't* lose Anderson, he told himself. *Pete will be fine, he'll be back to stuffing animals in no time.*

'DI Kirby?' said a voice.

Kirby looked up to see the man he recognised as the F part of F&G Architects. 'Sorry, yes. You must be Thadeus Finch.' He tried to push all thoughts of Anderson on the operating table out of his mind as he followed Finch through the office and out the other side. Except it wasn't outside at all. What Kirby had mistaken for an outside garden was, in fact, a beautiful indoor space with a glass roof. 'It'll be quieter out here,' said Finch, showing Kirby to a metal table and chairs.

No sooner had they sat down than de Souza appeared with a tray bearing a cafetière, cups and a carafe of water. Finch said nothing as the man laid the tray down, giving a curt nod of thanks instead. Kirby had read about the bullying that went on in some architectural circles and wondered whether it happened here.

'This looks a beautiful place to work, Mr Finch,' said Kirby, as the architect poured two coffees without asking if he wanted one.

'I've never yet met a policeman who didn't drink coffee,' said Finch. 'Milk?'

Kirby shook his head. 'Just some water. Thanks.'

Finch poured two glasses of water and then sat back in his chair. 'We were all devastated to hear about Will,' he said. 'He was only here on Friday.'

'How did he seem?' asked Kirby, taking a sip of coffee. Not espresso, but still pretty good.

'Seem? Fine. Same old Will.' Finch smiled.

'Can you tell me a bit about him? I gather he set up the firm with your father, Drew.'

'That's correct. Will started out as a local authority architect before setting up his own practice. After winning the Grasmere contract he then set up with my father once the estate was built. Stark Finch Partners. It brought quite a lot of work in as you can imagine. Then Dan joined the team in, gosh, that must've been in

167

the late eighties. He brought a whole new aesthetic to the practice and it went from strength to strength.'

'You said "after winning the Grasmere contract" – what do you mean?' Kirby had no idea how architects were chosen for such projects.

'The local authority held a competition for the estate. They whittled it down to six entrants and Will won.' Finch paused for a moment. 'Don't get me wrong, I still think the estate was a very bold design and I truly believe most of its problems were preventable, but it's by no means Will's best work. Nor, rumour has it, the best out of the final six entrants.' He shrugged. 'But something made them go for it over the others.'

Kirby hadn't known any of this. 'Who were the other entrants?'

'I'm afraid I don't recall. It was before my time.'

'Where would records be kept?'

'Goodness, I suppose Will might have kept some paperwork for nostalgic reasons. The council should have a record somewhere.'

'Okay, thanks.' Kirby made a note, thinking that this was Connie's territory. 'Did the practice experience any fallout from the estate when things started to go wrong?'

'Not that I know of. Outside of the architectural world, no one knew who'd designed it – not until the past decade at any rate. People usually have no idea who's designed the very building in which they live. It's always struck me as odd.'

'I doubt they know who designed their car or their kitchen table either,' said Kirby. 'So Mr Stark was here on Friday. Can you tell me why? I thought he'd retired.'

'He had, technically, but he liked to come in and keep up with things. He'd consulted on a few projects we have going on – nothing major, but he liked to be involved. We enjoyed having him here and his input was still valuable.'

'What time was he here?'

'He arrived at eleven,' said Finch. 'He sat in on our mid-morning meeting and then had a look at a new project we're working on down by the river. I had a sandwich with him out here at about one-ish and he left shortly after. He seemed perfectly fine.'

'Did he say if anything was bothering him? Or if anyone had threatened him?'

'Why on earth would anyone threaten Will?' asked Finch. 'But no, he didn't say anything like that.'

'Can you think of anyone who might have wanted to harm him? Perhaps a disgruntled client, a rival firm – did he owe money to anyone?'

'No. The whole thing is unfathomable. As for his finances, I can't comment. But the firm has never been in financial difficulty.'

'Do you know where he was going after he left here at lunchtime on Friday, did he say?'

Finch thought for a moment. 'He didn't say. I assumed he was going home.'

'I wanted to ask you about that,' said Kirby. 'Home was the estate, which strikes me as a little odd. Why did he stay there? I presume he could have afforded to live somewhere more salubrious than Grasmere.'

'Will was a very principled man. Sometimes, infuriatingly so. Yes, he could have moved somewhere far more upmarket but he felt compelled to live in the world he'd created.'

'He could have created another world for himself and his daughter, Alma, elsewhere,' said Kirby. 'It just strikes me as strange that they both stayed.' He noticed Finch stiffen slightly at the mention of Alma.

'I couldn't possibly say why Alma stayed. But she and her father were very close. You know what happened to Will's wife, don't you?'

'She took her own life by jumping off one of the blocks of flats on the estate.'

'That's right. Alma was only eleven at the time. It doesn't bear thinking about what they went through. My father ran the practice pretty much single-handed for six months after that, Will was in no fit state to return to the office. Alma was . . .' He paused. 'Difficult, after, shall we say.'

'In what way?'

'Will sort of smothered her. Walked or drove her everywhere. She could be very challenging if she didn't get her own way as a result. He indulged her – that was the problem. She's going to be in the hell of a mess after this. I can't really remember a time when they've been apart for longer than a couple of days.'

'Didn't Alma go to college or university?' Kirby tried to imagine growing up on the estate in Alma's shoes. Escape would have been his top priority. Reid had done it and so, it seemed, had Jason Roye.

'She did, yes, but here in London. She went to the AA.'

'AA?' Kirby's first thought was Alcoholics Anonymous.

'The Architectural Association School of Architecture. It's in Bedford Square. Alma inherited her father's talent for design. She even worked here for a year or so when she first graduated.'

'And after that?'

'She was at a firm in Camden for a bit, but working as part of a team didn't suit her. She left and began doing extremely detailed drawings of buildings. She tapped into a market no one else really had – an original of hers can sell for a fair whack. Rightly so. The detail is astounding and each one takes months to complete. You might have seen some of them for sale – she's done the Barbican, Trellick Tower, Preston Bus Station, Birmingham New Street Signal Box. All the iconic Brutalist buildings.'

'I've seen the map of London in her flat. It's quite extraordinary. Tell me, did Mr Stark still have a desk here?'

'Goodness, no. Nothing like that. He moved all his stuff out when he retired. But he did occasionally use one of the computers.'

Kirby's ears pricked up. 'I'm going to need to see that,' he said, and Finch nodded, making to get up. 'One more thing though,' said Kirby. 'What can you tell me about Mr Stark's involvement with the campaign to save Grasmere?'

Finch sat back down again. 'To be honest, he became quite obsessed. It was a waste of his energy – and I told him as much – but he wouldn't listen. He was never going to win against the developers, Paragon, no matter how good his arguments. Or, indeed, the right or wrong of it. The deal was done and nothing any committee could say or do was going to change that. It was wearing him down.' Finch took off his glasses and polished the lenses with a cloth he took from his pocket. Kirby sensed he had something to add, and waited as the architect cleaned his glasses and carefully repositioned them on his nose. 'You asked me if I could think of anyone who wanted to harm Will and I couldn't. This may sound a little off the wall, but the thing that posed the greatest threat to him was Grasmere. It may well have been the making of him, but it also damn near killed him. It was relentless once things started to go wrong. We're talking almost fifty years of constant pressure. From the physical deterioration of the estate to the societal and cultural breakdown – Will fought hard the entire time to make the people in power see it was them and not the estate that was at fault. But it all came down to economics in the end.' He shrugged. 'Eventually – and this sounds crazy – Grasmere seemed to develop a malevolence all of its own, and yet Will refused to see it.'

'I'll see the computer now, please,' said Kirby. As he stood, he thought of Anderson lying on the operating table fighting for his life and shuddered. Crazy or not, the malevolence felt real.

CHAPTER 30

Connie hadn't expected to feel so nervous. The anticipation of finally being able to meet Brian Kaplinsky, and possibly learn the truth about her sister's death, had almost made her turn around and leave. But she couldn't back out, not now. As she walked along the gangway towards the flat, she had the strangest sensation of being watched, but then, it was Grasmere. She turned and looked behind her at the long expanse of concrete walkway, but there was no one there. All the flats were boarded up so she put it down to nerves and continued on her way. She wondered what Kirby would think if he knew she was here. He'd be distinctly unimpressed, she decided.

When she reached flat 16 she stopped. Her heart was racing and she almost wished she'd had a stiff drink before coming. Just as she was poised to knock, the door opened and a man filled the doorframe. For a few seconds they stared at each other in silence. Connie's mind had suddenly gone blank and it was the man who spoke first.

'You Connie?'

'Yes. Are you . . . ?'

'Brian Kaplinsky. You better come in.' He stepped back into the hallway, holding the door open.

Connie hesitated. 'I'd rather talk out here,' she said, now regretting not telling anyone where she was.

'I don't bite,' said Kaplinsky.

Arsehole, thought Connie. 'People know I'm here.'

Kaplinsky rolled his eyes. 'I'm not going to do anything,' he said. 'But suit yourself.' He leant on the doorframe and folded his arms. 'Come on then. Say what you've got to say.'

'It's more what you've got to say. I want to know what happened the night my sister died at Blackwater. I know you were there.' The words tumbled out and hung between them awkwardly.

'Who told you that?'

'Another explorer. It doesn't matter who.'

'And you told the police. They questioned me about it yesterday. Thanks,' he said sarcastically.

'*Excuse me?*' Connie was confused.

'Yeah, DI Kirby, the same copper who was on the Blackwater case came to see me at work. A bloke was murdered here at the weekend, in the church. Which, I hasten to add, has nothing to do with me before you get any funny ideas about that too.'

For a second, Connie was speechless. Kirby had spoken to Kaplinsky and hadn't told her? She'd bloody kill him when she saw him next. 'I don't know anything about that. I'm here to talk about my sister. I want to know what happened. You owe me that at least.'

Kaplinsky regarded her for a moment. 'I don't know what you want me to say. That I was a dick? Okay, yeah, maybe I was. I didn't want to get caught by the police. I did the right thing though – I called the ambulance. I could have just left her there.'

'You *did* just leave her there,' said Connie, controlling the rage that had suddenly ignited. 'You don't "just leave" someone.'

'She was dead,' said Kaplinsky, bluntly.

His words stung and Connie felt herself flinch, her eyes threatening tears that she managed to blink away. Coming here had been a mistake. Kaplinsky was either in so much denial he couldn't see anything wrong in his actions, or he was a cold-hearted bastard. She felt like a mug for even thinking he would be anything otherwise.

He must have seen the hurt on her face. 'It wasn't like that,' he added. 'I'm sorry, I . . .'

'What the fuck was it like then?' said Connie, regaining some composure. 'I want to know. I want you to tell me why you left an injured woman alone. Dead, or dying, I want you to tell me what's okay about that. Go on!'

'There's nothing okay about it,' said Kaplinsky, who'd unfolded his arms now, his veneer of hostility beginning to slip. He shoved his hands deep into his jeans pockets. 'There's nothing okay about it. You're right. But she was definitely dead when I left. I swear.'

'So why'd you do it? It's not like you were going to get prosecuted for being there. You worked for the bloody developer for Christ's sake! You could easily have made up some story about being there at night if you'd needed to. Come on, I'm waiting. I want an explanation.'

He didn't answer immediately and when he did it was so quietly Connie thought she'd misheard him. 'Say that again?'

'There was someone else there that night. By the water tower.'

Connie's mind was racing. Another explorer? 'Who?'

'I don't know,' he said, looking up. 'Really, I don't.'

'So talk me through it. You go up the water tower together, Sarah somehow falls because the structure's unsafe. You presumably run down to see if she's okay and—'

'No,' interrupted Kaplinsky. 'I was never in the water tower. Sarah went up alone.'

Connie stared at him for a moment, uncomprehending. 'This other person – where were they?'

'Up there,' he whispered. 'Jesus.' He rubbed his eyes with his thumb and forefinger. 'There was someone up there with her.'

'No . . . you're lying,' said Connie. 'Fuck's sake. You're worse than I thought you were.'

'It's the truth,' said Kaplinsky. They were now both standing on the communal walkway. Connie was pacing up and down. She didn't want to believe what Kaplinsky had told her and yet . . .

'Whoever it was saw me,' Kaplinsky went on. 'They had to have done. I had a torch with me. Sarah . . . she waved at me from the top of the tower. And then . . .'

'What?' Connie was right in front of him now, she could feel his breath on her face. 'Tell me.'

'She fell. Just like that. One minute she was waving. The next . . . I . . . I didn't know what to do. I went over to her, of course I did. She wasn't breathing. The angle of her head . . . I knew she was gone. And then I heard a noise. I saw a light in the water tower. Whoever it was, they were coming down the stairs. I ran. I hid.'

'What did the person do?'

'They went over to your sister and just looked at her. They didn't crouch down or anything, just stood there, shining a light on her and . . . and just left.'

'Did you recognise them?'

Kaplinsky shook his head a bit too quickly. 'No. It was just a silhouette. You know how dark it gets there at night.'

That was one thing Kaplinsky had said that she did believe. The darkness. 'Why didn't you say anything?' she asked.

'I was scared, alright? I called the ambulance, didn't I?'

'Bully for you.'

'Look, I've got to go,' said Kaplinsky. 'I need to get my stuff. My wife's waiting.'

Connie grabbed hold of his sleeve. 'Does she know about this?'

'No.' A look of alarm crossed his face. 'No one does. You're the only person I've told.' He pulled his arm free and turned to go inside.

'Wait. You remember Raymond Sweet, the man who lives in the Old Lodge in the asylum's grounds?'

Kaplinsky stopped. 'What about him?'

'He saw someone creeping about the place. He called them The Creeper. He thought it was you.'

'I did try to scare him a few times – we wanted him off the land. Trying to sell luxury flats with a resident squatter wouldn't have been a good look. I used to move stuff about in his house for a laugh, hope he'd get freaked out. He was halfway there already.'

Connie had befriended Raymond last year during the Blackwater case and yes, he was eccentric, but he wasn't unbalanced. 'Did you ever come to my house at the Four Sails? Move things around there too? Huh?'

'What? Why would I do that? Look,' he said, lowering his voice as though they might be overheard. 'It's been eating away at me, okay? Your sister was . . . she was great.'

Connie waited, expecting more, but Kaplinsky had finished. 'Is that it?'

'You wanted to know what happened that night, and I've told you. I didn't hurt your sister. There was someone else there. I ran away and I called the ambulance. That's it.' He held his arms out. 'That's all I can give you. And now you've got to leave it alone.'

'But—'

'You heard. Leave it. For your own good.' He disappeared into the flat, slamming the door behind him.

Connie shook her head in disgust. 'You're such a fucking prick, Brian, d'you know that?'

CHAPTER 31

'Why didn't you tell me you'd spoken to Brian Kaplinsky?' Connie had been sitting on the deck of Kirby's boat for half an hour, waiting for him to come home. She'd taken herself for a very long walk after talking to Kaplinsky and then gone to the pub where she'd downed several pints.

'How the hell did you get in?' Kirby asked, ignoring her question and jumping on board, his keys jangling in his hand.

'Someone let me in.'

'Well they shouldn't have. The security gate to the mooring is there for a reason. Who was it? I'll have a word.'

'Actually, it was Isabel. On her way to Paris.'

Kirby stopped what he was doing for a second. 'Oh. Right. She's visiting her mother.'

Connie sensed there was more to it but wasn't interested in Kirby's domestic situation at that precise moment. 'So you spoke to Brian Kaplinsky. You knew where he worked and you didn't tell me.'

Kirby unlocked the door to the boat's quarters. 'I suppose you'd better come in.' He disappeared inside and Connie followed, irritation rising. He didn't seem to realise why she was so pissed off.

'I've got a killer headache,' said Kirby, throwing his keys on to the kitchen surface and opening the fridge. 'I need some water, and so do you judging by the smell of alcohol on your breath.'

Connie bristled at the comment but ignored it. 'Why didn't you tell me you were going to see him? You know how important this is to me.' She was going to get an answer whether Kirby liked it or not.

'Yes, I do know, and I told you on Sunday I'd have to interview him in connection to Stark's murder. But on Sunday I didn't know where he was. I haven't seen you since then. Plus, it's not actually any of your business.' He took out a cold bottle of fizzy water from the fridge and held it up. 'Want some?'

Connie nodded, annoyed he'd sussed her out.

'I could ask how you know that I've spoken to Kaplinsky,' said Kirby, pouring two glasses of water. 'I take it you've talked to him.'

Was that disapproval in his voice? Christ, she was spoiling for a fight and tried to quell the urge. She also didn't want to get kicked out of Livia's. 'He texted me this morning and said he'd be at the Grasmere flat at one thirty, so I went to see him.'

'Okay,' said Kirby, handing her a glass of ice-cold water before rummaging about in a kitchen drawer. 'And how did it go?'

'You make it sound like a fucking date. But since you ask, he admitted he'd been with Sarah when she had the accident. But he also said someone else was there too.' Connie recounted their conversation and felt her earlier irritation begin to subside.

'He could just be making it up to get you off his back,' said Kirby, popping two paracetamol in his mouth and swallowing them with a mouthful of water.

'That crossed my mind, but I think he's scared and that's why he warned me off.' She took a sip of the water and nearly spat it out. 'What in God's name is this? It tastes like sea water.'

'Don't you like it?'

'It's revolting.'

'Help yourself to tap water then.'

She went to the sink and filled up her glass. 'Christ, that's better. What's that stuff called?'

'It's Spanish.'

'Great, I'll remember the label so I never have to drink it again.'

Kirby shrugged and finished the rest of his water. Connie didn't know how he could drink it; it was rank.

'So what did Kaplinsky say to you?' she asked.

'He denied he was ever at Blackwater with your sister and said he didn't know a thing about her accident.' Kirby paused. 'But he was lying, I'm fairly sure.'

Connie felt a wave of relief. He believed her. 'So what happens next?' She downed her water and poured another, feeling the effects of the beer starting to wear off.

'Nothing.' Kirby sat down on one of the stools in the kitchen. 'Even if what he told you was true – that there was a third party at the water tower that night – there's no evidence anything suspicious happened. To have the case reopened would mean significant new evidence coming to light.'

'So there's nothing you can do?'

'With no new evidence, no. I'm sorry.'

'What if I could persuade Kaplinsky to make a statement saying he saw someone in the water tower with Sarah? Maybe they'd come forward.'

'It still doesn't suggest it was anything other than an accident.'

'But what if whoever was up there pushed her off?' She could feel her frustration growing.

'It's a big leap from having another witness to murder. And what possible motive would anyone have for killing Sarah? I get you want answers and that Kaplinsky has given you anything but, but you've got to be rational about this.'

'Rational? Look, I know I've had a couple of beers, but something's not right about this. Kaplinsky did admit to entering Raymond Sweet's house to scare him off, but swore he'd never broken into the Four Sails.'

'We don't know *anyone* did. You had no evidence for that either.'

'Come off it, you were there. You believed me.'

'True, I did. But that was based on nothing more than trust. I'm sorry, I honestly can't take this any further. Can we change the subject?' He rubbed his eyes. 'I've had a shit day and—'

'You and me both.'

'*And* I'd like your help with something.'

'You want my help? You won't help me but—'

'It's to do with Will Stark's murder,' Kirby interrupted her.

Despite her annoyance with him, Connie reluctantly found herself intrigued. 'What sort of help?'

'I visited Stark's old architectural practice today and found out he *won* the contract for Grasmere. There was some kind of competition, only I can't find any reference to it and I wondered if you could do some digging? I want to know who the other competitors were. It's probably not important but it needs checking and you're the perfect person to help.'

'Are you asking me to do this because you feel bad about not being able to help me with Sarah?'

'No,' said Kirby. 'I could genuinely use the help. Pete's in hospital. There was an accident at Grasmere and he was hit on the head by a piece of falling concrete.'

She'd been so preoccupied with Kaplinsky and being annoyed with Kirby that she hadn't noticed until now how strained he looked. 'Is he going to be okay?'

'Honestly? I don't know.'

'I'm so sorry. You should have said. Has he got family?'

'A wife. Eleanor. And a daughter in America.'

'What have the hospital told you – I mean, what's the prognosis?'

'He had a bleed on his brain, which got worse overnight and they had to operate this afternoon.'

Connie felt terrible now for charging in like a bull at a gate. The last thing Kirby needed was her going off into the deep end. 'I'm sorry. If I'd known . . . How did it go, the operation?'

'They managed to stop the bleeding but it's too early to tell whether there's been any damage. I'm going over there now – I only came home to change.'

The guilt was piling on. She was now holding him up. No wonder he was so snippy with her. She started towards the door. 'I'll get out of your hair.'

'So can you find out what you can on this competition?' asked Kirby. 'There has to be a record somewhere.'

'Probably the council archives. It was nearly fifty years ago though – the estate was built in the early seventies.'

'I know it's a long shot, but you're in a far better position than me to find out what went on – with Pete laid up, we're stretched.'

'Leave it with me,' she said. 'I'll see what I can do. And I'm sorry I was pissed off with you. Are you okay?' she asked tentatively. 'With Isabel away too . . .'

Before Kirby could answer his phone began ringing. 'Sorry,' he sighed, looking more tired than ever, 'I'd better get this.'

While Kirby took the call Connie mulled over the tin chapel again and whether or not she should mention it to Kirby. Probably not, given what a shit day they'd both had. She couldn't face another telling-off.

When Kirby finished the call it was obvious something had happened. 'It's not Pete, is it?' she asked with a feeling of dread.

He shook his head and picked up his keys from the kitchen counter and stood up. 'There's been another death at Grasmere. Someone set one of the garages alight and there was a body inside.'

CHAPTER 32

By the time Kirby reached the estate, Sally Shires' garage was nothing more than a dripping black hole in the row of graffitied metal doors that ran along the ground floor of Ullswater House. Arc lights set up by the fire department showed where soot had blackened the facade of the building above and around the garage door, which hung at an angle from its runners. A cordon had been placed around the entrance and neighbouring garages on each side. Outside the cordon he spotted the Falkes and the Hoffmanns huddled together. The Carmodys were just leaving. Standing alone, on the edge of the wood, was Vernon Reid. He was staring up at the first-floor balcony where Alma Stark stood silhouetted in her open doorway before disappearing inside.

'The fire started in the centre of the garage on an old sofa,' said the fire officer in charge. 'The victim looks as though he was lying on the sofa at the time the fire took hold. There's no sign he'd tried to escape, so I'd guess he died of smoke inhalation before the flames got to him. But obviously, Forensics will confirm that for you.'

'Any idea who it is?'

The fire officer shook his head. 'There might be something in his pocket but we'll have to wait for the forensic officer to get here. Do you know who the garage belongs to? I thought this place was empty.'

'There are still eight residents left,' said Kirby. 'Elliott and Michaela Falke, Pat and Ralph Carmody, Tobias and Mary Hoffmann, Alma Stark and Vernon Reid. But I've been told this garage belonged to a previous resident, Sally Shires.'

The officer's eyes widened. He was too young to remember the case but he'd probably read the article in the *Evening Standard*. 'Shit.'

'Who reported the fire?'

'One of the residents. He lives over there.' The fire officer pointed towards Coniston House.

'Vernon Reid?'

The fire officer nodded.

'Are you able to say yet whether this was started deliberately?' Kirby looked at the burnt-out garage. What had been stored here?

'The contents of the garage appear to be mainly clothes and boxes of old toys, so they burned quickly,' said the fire officer, as if reading Kirby's mind. 'The fire originated around the area of the sofa, so it's possible a cigarette caused it. There's nothing to indicate that petrol was stored here. Weirdly, some of the garages still have power, so it's possible it was an electrical fault of some kind but I can't be more specific than that at this point.'

'Is it safe to go in?'

'As long as you're suited and booted, yes.' From where he was standing, Kirby saw what looked like the twisted frame of a sofa, the fabric burnt away and a dark shape on the ground, and felt sick. He thanked the officer and trotted back to the car to change into his PPE kit. He was surprised to find Reid waiting for him.

'Evening, Mr Reid,' he said. 'I gather you called this in?'

Reid nodded. 'Was someone inside?' His voice trembled and Kirby realised he was in shock.

'A body has been found, yes.' Kirby looked in the direction of the Falkes who had started to walk home, their torch beams dancing in the dark, before turning back to Reid. 'Dan Scribbs moved out on Monday and everyone who still lives here is accounted for. Which leaves one person.'

Reid swallowed. 'You think it's Jason?'

'Do you?'

Reid couldn't hold Kirby's gaze any longer and looked around nervously. He probably hadn't been near so many people in uniform since his spell in prison. 'Sunday night. I saw light under the garage door and realised where he'd gone. I went down there early on Monday morning and found him.'

'You found Jason in the Shires' garage? How did he get in?'

'Sally gave him a key when he visited her in hospital.'

'Why didn't he stay with you? He'd stayed on Saturday night.'

Reid shuffled on his feet uneasily. 'I like being alone. He knew I was uncomfortable having him in the flat.'

Kirby didn't believe him – not completely – and Reid must have understood his look.

'I didn't say he couldn't stay – in fact I'd planned on telling him that he could – but when I got back on Sunday . . . the police were here and . . . Jason was gone. Then I saw the light.'

'Let me get this straight. Jason rolls up unannounced on Saturday evening and you let him stay at yours?' He looked at Reid who nodded in confirmation. 'Then on Sunday, you got up early to go to work. You then returned back here in the evening to find Jason gone and William Stark murdered. And as far as you know, Jason slept in the garage that night.' Reid nodded again. 'So where's he been since then?'

'I don't know.'

'Don't lie to me, Mr Reid.' They stared at each other for a few moments. 'Okay, I tell you what. I want you to go home and think very carefully about what you've told me and what you haven't told me, because we have a dead body in that garage and from what you've said the odds are looking pretty high it belongs to your friend.'

'I—' Reid started to say something but stumbled back and bumped into the front wing of the Corsa. He leant on the car, his breathing coming in heavy, rapid breaths and his face damp with sweat. He was having a panic attack.

'Mr Reid – Vernon? Take some deep breaths for me now,' said Kirby, stepping into his sightline so Reid couldn't see into the burnt-out garage. 'Concentrate on your breathing, try to forget what's going on around you.'

Kirby waited as Reid tried to calm himself. After a couple of minutes his breath had slowed but he was still leaning on the car for support. Kirby reached inside and took out an unopened bottle of water that he handed to Reid, who unscrewed the top and took several long gulps.

'I need to go for a walk . . .' said Reid, pushing himself off the car and standing unsteadily.

'That's a good idea. I'll see you back at your flat in an hour. We need to talk.'

Knowing how the Waco siege had ended – in a fierce blaze that had claimed seventy-six lives – it was hardly surprising the burnt-out garage had triggered Reid's panic attack, let alone the idea that his friend might have been inside.

'*Fuck*,' Kirby muttered to himself as he unlocked the car boot and took out his PPE kit.

CHAPTER 33

After picking his way through the charred remains of Sally Shires' garage and moving carefully around the blackened body of the man he believed to be Jason Roye, Kirby was only too glad to be back outside in the fresh air. Even though the garage was small, the smell of smoke followed him to the car where he reached for the bottled water only to remember he'd given it to Vernon Reid. Reid was his next port of call and for once he hoped he would be offered a drink of some kind. He wanted to wash away the acrid taste of smoke in his mouth. It had seeped into his body leaving its pungent trail in its wake. Carter Jenks had arrived as well as an ambulance and there wasn't much room in the garage, so he'd left him to it.

As he locked the Corsa, he glanced in the direction of the walkway where Anderson had had his accident. It was shrouded in darkness, only revealing itself briefly when the blue light of the ambulance grazed its angular features, and he shivered involuntarily. Hamer had called earlier to confirm what the council official had told him yesterday – that it looked as though Anderson had been the victim of bad luck and that so far there was nothing to suggest foul play. Alma's words about how the estate had taken her father came flooding back and he wondered what the impact of living somewhere like this was, where lives could so suddenly be altered whether by accident or, in some cases, design. He pictured

Eleanor alone at the hospital by her husband's side and wished he could be there for her.

Connie's earlier comment about Isabel being away had also hit a nerve. When Isabel had called to tell him she was going to visit her mother in Paris for a few days to clear her head, Kirby had been relieved. Now all he wanted to do was race back to the red Dutch barge and take her in his arms as the possibility she might not come back reared its head. The realisation that if he were ever to have children he would want them with Isabel had been growing ever since. He couldn't conceive of being a parent with anyone else. And yet, at that precise moment he experienced a bleakness he hadn't felt in years.

Reid was in the polytunnel watering his seedlings by torchlight when Kirby arrived, a worried look on his face. 'Is it Jason?' he asked.

'It's too early to tell, but as soon as I hear anything I'll let you know. We need to talk, Mr Reid.'

Reid grunted, resigned. 'You'd better come in then.'

Kirby followed him through the polytunnel and back to his flat where he turned off the hosepipe he'd attached to the kitchen tap. He began busying himself at the sink washing his hands and filling a kettle. Kirby noticed his hands were shaking again and he'd also spotted a cricket bat propped up by the front door that he'd missed on the first visit. In the kitchen, Kirby deliberately sat with his back to the door so Reid could take the seat opposite with a clear view to the hall and front door. He was sure Reid was suffering from PTSD.

He gratefully took the tea Reid made him. 'The smell of smoke stays with you,' he said, raising his mug in a gesture of thanks before taking a sip. 'But then you'd know that, wouldn't you? After Waco.' He watched Reid carefully for a reaction.

'So you know then. It's hardly a secret; I just don't broadcast it for obvious reasons. Especially not to people like you.'

'You mean the police?'

Reid nodded. 'You'll forgive me if I don't trust you. You know what they did, don't you? Those people died because of men like you.'

'With respect, Mr Reid, this isn't America and I'm not the FBI. I appreciate your point though.' And Kirby did. From what he'd read about the siege at Waco it appeared to have been an unmitigated disaster on the part of the FBI, with the most tragic of consequences, and he wondered how a similar situation would be handled today. He'd like to think differently, although given how recent civil unrest and several high-profile cases of police brutality in the States had been handled, he wasn't so sure. 'Do you get any help?'

'Help?'

'Counselling. Therapy. You do suffer from PTSD.'

'You said we needed to talk, but I didn't realise you meant dissecting my life.'

Kirby put his tea down. 'Tell me what Jason was doing in Sally Shires' garage. You told me she'd given him the key. Why?'

'It's full—' he stopped to correct himself, '*was* full of Kev's things. Sally couldn't bear to get rid of it all, so she stored it in the garage. Then she became ill and it just sat there. Jason turned up and . . .' Reid shrugged his shoulders. 'She said he could take whatever he wanted.'

'Is that the only reason?'

'Why are you so interested? You probably just want to pin Kev's disappearance on him. Kill two birds with one stone.'

'Why would I want to do that?' said Kirby, evenly.

'Because that's what people did. Some folk who are still here think it was Jason's fault.'

'But Sally Shires doesn't.'

189

'Of course not. She knows Kev and Jason were like that.' He held up crossed fingers.

'Look, Mr Reid, I haven't read the case notes, but I can assure you if the police thought Jason was involved in whatever happened to Kevin then they would have had a very good reason. But to my knowledge that wasn't the case. People talk. They gossip. They like to have someone to blame when the unthinkable happens. Places like this, like Grasmere, are cauldrons of rumour. And you know what it's like being on the receiving end of that, I imagine. Now please, just tell me what Jason was doing.'

'He wanted to go through Kev's stuff looking for something the police might've missed when he disappeared. Anything that might give him a clue as to what happened to him. I know you lot would have gone through it at the time but no one who knew Kev like he did would have done. Jason just hoped to find something that had been missed.'

'And did he?'

'I don't know,' said Reid, hesitantly. 'It might be nothing but there was a birthday card from someone we didn't recognise.'

'Was it signed?'

Reid shook his head. 'Someone had drawn the peace sign on it. Everyone used it back in the nineties.'

'An anonymous card isn't proof of anything,' said Kirby. 'Maybe Kevin had a secret girlfriend.'

'He didn't,' Reid said. 'If he had, Jason would have known.'

'What about you? Would you have known?'

'Maybe. I don't know.'

'Where's this card now?'

'It's probably ashes. Last I saw, Jason put the card in his pocket.'

'Was there anything in the garage that you remember that could have started the fire? Was Jason using a heater in there?'

'I . . . I don't think so. It was cold in there on Sunday morning when I went to talk to him, so I guess he wasn't.'

'Did he smoke in the garage?'

Reid nodded. 'I saw him do it once. You think that's what happened? The fire started with a cigarette?'

'It's one possibility.'

Reid's eyes narrowed to a question mark. 'And another possibility?'

'That the fire was started deliberately.'

'Dear Lord. May his spirit rest in peace.' Reid crossed himself.

'Did anyone else know Jason was hanging out in the garage?'

'I . . . I don't know. It's feasible someone saw him coming or going. I don't think he told anyone.'

Kirby thought of Mrs Carmody with her binoculars. 'Did Jason speak to any of the other residents while he was here?'

'He said he spoke to Tobias. He didn't mention talking to anyone else but that doesn't mean he didn't.'

'Do you know what he and Tobias talked about?'

'Nothing much. Although he did ask Tobias how Michaela was. Jason said he looked like he'd seen a ghost.'

'Why would that be?'

'None of my business,' Reid said, dismissively.

'Come on, Mr Reid. If you know something that could help you need to tell me.'

'Tobias and Michaela – they had an affair.'

'When?'

'Years ago – we were teenagers. We saw them one day in the church.'

'Who's "we"?'

'Me, Jason and Kevin.'

'Did they know they'd been seen?'

'I don't think so. Maybe. I don't see what that has to do with Jason's death.'

'Could they still be having an affair?' asked Kirby, remembering Michaela's embrace in the woods.

Reid shook his head. 'You'd have to ask them that. I have nothing to do with them.'

'Can you think of anyone who might have used the church for an illicit rendezvous recently?'

'You mean someone here?'

'Anyone.'

'No.' A smile crept over Reid's lips. 'Elliott won't like that at all.'

No, thought Kirby. *Especially if it turns out to be his wife.*

Reid stood up and rinsed his mug in the sink, his head bowed. Kirby sensed he was mulling something over and waited.

'Jason called me this morning,' said Reid eventually, turning around to face Kirby. 'He said he'd found something else.'

'What?'

'He didn't say. Only that it was important.'

'What time was this?'

'Nine? It was before I left here.'

'Where was he when he called?'

'I assumed the garage . . . but I can't be sure.'

'What kind of mobile did he have?'

'Nothing smart like an iPhone. A cheap Android maybe?'

Kirby took out his own phone and called Jenks. 'Carter, are you still in the garage?'

'Yes. Why?'

'Did you find a mobile phone on the victim?'

'Not on the victim, no, but on the bench so it's not too badly damaged. It looks like a Doro, one of the cheap models you buy from those shops on Oxford Street. Remarkably, it still seems to work.'

'Give me a sec, will you?' Kirby looked over to Reid who was watching him intently. 'Have you got Jason's number?'

Reid nodded and took out his phone. 'Call it,' said Kirby. Reid did as instructed and after a few seconds Kirby heard a distant ringtone down the line from Jenks.

'It says "Vern calling",' said Jenks.

Kirby nodded to Reid to end the call and then spoke to Jenks. 'The phone belongs to Jason Roye, our missing schoolboy from the nineties. I need that body ID'd as soon as possible.'

Reid had sat down, his head in his hands, and looked up when Kirby ended the call. 'It's Jason, isn't it?'

'It's his phone but we need more than that.'

Reid shook his head. 'The devil is walking this estate as if it were his kingdom. He took Kevin and now he's taken Jason.'

'What about Will Stark – did the devil take him, too?'

'The devil will take whoever he sees fit,' said Reid, pausing for a moment. 'Even if it's one of his own.'

CHAPTER 34

If Kirby had felt tired the day before, the next morning he felt like death warmed up. He was sitting in Hamer's office being grilled by his boss about the fire. He hadn't left the Grasmere Estate until gone two in the morning. All notions of visiting Anderson had gone out of the window. Being a policeman's wife Eleanor had understood, but he'd heard the disappointment in her voice when he'd told her he wouldn't make it. The doctors were being very guarded in their prognosis which was causing her to fret even more. When he'd got back to the boat he'd showered to get rid of the smell of smoke and fallen into bed where – just to add insult to injury – he'd dreamt about Bob Dylan. Anderson was firmly with Isabel on the Dylan debate and would have gleefully viewed the dream as a prelude to a Damascene conversion, as he worshipped Dylan almost as much as he did his taxidermy victims. Kirby was feeling the absence of his partner acutely as Hamer fired questions at him.

'Is there anything to suggest this is connected to William Stark's murder?' asked his boss. Hamer was always a smart dresser but an appearance at the Old Bailey meant he was in uniform today, which only added to Kirby's feeling of tawdriness.

'Not immediately but it does seem a big coincidence,' said Kirby, swallowing a yawn.

'And we don't like coincidences. You do know if the body in the garage does turn out to be that of Jason Roye the press will be all over it?' His boss glared at him as though the fire in the garage was somehow his fault.

'At least we know Reid won't talk to the press – they're probably second on his shit-list after us – and I can't see the Falkes or the Hoffmanns talking to them either.'

'They'll find someone, they always do. Were the fire crew able to tell you anything?'

'It looks as though the fire originated on, or near, the sofa. They can't really tell us much more than that at the moment – not even if it was an accident or deliberate. Reid told me Roye did smoke, so it might have started with a cigarette. The sofa was ancient, probably early eighties, if not earlier.'

'So before the rules on soft furnishings came into force,' said Hamer. 'Nasty.'

'Quite.'

'Do we know if Roye had changed much, physically? I'm just wondering whether people would have recognised him had they seen him.'

'Reid says he hadn't. But it's a long time ago. Unless they knew him well as a boy then there's no reason why they'd put two and two together now.' While he spoke, something was bothering him. 'Michaela Falke seemed to think the person they saw going into Reid's block of flats could be Brian Kaplinsky, even though she hardly knew him, whereas her husband was positive it was someone else. I wonder whether she recognised Roye but didn't want us – or her husband – to know.'

'Why would she do that?' asked Hamer.

'Reid says Michaela and Toby Hoffmann had an affair back in the nineties, and I saw her with someone in the woods on Tuesday

195

who wasn't Elliott. If Roye was back, she might have been worried he'd stir things up.'

Hamer raised an eyebrow. 'That's a long time to have an affair. Do you think they could be our mystery couple in the church?'

'It's possible, I suppose.' Kirby couldn't envisage it though. Then again, Michaela had seemed embarrassed by the idea of the church being used for illicit meetings when he'd mentioned it in the woods.

'Has anything linking William Stark to Jason Roye or Kevin Shires cropped up in the investigation?' asked Hamer.

'No, but we weren't looking. Reid said Roye knew Stark's name but that they didn't know each other. I'd better talk to Sally Shires again. If it is Roye's body then she needs to know before the press get hold of it.'

Hamer agreed. 'Even if they didn't know each other when Roye was a teenager they could have met as adults. Reid was out of the country for over fifteen years, remember, so how do we know Roye didn't return to the estate at some point then? Reid would never have known.'

'True, but Reid's story that Roye came back to find out what happened to Kevin after reading Sally Shires' *Evening Standard* article rings true to me.'

'We only have Reid's word for that,' Hamer reminded him. 'Do we have the case files on the boys' disappearance yet?'

Kirby shook his head. 'I've put a request in, but God knows when they'll come through. They're pre-digital era so I had to go via the General Register.'

'The rumour Roye had done away with his best friend was cooked up by one or two papers – or at least that's what I remember of the case. But if there is anything to suggest otherwise we need to know about it. Who was the SIO?'

'Ted Harper. He's retired now, lives in Kent.' Kirby had been on to HR earlier.

'Talk to him. And ask if he remembers Stark – whether he cropped up in the investigation or not. How long until we get a positive ID on the garage victim?'

'Jenks said he'd work on it asap, so I'm hoping later today.'

'That man works miracles sometimes.' Hamer gathered up his things – mobile and keys – and smoothed the sleeves of his jacket.

'Is this the Stankevič case?' asked Kirby. Paul Stankevič had been a bouncer at the Tops Nightclub in Peckham, stabbed in the early hours of the morning as he left work.

Hamer nodded, grimly. 'The parents need our support today. The trial's at a delicate stage.'

Kirby knew the Stankevičs had lost their other two children to illness and a road accident. Paul had been the apple of their eye, his death making the unimaginable horror of outliving all three of their offspring a reality. Kirby thought about Isabel and the child she was carrying and wondered whether he could bear being a parent.

'Did William Stark leave a will?' asked Hamer, as he and Kirby left his office.

'It was something Pete had been looking into – I'll get on it.'

'I heard they had to put a drain in,' said Hamer, his face sombre. 'I spoke to Eleanor earlier.'

'I should have been with her last night but then I got the call about the fire . . .' Kirby shook his head.

Hamer patted Kirby on the shoulder in a rare display of fondness. 'You can't be in two places at once, Lew. He'll be fine, I know he will.' Hamer approached the lift and jabbed at the button, all business again. 'Architects – especially one of Stark's standing – aren't usually badly paid. The rent for Grasmere must have been minimal for someone like him, so where did his money go? His daughter might be getting a nice lump sum.' The lift doors slid open and Hamer was about to get in when he paused. 'And where did the two boys get their money to go to Glasgow?' He stepped into the lift and admired himself in its mirrored walls as the doors slid shut, leaving Kirby pondering the question.

He went and sat down, his eyes drawn to the empty desk opposite, where Anderson usually sat. The room was quiet without him. Anderson's entrances were legendary and once he was in a room he seemed to fill it. It wasn't just his physical bulk but the constant barrage of bad-taste jokes or ribbing. Kirby found himself yearning to have the piss ripped out of him for eating something as innocuous as, say, a fruit salad. He smiled at the memory of the chia pot incident. 'Fuck that shit' had been Anderson's assessment of the vegan concoction of chia seeds and coconut yoghurt, which Kirby had bought by accident. It had been surprisingly good, but he'd kept his mouth shut knowing Anderson would have ribbed him mercilessly for months had he said anything. Now he positively longed to be on the receiving end of his partner's teasing.

'You mentioned Stark's finances just now,' said Masters, who suddenly appeared by his desk. 'The boss was right; Stark wasn't badly off. Private pension by the looks of things. And I did find another account. Want to take a look?'

Kirby followed her over to her computer where she brought up Stark's statements. 'These are his bank statements, which you already know about. It's all pretty standard stuff,' said Masters as they scanned the transactions. 'Mobile bill, broadband, council tax, Marks & Spencer, his Oyster card top-up, Pret. He had subscriptions to *Architects' Journal* and *Wallpaper** magazine. The only interesting thing about this is what's not here.'

'His council rent. Or did he buy his flat?'

'Nope. He didn't own it, I checked. But neither did he pay any rent that I can see – not out of this account or' – she paused, bringing up another account on screen – 'from this.' It was a Nationwide account that had getting on for a hundred grand in it. 'He also had various investments, ISAs and so on. He wasn't a millionaire, but he was certainly comfortable. No suspicious withdrawals – or deposits.'

'Any sign of a will?'

Masters shook her head. 'It's probably with his solicitors, whoever they are.'

Kirby made a mental note to ask Alma. 'Did Mark get anywhere with Stark's friend yesterday? Where is he?' Kirby looked around the office but Drayton was nowhere to be seen.

'No idea. He wouldn't tell me in any case. I don't think he likes me.'

'Ignore him, Romy,' said Kirby, who'd noticed Drayton's nose had been out of joint recently. 'He's been a grumpy sod for the past two months.' Kirby's phone began ringing and he recognised the area code for Kent. 'I need to take this.'

'It's Ted Harper, you left me a message,' said a voice when Kirby picked up.

'Thanks for calling back so promptly. I wanted to pick your brains about the Jason Roye and Kevin Shires case.'

'I've been expecting a call as I saw the *Mail* story. I'm actually going to be in London tomorrow – I could meet you then,' said Harper.

Kirby arranged to meet the retired detective at a small pub in Belgravia. It was a well-known police hang-out and had frequent lock-ins but during the day was quiet. Hanging up, Kirby's eyes fell on his computer screen. His inbox was full of unanswered emails and he reluctantly began to sift through them. Computer updates. Delete. Health and Safety training. Delete. He skimmed over the daily intelligence briefing, the local borough news and Wandsworth's most wanted. Then he came to an email with the subject 'Fitness Test'. He was due one at the end of the month and he'd pass, that wasn't a problem. However, before taking the fitness test he had to sign a health assessment form. He clicked on the attached form and began filling it in. The last question was 'Do you have any known medical conditions?' A lot of officers lied. Kirby had never had cause to – and he didn't know whether he had cause now. Raising the spectre of the FFI with the medical officer would open a whole can of worms – he might be forced into taking the gene test, maybe even into early retirement if it came back positive. He clicked 'no' and then 'send'. There was no point making life more complicated. It was complicated enough as it was.

CHAPTER 35

After the events of the previous night, Reid had retreated up to the roof and his birds. He'd needed some sanctuary, somewhere away from the horrors going on in Sally's garage. He'd sat in darkness next to the pigeon coop, watching the illuminated scene below, the gentle noise of the birds soothing. He'd eventually gone down to bed at around 4 a.m. but had been unable to sleep. He'd made a flask of tea and taken it back up, where he'd let the birds out at dawn. It was his favourite time of day on the roof – that and sunset – and he finally felt himself becoming drowsy.

When the pigeons returned, he fed and watered them and made his way back to the flat. If he was lucky he might get a few hours' sleep. He hoped the demolition wouldn't disturb him too much, and when he got home he went straight to the bedroom where he lay staring at the ceiling. Every single crack on it was familiar. Like the ceiling of his cell in the penitentiary. How many times had he traced those lines looking for the truth? Trying to make sense out of what had happened? The final day of the stand-off at Waco still haunted him. He could recall the smell of fear as people took shelter, mingled with tear gas and burning, smells that would stay with him forever. The way the tanks had crashed through the walls, destroying everything in their path, was still as vivid today as it had been then. The panic to get the children to safety. Some of the children had left, but there were still a good number in the compound when the FBI had come in on that fateful morning in April 1993. And his mother, begging, pleading with him as she lay trapped beneath a collapsed wall. He closed his eyes and swallowed hard, not wanting to relive that moment as he had done so many times. Sleep was now as unlikely as an apology from the FBI.

He got up and went through to the kitchen where he switched on the radio; anything to block out the thoughts crowding his mind. Despite his tiredness he needed to focus. If the body in the garage was Jason's and the fire had been deliberately set then the police would be asking two questions: was Jason the target and who would want to kill him? Reid began making beans on toast as he mulled over these two questions. He tipped the beans into a small pan and set the heat low. The only reason he could think of to burn out Sally Shires' garage was because it contained something that someone didn't want found. It would be difficult not to notice a person was in there, which led to an uncomfortable conclusion. He carefully sliced a round of bread and stuck it in the toaster. He stirred the beans as they began to bubble around the edges and shook in a few drops of Tabasco.

While he ate, he thought over everything he and Jason had looked at in the garage, and kept coming back to the card. It had to be important. Had it still been in Jason's pocket when the fire started? Where else would it be?

Suddenly, Reid remembered something completely out of the blue. Jason's reappearance with the news that Kev hadn't left with him that day and that something must have happened to prevent him – plus going through Kev's belongings – had begun to trigger memories. This particular one being so vivid Reid put down his knife and fork for a second. It hadn't meant anything at the time because he'd been so preoccupied with leaving for America. Those last few weeks of the summer of 1992 before he and his mother had left to live at Mount Carmel had been a blur. Even the night before they left – the night Kevin and Jason were running away – seemed like a dream. Except now one thing stood out.

He and his mother had had several visitors that night. People coming to say goodbye, to wish them well – ironic, looking back on it, given what had happened – but Reid remembered one visitor in particular: Will Stark. Stark had always been kind to Reid and his mother, and after Stark had talked to Frances for a few minutes in the sitting room, he'd slipped into Reid's room to say goodbye. But that wasn't the only reason he'd come to see Reid. He'd asked about Reid's keys to the garden on The Drive. Reid should have dropped them through the letterbox when he was there the day before, but he'd forgotten. It had been Stark who'd got him the job tending the actress's garden – she was Alma's godmother – and so Stark had offered to return them for him. Reid vividly remembered Stark holding out his hand for the keys, and that's when he'd seen the blood on his cuff. Perhaps, had he not been so preoccupied with packing and his impending trip, he might have asked him about it.

But he hadn't, and the next morning Reid was in a taxi to Heathrow, the incident forgotten. The knowledge that his two friends, Jason and Kev, were off on their own adventure had given him hope and excitement for the future. Jason and Kev hadn't had anything to run to in America – nor the funds – so they'd improvised with stolen money and overnight train tickets to Glasgow.

For once, life had felt as though it held promise. Except that it hadn't. Certainly not for Reid and his mother, who found themselves embroiled in what became a dark event in America's history. Nor, as it turned out, for Kevin. Reid felt a tear run down his cheek and realised he was crying.

CHAPTER 36

It didn't take Connie long to find out the competition won by William Stark for the Grasmere Estate had gone virtually unrecorded. The local archive at Battersea Library held nothing, and after a frustrating half hour on the phone of being passed from one department to another she learned there was no trace of it in the council records held at an off-site storage facility either. Next, she tried the *Architects' Journal* website and was rewarded with a hit. The excitement was short-lived. The estate was only given a brief mention and the other entrants in the competition weren't even named. Such was the lack of information she began to wonder whether this mythical competition had ever actually taken place. She sat back in her chair, frustrated. After a few minutes she picked up the phone.

'Connie, Jean and I were just talking about you,' said Art.

Although she'd been determined to wait for Art to call her about the future of the archive, she'd remembered he'd known Stark and mentioned something about a party Stark had held at the estate. If she couldn't get the information she wanted online then she had little choice but to ask her boss. 'My ears must have been burning. I'm not act—'

'Look,' said Art, talking over her. 'We've had a discussion about your position at the archive and your ultimatum.'

Connie hadn't really thought of it in those terms, but supposed she had given him an ultimatum of sorts and suddenly felt nervous. 'Oh. And?'

'We completely understand your concerns. If we do have to close the archive but you somehow manage to raise funds to keep it in place then of course you want to know your future is secure. Bearing that in mind, we would like to offer you a place on the board, along with Jean and myself, and the curatorship. What do you think?'

For a moment Connie was speechless. All she'd expected was some kind of legal assurance that Ethan Blunt couldn't sell off the family archive when he inherited it. Based on what she knew about him, she wouldn't trust him as far as she could throw him. But the curatorship?

'Well?' said Art. 'Actually, no, don't say anything. Think about it and come back to me. It's a lot to take on board.'

'Yes,' she blurted out. 'I mean, that's wonderful, Art. I don't know what to say.'

'Of course,' said Art. 'This is all dependent on us being able to raise the funds – if and when I have to bail out Ethan.'

'Is there any news on that?'

'It's looking likely, I'm afraid. I should know in the next day or so. Ethan has a prospective investor interested but I'm not holding my breath.'

'Really,' said Connie, doing her best to keep the sarcasm from her voice. 'Well, let's hope this new investor comes through.'

'Ethan's trying his best and we have every faith in him. But I hope I've put your mind at rest, at least a little bit – I presume that's why you were calling?'

'Actually, it was about something else. William Stark – you said you knew him?'

'Oh, I see,' said Art, sounding a little affronted she hadn't been calling about the job. 'Yes, I did know Will. We lost touch and I hadn't seen him for, oh, five, ten years.'

'I'm trying to find out about the competition for the Grasmere site. Stark won and I can't seem to find much about it.'

Art was silent for a few moments. 'Damned if I can remember much either. I do recall it being thought of as a bit of a poisoned chalice. The whole thing had to be designed around Pinder Wood. Bloody awkward.'

'Pinder Wood?'

'The wooded area at the centre of the estate is called Pinder Wood. Not that it's been called that for many years. The competition was pretty low-key and I doubt anyone apart from the council knew about it.'

'How did people enter then? It must have been advertised somewhere.'

'I have no idea. I do remember one thing though: people were very surprised William won. I mean, he was a friend and all that, and I don't like to speak ill of the dead, but rumour had it his wasn't the best design by a mile.'

'Who were the other entrants?'

'I really can't remember. Most were young architects starting out – they saw Grasmere as a career opportunity.'

'You mentioned going to a party on the estate. When was that?'

'It must have been the year it was completed, or the year after. William entertained quite a few people in those days. He was keen to show off his work. And to prove the estate was a great place to live.'

'Who went to these parties?'

'Residents – he canvassed them to find out what they thought of it – architects, local council people. Why, what's this about?'

'Oh, nothing really.' She didn't want Art to know she was helping the police. And she was sure Kirby wouldn't want him to know, either. 'Don't you think it would be interesting to see the other entries? It would put our drawings in context.'

'Possibly, but I doubt that will ever happen. They were probably destroyed years ago. A good acquisition if you can find them.' Art paused. 'There is one person who might be able to help you. He wrote an article for the *RIBA Journal* about architectural competitions and I'm sure he refers to the Grasmere Estate there. Not favourably, if I recall.'

'Who?' asked Connie, wondering why she hadn't checked the *RIBA Journal's* online archive herself.

'Dan Quatremaine.'

Connie's heart sank. Hopefully she could find the article online and it would tell her what she needed to know without the need to speak to Quatremaine in person.

'Did you ask Bonaro about fundraising, by the way?' asked Art.

Connie thought it prudent not to tell him what Bonaro's reaction to that request had been, so she said, 'He'll think about it.' They chatted for a few more minutes and then Connie went online and searched for Quatremaine's article. After a bit of digging, she located it and skimmed the piece for any mention of the estate. About three-quarters of the way through she found it:

The hideous and generally denigrated Grasmere Estate was designed by William Stark, winner of a competition held by the local council in partnership with the Pinder Estate. Twenty-six practices expressed interest in designing housing for the awkward triangular site which incorporates Pinder Wood at its centre and six were chosen to submit plans. Of those six it's hard to see why William Stark's design won. Although initially celebrated, the estate soon fell into disrepair and became what is known as a 'sink' estate.

She glanced over the rest of the piece but that was the only mention of the housing development. Her first question was, who were the Pinder Estate? Presumably they owned Pinder Wood – and what about Pinder Hill? A quick google revealed very little about them apart from one interesting fact: Pinder Estate's registered address at Companies House was 46 The Drive. It couldn't be coincidence, surely? And what about the derelict land on which the tin church stood? Did they own that too? She went back to Quatremaine's article and scrolled down to the part about Stark and began to reread it, stopping halfway.

Of those six it's hard to see why William Stark's design won.

Quatremaine must have seen the other entries to make a statement like that and Connie suddenly remembered his comment about Stark only getting the Grasmere job because— and then the doorbell had interrupted them. After several attempts to find the information online – or, indeed anywhere else – Connie came to a reluctant conclusion. If she wanted to find out more she was going to have to speak with Quatremaine herself.

CHAPTER 37

Quatremaine being Quatremaine meant that he would only talk to Connie in person. He disliked phones, and in any case, he'd heard a rumour about the archive being in trouble and that perhaps it would be useful to 'bat a few ideas about'. How he'd found out about the fundraising, Connie didn't know, although she suspected Bonaro was probably behind it. She'd agreed to meet him for coffee in a café of his choosing. Connie arrived early and saw it was an expensive, old-school French-style patisserie. Of course it was. She was paying so he was hardly going to choose a greasy spoon. Connie ordered an overpriced café au lait and sat at a corner table with a view of the door. Quatremaine arrived bang on time and greeted Connie with an effusiveness that she'd not encountered from him before. Perhaps he smelt blood and was on a charm offensive to extract as much information as possible. After ordering a coffee and a pain au chocolat, he sat down.

'I hear Richard's not coming back,' he said, before his backside had settled on the seat.

'Really? And where did you hear that?' She bristled.

'From the horse's mouth. Shame, he was such an asset to RADE. Art must be desperate to fill his shoes.' He raised his eyebrows before taking a sip of coffee.

'I suppose so.' What had Bonaro been thinking of, confiding in a man like Dan Quatremaine? Connie certainly wasn't going to tell him about her arrangement with Art or the financial trouble they were in. Unless, of course, Bonaro had told him that too.

'Richard and I studied at the Courtauld Institute together,' Quatremaine went on, providing her with the answer. 'We had quite a boys' club.'

Connie wasn't quite sure what he was trying to say, and she wasn't sure she wanted to know. Had Bonaro and Quatremaine been in a relationship? Or was it like some Eton boys' club, all pigs' heads and rugby? Either scenario was enough to make her push her coffee cup away and change the subject. 'I'm sure you had a great time,' she said. 'But I wanted to talk to you about Will Stark and the competition he won for the Grasmere contract.'

'You've read my article, so you know I'm not a fan of the estate. Declan Jones had the right idea.'

'You can't be serious?' said Connie, aghast. Declan Jones was a character in a low-budget film that had been shot on the estate about a vigilante who went on a killing spree to avenge his daughter's death after taking bad drugs. It made *Death Wish* look like Beatrix Potter.

'It's what happens when architecture fails the state. Declan Jones did what was necessary. Had Stark been a character in that film he'd have died too.' Quatremaine sipped his coffee and smiled.

'Are you suggesting Stark was responsible for everything that's happened on the estate?' It was impossible to tell whether Quatremaine was winding her up or not.

'Who else? I agree that the council's actions, or lack of, have accelerated matters, but in the end, the buildings failed. It's also an aesthetic abomination.'

'But you knew William Stark,' said Connie, trying to keep the conversation on track. 'You said you liked him.'

'I did. That doesn't mean I approved of all his work. I'm quite capable of getting on with someone even if their views oppose mine. That's something people these days seem to have forgotten how to do. No one listens any more; people exist in bubbles.'

'On that we can agree,' said Connie. 'In your article you mention that of the six entries it was hard to see how Stark's won. Did you see the other designs?'

'Of course. Otherwise I would never have made the comment. It's called research, Connie.'

If he was winding her up on purpose he was doing a very good job. 'Do you know what happened to them?' she asked, wondering just how much he'd enjoy a conversation with someone of her age outside his bubble.

'Why are you so interested?' Quatremaine drained his coffee without taking his eyes off her.

'Professional curiosity. They'd also be a good acquisition for the archive.'

'Playing curator, I see.'

'You do know we have the Grasmere drawings in the collection, don't you?'

'Really? No, I didn't. But then again, why would I? It's hardly my area of expertise. Now the Victorians knew a thing or two about architecture.'

'The Victorians built what became slums, Dan.'

'Yes, but they did it with such style. Anyhow, going back to the competition. I didn't see the actual drawings – I'm not sure they survived – but I did see photographs of the main plans and elevations.'

'Where?' asked Connie.

'A man called Zeke Wardell. He was a local historian – dead now – and worked at the Town Hall at the time of the competition. They displayed the six entries for a few days and he took photographs. I went to visit him to look at some old photos he had of Battersea Park when it was first built. The Grasmere pictures just happened to be in the same folder.'

'What happened to Zeke's collection when he died?'

'Split up by his kids. Some of it was sold, most of it went in the bin and I'd wager those photographs did.'

'Can you remember who the other entrants were for the competition?'

'I wrote them down before I came out.' Quatremaine smiled and produced a slip of paper from his jacket. He held it between his index and middle fingers. 'What's it worth?'

'Worth?' asked Connie, slightly taken aback. 'What do you mean?'

'I'm helping you out, but will you help me?' He waggled the slip of paper.

How she could be of use to Dan Quatremaine, Connie couldn't imagine. 'Help you with what?'

'The position of curator at RADE.' He smiled again. 'I've had my eye on it for a while – Richard knew I was green with envy when he landed the role. Not that it spoiled our friendship you understand, we have an amicable rivalry.'

'What makes you think I can help? I'm just the assistant,' said Connie, who'd once overheard Quatremaine call her just that to Bonaro.

'Well, you are. Or were. But Art must rate you a great deal – he's left you in charge while Richard's been on sabbatical which says a lot about you. You must have his ear, surely? I've written to Art expressing my interest but perhaps a little word from you might help? It would also be useful to get the inside track. That you hold the Grasmere plans is very useful to know. I'm well aware of my weak spots when it comes to the overall collection.'

'Well . . .' Connie eyed the list of names in his hand, at the same time thinking that if Dan Quatremaine became curator of RADE she'd have no choice but to leave. 'I suppose I could speak to Art. Put in a good word or two.' *Followed by ten bad ones.* She was definitely going to hell for this.

'Be subtle about it, obviously. Perhaps you could suggest I'd be a most suitable successor to Richard in your opinion. And maybe not mention this conversation.' He held out the slip of paper.

'Naturally,' said Connie, snatching the names before Quatremaine changed his mind.

'Excellent. You won't regret this, Connie. I think we'd work well together, despite our differing views on municipal housing and films – no, I shall rephrase that, *because* of our differing views.'

The waitress came over to see if they wanted anything else and Connie asked for the bill.

'Thank you, Connie, a most productive meeting. We both got what we wanted.' Quatremaine stood up to leave.

'There is something else, Dan. When we spoke at the archive the other day, you began saying Will Stark only won the competition because – and then we were interrupted. Because of what?'

'Oh, that.' He sat down again, a conspiratorial look on his face. 'It's just gossip really. But because of Pinder Wood.'

For a moment Connie was confused before she remembered Art using the same name. 'The trees at the centre of the estate.'

'Correct. I'm impressed,' said Quatremaine, surprised. 'No one calls it that any more. Anyhow, there were rumours he won the contract because of some legal loophole connected to the wood only he was able to surmount. I asked him about it once but he brushed it off. Said it was rubbish and that he won because his design was the best. Take it from me, it wasn't, but there's no accounting for taste.'

'What was the legal loophole with the wood?'

'I believe it was right of way, or something. It didn't interest me enough to try and find out.'

'And that's because it's privately owned by the Pinder Estate?' said Connie.

'Exactly. I have no idea how Will swung it, but he did. Maybe it was good old nepotism – both his grandparents were born in the area.'

'Do you know anything about the Pinder Estate? Who are they?'

'You're asking a lot of questions, young lady,' said Quatremaine, feigning disapproval. He was enjoying every minute of this, Connie could tell. 'The Pinders used to own that whole area at one time. There's only one Pinder left now – at least I think she's still alive. Mad old bat who lives up on The Drive. And on that note, I really must leave you. I think I've given you more than your fair share of information. I expect you to hold your end of the bargain.'

'You can rely on me, Dan.'

Quatremaine looked satisfied and she watched him leave the café and disappear around the corner before looking at the list of names he'd given her. Only one was familiar – a large corporate practice in the city. She folded the list and slipped it into her wallet, wondering just how difficult Quatremaine could make her life if she reneged. Probably very, but it might be a price worth paying.

CHAPTER 38

David Koresh had come to Reid in a dream that morning. The man who had simultaneously destroyed and given meaning to his life all those years ago in Waco. Reid had eventually fallen asleep at the kitchen table, his head resting on his arms, until a loud crash from outside had woken him with a start. In the dream he'd been by the sea – he didn't know where, it wasn't a place he recognised – and David had emerged out of the water and walked towards him. His feet had barely been wet. He glided through the waves with ease, reaching the shore with his arms open. 'My friend,' he'd said to Reid. 'I've come to tell you it's almost time. The End of Days is fast approaching. Sally will be with Kevin very soon. You will see your mother.'

'What about Kevin's killer? Jason's?' Reid had asked. 'What about the sinners?'

David had moved closer to him then, reciting Matthew's Gospel 13, the words as familiar as his own name. '"The Son of Man will send out his angels, and they will weed out of his kingdom everything that causes sin and all who do evil. They will throw them into the blazing furnace, where there will be weeping and gnashing of teeth." Weed out the sinners, Vernon, and seek the truth in the name of God.' Koresh had then turned and walked back into the sea until his head disappeared under the waves. Reid had woken with a start. Unlike a lot of dreams that were vivid only for a few minutes after waking before fading quickly, this one stayed with him, its message clear: find Kevin and Jason's killer.

The demolition site was quiet and Reid savoured the fresh morning air as he walked through the wood. He didn't want to see the burnt-out garage where Jason's body had been found because it hadn't only been Koresh who'd visited Reid in his dreams. The charred bodies of his mother, their friends and children from the compound had also come. He thought how strange it was that the body could be transformed into something so grotesque and inhuman so quickly. How fire devoured life and anything in its way with an ease he found unfathomable. He'd been walking, lost in thought, when he suddenly found himself near what was left of Jason's camp. Police tape hung limply from the surrounding trees and fluttered in the breeze. The police had taken away the tarpaulin and the litter, and it pained him to think that Jason's life had now been reduced to forensic evidence and a charred corpse. Why did everyone he cared about end up burning?

A twig snapped nearby and he turned to see Tobias Hoffmann walking along the path with his head down. He, too, appeared deep in thought and hadn't yet noticed Reid. The events of the past week had weighed heavily on everyone, although some more than others and possibly for different reasons. Hoffmann and Stark had been close once – before Reid left for Texas – but when Reid had returned to the estate in 2008 something had changed. They had still been friendly and yet there was a distinct shift that Reid couldn't put his finger on. He'd tried asking Stark about it but had been met with a puzzled look. *Nothing's changed, Vern, it's you who's changed.* Reid had left it there. Perhaps he was imagining it because Stark had been right: he had changed. You didn't live through something like Waco and fourteen years in prison and not be changed. When Hoffmann did finally see him, he looked bewildered for a few seconds. He then seemed to come to, as though he'd drifted back from some distant world.

'Vernon, I didn't expect to see you here.'

Reid shrugged. He didn't have a response.

'I heard it was Jason Roye's body in the garage,' said Hoffmann. Reid could tell he was trying to be casual, but something was bothering him. 'A terrible thing. We prayed for him last night, Mary and I.' Hoffmann paused for a moment, rubbing his bald head. 'I saw him, Jason.' His eyes drifted to the remains of the camp then back to Reid. 'He said he was looking for Kevin. What did he mean – did you speak to him?'

Reid nodded slowly, remembering his conversation with Jason in the Shires' garage. An image of Hoffmann's arse as he fucked Michaela Falke flashed through his mind. 'He meant exactly what he said. He was looking for Kev.'

Hoffmann frowned. 'You mean Jason had nothing to do with his disappearance?'

'I never believed that,' said Reid.

Hoffmann considered this for a moment. 'What was he doing in the Shires' garage?'

'Going though Kev's things in case the police missed something.'

'And had they? The police were very thorough when it happened. I'm sure they'd've found something if it was there.'

'That depends on what they were looking for,' said Reid. 'Jason thought Kevin never left. That he's still here.'

Hoffmann blanched at the suggestion. 'What? Surely he didn't think . . .' He swallowed. 'He's literally *here*?'

Reid nodded. 'Why, do you think that's crazy?'

'Well, yes, obviously. Don't you?'

'Not really, no.' Hoffmann was now looking very uncomfortable and Reid couldn't resist stirring the pot. 'Jason said he'd seen you. In fact, he asked me whether you were still seeing Michaela Falke.'

'I beg your pardon?'

'You and Michaela. We saw you. Jason remembered.'

Hoffmann's face had now turned completely white. 'You and Jason . . .' He trailed off. 'Where? When?'

'At the back of the church. You'd forgotten to lock the door. You were lucky it was us and not Elliott.' He paused. 'It was back in the nineties, Kev was with us too.'

'Oh, I thought you meant . . . I mean, that was a long time ago.' Hoffmann laughed nervously.

Hoffmann had done his best to cover up his blunder but it was too late and Reid smiled to himself. *You thought I meant recently. You're still at it.*

'So it was you who told Will about us then,' said Hoffmann, as if some long-forgotten penny was finally dropping.

Reid shook his head. 'Why would I do that?'

'Someone did,' said Hoffmann. 'Who else would it be? Jason?'

'Not Jason – he didn't even know Will. Didn't you ask him?'

'Of course I did, but he wouldn't say. Must have been Kevin then, the little bastard.'

Reid's hand shot out, stopping an inch from Hoffmann's face.

'I didn't mean that, I'm sorry.' Hoffmann held up his hands apologetically. 'Vern, you won't tell anyone about this, will you? Our conversation? Only I hope to take over from Elliott when he retires at the church in Earlsfield. If it came out . . .'

'I've not said a word all this time – why would I do so now? In any case, it's not me who you have to worry about.'

'Why?' Hoffmann looked alarmed. 'Who else knows?'

'God, Tobias. *One who conceals his wrongdoings will not prosper, but one who confesses and abandons them will find compassion.*' Reid wondered how devout Hoffmann actually was. Or perhaps he was just stupid. 'It's God you need to make your peace with. And if I were you I'd hurry up because soon all this will be gone – the woods, the estate and your new church. Everything. I know you don't believe like me, that you think I was the victim of a cult, that I was brainwashed.' Reid took a step closer. 'I'm no more brain-washed than you are. Whatever your sins, Tobias, make good now. When the time comes you'll think back to this conversation and thank me.'

'I'm not even going to try to argue with you, Vern, but you're wrong. This is a new beginning for me, for the church, for God's work. The estate and everything that's happened here will soon be in the past.'

'I wouldn't be so sure,' said Reid.

'What do you mean by that?' Hoffmann tried to move back but found himself blocked by a tree.

'The night Jason and Kevin disappeared, Will came to see us. My mother and I. Did you know that?'

'Um, no, I don't think I did,' he said hesitantly. 'What's that got to do with anything?'

'He came to say goodbye. He seemed upset.'

'Oh, well, Will was very fond of your mother. He was good to you too. He saw you as one of the good things on the estate.'

'It's funny though, because we saw him earlier that day. We said our goodbyes then.'

'I . . . I don't know what to say. Maybe he realised how much he was going to miss you.'

'We weren't that close, Tobias. No, he had another reason for coming. He took my keys to Miss Fontaine's house, up on The Drive. Or, to be precise, the keys to her land.'

Hoffmann swallowed. 'He did? Well, he was probably doing a good deed – she was Alma's godmother, after all. Her keys would have been no good to her on the other side of the world, would they?'

'He had blood on his sleeve, Tobias.' Reid was now standing so close to Hoffmann he could smell the fear coming off him. 'Do you know how it got there?'

'Me? Why would I know?' Hoffmann had backed himself against the tree and had nowhere to go.

'Because I saw him get into your car after he left.' Reid stood for a moment before turning and walking away. He heard Hoffmann's coat catch on the bark as he slid to the ground.

CHAPTER 39

The Drive was quiet apart from the odd courier van making deliveries. There were fewer than ten houses on the whole road and it had the surreal quality of a film set. The house numbering appeared totally random and when Connie stopped outside number 46 and gazed up she half-expected to see a ghostly apparition of a child appear in one of the upper windows, the area was so other-worldly. A postman rounded the corner from Traps Lane, and she lingered by the gate.

'I can take those,' she said, nodding at the bundle of post in his hand.

'Actually, it's just junk,' he said, holding out a fistful of glossy catalogues and leaflets. 'Waste of paper if you ask me.'

'Couldn't agree more,' she said, taking the leaflets from him and opening the gate.

'Visiting, are you?'

'Well . . . yes. Long-lost relation of the family. I'm not even sure if they're still here.'

'Reclusive is the word I'd use. I've been delivering mail here for two years and never seen a soul,' said the postman. 'An actress, I gather.'

'That's right. Brilliant stage career,' said Connie, bluffing madly.

'I saw one of her early films once, *The Thief and His Mistress*. She played the mistress. Smouldering. And what a figure. What she looks like now though . . .' He trailed off. 'Sorry, I didn't mean . . . the accident . . . you know.' He made a circular gesture round his eye. 'I must get on,' he said. 'These won't post themselves.' He patted his bag and left.

Connie looked at the sheaf of junk mail in her hand – leaflets mainly, but there was a catalogue from a gardening company that was addressed to Miss Irene Fontaine and what looked like a letter from Thames Water addressed to Miss Irene Pinder. The fact post was still being addressed here didn't mean very much; the property could still be empty and the post collected by a third party. Conversely, the house could still be occupied, so she walked purposefully up the drive and rang the doorbell. She heard it echo in the hall and when she got no reply, she pushed the junk mail through the letterbox and peered in. The hall had a parquet floor and the leaflets had slid along the polished wood and lay marooned. There was no sign of any other mail there, so it had been collected recently. She listened for any sounds within the house, but it was as silent as the grave. If there was anyone at home they clearly weren't going to answer the door so she retreated back down the drive, making sure to close the front gate, and walked around the corner to Traps Lane.

The electricity substation was still humming and the gap she'd squeezed through on Tuesday night looked a lot smaller in daylight than it had at dusk. No wonder she'd torn her coat. She'd worn the same one again today – no point in ruining another. The traffic was light and she slipped through the gap without worrying about being seen by a passing driver, pulling her small rucksack in after her. Today she'd come prepared – or as prepared as she could be – with a torch, a personal alarm and a water spray laced with chilli. She'd never used the water spray but given Mace wasn't an option this would do. It was a prop she hoped never to have recourse to use.

Her plan today was twofold: to get into the tin church and to scope out the rear of the house. Before heading into the depths of the overgrown plot, Connie stopped for a quick Google search for 'actress Irene Pinder' and 'actress Irene Fontaine' and was surprised when she got several hits. Fontaine was her stage name and she'd had a prolific theatrical career before moving into film. Her career had been cut short when she lost an eye in a road accident in 2002; presumably what the postman was alluding to with his terrible mime. None of the sites Connie looked at gave mention of her current whereabouts other than to say she was still alive. It had to be the mad old bat Quatremaine had referred to, the last member of the Pinder family. Interestingly, her father had been a man of the cloth and when Connie googled him, it turned out he'd run his own church called the Healing Waters Chapel. Hadn't the tin church been built near a natural spring said to have healing properties? Connie switched her phone to silent, wondering whether the Reverend Pinder was the same minister that Joe with the Staffie had mentioned on her previous visit.

In daylight she was able to follow the path she'd taken previously and reached the tin church within a couple of minutes. Without the eerie pink light of sunset the small building looked a lot less creepy than it had done. As she approached the door she scanned her surroundings for any sign someone had been there. She spotted a trampled path she hadn't noticed in the fading light on Tuesday and followed it around the church in the opposite direction to the one she'd taken – there was a definite trail leading towards the house. Someone had been there recently by the looks of things. Was whoever pushed past her on Tuesday night connected to number 46? Or had they hidden here and waited for her to leave?

Making her way back to the church door, she found it unlocked and gently pushed it open.

'Hello?' she called. Complete and utter silence greeted her, so she stepped inside. The interior was simple. Three small Gothic arched windows ran down both sides of the church, the glass dirty and partly obscured by the foliage clambering over the exterior. The walls were made up of wooden panels, as was usual with tin churches, and the roof was a series of wooden trusses. The impression was of a picturesque village hall that had been sealed in a time capsule from the 1930s. What looked like an old camping chair stood in the middle of the floor and to the rear there was a raised area, with a primitive wooden altar. Behind that at the far end – all of a few feet away – was another Gothic arched window that had a simple stained-glass design of a cross within an inverted triangle – like the one carved on the door. As a functioning church it would probably have held fifty people at most, more suited to a rural community than south London.

Scattered around the small room were various bits of garden machinery and tools including a vintage lawnmower – one of the old manual types with a large cast-iron roller. A man's coat was draped over the handle. Other tools from a similar era lay scattered about – hoes, rakes and digging forks.

As she moved around the small interior she spotted a carrier bag full of what looked like magazines. Her first thought was she'd stumbled on a stash of porn, but on taking one out she saw they were old editions of some kind of fanzine. It was called *High Rize* and by today's standards looked amateurish. It was dated November 1992 and featured, among other things, a comic strip set on a housing estate that bore a remarkable resemblance to Grasmere. She flicked through it and noticed someone had scribbled in the margins. She didn't know much about fanzines – they'd all but gone by the time she was a teenager and everyone had access to the internet

– but it was a strange thing to find in an old church being used as a garden shed on a derelict piece of land. Like the vintage gardening equipment, some fanzines were now collectible and it struck her that the contents of the small church were possibly quite valuable.

After poking about a bit more and taking a few pictures she left the church and followed the second path back towards the house. It brought her to a small gate set in the wooden pillar-and-post fence. Although she was obviously trespassing right now, entering someone's garden was a different matter. But her curiosity was piqued and finding a small hole where a knot of wood had fallen out of the fence she put her eye to it. Beyond lay what could only be described as a jungle. It was overrun and wild-looking and yet simultaneously had the appearance of being well maintained.

It was also irresistible and – as with the church door on Tuesday night – Connie felt her hand on the latch of the gate as if operating of its own free will. She pressed the metal latch and felt the gate swing open as if some magical force were willing her to step through. Before she had time to even think what a bad idea it was, a figure had stepped out from behind the gate. For a moment, all Connie could focus on was the burning red Cyclops eye staring at her before she heard a voice – full and rich, almost Shakespearian – 'Halt!' And then came the cane, black and sleek, crashing down on her shoulder.

CHAPTER 40

'This hides a blade,' said the woman, brandishing the cane that had just smashed down on Connie's shoulder. 'Don't think I won't use it if I feel threatened.'

Connie was in no doubt the woman meant business and backed away with her hands held up in a gesture of surrender. 'I'm sorry, I wasn't sure anyone still lived here.'

'Well, they bloody well do. I live here. This is my house.'

'Are you Irene Pinder?'

'Pinder? I haven't been called that for years. But yes, I suppose I am. More's the point, who are you and what do you want?' She jabbed the cane in Connie's direction.

Irene Pinder – or Irene Fontaine – had to be eighty if a day. An eyepatch covered one eye and was adorned with iridescent red sequins that caught the light, lending her a devilish air, while her other, good eye twinkled with mischievousness. Quatremaine's description of a mad old bat was so far accurate. Connie rubbed her shoulder – she'd have a lovely bruise there in the morning. 'My name's Connie Darke,' she began, deciding honesty was the best policy. 'I work for an archive called RADE. I was researching the tin chapel that used to be where the Grasmere Estate now is and found an invoice for the removal of an iron structure to Traps Lane, so I came to take a look.'

'I see,' said the woman, whose good eye was roving over Connie as she spoke. 'Well, now you've found it. Was there something else? Only you're in my garden.'

'Actually, yes,' said Connie. There was clearly no point in beating around the bush with Irene. 'The wood at the centre of the Grasmere Estate, I gather you own it.'

'Why do you want to know?'

'A competition was held for the estate and I heard the winner was granted access to your land.'

The woman's eye narrowed. 'Who told you that?'

'A colleague,' said Connie, although Quatremaine was hardly a colleague. Rival, more like. 'I was researching the competition for a friend. The architect who built the estate died recently.'

'Indeed,' said the old woman. 'What's that got to do with you?'

'It was me who found the body.'

The woman peered at Connie with her one good eye as though seeing her properly for the first time. 'How unpleasant for you. He was in the church, I gather.'

Connie nodded. 'There was a storm and I was sheltering under the church porch and noticed the door ajar so I went in and . . .' Connie shivered. 'There he was.'

The old woman nodded as though it all made perfect sense. 'Poor William,' she sighed, producing a key from her pocket. 'I did know him, yes. You'd better come in and tell me exactly what happened.' She locked the gate and then gestured for Connie to follow her up through the garden towards the back of the house. Connie didn't have much choice.

Ten minutes later and Connie was perched on a velvet chaise overlooking the garden, while Irene rattled bottles on the top of a drinks cabinet. After a few moments she handed Connie a glass of brown liquid. 'Drink that,' she said. 'I don't know about you, but I certainly need one.' She picked up her own glass and sat down opposite Connie before taking a sip. Connie put the glass to her mouth with a vague feeling of being in a fairy tale as she touched the brown liquid to her lips. Was it poisoned? She had no idea exactly how batty Irene Pinder was. Or whether they were alone in the house. The garden gate was locked and the fence was high – escaping over that would be a last resort.

'Do you like it?' asked Irene.

Connie ran her tongue over her lips and tasted something medicinal, herbal in origin. It was what she'd call an acquired taste if she was being generous. 'What is it?'

'Fernet-Branca. It won't kill you.' Irene smiled. 'If I'd wanted to do that I'd have done it in the garden.'

'That's reassuring.' Connie put the drink down. 'Look, I really am sorry about trespassing. I did try to find out who owns the Traps Lane plot from the Land Registry but nothing was listed online. Nor for this house, as I thought the two might be connected.'

'No, they wouldn't be. That plot of land and this house have been in my family for over a century.'

'What about the land at the centre of the estate – is that really yours? From what little I've been able to piece together, William Stark's design wasn't the best and yet it won the contest to build the estate. There are rumours he only won because he managed to navigate some legal loophole regarding access to that land. I'm curious to know if that's true.'

'And why is that, may I ask?'

Again, Connie decided to be honest. 'Two reasons. The first is that I love architectural mysteries – land disputes, all that kind of stuff. I'm an urban explorer in my spare time and—'

'An urban what?' interrupted Irene.

'Explorer. I explore derelict and abandoned buildings. It's another reason I wanted to see the church.'

'And you thought my house might be abandoned too.'

'Not exactly . . .' said Connie, floundering. Irene began to smile.

'Your discomfort is quite endearing,' she said. 'You break into my land, enter my garden and then imply my house is in a state of dereliction. That's quite impressive.'

'What's impressive is you haven't thrown me out. Or called the police,' said Connie, hoping she wouldn't give Irene any ideas.

'And what was the second reason you're so interested in the land and the competition? So far you've only given me some half-arsed excuse about it being a hobby.' She sniffed.

'The police think it might be connected to William Stark's murder. Maybe a long-held grudge. It's unlikely, of course, but I said I'd dig up some information for them about the competition. Only there isn't any. Or very little.'

Irene considered what she'd said for a few moments. 'So you're working for the police and decided to come and have a good poke around my property off your own bat.'

That pretty much summed it up and Connie crossed her fingers Irene wasn't going to make a complaint about her. Kirby would hit the roof and she was willing to bet his boss didn't know about her research project either. 'For the record, I did knock at the front door and I did try the Land Registry.' It was a feeble excuse.

'What did you say the name of this place you work for was called, RAVE?' From the side of her armchair Irene produced an iPad.

'RADE,' corrected Connie, although if Ethan Blunt got his hands on the place it probably would end up being a nightclub. 'The Repository of Architectural Drawings and Ephemera. It's totally legit.'

With an arthritic finger Irene tapped at the iPad and then waved the screen towards Connie. 'This place?'

RADE's homepage filled the screen and she nodded. Connie watched as Irene navigated the website for a minute or so before closing it down. 'You're the assistant,' she said.

God, she was as bad as Quatremaine. 'Officially, yes, I am the assistant, but Mr Bonaro has been on sabbatical and he's not coming back. I've been running the place in his absence for nearly a year now.'

'Hmm,' said Irene, who seemed to be reappraising her morning catch as though she'd caught a bigger, more interesting fish than she first thought. 'Will you replace this Mr Bonaro if he's not returning to his post?'

'I . . . I don't know,' said Connie. 'It's complicated.'

'I'd like to come and see this RADE of yours,' said Irene, suddenly.

'Why? I mean . . . you're welcome, but . . .'

'But, what? You want to know about the land and the competition and I want to see this archive of yours.'

'Well, yes, of course then. When?'

'Tomorrow morning? Nine o'clock?'

Connie was about to say they didn't open until ten and thought better of it. 'Perfect.'

'That's settled then.' Irene hauled herself out of her chair, grasping her cane. It was obviously time for Connie to leave and she stood up too. A drawing of Irene on the wall caught her eye. 'That's a very good likeness,' she said.

'My god-daughter drew it. You didn't finish your drink.' Irene's eye rested on Connie's untouched glass.

'Sorry, I . . .' She made a mental note to add it to the list containing Kirby's disgusting mineral water of drinks to avoid.

'Never mind. The next time you're here.'

Connie half-expected Irene to lead her back to the garden and make her leave via the broken fence on Traps Lane – it was probably what she deserved – but instead Irene took her to the kitchen and let her out via a side entrance that opened into a carport where a battered Volvo was parked.

'That's The Drive up there.' She pointed. 'I never use the main entrance. This is far more private.'

Connie stepped outside and thanked the old lady. 'I'll see you tomorrow at nine then.'

'I look forward to it,' said Irene, waving her cane to say goodbye. 'And I'm sorry about bashing you on the shoulder.'

'Is there really a blade in that?'

Irene grabbed the shaft with her free hand and rather clumsily, because she couldn't grasp it very well with her arthritic fingers, pulled out a short, thin blade. 'People underestimate you when you're my age,' she said, returning the blade to its case. 'And it's always a mistake.'

CHAPTER 41

There was something about his conversation with Tobias Hoffmann in the woods that had unsettled Reid. He didn't believe any of Hoffmann's claptrap about new beginnings and that the past was now in the past. On the contrary, Reid could feel the past snapping at his heels. The nearer demolition came the more this feeling had escalated, reinforced by Jason's sudden reappearance. Not only that, two people were dead, including Jason, and although Reid struggled to see a link he couldn't help but feel in his gut that the deaths were connected.

He tried to disentangle what was really going on as he climbed the stairs in Ullswater House on his way to see Alma Stark. Jason had returned to the estate and then a day later Will Stark had been killed. A few days on from that and Jason was dead too. William Cowper had written that God moves in a mysterious way and Reid had been through enough in his life to know this more than most. Waco had burned to the ground, innocent people lost, and yet God had allowed it to happen. The Book of Job said it wasn't ours to question why but human nature being what it was, Reid had asked himself the question many times in the intervening years, especially during his periods of solitary confinement. And he asked the same question again now: why had God allowed Stark and Jason to die?

When he reached Alma's floor Reid paused for a moment. He hadn't seen her since her father died and felt a stab of guilt. Stark had been good to him and despite his growing unease about the night Kevin disappeared, Reid had liked him. But he'd never been close to Alma despite their similar age. That was no excuse, he told himself, and began walking purposefully along the walkway towards her flat where he knocked on the front door and waited. After his conversation with Hoffmann, he also had another reason for visiting Alma. It was connected to Hoffmann's affair with Michaela Falke and the fact that somehow Stark had known about it. Alma had spent a lot of time at the Hoffmanns' after her mother died and Stark had struggled to cope. She'd been close to both Mary and Tobias – had she found out about the affair and told her father? It seemed perfectly possible, but what Reid wanted to know was *how* she'd found out. Had she seen them, like he, Jason and Kevin had? Or had someone told her? And that's what was needling him because an unpleasant thought had crossed his mind. What if that someone had been Kevin?

'Vernon. What are you doing here?' said Alma, on opening the door.

Reid's first thought was how terrible she looked, pale and drawn, her hair hanging wildly around her face. Then again, he hadn't seen her close up for some time. Perhaps she always looked like this.

'I came to offer my condolences,' said Reid. 'I'm sorry, I should have come sooner.'

'It's not like we're close, Vernon, it's fine. But come in now you're here.' Not waiting for a response, Alma retreated inside leaving Reid to follow. He closed the door behind him and followed her through the dimly lit hall. He thought he smelt a faint whiff of cannabis as he entered the kitchen and could feel his skin beginning to prickle, anxiety edging its way forward, being on unfamiliar territory. Except it wasn't completely unfamiliar – the kitchen had the same layout as his. But the light was different – brighter – and made the space appear bigger.

'Would you like a drink?' she asked.

'Water. Thanks.' His throat was dry and he tried swallowing but that only made it worse. He wasn't used to this, being in someone else's home. It made him nervous.

'Here you are,' said Alma, handing him a glass of water.

'I won't stay long. I just wanted to say how sorry I was to hear about Will. I've been praying for him.' The water felt blissfully cool as it slipped down his throat.

'Why don't you sit down?' She indicated a seat at the kitchen table, and sank into one on the opposite side. Reid had no choice but to take the one with its back to the door and he felt his anxiety go up a notch.

'I'm not sure how I feel,' Alma was saying. 'I think I'm still in shock.'

'Have the police told you anything?'

'Mary asked me the same thing earlier. I don't think they have a clue. They wanted to know if my dad had any enemies. You knew him, it's a ludicrous notion.'

'Your father was a good man. He was very generous to me and I'll never forget that. I find it hard to believe he did something so awful it drove someone to take his life.' They lapsed into silence and Reid desperately wanted to leave and yet he somehow needed to steer the conversation around to Hoffmann's affair. He wasn't good at this, poking about people's personal lives, and took another sip of water to try and quell his nerves.

'I heard about the fire,' said Alma. 'Someone told me it was Jason Roye. Is it true?'

Reid nodded. 'It looks that way. He came to see me.'

'So you must know what he was doing in the Shires' garage then.' Alma cocked her head to one side and stared at him.

Reid shifted in his seat uncomfortably. 'Sally kept all Kev's things there – we were going through them together. I think he hoped to find a clue as to what happened to him.'

'And did you?'

'Not really,' said Reid, clearing his throat and taking another sip of water. 'It was good to see him again. Brought back a lot of memories. The three of us hanging out in the woods. Getting up to mischief.'

'There was no shortage of that here. Everyone had a secret.'

'Some of them still do,' said Reid. 'Even Tobias.'

'Toby?' said Alma. 'What do you mean?'

Reid felt so outside of his comfort zone he almost got up and walked out. 'His affair with Michaela.'

Something flashed across Alma's face – recognition – but she said nothing.

'We saw them together in the church, me, Kev and Jason. Idiots had forgotten to lock the door,' said Reid, attempting to make light of it.

Alma laughed for the first time since he'd arrived and Reid relaxed a little. Then she stopped, suddenly serious again. 'We really shouldn't be talking like this. Toby and Mary were really good to me when I was a teenager.'

'You're right. I'm sure Tobias is a different man today and has paid his dues.' He drank the last of his water. *Come on Vernon, the Lord is with you. He'll guide you.* 'So you knew about the affair then? Don't tell me you saw them too.'

'I . . . no. Someone must have told me, I honestly can't remember.' Alma picked up his now empty glass and went to the sink, suddenly keen to end the conversation. 'Thanks for stopping by, Vernon. It was kind of you.' She put the glass in the sink and turned around. 'Whoever did this must have had their reasons. People are so very unpredictable, aren't they? We're all probably capable if pushed. Even you.' Her voice was flat, but something in her eyes told him she was testing him. 'The siege must have been a terrible ordeal. Your poor mother. I can't begin to imagine.'

'No,' said Reid, carefully, forcing down the paranoia that was rising. 'And you don't want to.' He'd never told anyone what had happened in Texas and it was staying that way. 'When's the funeral?'

'The body hasn't been released yet, so I can't make any arrangements.'

'Will you ask Tobias to officiate?'

'I haven't really thought about it. My dad wasn't religious in the slightest and neither am I. I'm going to have him cremated. Scatter his ashes.'

'Where?' Reid asked, pushing images of yet another burning corpse out of his mind. Too many fires.

'I have somewhere in mind.'

Where, Reid wondered. On the estate? 'If you have a memorial service, I'd like to come.'

Alma nodded and they wandered into the hall. 'What about Jason? What will happen to him?' she asked.

'I don't know.' It was true, Reid didn't. Jason had mentioned an estranged wife to him on his first night back but there had been no mention of children. Both his parents were dead, but had they been alive Reid doubted they'd have stumped up to bury the son who ran away from them. He often wondered whether they ever really noticed he'd gone; they were so caught up in their own sordid lives.

'I'm sorry,' said Alma.

'For what?' Reid was confused.

'About Jason. I'm sorry he had to die like that. It can't be easy for you.' They were standing by the front door when Alma suddenly touched his arm. 'Your number. If I'm going to let you know about the memorial I'll need it. Wait here.'

She left Reid in the darkened hall to fetch her phone. A framed collage hung on the wall and he moved closer for a better look. Someone, presumably Alma, had made a montage of old concert tickets. They were mainly from the nineties – Mudhoney, Bon Jovi, Ice T, Sex Pistols and loads of other bands Reid had never heard of – and scattered among them were a few odd train tickets, presumably from memorable journeys: Bristol, Manchester, Birmingham. It was like seeing Alma's youth encapsulated in a frame. His would have been dull by comparison; a one-way ticket to Texas and the return fourteen years later. He did see some bands in Texas – Koresh liked to play himself, and they'd go into town sometimes to catch a live show – but nothing like The Ramones or Sex Pistols.

He scanned the montage again and found himself drawn to one of the train tickets. He blinked in the dim light just to be sure he was reading the small text correctly. The air around him seemed to suddenly thicken, the smell of cannabis when he'd arrived now cloying in the back of his throat. The drowning sensation came over him, he couldn't breathe properly and could have sworn the walls of the hall were moving. He reached for the door and fumbled with the lock. He heard Alma calling his name as he lurched on to the walkway outside, his heart thumping in his chest.

'What's wrong?' Alma was standing in the hallway next to the montage.

'Panic attack,' he gasped. 'I'm sorry, I have to go.'

Reid didn't wait for a response. He needed to get away from Alma and her flat right now. He walked quickly towards the stairs, glancing over his shoulder to see if she was following him and was relieved when she wasn't. At Coniston House, instead of going to his flat Reid headed straight for the roof. The birds were excited to see him, expecting more food, so when he opened the doors they looked momentarily confused before taking flight. He watched them circle overhead a few times before disappearing into the distance. Watching them fly soothed him a little, but what he'd seen in Alma's flat had shaken him to the core. As his breathing became more regular his eyes drifted downwards where he saw a figure on the walkway of Ullswater House.

Alma was standing outside her flat, staring up at him, rigid, arms by her sides. He saw her reach out with her right arm as though to hand him something across the abyss that separated them. Then something was fluttering in the breeze – a piece of paper – and he watched, fascinated, as it was swept around by the wind. It fluttered towards the ground before sailing back up and travelling in the direction of Coniston House and then back down again, where Reid lost sight of it.

He thought about running down ten flights of stairs to see if he could find it but knew it would be useless. When he looked back at the spot where Alma had been standing, she was gone. And so was Kevin's train ticket to Glasgow that Reid had seen framed in her hall. That's what Alma had thrown to the wind: the one piece of evidence that she'd been involved in Kevin's disappearance – or at least one of the last people to see him. The ticket was now just another piece of detritus to be whipped around the desolate estate that had once been Kevin's home.

CHAPTER 42

'So we now have two deaths on the Grasmere Estate.' Hamer was standing in front of the Grasmere team looking none too pleased. He'd ditched his uniform jacket after his Old Bailey appearance that morning and despite being in shirtsleeves rolled to the elbows, he still managed to look smart. 'The preliminary report on the garage fire suggests the point of origin was the sofa, where the victim was found. The fire was probably started by a firelighter.'

Kirby stifled a yawn and rubbed his eyes, which had felt bad enough that morning but now as though they needed propping open. Tomorrow would be Friday, almost a week since Stark's murder and now they had another suspicious death on their plate. A lie-in was looking about as likely as him capitulating about Bob Dylan.

'So it was definitely arson?' said Drayton.

Hamer nodded. 'Yes. If the victim was asleep when the fire started then it's possible they were overcome by toxic fumes before having a chance to escape. However, it's also possible they were incapacitated in some way before the fire began. We should have the lab results by the end of the day and if they indicate the latter, then we need to ask ourselves whether this death is linked to that of William Stark.'

'Do we know for sure it's Jason Roye?' asked Masters.

'Not yet. We're getting dental records from Glasgow which is where he'd been living.' Kirby had spent a gruelling day trying to trace Roye's whereabouts for the last few decades. 'We know from Vernon Reid that Roye slept in the garage on at least one occasion and his phone was found at the scene so it's a strong possibility it is him.'

'Mark, did you find anything out from Stark's best friend?' asked Hamer.

'Joost Larrsen,' said Drayton. 'He saw Stark last week – they have lunch regularly. Larrsen said he was worn down by the estate business. To begin with he was full of fight, but as time went on, and it became clear the estate couldn't be saved, he became more and more withdrawn. Larrsen did say one interesting thing. At their last lunch, Stark told him all he'd ever wanted was to do the right thing but he'd failed. He finished by telling Larrsen there was still time to put some things right. When Larrsen asked what he meant he waved it off.'

'There's nothing he could have done about the estate so he must have been talking about something else,' said Kirby, wondering what it could have been. 'Did you ask him about Stark's wife's death?'

Drayton nodded. 'Larrsen was out of the country when it happened – he's a retired pilot – but he said he was surprised by the news when he heard. Louisa – that's the wife – hadn't struck him as the suicidal type. But he did say she was unhappy at Grasmere. Larrsen wondered if she was planning on leaving.'

'It really does make you wonder why they stayed. And why Stark stayed on after Louisa's death,' said Hamer. 'Did Larrsen shed any light on that?'

'No. He'd asked Stark the same question and never got a satisfactory answer. Stark always replied he had a moral obligation to stay and see his work through – whatever that meant – and he couldn't leave because it would look like he was abandoning the estate and everyone there. A double-standard thing. When Louisa died Larrsen pushed him to leave, but if anything Stark became more stubborn.'

'What about Alma? How did she feel?'

'Larrsen never really spoke to her about it. I got the impression they didn't get on, although Larrsen didn't say so explicitly. When her mother died she withdrew, didn't seem to care about leaving or staying. Stark wrapped her in cotton wool.'

'That's pretty much what Tad Finch said to me at Stark's old practice,' said Kirby. 'There's something else.' He'd told Hamer about Hoffmann's affair with Michaela Falke but not the rest of the group. 'According to Vernon Reid, Tobias Hoffmann and Michaela Falke had an affair in the 1990s. He, Jason and Kevin saw them having sex in the church one evening.'

The small group exchanged glances but it was Drayton who spoke up first. 'Surely they're not still at it all these years later, in the same place? I mean, how old are they?'

'Michaela must be late sixties,' said Kirby. 'Hoffmann's maybe ten years younger. People do still have sex over the age of fifty, you know.'

'But in a church?' Drayton's face was a vision of pure distaste.

'Could William Stark have known about the affair?' asked Masters. 'Maybe he was threatening to tell the partners, Elliott and Mary. We know Roye knew about it, so it's something that would link our two victims if he did.'

'Why now though? It happened eons ago. And as far as we're aware, Roye had come back to find out what happened to his mate, not stir up decades-old gossip,' said Drayton, in a less-than-friendly way. Kirby really must talk to him about his problem with Masters.

'We don't know much about Roye's circumstances yet,' said Kirby. 'He slept rough for at least one night which suggests he didn't have much money. He might have thought he could black-mail Hoffmann. But I agree, it would be a massive coincidence for both Stark and Roye to bring it up at the same time unless something prompted them.'

'Have you spoken to Hoffmann about it?' Hamer asked Kirby.

'Not yet. I did see Michaela Falke embrace someone in the woods, but it was too dark to see who it was.'

'Could have been her husband,' said Masters.

'I don't think so. He doesn't strike me as the kind of man who'd embrace in public, let alone in the woods. In fact, he doesn't like her going there at all.'

'What's the relationship between the Hoffmanns and the Falkes?' asked Hamer.

'Michaela's good friends with Mary Hoffmann,' said Kirby. 'I got the impression the four of them are close and the Hoffmanns worshipped at Falke's church, which makes committing adultery there rather personal if you ask me.'

'It's private though,' said Masters. 'Where else could they go that's nearby? Mind you, it is risky.'

'Maybe that was part of the attraction to begin with. If they turn out to be our recent lovebirds then perhaps it's purely practical.'

'You'd think they'd use one of the empty flats if they were that desperate,' said Drayton. 'Didn't Kaplinsky say Hoffmann had keys to all sorts on the estate?'

'So did Dan Scribbs. I'm sure he'd have parted with a key to an empty flat for a price. Although once they were all boarded up they'd have been stuck for a venue.'

'So at the moment, Tobias and Michaela's affair is a possible motive for one or both murders,' said Hamer. 'Scribbs also had motive if Stark had found out what he was doing in the church and threatened to report him. Speak to the daughter again and see if she knows anything about either of these and whether her father did.'

Kirby nodded. He may as well move into one of the empty flats at Grasmere himself at this rate. 'We haven't talked about the elephant in the room yet,' he said. 'And that's the disappearance of Kevin Shires.'

'You think Roye's death could be linked to that?' asked Masters. 'If it really is him in the garage?'

'It's the reason he came back to the estate. And Reid did say Roye had found something, so the fire might have been an attempt to destroy evidence. I'm seeing the SIO on the boys' case tomorrow who can hopefully fill in a few blanks.' Kirby felt his phone vibrate. 'It's Carter Jenks.'

He wandered over to the murder board as he took the call, his colleagues' voices drifting out of focus. He stared at Stark's hanging body and the charred remains in the Shires' garage as Jenks talked. When he'd finished, Kirby thanked the pathologist and hung up. He suddenly became aware that everyone had fallen silent behind him.

'Well?' asked Hamer, impatiently.

'Our garage victim is definitely Jason Roye,' said Kirby, tapping the photo on the murder board. 'But there's something else,' he said, turning. 'Someone drugged him before setting the fire. He was full of ketamine.'

CHAPTER 43

Broken glass glinted on the carpet in the hallway and a whiff of cannabis wafted out through the letterbox as Kirby peered into Alma Stark's flat. It was still quite early so if she'd had a heavy night there was every chance she was still in bed. He'd knocked several times and got no reply. He let the letterbox snap shut and stood up. The broken glass was a slight worry but nothing else looked out of place from what he could see. He turned to walk away, deciding to go and see Michaela Falke and come back later, when he heard the door being unlocked.

'What do you want?' Alma's voice was croaky as if she'd just woken after a long night. She cleared her throat. 'Have you found out who killed my father yet?'

'We're still working on that. May I come in for a moment?' he asked.

After a slight hesitation, she opened the door. 'Excuse the mess, I was packing all last night. Watch out,' she said, indicating the broken glass Kirby had seen through the letterbox. 'I knocked a picture off the wall moving stuff about.' She led him into the kitchen which had the same layout as Reid's. 'Take a seat. You want coffee?'

'No, I'm fine thanks,' said Kirby, sitting down. Unlike Reid's seventies' padded vinyl, Alma had modern bent-plywood chairs. In fact, everything about the kitchen, apart from its layout, was the opposite of Reid's. It looked like something out of a catalogue, albeit small. Gleaming white cupboards hid everything, sleek appliances stood on the marble-topped work surface. Kirby's eyes roamed for a coffee machine in case he'd been too hasty in refusing but he couldn't see one.

Alma opened a cupboard and took out a jar of instant. 'Or would you prefer tea?'

'No, I'm good. Is this the picture you broke?' A frame, still intact but with several jagged pieces of glass still in situ, lay on the table. Inside was a montage of old concert and train tickets, some of which had come loose.

'Let me move that,' said Alma quickly picking up the montage and placing it on the kitchen counter next to her car keys. 'It's junk.'

'Concert tickets hold a lot of memories. I leave them in old books to find years later – it's a nice surprise.'

'Only if you like surprises,' said Alma. She poured water into the mug and the smell of instant coffee filled the kitchen. 'If you haven't found my father's killer then why are you here?' she asked, taking a seat opposite. 'I've told you everything I can.' She took a sip of the black coffee and winced. 'Shit, that's hot.'

'There's something I wanted to ask you – it's about Tobias Hoffmann.'

'Really?' Alma blew on her coffee before taking another more tentative sip. 'What about him?'

'Did you know about his affair with Michaela Falke?'

Alma put down her coffee. 'I'm sorry?'

'They had an affair in the early nineties. I wondered whether you and your father knew?'

'What's this got to do with finding his killer?'

'It may have nothing to do with it,' said Kirby. 'But I'd like to know if you knew, nevertheless.'

Alma leant back in her chair, her hands wrapped around her mug as though she were cold. *She must have Teflon hands*, thought Kirby, noticing a cut on one of her knuckles. 'You think my father could have been murdered over an affair that happened that long ago?'

'We don't know the affair ended.'

Leaning forward, Alma stared into her coffee for a moment before looking up. 'I spent a lot of time with the Hoffmanns. They were very good to me. But yes, I did know Toby was seeing Michaela on the side.'

'How come?'

Alma shrugged. 'I saw them at it.' She took a sip of coffee, a smile creeping over her lips. 'I told Dad and he said, don't get involved. Don't say a word. So I didn't.'

'Where did you see them?'

'In the church. Funny place to choose but, hey. I only saw them once.'

'Was anyone with you?'

'No, why?'

'No reason,' said Kirby. 'And you never spoke to Tobias about what you'd seen, or mentioned it to anyone else?'

'No, I just said. I told Dad because I thought it was funny – I was only about fifteen or sixteen at the time. He didn't find it funny, but that's grown-ups for you. In fact he took it quite seriously, said he'd talk to Tobias about it. I think he was a bit hurt Tobias hadn't told him.'

'What about Elliott Falke?'

Alma shrugged. 'What about him? Tobias was my father's friend and that's where his loyalty lay.'

'So he didn't tell Elliott Falke what was going on?'

'No. Why would he?'

'And did the affair end?'

'Yes. My dad spoke to Tobias and that was that.'

Kirby wasn't so sure but let it go for the moment, sensing there was more to it. 'Dan Scribbs had been hiding illegal material in the church. Did you know that?'

'No, but it doesn't surprise me. Dad never trusted him to do any work in his flat and neither did I.'

'Did your father know what he was up to in the church?'

'No. Or if he did he didn't mention it. You can't seriously think Dan Scribbs killed my father?' Alma snorted. 'If he did he'd have left plenty of evidence. He's as thick as pig shit.'

That thought had crossed Kirby's mind, although Scribbs certainly had the strength to hoist Stark up from the scaffolding. 'There was something else I wanted to ask you. The fire in Sally Shires' garage; did you see anyone near the garage on Wednesday or see anyone go in?'

'No, and I can't think why anyone would set it alight. The bulldozers will do the same job in a few weeks.'

'Not entirely. We found a body inside.'

Alma blinked. 'Who?'

'Jason Roye.'

'What on earth was he doing there?'

'You don't sound very surprised at hearing his name.'

'Someone must have told me he was back. There may not be many of us left but news travels fast.'

'He'd been back for a few days. You didn't see him at all?'

'No . . . I'm not sure I'd even recognise him. I mean, I hardly knew him. Nor Kevin. Was it him sleeping rough in the wood?'

'Possibly. Did your father know Jason?'

'I doubt it.' Alma hesitated. 'Are you implying he had something to do with my father's murder?'

'Not at all,' said Kirby. 'We're just looking for any possible link between the two deaths.'

'But the fire was an accident, surely?'

'No, it was started deliberately.' Kirby paused for a moment. 'It could be coincidence, but it's odd Jason came back here after so many years and your father was killed the next night, don't you think?'

'Plenty of odd things happen here, so I wouldn't set too much store by it,' said Alma dismissively.

'So I'm learning. Out of interest, do you remember the night Kevin and Jason disappeared?'

'Of course I do. Everyone does. It's like people remembering where they were when Lennon was shot, or Kennedy. I was at home with my dad.'

'One final question: do you know who your father's solicitors are?'

'Penrose and Lodge. Why?'

'Have you been in touch with them yet about your father's will?'

Alma shook her head. 'But it will all come to me, whatever he had. There isn't anyone else.'

◆ ◆ ◆

Outside it had begun to rain. Large drops carried on the wind spattered Kirby's face as he made his way to the stairwell and up to the ninth floor and the Falkes' flat. He didn't know what to make of Alma Stark, only that she was holding back. Not necessarily information, although his instinct told him that was likely, but on a personal level. Her reaction to Tobias Hoffmann's affair was blasé. She was also totally unfazed by the mention of Jason Roye's name. She might have read the *Mail* story, in which case she'd have known he was back, but Kirby had expected some surprise that it could be his body in the garage, or even curiosity. And yet there had been neither. Perhaps she was still in shock after her father's death. Losing a loved one affected everyone differently so it could just be she'd closed down emotionally. The picture bothered him too. The hallway was carpeted. It was unlikely that knocking the picture off the wall would break the glass, unless it had been damaged before. And there was the fresh cut on her knuckle. He looked up as he heard heavy footsteps on the stairs above. Someone was coming in the opposite direction.

Elliott Falke appeared on the next landing and looked up from his phone. 'Detective. I've important church business to attend to in Earlsfield. If you want to talk to me I'm afraid you'll have to turn around.'

'No, that's fine, Mr Falke. It's not you I'm here to see.' Kirby carried on walking.

'Wait,' said Falke. 'My wife?'

'Just routine questions. Nothing to worry about. She can update you later.' He heard Falke sigh loudly, as if to register his annoyance, and was relieved when the clergyman didn't change his mind and turn back. When Michaela Falke opened her front door she checked the walkway in both directions as though looking for her husband.

'I just passed him,' said Kirby. 'He was in a rush. I told him you'd fill him in on our chat later. May I come in?'

'Well, yes, I suppose so.'

'I'm glad to have caught you alone,' said Kirby. 'Because I need to ask you about a personal matter.' Michaela blanched. *She knows what's coming*, thought Kirby. They sat in the living room, which wasn't so cosy this time. The walls had been stripped of pictures, the antimacassars had been removed and acrid notes of burnt toast lingered in the air.

'What is it you want to ask me about?'

'Your affair with Tobias Hoffmann.' Michaela's face flushed red and she looked away. 'Does Elliott know?' he asked.

'No,' replied Michaela. It came out as a whisper as though Elliott might be listening outside the door.

'Did William Stark know?'

Michaela dragged her eyes back to Kirby. 'Why do you ask?'

'Because on Wednesday we found a body in Sally Shires' old garage. It belongs to Jason Roye. You know who I'm talking about?'

Michaela nodded.

'Jason knew about your affair – he saw the two of you in the church. We also have reason to believe William Stark knew too. Is that true?'

It took Michaela a few moments to collect herself. 'Yes, it is. But you can't be implying I had something to do with his death? That I'd kill someone to protect myself? What kind of person do you think I am?' Her voice was shaking.

'The kind that takes a huge risk by cheating on their husband in his own church with one of his close friends. Whatever your reasons.'

Michaela opened her mouth but nothing came out.

'I also suspect the affair is still going on, that it wasn't a quick fling that's forgotten about and everyone pretends didn't happen. I saw you with Tobias in the wood on Tuesday.'

Michaela stood up and went to the window. She didn't say anything for a few moments and just stared out, chewing the knuckle of her index finger. 'My husband mustn't find out about this,' she said, eventually. 'He's retiring soon, as you know, and the church elders are voting on his successor next week.' She turned around to face Kirby. 'Tobias is expected to win but if Elliott finds out about the affair, he'll ruin him. Not only that, he'll make my life hell.'

CHAPTER 44

Once Michaela Falke had admitted to her affair with Tobias Hoffmann there had been no stopping her talking, and Kirby thought he'd be late for his meeting with Ted Harper, the retired SIO on the Roye/Shires case. Michaela and Hoffmann's affair had ended – soon after the two boys went missing – and for a period of time the Falkes had carried out missionary work in Ghana. When they returned to Grasmere, Falke had reclaimed his post as head of All Hallows and for a while, things carried on as normal. Then the affair had started up again, this time in empty flats and eventually the boarded-up church. That Hoffmann was likely to succeed Falke as church leader seemed as unlikely as it did naive. Michaela had been adamant her husband knew nothing about their affair, something Kirby found extremely difficult to believe. She was also scared of him and Kirby wouldn't put it past Elliott to know exactly what was going on but be biding his time until he could exert maximum revenge. What bearing it had, if any, on Stark's or Roye's murders, Kirby didn't know.

The Star and Garter pub was tucked away in a small mews in Belgravia and when Kirby walked in he spotted Ted Harper straight away. It wasn't a case of 'once a copper, always a copper' but more that he was the only punter in the small, cosy hostelry. Harper was in his seventies but Kirby would never have guessed from looking at him. Lean and fit, with close-cropped grey hair and a neatly trimmed beard, Harper clearly took care of himself.

'How's retirement?' Kirby asked, as they shook hands.

'Everything it's cracked up to be,' said Harper. 'Although you can never leave behind what you've seen no matter how hard you try.'

'No,' said Kirby. 'In that case I'm sorry to be here raking up an old case.' He'd have killed for a pint but instead ordered a mineral water before filling Harper in on Stark's murder and the fire in Sally Shires' garage. 'The body inside belongs to Jason Roye. He was drugged before the garage was set alight.'

'Shit,' said Harper, rubbing his forehead.

'He'd been going through Kevin's things looking for clues as to what might have happened to him.'

Kirby could see Harper's mind working its way through the implications. 'So you're looking for a link between William Stark and Jason Roye?'

Kirby nodded. 'Did Stark crop up in your investigation at all? Or his daughter, Alma?'

Harper thought for a moment. 'He would have been questioned – everyone on the estate was – but I don't recall anything specific, although he did help organise a search. The woods on the estate, all the empty garages and vacant flats, the surrounding roads, verges. He knew the place like the back of his hand – obviously.'

'Did he initiate that, or did you ask him?'

'He came to us. He took everything that happened on the estate very personally. I know what you're thinking and we did look at him for that very reason, the perpetrator inserting themselves into an investigation, but we didn't find anything untoward.'

'Did he know Jason and Kevin?'

'Not really. He knew who they were, but their paths didn't cross.'

'What about Alma, was she friends with the boys? They were about the same age.'

Harper shook his head. 'I don't think so. Alma went to a different school, and I can't imagine her dad would want her hanging about with the likes of Kevin and Jason.'

'Why not?'

'Jason had been in trouble with the police a few times – joyriding, nicking stuff from the local shop. He wasn't exactly a boy to take home to meet the parents.'

'Or parent, in Alma's case. Louisa Stark died.'

Harper clicked his fingers as the memory came back. 'That's it; she threw herself off Windermere House. By all accounts she hated living on the estate but Stark wouldn't leave. Christ, I'd forgotten about that.' Harper took a long sip of his beer.

'Can you remember what they were like as a family, Alma and her father?'

Harper shook his head. 'Like I said, we questioned everyone, but we focused on the boys' friends and family. Alma and her father didn't feature in the investigation beyond general enquiries. Apart from helping with the search, I honestly can't think of a connection between Stark and Jason. Or Kevin, for that matter. Although Kevin wasn't so much of a tearaway as Jason.'

'A story ran in the press suggesting Jason might have harmed Kevin. Was there any truth in that?'

'None that I saw. They were best friends.'

'Where did it come from then?'

'Jason was no saint but his dad, Tommy Glitch, was a right bastard. His nickname was "Milk", because he sold drugs off the back of his milk cart. He was in and out of trouble like a rosary out of a nun's pocket. People on the estate started talking, all that "like father, like son" business. You know how those places are, bloody rumour mills. Anyhow, some local busybody mouthed off to a *Sun* reporter. Said they'd seen Jason pushing Kevin about a bit a few days before. It just escalated. We never thought Jason had harmed Kevin and neither did Sally Shires.'

'It could have been an accident. Two boys mucking about. It wouldn't be the first time,' said Kirby.

'We considered it, of course. But we had no evidence. Where would this accident have happened? If it had taken place on the estate then we'd have found something. And where was the body? We searched all the places the boys were known to hang out and found nothing. I also reckon Jason would have turned up in a few days had that been the case.'

Kirby agreed with him. A sixteen-year-old boy who'd accidentally killed his best friend wasn't going to find it easy hiding from the authorities. Never mind he had a body to dispose of. 'You mentioned Jason's father; what about his mother?'

'Tricia? Let's put it this way, she sampled the goods off Glitch's milk float. She meant well, but . . .' Harper shook his head. 'She'd had a tough life herself, in and out of care, and Jason was more than she could handle. She spent most of the days following their disappearance off her head. She's dead now.'

'What happened to Kevin's dad?'

'Rick Shires. He lost his job during the Wapping dispute in '87 when Kevin was about ten or eleven. He took it very badly, had mental health issues as a result. He was out of work for several years then eventually got a job with the railway and was killed working on the tracks. That must have been a few years after Kevin disappeared.'

'Sounds like Jason had his reasons for wanting to run away, but Kevin?'

'You know what sixteen-year-old lads are like. Probably seemed like an adventure to him. And remember, their other best mate – Vernon Reid – was heading for the Lone Star State with his mother.

I could see Kevin getting caught up in the whole adventure of it. Maybe Jason was right and he had changed his mind, but either way something happened to him . . .' Harper trailed off.

'So tell me what happened the day they went missing. I haven't read the original case files yet,' said Kirby.

'It was a Thursday night. The boys had both told their parents – or in Jason's case, his mother – they were at each other's houses. That was at about 7 p.m. They weren't missed until they didn't turn up at school the next day. Even then people thought they were bunking off school so the police weren't called until the Friday evening.'

'Christ. By which point you'd lost hours. When did Reid and his mother leave?'

'Friday morning. Reid was a year older so wasn't in school. By the time we got involved he was on a plane.'

'Where had he been the previous night?'

'He was at home with his mother doing last-minute packing. They had several visitors that evening, all of whom saw Vernon in the flat.'

'Were you able to question him at all?'

'We eventually spoke to him and his mother by phone about a week later. Vernon didn't mention anything about the boys planning to run away. We did consider that scenario but then the whole Walter Flynn thing blew up.'

A memory stirred in Kirby's mind. Walter Flynn, a convicted paedophile, had been living on the estate under a new name and no one had known. Not even the police. It had been a public-relations disaster.

'It wasn't until the two boys went missing that someone on the estate discovered who Flynn actually was and spray-painted the front of his flat with "paedo". We didn't have centralised records in those days and Scotland didn't think to tell us. It was a right fucking mess.'

'Do you know who tagged his house?'

'We never found out,' said Harper. 'I did wonder whether Elliott Falke learned his real identity but was bound by clergy-penitent privilege and took matters into his own hands by "accidentally" letting it slip.'

'What happened?'

'Someone set Flynn's flat on fire and he burned to death.'

Kirby could only too easily imagine the vigilante mentality on an estate like Grasmere when news of a convicted paedophile was living there got out. 'Did you think Flynn could have killed Kevin?'

'He fitted the profile perfectly. He had a record for the attempted abduction of teenage boys in Scotland – that's a pretty rare offence – as well as a string of other sex offences to his name.'

'That's a strong reason to look at him,' said Kirby, thinking he might have done the same. 'Did he know the boys?'

'Oh yes, that's why I mentioned Elliott Falke. Flynn helped at the local community centre, which was run by Elliott and his wife.' Harper's look said it all. 'Flynn was very nervous when we brought him in – who the fuck wouldn't be with a rap sheet like his – and his alibi was non-existent. I think he was scared we'd fit him up for it. In the end we didn't need to.'

Kirby stared at Harper trying to figure out if he was serious or not.

'I'm joking,' said Harper, with a sarcastic smile. 'There was no evidence to link him with the two boys other than that they knew each other. Do I think he could have killed Kevin?' He raised his eyebrows. 'It's certainly possible. He'd have had trouble subduing two teenage boys, but one is another matter. Kevin wasn't a big lad.'

'Was anyone else in the frame?'

Harper shook his head. 'We looked at family and friends, known criminals in the area – there were a lot of those, I can tell you, Jason's dad being one – but nada.' Harper finished his pint. 'Sure I can't tempt you?' he asked, on his way to the bar.

Kirby shook his head and waited while Harper was served. When he came back, Kirby asked, 'When you searched the boys' rooms did you see any evidence they'd planned to run away? Clothes missing?'

'Not really.'

'What about stuff like birth certificates? The parents would have had those – were they missing?'

'Look, Tricia Roye was all over the place. She couldn't find a shopping list, never mind a birth certificate.'

'But you did ask?'

Harper sighed. 'It'll be in the report. I honestly can't remember. Neither of the boys had a passport.'

Kirby wondered whether Jason had a bank account and if he had, how he'd managed to open it without a birth certificate. If he and Kevin had planned to run away then personal documents like that would have been very useful. Kirby wasn't sure there was much else to be had from Harper, although there was one thing he hadn't asked him about. 'You mentioned Elliott Falke. Do you remember Mary and Tobias Hoffmann? They were close, connected to the church.'

'I do, yes. Toby Hoffmann was the caretaker at the time. He helped us check places like the lift shafts and boiler room. Nice bloke, I seem to remember. Why?'

'He was having an affair with Falke's wife, Michaela.'

The surprise on Harper's face was genuine. 'You're fucking kidding me.'

'Jason, Kevin and Vernon saw them in the church together.'

'I'll be damned.' Harper chuckled. 'Talk about shitting on your own doorstep.'

'On the subject of the Hoffmanns, they had a foster daughter who died.'

Harper nodded. 'Angela Barton. She was a close friend of Alma's now I think about it. It was only a few months before the boys disappeared. Tragic for all concerned, obviously, but I did feel for Alma. First she loses her mother, then her best friend dies and then the two lads went missing.'

'I thought you said she didn't know Jason and Kevin?'

'I don't think she did. But she was still very upset – everyone was.'

'Steve, do me a favour and run another background check on Alma Stark.' Kirby was on the phone to Kobrak as he sat in the Fucking Corsa eating a doughnut and drinking coffee after his chat with Harper. He'd resisted the pint and doughnuts weren't something he made a habit of, but they reminded him of Anderson and he was missing his partner. *C'mon, Lew, it's what cops do!* his partner used to say to him when he'd moaned about the calories. Today he didn't give a rat's arse about the calories. He might be dead in a few years from insomnia, so what the hell?

'Am I looking for anything in particular?' asked Kobrak.

'Anything unusual. Places she used to work – Tad Finch mentioned an architectural practice in Camden. She didn't fit in, apparently, and left. I'd like to know why.'

'I'll get on to it.'

'Also, can you get on to the Central Registry and chase up Jason and Kevin's case files? And when you speak to them ask for the files on Stark's wife, Louisa, and also a girl called Angela Barton. Tell them it's urgent. Angela was one of Hoffmann's foster kids and close friends with Alma. She died just a few months before Jason and Kevin disappeared. Alma may just be unlucky, but a lot of people seem to die around her.'

'Okay, will do. By the way, Romy found something interesting in Stark's personal papers. Some kind of weird rental arrangement with the council.'

'What do you mean, weird?' He took a bite of his doughnut and licked the sugar from his lips. Anderson would have been impressed.

'Weird as in it was a non-rental agreement.'

'Non-rental?' said Kirby through a mouthful of doughnut. 'What the hell does that mean?'

'It means he wasn't paying any rent. Never did the entire time he was there.'

CHAPTER 45

'It is a splendid place that you have here.' Irene Fontaine – as she preferred to be known – was standing in the reading room at RADE looking out of the French windows down to the square below. She turned to Connie, who had just finished giving her the grand tour, and smiled. 'I'm impressed.'

Connie had arrived at the archive early and laid out some of the jewels in the collection's crown. Works by George Gilbert Scott, Edwin Lutyens and George Aitchison lay alongside those of Zaha Hadid and Renzo Piano. As well as work by the late William Stark. She'd left the drawings of Grasmere out on purpose. So far, Grasmere Estate and Pinder Wood hadn't been mentioned, but now the guided tour was over, Connie was itching to get to the real purpose of the visit – Irene's involvement with the land at the estate's heart and the architectural competition William Stark had won in order to build it.

'These are the drawings of the Grasmere Estate,' said Connie, spreading some of them out. 'Stark certainly made good use of the woods in the middle. Every flat on the estate must have a view of trees.'

Irene joined Connie at the table and lowered herself into a chair. Today's walking stick looked like ebony, with a carved horse hoof handle, and Connie wondered whether that, too, housed a blade.

Irene studied a plan of the estate, which showed the three main perimeter blocks surrounding Pinder Wood. The maisonettes jutted out at angles from the main blocks and on Stark's original drawings the area around them had been landscaped to transition into the denser nature of the wood. But Connie's eyes kept being pulled back to the church, sitting on the edge of the wood, disconnected from the rest of the estate that was tethered together by a string of walkways and pedestrian bridges.

'Bloody ugly, if you ask me,' said Irene.

Connie sat down next to her guest. 'I've shown you around the archive as we agreed, so now will you tell me about the land and the competition?'

'I always keep my end of a bargain,' she said. 'What do you want to know?'

It was hard to know where to begin so Connie decided to start with what Quatremaine had told her. 'Is it true Stark only won the competition because he overcame a legal loophole granting access to your land?'

'It is,' said Irene. 'I should preface everything I'm about to tell you with the fact that it was all my father's idea, not mine. I simply inherited the aftermath. In the first instance, my father wanted someone sympathetic to preserving the church – the tin chapel you're so fixated with – as well as respecting Pinder Wood. The church wasn't so much of an issue, although my father had impractical dreams of it remaining in situ, which was never going to happen. As a compromise, William agreed to dismantle it and rebuild it on the Traps Lane plot.'

'Anyone could have done that,' said Connie.

'They could, yes, but they didn't.'

261

'Why not?' Connie was struggling to see what had set Stark apart from the other entrants.

'Because in return for granting access to the wood my father wanted something back. Something the other entrants weren't willing to give.'

'What?' Connie was thinking of some compromise on the design and wasn't expecting what came next.

'Undivided loyalty.'

'I don't understand,' said Connie, confused. 'How? By joining his church?'

'Oh no, far worse.' Irene fixed her with her one functioning eye. 'By living on the estate.'

'Living on the estate?' Connie repeated, just to be sure she was getting this right. 'For how long?'

'Fifty years.'

'*Fifty* years?' She was starting to sound like a parrot. 'Why?'

'My father's father was badly injured in the First World War and it was only down to the loyalty and bravery of his fellow officers he came back alive. It had a profound effect on my father, who was a young teenager at the time. So much so, he devoted himself to the church and went through life demanding similar adherence from those around him. The Grasmere competition was no exception; if he couldn't find someone who was fully committed to the project then he'd simply withdraw his support – and access to Pinder Wood. He knew he'd never get that sort of loyalty from the council, but he hoped he might get it from the estate's creator. My father was eccentric, to say the least.' Irene smiled.

'And William Stark was the only one who agreed?'

Irene nodded. 'He was a very ambitious and complex man, but the bottom line was he wanted that contract. He wanted to set up his career, and he thought a new state-of-the-art housing estate in south London would be the first step. In many ways it was and yet . . . well, we all know what happened.'

'He lost his wife and the estate turned into crime central.'

'Personally, I believe he lost a lot more.' Irene tapped the side of her head. 'He lost his mind. He was a very serious man and principled. However, he had an ego the size of the British Museum. When he signed the contract with my father I don't believe he really knew what he was getting into, or rather, that his ego was so massive it never occurred to him he might fail.'

'What would have happened if he'd broken the contract and left the estate?'

'At the end of the fifty-year period he was due a large sum of money – another reason he wanted the contract so badly – a percentage of the money earned from leasing the land to the council. It would have been forfeited had he broken the contract. I don't know the exact sum, but it runs well into six figures. A very comfortable retirement pot.'

Connie wasn't a legal expert but surely Stark could have found some way out of the contract. 'What about when your father died? You said that you inherited this – couldn't you have released Will from the paperwork?'

'My father was very clear, the contract must be seen through. After that William was free to do as he pleased. As was I with the land.'

'Why did the council agree to any of this?' asked Connie. 'With respect, it's insane.'

'I doubt they had a clue,' said Irene. 'I think William presented them with his design, with access to the woods and a reasonable lease and they grabbed it. They were so desperate to build new housing at the end of the sixties they'd have done anything. People were still living in back-to-backs with outdoor toilets. Grasmere was going to be a shiny new estate taking the borough into the future.'

Connie still couldn't get her head around why William Stark would agree to such a thing. Money? He'd literally signed away half a century of his life. And for what? A successful architectural practice, yes, but he was hardly Norman Foster. Plus, he could have walked away and lost the money but at least he would have gained his freedom. None of it made any sense. 'What happens now Stark's dead?'

'There are stipulations, but the money goes to his daughter.'

Connie thought back to her visit to Alma and wondered whether she was aware of any of this. 'And Pinder Wood?'

'I've sold it.'

Connie felt her jaw drop. 'Why?'

'The redevelopment. William was going to get his money after being evicted and the land was free. I could have hung on to it, leased it out to the new owners, but . . .' Irene sighed. 'I'm too old to start buggering about with new business deals.'

'But your father went to all that trouble to protect the land – and basically sacrificed William Stark's freedom – and you've just sold it?'

'What else would I do with it? I can't use it. And it's been sold with caveats, obviously – it'll never be built on.'

Connie couldn't begin to imagine how much Pinder Wood was worth. If Irene had been well off before, she must now be positively rolling in it.

'Look.' Irene leaned in closer. 'What happened to William changes none of this. The land would be released back to me whether he was alive or dead. William made a choice though – he became fixated on saving the estate. He didn't *want* to leave. He was never going to beat the council but he certainly prolonged the process. The place could have been rubble by now and yet he clung on. Had I been in his shoes I'd have jumped for joy at the prospect of being forced out before the contract ended. That's what I meant when I said I think he lost his mind.'

'Wasn't he just being loyal, like your father wanted?'

Irene smiled. 'Loyalty is often misguided.'

'What about Alma?'

Irene's eye narrowed. Today's eyepatch was a sequinned bullseye. 'You know her?'

'Not really. I went to offer my condolences. That's all.'

'Alma's my god-daughter. Did you know that?'

Connie shook her head. This was getting crazier by the second.

'My father and William became close friends, in fact we all did. William, his wife Louisa and me. When Alma was born they asked me to be her godmother. Alma and I got on very well when she was a child. In fact, she loved playing in the tin church.'

'What happened?'

Irene thought for a moment. 'She was never the same after her mother died, but something else changed. It was after I'd been on tour playing Sybil Birling in *An Inspector Calls*. I came back to London and Alma was different. She stopped coming to see me – I hardly saw her.'

'How about now?'

Irene shook her head. 'We see each other very rarely, maybe at Christmas but that's about it.'

'When was this change?' asked Connie.

'It was 1992. I remember clearly because I came back to the news of those two boys going missing. It was all over the London papers.'

'Do you remember their names?'

'Of course,' said Irene. 'One of them used to deliver my papers – that was Kevin Shires. His friend was Jason Roye.'

CHAPTER 46

Connie was sitting in Kirby's boat, nursing one of the best hot chocolates she'd ever had. It was thick enough to stand a spoon in, not the thin watery stuff she'd grown up with. When she'd called him with news about the competition he'd invited her over and she'd agreed, on the proviso she didn't have to drink the disgusting salty bottled water. So far, the conversation was going far better than on her previous visit.

'The competition Stark won was organised by the local council in partnership with the Pinder Estate,' said Connie, licking the delicious sweet chocolate off her spoon, before handing Kirby the list of competition entrants Quatremaine had given her. 'Pinder owned the wood at the centre of the estate and the tin church I mentioned to you. What the council didn't know was that in return for granting access to the land the Pinder Estate wanted the contest winner to live on the new estate. It was sold as showing true commitment to the project, the theory being no one was going to design a place they wouldn't want to live in themselves.'

'How long did they expect them to stay?' asked Kirby, scanning the list she'd given him.

'Fifty years,' said Connie.

'Fifty? That's one hell of a commitment. It's more than that – it's mad.'

'It is and it isn't,' said Connie, who'd been doing some research. 'The architect Ernö Goldfinger lived in Balfron Tower in east London for a couple of months. In his case he wanted to experience first-hand the advantages and disadvantages of high-rise living.'

'That I can understand. But fifty years is taking it to an extreme.'

'I found a few other examples – there was a housing project in Norway where the architect lived and another in Germany. It's a small exclusive club, granted, and no one has stayed as long as Stark did. Anyhow, none of the other applicants were prepared to accept the challenge, despite having better designs. It's daft really. Enforcing such dedication meant an inferior design was built, totally defeating the object.'

'We found a contract in Stark's flat. He lived at Grasmere rent-free. That would have saved him a fortune over the years.'

'Not only that,' said Connie. 'He was also due a whopping sum when he was finally evicted. Had he broken his agreement with the Pinder Estate he'd have forfeited the money. So another incentive to stay.'

'How much are we talking?'

'I'm not sure of the exact amount, but six figures at least.' Connie finished the chocolate. 'That was amazing. Far better than the water you tried to palm off on me the last time.'

'What happens to the money now he's dead?' asked Kirby, rinsing her mug.

Connie smiled. 'It goes to the daughter. There's your motive if you want one.' Not that Alma had struck her as the type to kill her own father, if there was such a thing.

Kirby returned to his stool. 'I've never heard of this Pinder Estate, who are they?'

'The Pinder family owned quite a lot of land in that area and gradually sold it off, but they kept the wood and the tin church.

Richard Pinder, who sponsored the contest for the estate, was a bit of a self-styled evangelist and ran the tin church under the name Dick Fontaine. He's dead now, but his daughter Irene is still alive and that's where I got all this information. She took the name Fontaine as well; she's an actress.'

'Irene Fontaine sounds vaguely familiar. Does she know Stark's daughter, Alma?'

Connie nodded – she and Irene had talked for hours. 'Irene became friends with Stark's wife, Louisa, and when Alma was born they asked her to be godmother.'

'Irene's Alma's godmother?'

'Yes. Alma used to play in the church as a kid. Irene's garden is something else – to a kid living on Grasmere it must have been a magical place. Then Louisa and Irene fell out.'

'Why?'

'Because Stark hadn't told Louisa about the agreement with Irene's father. He'd strung her along for a good few years, promising they'd leave when the time was right. When she found out about it she was furious – can you imagine finding out you're stuck in a place like that? Louisa also challenged Irene about it, who admitted she'd known about the arrangement, even though she had nothing to do with it. Irene tried to distance herself from her father's business dealings but it was too late; her friendship with Louisa was damaged. Then Louisa killed herself.'

'This all sounds like something from the feudal system, not the twentieth century. Did Irene say how Louisa's death affected Alma and her father?'

'Not really. I was more interested in the competition. I mean, she said it was terrible. Richard Pinder – or Dick Fontaine – died a year later and Stark began visiting more, possibly in the hope Irene might be able to release him from the agreement, but she couldn't. She and Alma were quite close by that point – she used to let Alma

268

smoke in the church and that sort of thing. She must have seemed like the coolest godmother ever. Then something happened. Irene had been away on a regional theatre tour and when she got back Alma had changed.'

'In what way?'

'She stopped visiting. Even lost interest in hanging out in the church. Irene put it down to being a teenager.'

'When was this?'

'Irene said it was around the time those boys went missing, so early nineties.'

Kirby looked thoughtful. 'The body we found in the garage at Grasmere belonged to one of them, Jason Roye. He'd come back to the estate to try and find out what happened to his friend, Kevin.'

'You're joking – he was alive all along?'

Kirby nodded. 'He ran away. He and Kevin had planned to do it together, only something – or someone – prevented Kevin from going. Jason left without him. We're trying to piece together Jason's life but we know he went to Scotland – Glasgow – and didn't find out for a few months that Kevin was also officially missing.'

'Didn't he see the papers? Or the news?' Connie was too young to remember any media coverage for the story.

'This was the early nineties, remember. The story only ran briefly in a couple of the nationals and wouldn't have run in the regional press. It was also pre-internet. My guess is Jason spent his time simply getting by and didn't see the news much. Or maybe he didn't want to see it in case he was on it. Either way, he had no idea Kevin was missing.'

'And you think Alma might have had something to do with Kevin's disappearance?' Connie wondered how Irene would take the news if it turned out to be the case.

Kirby hesitated before replying. 'It's only a hunch, but it's possible. It looks like Kevin was keeping something from Jason.

269

Reid had found a handmade birthday card in Kevin's old garage. Someone had illustrated it with the peace sign.'

'Alma draws,' said Connie, thinking of the portrait hanging in Irene's front room. 'Do you have the card?'

'No. It was probably burned with everything else in the garage.'

Connie checked the time; it was getting late and she had to be in work early the following morning, even though it was a Saturday. A group of visiting architectural students from Japan had been booked in for months and it wasn't something she could cancel. They'd paid good money for a full tour and she needed to prep. 'Any news on Pete?' she asked, slipping off the kitchen stool.

'Groggy and conscious.'

'So that's good then?'

'I'll take it over unconscious and bleeding. The surgery seems to have been successful but it's early days.'

'You must be relieved.'

'He's not out of the woods yet but it's certainly better news than on Wednesday.'

Connie put on her coat. 'I'd better get going. I've got an early start.'

'And I'll have a late finish,' said Kirby, looking up from a text that had pinged into his phone. 'Kobrak's bringing Jason and Kevin's case files over.'

'About Stark,' said Connie, as Kirby walked her to the mooring's security gate in the cool evening air. 'What was his flat like?'

'Actually, rather nice. It's huge. He'd knocked two flats together. He wasn't exactly slumming it in terms of living space.'

'I'd love to see inside before it's bulldozed.'

'You'd have to square that with Alma,' said Kirby, opening the gate for her. 'Or wait until everyone's moved out and break in, like you usually do.'

CHAPTER 47

Kirby had stayed up half the night going through Jason and Kevin's case files. When he'd finished that, he'd looked at Louisa Stark's and Angela Barton's files, which by comparison were meagre. The architect's wife's death had been treated as suicide, which was what Kirby had been expecting. What he hadn't known was the eleven-year-old Alma had been with her mother at the time. There had been talk Louisa had planned on taking Alma with her when she jumped, but she'd either changed her mind, or something had happened to prevent her from doing so. Whatever had taken place that summer's day, Louisa had jumped, leaving little Alma alone on the hot roof until someone realised she was there and brought her down. The toxicology reports showed Louisa Stark had been on antidepressants, something her husband had been unaware of. Angela Barton had died in a far less spectacular fashion, her body found slumped in one of the many dark corners of Grasmere's concrete walkways, after taking ecstasy, or MDMA, with a higher than usual percentage of PMA. No one knew where she'd got it from. The tragedy had been heightened when it transpired she had been due to return to the care of her mother that very week.

The files on the two boys were complex, and as he drove to the hospital to see Sally Shires again he thought about what he'd learned. One of the key things was that the estate had been undergoing some rare refurbishment. The three main blocks had been covered in scaffolding and some parts had also been clad in green debris netting, therefore significantly reducing visibility. For two boys intent on running away, this was either good luck or good timing. It had likely also proved useful in obscuring whatever had happened to Kevin. Harper had been convinced whatever it was hadn't taken place on the estate. The case files showed a thorough search had taken place and no evidence had been found to suggest anything had happened to the boys on site. And, as Harper had said, locations the boys were known to have frequented – such as the woods at the centre of the estate, a rundown bus shelter and the railway bridge – were all searched and yielded nothing.

It took Kirby several tours of the hospital car park to find a space. It was Saturday and busy with weekend visitors – more so than usual due to a Tube strike that had brought parts of the underground system to a halt and doubled the amount of traffic. He wasn't looking forward to delivering the news of Jason's death to Sally Shires. As he rode the elevator up to her ward, he realised she'd probably viewed Jason as her last hope of finding out what had happened to her son. He stepped out into the corridor with renewed determination to try and rectify that if he possibly could. Arriving at ward reception, he was told Sally had been moved and it took him twenty minutes to locate her. When he eventually found her on the floor below, she looked worse than she had the first time they'd met and he questioned the wisdom of his visit.

'Sally, it's DI Kirby. I came to see you on Wednesday, do you remember?'

A slow nod was her reply.

He sat down beside her bed. 'I'm afraid I have some bad news. I wanted you to hear it from me before the press get hold of it. It's about Jason. I'm very sorry to have to tell you he's been killed.'

Sally's eyes widened and then blinked closed, tears puddling in the corners. 'I need to ask you a couple of questions if you're up to it, as we don't think his death was an accident,' Kirby said gently.

Sally nodded her head, followed by a sob. Kirby handed her a tissue and helped her sit up. When she was comfortable, he continued. 'We found Jason's body in your garage. Someone had set it alight. We don't know yet, but we think it might be connected to the death of William Stark. Do you know if Kevin or Jason knew Mr Stark?'

'Maybe by name,' croaked Sally.

'When I was here last, you told me Will Stark promised to keep the candle burning for Kevin. How come?'

'He organised a search for the boys. He was a kind man – he knew what it was like to lose someone, what with his wife dying like that. And his daughter was very upset, or she pretended to be. She was trouble, that one. Anything to get attention from her dad. Kev had a crush on her – he didn't know I knew, but, well, mother's intuition. I kept quiet, Kev was a sensitive lad underneath it all.'

'Was the crush reciprocated?'

'I doubt it.' Sally thought for a moment. 'But it could have been, I suppose.'

'Did Jason know about this?'

'I don't think so. Kev would have been embarrassed.'

'When you say Alma was trouble, what did you mean?'

'I used to see her slipping out of her bedroom window at night. I worked night shifts, you see. Don't know where she went but I'm bloody sure her dad didn't know. Had him wrapped around her finger after her mother jumped. I felt sorry for him – he was devoted to her, but he was blind to what she was really like.'

'I hate to ask you this, but did Kevin ever sneak out at night?'

Sally didn't answer immediately. 'He did once or twice. Rick, his dad, went mental. Tried grounding him for a week but it only made it worse.'

'Do you know where he went?'

Sally shook her head. 'Just out, was all he'd say. I assumed he was off with Jason. Jase was out all hours – Tricia, his mum, had no control over him. Then it all sort of fizzled out and Kev went a bit quiet. Was a bit withdrawn for a week or two. And then he disappeared. Just like that.'

'This period of being withdrawn, when was that exactly – two weeks before he disappeared, three?'

'More like a couple of months, maybe longer. Hang on, it was—' Sally was interrupted by a coughing fit. 'It was just after that girl died.'

'Which girl – not Angela Barton, Tobias and Mary Hoffmann's foster daughter?'

'That's her. Poor lass. Alma was upset about that too, although that was more understandable. She and Angela were tight, although she was set to lose her as well.'

'Because she was going back to her real mother?'

'That's what I heard.'

'Did Kevin and Alma ever meet up? Did you see them together?'

Sally frowned. 'I only saw them together once. Kevin had a newspaper round, not on the estate, but the big houses up on Pinder Hill. I'd got a lift home from my shift one morning – it must have been about 6 a.m. – and I saw them together on Traps Lane, the road that cuts down from The Drive.'

'What were they doing?' asked Kirby.

'Just talking. They were looking at something, a magazine or newspaper. It did cross my mind whether they'd been out all night.'

'Does the name Irene Fontaine or Irene Pinder mean anything to you?'

Sally shook her head. 'Should it?'

'She's Alma's godmother. She lives at the top of Traps Lane on The Drive. That might explain what Alma was doing there and perhaps Kevin was delivering papers.'

'The Drive was on his round, yes.'

'Before I leave you, Jason and Vernon Reid had been going through Kevin's things in the garage. Vernon mentioned a birthday card – someone had signed the card with a peace sign. Do you have any idea who it was from?'

'He said it was a present from one of the people involved in that fanzine he collected – *High Rize*. He loved his magazines and *High Rize* was his favourite. They kept coming after he disappeared and I couldn't bear to open them. They were all still in their envelopes in the garage.'

After a few more minutes, Kirby left Sally. As he was in the hospital he thought he'd take the opportunity to visit Anderson, and began to follow the colour-coded signs to his partner's ward. Reid had made no mention of the fanzine. Presumably, he and Jason had found the copies Sally had mentioned in the garage and not made the connection to the birthday card. Or was that what Jason had discovered when he phoned Reid to tell him he'd found something? If only they had that damned card. It felt like an important piece of the jigsaw. But they didn't have it. Someone had seen to that.

CHAPTER 48

Irene Fontaine was asleep on the chaise longue. Her eyepatch had slipped and the hollow where her eyeball should have been was a dark concave shadow. In sleep, she looked older than her eighty-three years, her face slack, lipstick faded. A thin sliver of drool hung from her mouth and her cane, the one with the blade, had fallen and rolled across the floor out of reach. She looked small and frag-ile – vulnerable. Reid tapped gently on the window, not wanting to startle her. As soon as she heard him she was alert, like a bird, her good eye darting around searching for the source of the sound. She may only have had one eye but there was nothing wrong with her hearing. Reid moved closer to the window and tapped again, louder. 'Miss Fontaine,' he called. 'It's me, Vernon.'

He made a fuss of opening the French window and wiping his feet, and by the time he stepped into the room and pulled the door shut behind him she was sitting up, the cane across her knees and the eyepatch in its proper position. Dignity restored.

'Vernon, this is unusual. To what do I owe the pleasure? Sit down.'

Reid had only stepped foot in the house a handful of times since he'd started working for Irene over thirty years ago. He'd been fourteen when Will Stark had suggested he work for Alma's god-mother. She'd wanted someone to help in the garden and to take care of general maintenance. The fourteen-year-old Reid had been terrified of Irene at first, but then the love of plants had transcended everything and he spent nearly three blissful years working there tending her jungle-like garden and the land beyond, where the tin church stood. While he was at school he'd only been able to work on Saturdays and the odd evening in summer, but when he'd returned from the States and Stark had suggested he approach Irene about working for her again, Irene had been happy to have him for as many hours as he wanted. To say he owed her his sanity was an understatement.

Reid wasn't the only one to have changed in the intervening years – Irene had lost an eye in a car accident that almost took her life and impacted her acting career. The garden had fallen into ruin, but Reid's reappearance had ignited something in the old actress and he'd restored the garden. He owed Irene a huge debt of gratitude, which made what he was about to say difficult.

'Would you like some tea?' Irene held up a flask. She always had a flask of tea with her in the house as it saved her from constantly going to the kitchen.

Reid held up his hand. 'Thank you, but no. There's something I need to speak to you about.'

'That sounds very serious, Vernon. Is something wrong? If it's the travel you're worried about when you leave Grasmere I can—'

'No, it's not that,' he cut in. 'It's something else.'

'I see,' said Irene. 'Go on then.'

'You heard about the fire?'

'No, what fire?'

'There was a fire at Grasmere. One of the garages was set alight. Someone died.'

'Dear me, how awful. Who?'

'A man called Jason Roye.'

Irene looked shocked. 'As in your friend Jason – the one who disappeared with Kevin Shires? Kevin used to deliver my newspapers, remember that?'

'I do.' Reid smiled. 'Kevin thought your house was creepy. He'd run up the drive and throw the paper on to the doorstep and run away again. Jason turned up at my flat out of the blue last week. He'd read about the estate being pulled down and had seen the interview with Kevin's mother in the paper. He came back to try and find out what happened to Kevin. I'd been helping him.'

'You're going to have to explain, Vernon. Where had he been? What happened to him?'

'I'll get to all that later,' said Reid, not quite sure how to proceed. 'When I left for America, you were away, remember?'

'I do. *An Inspector Calls*; I played Sybil Birling. I was away for six months.'

'I forgot to return your keys. I gave them to Will Stark to give back to you before I left.'

'Gosh, yes, I'd forgotten. What a memory you have.'

'So Will and Alma didn't have keys to this house?'

'No. Why are you asking me all this?'

'Bear with me, and I'll explain. When you came back from that tour, did you go into the tin church?'

'I would have done at some point, but not immediately. You know I don't spend time there and never have.' Irene looked totally bewildered at his questions.

Reid looked down at his hands, which were clasped tightly, his knuckles white, and began. 'That night, the night the boys disappeared, they didn't really disappear. They ran away, or at least Jason did. They'd been planning it for weeks. I was going to America, escaping the estate, and they wanted to do the same. I didn't blame them. We promised each other we'd meet up in a few years' time but, well, that never happened. Anyhow, that night while Mum and I were packing, Will turned up at our flat. Mum let him in. He wanted to know if I'd returned your keys and when I said no, he offered to take them. He seemed' – Reid searched for the right word – 'agitated. When he reached out for the keys I noticed blood on his sleeve.'

Irene was now staring at him with her one eye, transfixed.

Reid continued. 'When he left the flat he said he was going home, back to Alma, only I saw him get into Tobias Hoffmann's car – you remember him?'

Irene nodded. 'Alma spent a lot of time with him and his wife – and their foster daughter, the one who died.'

Reid nodded. There was nothing wrong with Irene's memory. 'Tobias was parked behind Coniston House. I thought he was going to drive Stark round to Ullswater and back to his flat, but he didn't, he drove off the estate and I didn't give it too much thought. The next day Mum and I left for America and I forgot about it.'

'What are you saying?'

'When I came back, Will was very kind to me. He spoke to you about giving me a job. He made sure I was okay, that I wasn't struggling. He also made a point of telling me what a terrible few months it had been after I left. About Kevin and Jason disappearing, how the whole estate was questioned by the police. How he'd gone straight home after saying goodbye to me and Mum with no idea of what had happened.'

'Did you tell him you'd seen him leave with Tobias Hoffmann?'

Reid shook his head. 'I had no reason to. I didn't even think about it – at that point as far as I knew Kevin and Jason had run away together as planned. It was only when Jason came back last week and told me Kevin didn't go with him that I started to remember what happened that night.'

Irene was silent, her face giving away nothing. 'What exactly is it you're trying to articulate, Vernon? That Will and Tobias

Hoffmann were somehow involved with whatever happened to Kevin?'

'I don't know. Maybe.' He took a copy of *High Rize* out of his pocket and flicked though the small fanzine until he came to the page he wanted. He'd found it in the old chapel along with Jason's rucksack. Jason must have taken them from the garage on Tuesday when Reid had insisted he leave the estate until things quietened down. He hadn't found the birthday card or drawing of Kevin though. 'Do you recognise this?' He held out the fanzine for Irene.

'What is it?' she asked, taking the copy of *High Rize*.

'It's a fanzine from the nineties. Look at the story.'

Irene examined the fanzine and turned the page, following the comic strip Reid had indicated of a young girl killing her lover. When she looked up, he could have sworn her face was a shade paler. 'Where did you get this?'

'Jason and I found it in Sally Shires' garage. It was Kevin's. He subscribed – that issue arrived after he vanished. It was still in its envelope, unopened.'

Irene said nothing as she stared at the comic-strip images. After a bit she closed the fanzine. 'Has anyone else seen this?'

Reid shook his head. 'Only Jason.'

'There has to be an explanation,' said Irene. 'Someone else could have drawn this.'

Reid's eyes wandered to a framed picture on the wall, a pen and ink drawing of Irene before her accident. He may not have been in Irene's house very often, but it was hard to miss Alma's illustration. And stylistically, it was hard to miss the likeness to the comic in Irene's hands. She followed his gaze.

'It doesn't prove anything,' she said after a few moments.

'There are more,' said Reid. 'More stories. All published after Kevin disappeared. It's all there. A woman falling from the roof. A girl dying in the stairwell. They're all Alma's stories. It's *her*.' He nodded towards the fanzine in her hand. 'The Lady Electra character in that strip is Alma.' Reid paused for a moment before going on. 'David Koresh came to me in a dream a couple of days ago. The world is going to end very soon and I need to put this right before we're all gone.'

'What do you intend to do?' asked Irene, handing the fanzine back.

The one piece of physical evidence that would have proved Alma's involvement with Kevin – the train ticket to Glasgow, which Reid had seen framed in her hall – was now another piece of litter on the estate. Jason had bought the tickets in advance and the ticket in Alma's hall was dated the day he and Kevin planned to run away. What else would Alma be doing with it if she hadn't taken it from Kevin? As far as Reid could see, he only had one option.

'I'm going to find Kevin's body and I think this tells me where he is.' He held it up before slipping the fanzine back in his pocket. 'If I'm right . . .' He didn't need to finish the sentence because Irene understood perfectly well what that would mean. It would mean that her god-daughter was guilty.

CHAPTER 49

Since Irene's visit to RADE an idea had been forming in Connie's mind, which at first had seemed so unlikely she'd actually told herself out loud to get a grip. But the more she thought about it the more she wondered whether it might actually be a possibility. Would Irene be prepared to invest in RADE with some of the money she'd made from the Pinder Wood sale? Of course, and nothing would surprise her about the elderly actress, Irene could be mired in debt. People's private lives were never straightforward. The thought of asking Irene for money made Connie's blood run cold – it wasn't her style and was one of the reasons Bonaro had made such a brilliant custodian of the archive. He was charming and brazen in equal measure. But Connie had to face hard facts: there was a very strong chance she'd be out of a job in three months' time. Even if she wasn't, the situation could easily arise again as she didn't trust Ethan Blunt not to fuck up another business deal. Irene was probably the only rich person Connie knew. What harm could it do to ask?

She'd stayed on late at the archive. The visiting students from Japan had taken up more time than she'd anticipated. When they'd eventually gone it had taken several hours to put everything away. She could have left it until Monday but in truth she was glad of the distraction. Eventually, she decided enough was enough and closed down her computer before pulling down the blinds and switching off the lights. With only the streetlight filtering in from outside, the archive's reading room was full of shadows, the busts in particular forming dark silhouettes of men long dead, and she was glad when she closed the door and made her way downstairs.

It was almost a week since she'd found Will Stark's body hanging in the church at Grasmere and she was still having nightmares about his bloated face. She'd also had several dreams about the estate that had slipped into her subconscious like a poisonous snake. Kevin and Jason had also become a constant presence, ghostly apparitions that hovered at the end of corridors, their faces pale, hands outstretched as if begging for help. However, the dream that had disturbed her most had been about her sister. In the dream, Connie was inhabiting Sarah's body as she climbed the water tower at Blackwater. At the top, she'd looked down and seen the light of Kaplinsky's phone and waved, but next to him were the two pale oval faces of Jason and Kevin. At first Connie had thought they were staring at her, but they weren't. It was at something behind her. Connie woke in a silent scream just as she hit the ground as whatever it was pushed her off the tower. Was this what death felt like? The sensation had been so real she was willing to believe it was. It also prompted her to reconsider meeting with Kaplinsky again to try and persuade him to talk to the police.

She set the alarm in the downstairs hall and stepped outside into the cool evening air, pulling the big oak door closed behind her. Once the alarm had stopped beeping she stood on the pavement for a moment deciding what to do. Go for a drink? It was Saturday night, after all, and there was usually someone she knew in the Pipe and Optic Bar – or the Poptic as it was known to regulars. But she wasn't in the mood, and instead pulled out her phone and brought up Irene's number. She began walking towards the bus stop, and at the end of the street, she finally tapped 'call'. It rang several times before Irene picked up.

'Hello?' said Irene.

'Hi, it's Connie. I wondered whether I could drop by? There's something I wanted to talk to you about.' As soon as she'd asked, Connie regretted not thinking things through before calling. She didn't have a business plan or anything for Irene.

'You mean tonight?' said Irene. Her voice sounded strained.

'Yes, only if it's convenient.'

'I'm afraid that it isn't. Not tonight.' The words were clipped.

'Sorry. I shouldn't have rung on the spur of the moment. Perhaps one day next week.' *You idiot.* At least it would give her some time to prepare what she was going to say. She couldn't expect Irene to agree to hand over a sum of cash without knowing exactly how it would be spent. 'I'll call you after the weekend then.' There was no response although she could hear Irene's gentle breathing. 'Irene, is everything okay?'

'Actually, no, I'm afraid it isn't,' came the reply, after a long pause.

'Is there anything I can do?'

'I don't know . . .'

'What's happened?'

'It's Vernon, my gardener. He's got it into his head my god-daughter, Alma, had something to do with the disappearance of that boy from Grasmere back in the nineties, Kevin.'

Connie's heart skipped a beat, remembering her conversation with Kirby and his suspicions about Alma. 'What makes him think that?' she asked, carefully.

'He's got some old fanzine from the nineties and says the comic strips inside are based on real events that happened on the estate, including Kevin's disappearance. He's convinced Alma drew it.' Irene paused. 'Vernon thinks the world is about to end – that damned Koresh nonsense he believes in – and he's not thinking straight.'

'I still don't understand why he thinks Alma's involved.'

'Because Vernon is convinced one of the comic strips shows where the body of that poor boy Kevin is.' Connie could hear the exasperation in Irene's voice. 'He also mentioned something about a train ticket to Glasgow – apparently that's where the boys were going – and he saw a similar one in Alma's flat dated the day they planned to go.'

'Maybe Alma went to Glasgow at the same time.'

There was a pause. 'No,' said Irene. 'She didn't.'

'Where is the ticket now?' asked Connie, knowing Kirby would want evidence.

'Vernon said Alma threw it away. Let the wind take it from her hand on the balcony outside her flat.'

Bang went Kirby's evidence. 'Did Vernon say where he thinks the body might be?'

'He said the old well – where the tin chapel once stood.'

'A well?' asked Connie. 'I thought the church was built near a spring?'

'There was a well there too. The church was built over it as a sort of protection – people were desperate to take its waters.'

Connie thought for moment, trying to visualise where the tin chapel had stood in relation to the rest of the estate. 'Do you know where this well is, exactly?'

'I don't think it's far from the church that stands on the estate today, but I couldn't tell you any more than that. It was a long time ago and I was younger, my acting career taking off. Vernon said he wants to put things right before it's "too late". I'm worried what he'll do – I've a mind to go to Grasmere myself with my cane and make sure he doesn't do anything stupid.'

'I don't think that's a good idea,' said Connie firmly.

'What if he goes after Alma?'

He'll only do that if he finds something, thought Connie. 'Have you called the police?'

'Vernon made me promise not to. He means to deal with it on his own.'

Connie framed her next question carefully. 'I know it's unpalatable, but is it possible Alma could have had something to do with Kevin's disappearance? You did tell me she changed around that time.' Connie wondered about Will Stark too – could Alma have killed her own father? She was the beneficiary of his pact with Irene's father, after all.

'I don't know what to think . . . Vernon said Will had blood on his clothes that night and he drove off the estate after collecting his spare key to my house.'

'Hang on, Vernon gave Will the keys to your house? Why?'

'Vernon was leaving for America the next day and he'd forgotten to drop them off. Will turned up unannounced while Vernon and his mother were packing and said he'd return them for him.'

'And did he?'

'Yes, when I got back from touring. I'd forgotten all about it but when Vernon mentioned it tonight I remembered Will handing them back. They weren't even for the house, just the main gate and into the grounds so Vernon could work on the garden while I was touring.'

What possible reason could Stark have had for wanting Reid's keys to Irene's garden? He'd collected them – which had to be a gamble because he presumably had no way of knowing Reid had forgotten to drop them off as planned – and then immediately driven off the estate. And he'd had blood on his clothes. It didn't make much sense, unless . . . Connie stopped suddenly in the middle of the pavement as a thought occurred to her, causing a man behind to walk straight into her. He tutted loudly as she stepped aside.

'I'm going to call the police,' she told Irene.

'But—'

'No buts.' After making Irene promise she would not go to Grasmere, Connie hung up and rang Kirby's number as she began to retrace her steps back to the archive. The most plausible version of events was that Vernon had lost the plot – the demolition of Windermere House and then the death of his school friend in a fire seemed like pretty tangible triggers for someone who Kirby said suffered from PTSD. However, if Reid *did* find Kevin's body at the location shown in the comic strip – the old well – that would change everything. After ringing for what seemed like an age, Kirby's phone went to voicemail, so Connie left a message trying to be as succinct as possible, but still managed to sound like she'd swallowed a script to a B-movie.

After disabling the alarm at RADE, Connie raced up the stairs to the main reading room and rifled through the Grasmere drawings until she found a plan of the area around Pinder Wood before it was cleared to make way for the estate. The tin church had originally stood on Chalfont Street, which no longer existed, but Connie had no idea where this actually was in relation to the estate now. She rummaged about a bit more and eventually came across a plan of Grasmere that had been superimposed over an old map of the area, so it was possible to see the original street layouts in relation to the new buildings. It only took her a moment or two to locate Chalfont Street, and as she traced its path with her finger she suddenly realised where it was leading.

'*Got you,*' she whispered.

CHAPTER 50

Reid was nervous. Irene had promised not to call the police but she would eventually, he knew. He just had to hope that she would give him enough time. He'd jimmied his way into the church where Stark's body had been found and was standing in the darkness of the disused building taking in the sounds and smells. He heard an animal – probably a mouse or a rat – somewhere off to his left. A vague whiff of incense hung in the air despite the to-ings and fro-ings of recent days, and he had a flashback to his childhood and the first time his grandmother had taken him to church. He remembered very little of the experience apart from the smell which had stayed with him. He flicked on his torch and ran its beam around the interior, pausing for a moment as it passed over the scaffolding where Stark's body had been found, and shivered.

Now he was here the magnitude of what he was about to do hit him and the beam of light began jumping as his hand shook. Self-doubt was shouldering its way to the front of his thoughts. The voice that could talk you out of doing even the most well-intentioned thing. The anxiety you'd fuck it up so crippling it was easier not to even try. PTSD did that. He'd been so sure about everything when he'd gone to see Irene, but after verbalising his theory out loud even he could see how crazy it sounded. That Alma had killed Kevin and hidden his body on the estate; that the location of the dump site was shown in one of her comic strips in the *High Rize* fanzine; that Alma hadn't just killed Kevin, but possibly Angela Barton, one of the Hoffmanns' foster kids, as well. What part Will Stark and Tobias Hoffmann had played in any of this Reid wasn't entirely sure yet, but what he'd seen on the night Kevin and Jason disappeared gave him cause to think they'd certainly helped cover up whatever had happened to Kev.

With a trembling hand he pulled out the copy of *High Rize* from his pocket and clumsily flicked through the pages until he came to the comic strip that had finally convinced him of Alma's guilt. The images stood out bright under the glare of his torch. In this particular episode, Lady Electra had found out she'd been betrayed by her lover and had killed him in a fit of rage. The drawings showed her taking the body to a small building, a tin church, its corrugated iron exterior a riot of graffiti. Inside, Electra had dragged her dead lover to the font where she lifted the lid and proceeded to push the limp body inside. The next drawing showed her leaving the church and for the first time Reid noticed the graffiti on its door: a depiction of hands clasped in prayer. It was the same drawing that had appeared on the Shires' garage after Kevin's disappearance. So Alma had been responsible for that, too. He felt sick and shoved the fanzine back into his pocket and thought about where to start his search.

He remembered Stark telling him once how he'd tried to build the new church as near as possible to where the old one had stood. In the end it hadn't been feasible to match the location exactly, although the buildings' footprints had overlapped. The belief that healing water sprang from a well situated in the tin church had been the start of its fortune. Miracles were said to happen to those who'd been anointed by water drawn from the well and soon the church was thriving. When the well dried up, the church's fortune reversed. Reid was sure this was where Kevin's body was hidden, in the old healing well. All he had to do was find it.

From what he recalled of Stark's words, the two buildings had only overlapped by a small margin so the old well had to be somewhere near the edge of the current building. It couldn't be outside – there were no outbuildings and there was no way Alma or her father could have concealed a body on a busy estate like Grasmere unless they themselves were hidden in some way. Hoffmann, who was a church elder, would have had a key to the church, and no one would have thought twice about seeing him entering or leaving, even at night. Even if Hoffmann hadn't physically helped – and Reid didn't know if he had – he could certainly have aided the Starks by giving them access to the church.

Reid began walking the periphery of the building, aiming his torch at the ground. He wondered how Kevin's death had actually played out and thought through possible scenarios as he scoured the floor for anything resembling a capped-off well. Had Kevin gone to meet Alma in the tin church on Irene's land? She hung out there sometimes, he knew, because he'd seen her. He listened for any change in the sound of his footsteps on the wooden floor. He wasn't even sure what he was looking for – there was hardly going to be an obvious opening to the old well. Had there been, the police would have found it when they searched the building in the wake of Stark's murder. As he walked around the church, moving chairs and other bits of detritus that had been left behind, his torch fell on the font itself.

The font was near the entrance of the church. On a whim he went over and gave it a hard push. Had this been a scene in *High Rize* it would have slid seamlessly to one side revealing the well below. But of course, it didn't. This was real life. He carried on, occasionally stamping his feet when he thought the ground sounded more hollow than usual, but he saw no hidden doors in the church's floor anywhere. After circling the whole building, he moved to the kitchen area. Here the floor was linoleum, worn and scuffed. It felt solid underfoot, like concrete, with none of the slight give that wood had. A torn patch caught his eye and, crouching down, he began pulling at the corner. The linoleum was brittle and broke off in his hand when he tried to peel it back, but he eventually managed to pull a long strip off and shone his torch on the cracked concrete underneath where small insects scurried away. Nothing. He checked under the sink. He pulled out the old refrigerator where he found the corpses of several dead mice. But there was still no sign of anything that resembled the well.

The only place he hadn't checked was the vestry. It was a small room leading off the main church and had in later years been used to store the old pews. Shining the torch into the small room he now found it full of pigeon droppings. The birds had somehow found a way in before it had been boarded up. It didn't look as though the police had been in here much as the floor was undisturbed. An old pew sat in one corner and at the other end a dusty wooden desk, which had presumably once been Falke's. It was covered in box files and bundles of papers. Reid swept his foot over the floor, leaving an arc through the pigeon droppings, and revealing wooden boards below. He walked up and down, tapping his feet on the ground as he went. He crouched and knocked the floor beneath the desk with his torch. Nothing. He stood up, frustrated. Short of taking up the entire floor he couldn't think what to do next. The floorboards had been laid lengthways, so he could just pull up one or two to see what was beneath the whole length of the room. The crowbar he'd used to break into the church was in the main building, and as he turned to go he noticed a built-in wooden cupboard. It must be where Falke had kept his paraphernalia. The door had a padlock on it, so Reid went back into the church and got the crowbar.

The padlock came off easily and as the doors swung open the musty scent of incense he'd smelt earlier became stronger. Shining his torch inside the cupboard he saw boxes of incense, some nibbled open by mice. The cupboard was quite big. Vestments hung on a rail, but some had been thrown in and lay in a pile on the floor. He moved them to one side and felt a flicker of anticipation as his torch picked out a small, round hole in the floor. On his hands and knees he threw the vestments into the room behind him until he could see properly. A round concrete cover about a metre wide lay flush to the ground, but a small notch had been cut out from the edge that he could easily get two fingers into. Straddling the lid, he hooked his fingers into the small space and pulled. It didn't so much as budge. He grabbed the crowbar and jammed the end of it into the small hole and pushed with all his weight to lever the lid up. He felt it lift slightly. He shone the torch around the room and spotted a broken chair, its wooden legs loose. He had no trouble pulling one off and levering the concrete lid up with his foot on the crowbar, and he managed to slip the chair leg into the gap. Now that he had a better grip, he braced himself and slid the lid to one side.

Reid paused for a moment, panting after the effort, the smell of damp and decay rising up from whatever was down there. The feeling of nausea returned as the full impact of what he was about to do gripped him. If he was right, then he was metres away from the corpse of his old friend. And if he was wrong? Then all of this was for nothing. He'd never be able to look Irene in the eye again, let alone work for her. *Lord, grant me strength,* he whispered.

Steeling himself, he reached for the torch and aimed it at the black void in front of him. The side of the well was made of brick, and as he shone the torch beam down into the narrow shaft he saw something wrapped in black plastic. It was wedged in the narrow space about twenty feet down. But there was something else.

He angled the torch to get a better view.

The drowning sensation came over him so suddenly that he feared he might fall into the well. Where the plastic had ripped he could see a Converse trainer. It was the type Kevin used to wear. Attached to it was a leg.

He recoiled, dropping the torch, which clattered into the shaft. He scrabbled to get up, almost losing his footing as though the well were pulling him down. Stumbling out of the vestry he ran blindly towards the front entrance of the church. He could barely breathe, his lungs fighting for every breath. Tears streamed down his face. *Eternal rest grant unto them, Oh Lord. Amen. Amen.*

Bursting out into the fresh air he frantically gulped in deep breaths. His body numb with shock, he sank to his knees and began to pray. *Dear Lord, take Kevin into your Kingdom. Keep him safe until those that are left are called and can join him at your table. Amen.* He'd found Kevin. Sally would finally have her son back. His quest was almost over.

Slowly, he began to stand and as he did so something caught his eye in the distance. A flash of light on the other side of the wood. A firework? He moved to get a better sightline through the trees and saw a strange orange glow over Coniston House. Now it was moving, dancing in the night sky and a shiver ran down his spine as a new horror manifested itself.

Reid ran as fast as he could through Pinder Wood. He tripped on several occasions and by the time he emerged out of the trees at the other side, his face was scratched and bloodied. He stood for a moment on the edge of the children's playground to catch his breath and gazed up at his block of flats. Sparks were flying from the roof, shooting over the edge like molten rain. The pigeon loft was on fire. He sprinted across the old playground and straight into the main entrance where he took the stairs at breakneck speed. By the time he'd reached his floor the smell of smoke was pungent in his throat and he fought the panic that was threatening to take over. His legs felt weak and his body was now resisting every step as he climbed the last flight up to the roof.

He was almost at the top when he heard the noise. His gut twisted as he recognised the sound of terrified and injured birds and he raced up the final flight of stairs as fast as he could.

At the top, the fire door was open, and he lurched through it on to the roof where he was met by an apocalyptic scene. The blackened bodies of birds lay scattered across the flat roof, some still alive and flailing about. There was nothing he could do to save the pigeon coop, or the pigeons, and he watched helplessly as the wooden structure collapsed on itself, the fire crackling and popping like a box of popcorn in the oven.

The smoke was being blown towards him and he felt it catch in the back of his throat as he tried to see through it for any sign of who might have done this. He suddenly became aware of something moving behind him and turned back towards the stairwell, but it was too late. The door was closed. In front of it stood Alma, something heavy in her hand, coming towards him.

CHAPTER 51

'Alma Stark had a non-molestation order placed on her in 2010,' said Kobrak. 'Her ex-partner brought it on after their relationship broke down. He doesn't live in the UK any more but I managed to speak to him in Austria. He split up with Alma because he found her controlling and unreasonable. He had a daughter from a previous relationship and he was worried Alma might harm or interfere with her.'

'How long was the order in place?' asked Kirby. The Grasmere team – minus Hamer, who'd been held up by the traffic – had assembled to go over everything they had so far, which didn't feel like very much to Kirby. After talking to Sally Shires he'd tried to visit Anderson but his partner had been with the consultant and so he'd left without seeing him. He was tired and wanted nothing more than to be at home on the boat with a good film. The chances of that were slim until this case was over. On Monday the contractors would descend on Grasmere and begin their slow dismantling of the rest of the estate, and Kirby felt as though it would somehow signify the end of one part of their investigation.

'Three months,' said Kobrak, in answer to his question. 'It worked though. Alma didn't breach it and the ex didn't hear from her again.'

'Good work, Steve. Anything from the place in Camden where Alma worked?'

'I managed to track down someone who worked with her there who told me she was odd. She cited an incident where one of her co-workers, who Alma had been very friendly with, had been offered another job and had accepted it. Given the competitive nature of the environment, she'd kept it quiet – no one at the office knew until she announced it one evening in the pub. Alma went berserk. Threw her drink over her. Caused a right scene, apparently. People viewed her differently after and kept their distance. In the end, Alma left and set up her own business, EyeCons.'

'Okay,' said Drayton. 'So we know Alma can be volatile. So can a lot of folk, but they don't kill people.'

'True,' said Kirby, who was building a rather wild theory he wasn't sure he was quite ready to voice. 'But there is a pattern here. All those people – the ex and his kid, the friend from work, the Hoffmanns' foster daughter, Angela, and even Alma's mother – were leaving. They weren't all leaving Alma per se, but they were leaving the environment in which she knew them. And then there's Kevin. If Alma was his secret girlfriend, or just a close friend he kept hidden from Jason, then she was set to lose him as well, because he was planning on running away with his best mate. Only something stopped Kevin from going. Sally Shires saw them together so we know they knew one another.'

'But they're not all dead,' said Masters. 'And as far as we know, Will Stark wasn't about to abandon his daughter.'

'And why would she kill her father?' asked Drayton. 'And maybe Alma and Kevin didn't know each other well. Lew, mate, I hate to say this, but I think this business with Pete's accident is getting to you. Maybe Alma is a bit barmy, so what? None of this gets us any nearer finding out who killed William Stark and Jason Roye.'

The small group fell silent. Kirby hated it when Drayton called him mate, but perhaps he was right and Kirby was seeing connections when there weren't any. Yet he felt convinced that somehow it all linked up – he just didn't know how.

The silence was broken by the lift doors opening and Hamer strode out clutching a folder in his hand that he held up. 'Final results are in from the church and the garage.' He didn't even bother taking his coat off and came straight over to the small group.

'Have Forensics found something?' Drayton asked.

'They have,' said Hamer. 'The church, as we all know, was a nightmare to process – public building, covered in prints, some more recent than others but no way of knowing when any of them had been left. However' – he paused for effect – 'there was a hair. It was caught between Stark's neck and the rope – the follicle was intact.'

Kirby knew humans could shed up to a hundred hairs a day quite naturally, but not with the follicle attached. 'So someone got their hair caught as they were putting the noose around his neck.'

'Wouldn't they need long hair for it to get caught and pulled out like that?' asked Masters.

'However it got there,' said Hamer, 'it gives us DNA and it also tells us whoever it belongs to dyes their hair blond.'

Kirby mentally went through the residents on the estate and could only think of one person who visibly dyed their hair. 'Mary Hoffmann has blonde streaks. And her hair is long. Plus, we know Tobias Hoffmann went out that night. He was seen by Dan Scribbs.'

'Who's unreliable and doesn't like the Hoffmanns,' said Drayton, distracted by something on his phone.

'We still don't have enough to request a DNA sample from Mary Hoffmann,' said Hamer.

'Bingo,' said Drayton, brandishing his phone. 'Stark's mobile phone data and guess what? Stark had a call from Tobias Hoffmann the night he died.'

'What time?' asked Kirby, feeling the familiar surge of adrenaline that came with a breakthrough in a case.

'Seven forty-five. It lasted less than thirty seconds.'

'Any other calls that night? Or texts?' Hamer asked.

'Only his daughter. That was at seven, which backs up what she told us.'

'A call lasting thirty seconds is either the wrong number or just enough time to arrange to meet someone,' said Kirby. 'It's definitely time to pay the Hoffmanns a visit in their new home.'

'Agreed,' said Hamer. 'Mark, you go and take Romy with you. Lew, I want a word.'

Drayton's face looked like thunder as he and Masters gathered their things and headed towards the lift.

'Why did you do that?' Kirby asked his boss when they'd gone.

'Mark is a good detective but needs to get over his problem with Romy, whatever it is, and she can learn from him. Trust me, they'll be fine.'

That wasn't exactly what Kirby had meant when he'd asked. He was the one who'd spoken to the Hoffmanns previously and it seemed logical he should speak to them now, but something in Hamer's demeanour made him decide not to pursue it as he followed him into his office.

'Close the door and sit down,' said Hamer, taking off his coat and settling behind his desk, a serious look on his face.

'What's going on? It's not Pete, is it?' asked Kirby, suddenly worried.

'No, nothing like that. I had a call from Brian Kaplinsky earlier.'

'What the hell did he want?'

'He alleges you've been harassing him about Sarah Darke's accident.'

'That's not true,' said Kirby.

'He says you implied he had something to do with her death and said as much to his wife.'

'*What?*' Kirby thought back to his brief conversation with Kaplinsky's wife and although it had been tempting to drop him in the marital shit – somewhere he was obviously used to being, hence his stint at Grasmere – he'd refrained.

'He also said Sarah's sister, Connie Darke, spoke to him about it and accused him of being involved. But that's not all, Lew.' Hamer leant forward and lowered his voice, even though no one outside could hear. 'He knows about Patrick Calder.'

Fuck, thought Kirby. Patrick Calder had been a property developer Hamer had had an affair with a year or so ago. He'd also been Kaplinsky's boss at Blackwater. 'How?'

'I don't know but he says he has proof.'

Probably photographs or film. Kirby rubbed his eyes and was about to open his mouth to speak when Hamer cut him off.

'It means you have to leave him alone and so does Miss Darke. I'm not even going to ask what's going on with you two—'

Kirby held up his hand to interrupt his boss. 'Look, Kaplinsky told Connie there was someone else at Blackwater the night Sarah fell and that whoever it was, they were at the top of the water tower when the accident happened. Kaplinsky says he never went up the tower, that he stayed on the ground the whole time. He saw her fall.'

'And you believe him?'

Kirby shrugged. 'I don't know what to believe. Kaplinsky's lying about his wife though. I didn't mention any of what I've just told you in my conversation with her and I have no idea why he'd lie about it.'

Hamer regarded him. 'We have to leave this alone, Lew. Unless there's compelling new evidence to the contrary, Sarah Darke's accident was just that. Kaplinsky could make things very difficult for both of us.'

They sat in silence for a few moments, Kirby thinking over what Hamer had just said. He was right: if Kaplinsky went public with information that the DCI on the Blackwater case had had an affair with the prime suspect and one of his officers had known about it and said nothing, then all sorts of shit would hit the fan. Kirby stood up, keeping his anger in check. 'Is that all?'

'For now, yes. Go and do your job and find out who killed William Stark and Jason Roye.'

Kirby left Hamer's office and felt like punching something. Kaplinsky was one grade-A slippery bastard. That he'd lied to Hamer about what he'd said to his wife made Kirby more convinced than ever that he was hiding something about Sarah Darke's death. As if on cue his phone pinged and he saw Connie's name flash up. A missed call and a voicemail. He played back the message and didn't even get halfway to his desk before heading straight back to Hamer's office.

'What is it?' Hamer asked, looking up.

'Vernon Reid thinks he knows where Kevin Shires' body is. He's at Grasmere searching for it now.'

CHAPTER 52

Once Connie had decided to go to Grasmere she couldn't get there fast enough. The bus journey was painfully slow, and she reacquainted herself with several swear words she hadn't used in years as well as inventing a few new ones. Intermittent thunderstorms mixed with weekend roadworks and a strike on London's underground had slowed heavy traffic and shortened tempers. By the time she got off at the stop nearest to the estate she felt ready to scream with pent-up frustration. She quickly dodged through the pedestrian barrier at the Grayshott Road entrance and made her way on to the estate. It had stopped raining and she paused briefly and glanced towards Pinder Hill and Irene's house, hoping she had heeded Connie's advice to stay put.

Irene had been right when she said the tin chapel's original location hadn't been far from where the current church stood today. In fact, she'd been more than right – the footprints of the two churches overlapped, the current vestry situated on part of the plot the small chapel had once occupied. At a guess, this was where the old healing well had been situated. Circumventing the large puddles that had accumulated after the rain, Connie picked her way through the outskirts of the estate towards the church. She'd never been here at night and hadn't been prepared for how dark it was. The buildings cast thick shadows that seemed to physically cling to her. The open areas where she thought she could see more were deceptive and twice she tripped on loose tarmac, reminding her that her ankle was still tender from her fall at the tin chapel.

Passing the block of maisonettes she was momentarily grateful for a lone light outside one of the flats, but it was short-lived as it made everything around it disappear into a black void. She encountered no one as she made her way to the church. Her eyes finally adjusted to the differing shades of darkness, although Pinder Wood, which was now ahead of her, was the blackest of black, a dense foreboding mass of vegetation. Ullswater House was off to her left and she'd just veered to the right, towards the church, when a noise made her stop. Something moved in the shadows up ahead, and she heard the sound of footsteps. Someone was running. A figure tore into the woods from the direction of the church. It was too dark and Connie was too far away to be able to see who it was, or even if it was male or female. Could it be Reid? And what had made him run?

She cautiously continued along the path until she reached the entrance to the church. From here she had a clearer view across the estate and immediately saw the likely reason for the sprinting figure. Something was burning in Coniston House. Was it Reid's flat, or something on the roof? She couldn't tell. Without going through the woods – and there was no way she was doing that – it would take her a good ten minutes to get to there, if not more. The pedestrian walkways were bad enough during the day but at night they'd be lethal. She pulled out her phone and sent Kirby a short message, *Coniston Hs on fire*. She waited for a moment in case he replied, but when he didn't she turned her attention back to the church.

As soon as she reached the door she had that *Groundhog Day* feeling. Just as it had been on the day she found Will Stark's body, the door was ajar and the church interior pitch-black, but more so as there was no light to filter in from outside. Apart from a car engine in the distance it was silent. She switched on her torch and stepped inside. The first thing she saw was the scaffolding from which Stark had been hung and she shivered. From the church plans she knew the vestry was off to the right, and with a sense of foreboding she made her way across the church as quietly and quickly as she could.

As she neared the vestry her pace slowed. There was something about the quality of light beyond the door that gave her pause. Killing the light on her phone, she slipped it into her pocket and cautiously approached. She paused on the threshold, her eyes adjusting to the dimness. The room was still and silent but the sensation that someone had been there recently hung in the air. What looked like vestments lay scattered across the floor and in the corner something glowed, flickering every now and then. Stepping into the room, she moved closer to the source of the light and as she did so, the smell of church incense became stronger and stronger: pungent and musty.

The light was coming from below ground, in some sort of large cupboard, and as she drew closer Connie saw what she instinctively knew was the old healing well. A concrete cover had been pulled to one side and the light was coming from deep below. A sudden fear gripped her; in her mind's eye she could see a hand grasping the side of the hole, a body hauling itself out and a decaying Kevin Shires crawling across the floor towards her, shedding bone and skin as he went. '*Fuck's sake, get a grip,*' she muttered. After vowing to never watch another zombie movie again, she inched closer and peered into the well.

A small torch was wedged between a rotting Converse trainer and the brick wall of the shaft. The Converse was protruding from a black plastic wrapped package and with horror she realised there was a leg attached to it. She instinctively recoiled and stepped back, but a pair of hands gripped her arms from behind. Grasping her tightly, they propelled her towards the well, where she teetered on the edge. She let out a scream and tried to wriggle free, but it was too late. One foot was already over the void, and although she pushed back with all her might she was no match for whoever was holding her and she felt herself tipping forward.

Suddenly the hands let go, and she was falling. Her own hands shot up to grab hold of anything they could, only to graze the top ridge of the opening, then frantically claw at the brick wall of the well as she tumbled, bouncing off the sides, eventually landing on the body of Kevin Shires with a sickening snap of bone.

CHAPTER 53

When Reid blinked his eyes open it took him a few moments to remember what had happened. He recalled stepping on to the roof of the flats and feeling the heat of the fire, his beloved pigeons dead and dying across the roof. Then everything went blank. He was still on the roof and lying face down, the asphalt pressing uncomfortably into his cheek. From where he was lying he could see he was next to one of the two graffiti-tagged air vents that sat at each end of the roof of Coniston House. Slowly, more details filtered back. Alma had screamed like a wild banshee before hitting him full force with the fire extinguisher. How he'd got on this side of the air vent, he had no idea. Perhaps Alma had dragged him there. Or maybe they'd fought, he couldn't remember. But she hadn't killed him – yet.

One arm was flung out above his head; the other lay trapped under his chest. He gently eased it out, feeling pins and needles stab at the numb limb. When sensation had returned, he very carefully rolled on to his back, a sharp pain shooting through his temple as he moved. As the pain subsided and the feeling started to come back to the left side of his face he stared up into the night sky. Although his head was throbbing from Alma's blow, the anxiety he'd felt earlier had gone. In its place hyperreality, a symptom of his PTSD that exaggerated his senses. The stars above him seemed to shine more brightly than he'd ever seen, and the moon, a thin sliver, was like a glimpse into a bright world beyond the dark curtain of the sky. He imagined David Koresh there waiting for him. Suddenly a voice entered his perception, and for a brief moment he thought David was talking to him. But it wasn't David – it was Tobias Hoffmann. What the hell was he doing here?

Straining to hear what Hoffmann was saying, he then heard another voice. It was Alma's. She and Hoffmann were arguing. Reid tried to concentrate and piece together what they were talking about. Something about Tobias going to the church and finding someone there who he'd pushed into the well. *It has to be the police*, thought Reid. Who else could it be? Whoever it was, it wasn't his problem, although he was surprised to find himself hoping it wasn't DI Kirby. If anyone was going to untangle this sordid mess after Reid had finished it would be him. It was then he remembered the gun.

Coming up to the roof hadn't been part of Reid's plan and he realised with hindsight that Alma had lured him up there by setting the pigeon loft on fire. Still, as locations went, the roof was as good a place as any to put an end to all this, plus he now had the added bonus of Tobias being there too. Alma seemed to have forgotten him for the time being, distracted by Hoffmann's arrival. Reid didn't know how long that would last so he began crawling commando style around the air vent towards the box where he kept bits of paraphernalia for the birds. The asphalt felt like sandpaper on his hands and he stopped for a moment, lost in the beauty of its surface. Tiny shards of sand, each grain faceted and glinting in what little light there was. He was jolted out of his reverie by Tobias shouting at Alma. Time was running out.

The box contained bits of pigeon food, ankle tags for the birds, his blow torch – and a more recent acquisition. It never ceased to amaze Reid what people left behind on an estate like Grasmere.

The trick was knowing where to look, and Jason had known exactly where to look. Not that he had, but he'd regaled Reid with stories of his father's exploits on the estate which meant Jason knew every hiding place going. After he'd been killed in the fire, Reid had sought those hiding places out. Most had been empty, but not all. He'd found all sorts of things he wasn't interested in – drugs, small amounts of money, compromising photographs – but in one place he'd found what he was looking for and he'd taken it and stashed it.

One of the many things he'd learned in Texas was how to shoot, something, before he left the UK, he never thought he'd have cause to do. How wrong he'd been. When the FBI had first raided the compound in Waco in February 1993 – an operation that would lead to the full-blown siege – Reid had fought back against the ATF agents. He couldn't be sure he'd hit anyone but four federal agents had died during the two-hour confrontation and although killing anything – human or otherwise – was against his nature, defending himself and his fellow Branch Davidians in the compound was something he hadn't thought twice about. Later, as the siege neared its endgame, he'd also learned what it meant to kill in order to end suffering.

In the days and months following the siege at Mount Carmel his mother had dominated his dreams. He'd found her trapped and burned under the rubble of a wall demolished by one of the FBI's tanks. She'd been alive, just, and the look in her eyes when Reid had found her had been all he'd needed to end her pain. The dreams had eased over the years, but the demolition of Windermere House on his doorstep had brought them back, along with anxiety and panic attacks. That he was, once again, contemplating pulling the trigger was not something he took lightly.

But Alma had done a wicked, wicked thing in killing Kevin. Her involvement in the death of the Hoffmanns' foster daughter would never be proved and for a brief moment Reid wondered if

307

he could be wrong, but he didn't think so. The box was now within reach and still no one had come to look for him. He slowly lifted himself on to one elbow and carefully undid the catch on the box. Holding his breath, he eased his hand under the lid and groped inside for the gun. After what seemed like an age, he felt the cold metal barrel of the Russian Baikal pistol in his palm. As quietly as he could, he lifted it from the box.

CHAPTER 54

Kirby had seen the flames before they'd reached the estate. Kobrak was with him and they'd just come to a halt outside Coniston House when Kirby's phone rang. Drayton's name flashed on screen.

'Mark, what is it?'

'Tobias Hoffmann's not at the new place,' said Drayton. 'His wife says he's gone to Grasmere. Left over an hour ago.'

'Did she say why?'

'No. She's refusing to talk until he's back.'

'Damn it,' said Kirby. 'Have Romy stay with Mary Hoffmann and get yourself over to the estate. Steve and I have just arrived and there's a fire on the roof of Coniston House. It must be Reid's pigeon loft.'

'Okay. I'm—' The line went dead.

Kirby looked at his phone to find the signal had disappeared. *Damned place.*

'What's happened?' asked Kobrak.

'Hoffmann's not at home. He told Mary he was coming here,' said Kirby, noticing a WhatsApp message had come in from Connie about the fire. 'Connie sent a message about the fire earlier. It's only just come in.'

'She's here too?' Kobrak sounded incredulous.

'I bloody hope not. Come on,' said Kirby, getting out of the car. 'Stab vests – you never know.' He popped the boot and they both put on their standard-issue vests, cumbersome and uncomfortable, which could be the difference between life or death. A telltale plume of smoke spiralled into the sky from the top of the block of flats and sparks flew off the roof. Kirby doubted Reid would set fire to his own pigeon loft, not after what happened at Waco and more recently to Jason Roye in the Shires' garage. So that left Hoffmann – or Alma.

'Why would Hoffmann come back?' asked Kobrak as they approached the main entrance.

It was a good question. He'd called Stark on the night of his murder, they knew that. What they didn't know was why. Had they arranged to meet in the church and something went wrong? They'd come to the estate ostensibly to look for Reid in his quest to find Kevin's body, because if Irene Fontaine was to be believed, Reid was convinced Kevin Shires had been murdered by Alma Stark and his body hidden on the estate, possibly by her father. Kirby's suspicions about Alma had been mocked in the meeting, but if Reid could produce evidence then they might have enough to bring her in for questioning. None of it, however, explained what had brought Hoffmann back to the estate.

The lobby was dark and quiet as they entered but no sooner had they started up the stairs than they heard the lift on its way down. They paused and waited as it came to a stop with a deafening jangle of metal. The doors shuddered open, spilling flickering white light into the darkened foyer. A fox strolled out with something dark and smouldering in its mouth and ambled over to the front door where it squeezed itself through a hole in the broken glass. A faint whiff of barbeque lingered in its wake.

'I thought the lifts were out of action?' said Kobrak as they climbed the stairs.

'They seem to operate on a completely ad-hoc basis like everything around here.' Kirby couldn't help but think of his partner as Kobrak positively bounced up the stairs like a puppy. Had Anderson been there he'd have moaned continuously. The higher they climbed the stronger the smell of burning became. By the time they reached Reid's floor Kirby was getting breathless – if the FFI didn't kill him the stairs at Grasmere would – and he was glad when they reached the fire door to the roof and couldn't go any further. The door was ajar, the fire extinguisher that had propped it open on his previous visit was missing. This struck him as odd given the fire hadn't been put out. The smell of burnt meat and woodsmoke was pungent in the air.

'I can hear voices,' whispered Kobrak.

Kirby slowly pushed the fire door open and stepped on to the roof, Kobrak close behind. The voices drifted in and out of focus, carried by the wind, much like the smell. Smoke was drifting towards them from the pigeon loft making visibility difficult, but he could make out dark shapes on the ground. Some of them were moving and he realised they were Reid's pigeons. He stifled a gag when he understood what the fox had been carrying.

About ten feet away he spotted two figures on the roof. A lull in the wind afforded him snatches of conversation and he realised it was Alma and Hoffmann. They hadn't seen him or Kobrak yet and he indicated to the DS to hold back for a moment. He wanted to hear what they were saying.

'Did . . . see you . . .' Alma was asking.

'. . . I . . . chance,' Hoffmann replied.

'. . . sure?'

'Yes!' Hoffmann shouted this time. 'What are we going to do? Why did you have to . . .'

The next part was muffled and Kirby couldn't make out what was being said, but Hoffmann sounded upset. He scanned the roof, which was even bigger than he remembered, and wondered where Reid was. If he'd been searching for Kevin's body on the estate and seen the fire he would probably have come running. Reid also had a hose in his polytunnel which he ran on to the roof when he was cleaning the pigeon loft, but there was no sign of it now. Surely the first thing Reid would have done would be to extinguish the fire? There was something about this he didn't like. He cleared his throat. The sound made Alma and Hoffmann turn in unison.

'What happened?' asked Kirby, looking at what was left of the burning pigeon loft.

It was Alma who answered, greyhound fast. 'We saw the fire and came up here to help but . . .' She shrugged as though there was nothing to be done. She was wearing a pair of decorator's overalls covered in paint splashes, her hair in disarray.

Kirby's eyes rested on the fire extinguisher lying near the air vent. Something dark trickled down its side.

'It's like most things on the estate, it doesn't work any more,' Alma said, pre-empting his question.

Hoffmann looked terrible. Soot smudged his bald pate as he constantly rubbed it, and his eyes were red from smoke.

'I'm glad I've found you, Mr Hoffmann. Your wife said you'd be here somewhere.'

Hoffmann's eyes widened. 'You've spoken to Mary?'

'Two officers are with her now at your new address.'

'W-why? What is it you want?'

'We found out that you called Will Stark on the night he was killed. I was rather hoping you could tell me what you spoke about and why you failed to mention it.'

'Toby?' Alma turned to Hoffmann. 'You didn't tell me you'd spoken to Dad.'

'I . . . I must have forgotten.' He laughed. 'Silly me. I've been so tied up with the move. The new church . . . I must have . . .'

'Forgotten,' filled in Kirby. 'So you said. Well, perhaps you'd like to come with me and explain.'

'Um . . . tomorrow?' Hoffmann asked.

'No, Mr Hoffmann, now.' He glanced towards the pigeon coop which was still burning and suddenly remembered Reid's blow torch. It would have blown by now if it had been in the coop but nevertheless, Kirby wanted to get everyone off the roof as soon as possible. 'We should all head back downstairs. The fire brigade will be here soon. Have you seen Mr Reid? I need a word with him too.'

'I'll pass on the message,' said Alma. 'When I see him next.'

Kirby was about to usher Hoffmann and Alma towards the exit when a voice made him stop.

'That won't be necessary.'

The voice belonged to Reid, who'd appeared from behind the air vent, smoke curling around his body before slithering off into the night air. A large gash ran across the top of his left eye, which was swollen but still open. Blood dripped down the side of his face. But it was his hands that held Kirby's attention. Steady as a rock, they gripped a gun that he raised and pointed at Alma's head.

CHAPTER 55

Connie's throat was raw from screaming, her voice now little more than a croak. She'd been lucky; Kevin Shires' decomposing corpse had broken her fall into the old well. Not that it had felt like luck at the time. The torch that had drawn her to the well in the first place had broken when she fell, leaving her in complete darkness. Panic and revulsion had consumed her as she'd tried not to touch the remains, but it had been impossible. The tear in the plastic sheeting where she'd initially seen the foot must have ripped further, the body spilling out. In her frenzy to get away from Kevin's decaying skeleton she'd felt hair and bone and something soft that had caused her to retch repeatedly. It was like drowning without the water, a sense of continually being pulled down. Eventually, with her back rammed against the side of the well, she'd managed to brace both feet on the opposite side of the circular shaft and push herself about a foot up before her strength evaporated. It wasn't very comfortable, and she didn't know how long she'd be able to maintain the position, but it was better than the terror of trampling Kevin's dead body. It also gave her a moment to take stock and try to figure out what to do next.

Miraculously, apart from her hands, which were grazed raw and bleeding, she was mostly uninjured in any serious way. Her shoulder, still bruised from where Irene had bashed her with the cane, had been knocked in the fall, and her ankle was smarting, but it could have been a lot worse. Controlled breathing was usually her go-to for staying calm, but not wanting to breathe in any more of the fetid air than she had to meant her breaths were coming in short, sharp bursts. With great effort she concentrated on trying to regulate herself, angling her head upwards as far away from the corpse as possible. She needed to focus and stay calm. She had to get out.

Praying it hadn't slipped out of her pocket, she groped awkwardly with one hand for her phone, the other arm still pressed against the well's brickwork. When she felt the hard, flat shape of it she could have cried. Gripping it as though her life depended on it, she pulled it out. Using only one hand to navigate the screen was difficult, especially when that hand was shaking and smeared with blood, and she nearly dropped it several times before finally managing to swipe upwards to switch the torch on.

Deliberately avoiding shining the light downwards – she didn't want to see the horror of what lay below – she angled it up towards the top of the well. Relief flooded through her: whoever had pushed her in hadn't replaced the cover. She estimated she was probably about fifteen or twenty feet from the surface but in truth it could be much more. Her legs were now beginning to sing with the effort of holding her body in such a confined space so, gripping the phone between her teeth and pressing both hands against the back wall, she managed to adjust herself into a slightly more comfortable position. It wasn't going to be sustainable for long though, and she took the phone out of her mouth and checked the signal strength. Unsurprisingly, there wasn't any. Not only was she down a fucking well, but it was in the black hole of Grasmere where anything electrical or digital seemed to operate on some astral level no one could control. It was like the Bermuda Triangle of Wandsworth.

She tried to think rationally. Kirby had the map she'd sent him from RADE but who knew how long it would take him to get here? Right now, he was probably looking for Reid and Alma. It might take him hours to find her and that's if he'd even had time to read her text. What if he'd been too busy? Or had his phone switched off? Panic reared up again and she could feel herself starting to hyperventilate, a searing pain in her chest almost causing her to fall. *A heart attack now would be the icing on the fucking cake.* Then another thought occurred to her; what if her assailant returned and pulled the well cover back over? Salty tears ran down her face and she cried out again, a hoarse cry that bounced off the walls of the narrow shaft. But there was no one there to hear her. Only the twisted body of Kevin Shires, lying cold and silent below.

CHAPTER 56

There was little doubt in Kirby's mind that Reid knew how to handle a gun – probably most of Koresh's acolytes at Mount Carmel knew how to shoot.

'Why did you do it, Alma?' Reid asked. 'Why did you kill Kevin?'

Hoffmann gaped at her, and was about to speak when Reid continued.

'And don't think I don't know what part you played in this, Tobias. Kevin's blood is on your hands too – you helped hide his body.'

Hoffmann groaned but made no attempt at denying it.

'Vernon,' Kirby interjected. 'Give me the gun. It's not the way to solve this.' Reid looked more in control than Kirby had ever seen him.

'You know I'm not going to do that, DI Kirby, and I think you might even understand why.'

'Like I said before, this isn't America, Vernon. You need to put the gun down before the rest of the cavalry arrives. I won't shoot you, but I can't speak for the Armed Response Unit.' Out of the corner of his eye he saw Kobrak unclip his ASP baton.

'At least you're honest,' said Reid. 'But you and I both know that by the time they get here this will be over.'

Reid was probably right. At the moment no one knew what was happening on the roof. Drayton would turn up in the next half hour, but anything could happen between now and then. Before Kirby could respond, Reid turned his attention back to Alma.

'You haven't answered my question,' he said. 'Why did you kill Kevin?'

'Jesus, Vernon. You're like a stuck record with your crazy theories,' replied Alma. 'No one's going to believe you.'

At this, Reid took a step closer. 'I know about the well, Alma. I found Kevin's body.'

Although she did her best to disguise it, Alma took a sharp intake of breath.

'I'd just found him when I saw the fire up here,' Reid went on. 'And I was stupid enough to come running, just like you knew I would.' He turned to Kirby and Kobrak. 'Kevin's in the vestry. There's an old well. I'd planned on bringing him out, but instead I find myself up here with his murderer.'

Kirby's mind was racing. Reid had found a body, which changed everything. But he still had to be sure. 'How did you know where to look, Vernon?'

Keeping the gun trained on Alma, Reid reached into his pocket with his other hand and produced a small magazine. 'It's all here if you read the signs.' He threw the magazine towards Kirby, who caught it mid-air. 'Page twelve. The comic strip shows the church that used to be here, Saint Agatha's. But I knew Kevin wasn't there because that church now belongs to Alma's godmother. Will Stark had it moved.'

'For God's sake,' muttered Alma under her breath.

'But you'll notice the street name,' Reid went on. 'Chalfont Street is where Saint Agatha's once stood. It's where the current vestry of All Hallows now stands.' He turned to Alma. 'And you drew it.'

'What?' Hoffmann looked to Alma, confusion all over his face. 'This is ridiculous!' said Alma, ignoring Hoffmann as though he didn't exist. 'Aren't you going to do something, Detective? The man's mentally unstable. He thinks the world is about to end. He thinks David bloody Koresh is about to appear.' She was now gesticulating wildly in Reid's direction. 'It's all rubbish.' Beside her, Hoffmann looked as though he were about to have a coronary.

Kirby quickly skimmed the comic strip. A church; someone hiding a body beneath a font; the clasped hands graffitied on the outside of the church very similar to those on Sally Shires' garage door. 'So our handwriting and drawing analysts won't find any correlation between these,' Kirby held up the fanzine, 'and the drawings in your flat? Or the anonymous birthday card Kevin received signed with the peace sign?'

'Or the drawing of Kevin that was slipped inside,' cut in Reid. He glanced at Kirby. 'I didn't tell you about that but it was a very good likeness. Drawn by someone with talent.' His focus shifted back to Alma.

'What card? What drawing? I have no idea what you're on about.' Her voice was losing some of the assurance it had had before.

'You knew Kevin Shires, didn't you?' Kirby went on. 'He delivered newspapers to your godmother. You swapped fanzines, like this one.' Alma was becoming more and more agitated.

'No! I mean . . . you've got this all wrong. You're as mad as he is,' Alma said, looking at Reid.

'Not if we can prove you drew the comic strip showing the location of Kevin's body. And that's before we've even made a start on processing Kevin's remains.'

A dying pigeon fluttered at Alma's feet and with an air of barely concealed rage she casually stomped on its head, killing it. Hoffmann gagged, covering his mouth. Reid stared at Alma with pure hatred and in Kirby's mind the gesture confirmed what he and Reid already knew; Alma was a killer.

'You've known about this for years, haven't you, Tobias?' said Reid, now rounding on Hoffmann. 'You helped cover it up with Will. In fact, you went to the vestry tonight. I heard you telling Alma just now. What were you going to do? Move the body?'

'I . . . I . . . don't know what you're talking about,' Hoffmann said feebly.

'Don't lie to me Tobias, I heard you. Someone else was there too. Was it the police? Beat you to it, did they?'

Kirby had no idea what Reid was talking about. No officer had been despatched to the church and yet Hoffmann was shaking his head in the way only a guilty man could. Then an unpleasant thought occurred to him. 'Mr Hoffmann, who else was in the church this evening?'

'I . . . no one. I wasn't there. I . . .'

'I heard you!' shouted Reid and pointed the gun at him. 'I swear to God, Tobias, I will kill you right now—'

'The girl! The girl who found Will's body,' said Hoffmann, panicking. 'She was there when I arrived.'

'Where is she now?' demanded Kirby.

'I . . . oh God, it was an accident. I swear.' Hoffmann was holding up his hands as if he were in a Western.

Kirby had to stop himself lunging at him. 'What was an accident?' he asked, trying to keep his voice even. 'What have you done with her?'

Hoffmann was falling to pieces before their very eyes. 'She was just there, standing by the edge of the well. I'd gone there because . . .' He looked at Alma, who glared at him. 'Never mind . . . She didn't hear me, the girl. I saw her looking into the well, and then she suddenly stepped back . . . she bumped into me,

I . . . I grabbed her. I didn't push her . . . she just fell.' Hoffmann was crying now.

Kirby turned to Reid. He had to hope Reid was the man he thought he was. 'Vernon, listen to me. This is my DS, Steve Kobrak.' He gestured. 'You're going to let him leave right now, yes? He'll walk away and go straight to the church. You don't want another death on your conscience, I know you don't. The girl, whose name's Connie, by the way, has nothing to do with this. Let Steve go and help her.' Kirby could see Reid was torn. He needed to reach him. 'He'll bring Kevin up too. Then when all this is over you can call Sally Shires and tell her you found her boy.' He waited for what seemed like ages as Reid thought about what he'd said.

Eventually Reid nodded. 'Alright. And DS Kobrak?'

'Yes?' said Kobrak, pausing, halfway to the exit already.

'Look after Kevin.'

Kobrak dived for the fire door and was gone within seconds.

Now he was alone with Reid, Alma and Hoffmann, Kirby had to decide how to play it. Reid literally had nothing to lose. He'd found Kevin's body. Sally Shires would have closure of sorts before she died. Kirby didn't doubt for one second he would kill Alma or, indeed, Hoffmann for his part in Kevin's death. Somehow, he had to stop him.

CHAPTER 57

Connie shone her torch along the wall of the well, searching every inch for potential footholds. After her earlier outburst of hysteria, she'd talked herself down. If she didn't get a grip this might end very badly. Panic wasn't going to get her anywhere; she needed to think rationally and find a way out. The brickwork she'd admired before wasn't quite as good as she'd thought. Or rather, parts of it weren't. It had obviously been patched up at some point by someone not as skilled as the original builder. From her position deep in the well she could see where several bricks protruded from the wall. Whether they were loose or not she couldn't tell. If she could pull them out, they might give her a toehold. She couldn't stay where she was, that much was certain. Her legs were starting to go numb, the muscles in her thighs beginning to cramp. She had to move. Breathing was also becoming more difficult as she was almost bent double in the narrow space.

Desperate not to drop the phone she stuffed it into her bra. This also meant she was now back in darkness. Not that it mattered – she could hardly take a wrong turn. Next, she placed her palms flat against the wall behind her, just below her buttocks. Then, after taking a deep breath, she slowly moved her right foot off the opposite wall. Bracing herself, she pushed herself up using her hands and feet. She grunted with the effort. She'd barely moved and felt exhausted but no matter how small, it was progress. Steeling herself, she then performed the same manoeuvre but using her left foot instead of her right. The pins and needles were excruciating, and she gritted her teeth. A mountain climber would likely have had no problem in scaling the old well, but Connie's legs weren't used to such strain and after a few more efforts alternating between the right and left leg she had to stop. Thirst ravaged her throat, which was bone dry and sore. Who the fuck got trapped in a well with no water? She shook her head at the irony.

A few of her friends who explored sewers had navigated some very narrow spaces, but they'd been properly equipped, plus they hadn't had the extra icing of a dead body to contend with. As she psyched herself up for the next exertion, she tried not to think of the corpse beneath her. Kevin had been down here alone for decades, his mother Sally trying to piece her life back together no more than a stone's throw away, oblivious. Connie imagined her coming to the church to pray, not knowing how close she'd been to her son. '*Fucking Alma, I hope you pay for this,*' she mumbled under her breath. Connie wholeheartedly hoped Reid would find her and that justice would be meted one way or the other. The way she currently felt she didn't care how. The fire at Coniston House fleetingly crossed her mind. Had that been Alma's doing to lure Reid away? She now cursed herself for not calling 999.

Driving those thoughts away, she pressed her palms against the wall and braced her left foot on the brickwork behind her and pushed. As she did so a searing pain shot up her leg and she slipped as it failed to take her weight. Slamming her back against the wall behind her, she moved her foot to the wall in front, her right thigh taking most of the pressure. As she eased the weight back on to her left foot she cried out in pain. *Fuck.* Her injured ankle had finally given up. Her right leg wouldn't take the weight alone for much longer and panic once again threatened to take over. Connie could feel herself slipping, as though the well were sucking her back down. Just as the muscles in her right leg began to spasm, a noise suddenly made her look up. It had been deathly silent apart from her own grunts and groans but now she heard a distinct thud. The quality of the darkness above changed ever so slightly. Someone was coming.

'Help!' Connie screamed as much as her voice would allow. 'Help me!' She couldn't hear anything over the sound of her own heavy breathing but suddenly a light flashed overhead. 'Down here!' she yelled. A bright light dazzled her as someone shone a torch down the well. 'Who's there?' She almost didn't want to know in case it was the same person who'd pushed her in, come back to seal the well. Then she heard a voice she recognised.

'Connie, it's DS Kobrak. Hold on in there, I'm going to get you out.'

CHAPTER 58

'I appreciate you letting DS Kobrak leave,' said Kirby. 'You may well have saved a life tonight. It would be a shame if you blew it by doing something stupid with that gun.' As he said the words he couldn't help thinking if Connie died as a result of Hoffmann's actions then he'd happily pull the trigger himself.

Reid smiled. 'I know what you're trying to do, but it won't work. You're right, the girl has nothing to do with this and I sincerely hope she's okay. She was in the wrong place at the wrong time, that's all. But these two' – he gestured towards Alma and Hoffmann – 'they're different.'

'If that's the case, then let them be tried in a court of law. If we find evidence—'

'You don't understand,' said Reid, cutting him off. 'Alma's right, I do believe the world is about to end. It's coming very, very soon. It's what I've dreamed of for years and finally it's happening. I'll get to see my mother again, my friends from Texas, from the compound. David Koresh himself.'

'What if it doesn't? Just think about it for a moment.' Kirby had read that some Waco survivors had expected the world to end on the tenth anniversary of the siege, only to be disappointed. 'You'll go back to prison.'

'It won't come to that,' said Reid, turning to Hoffmann and Alma. 'This has to be settled now. David is waiting for me, and I want to meet him knowing I did the right thing.'

'Please, Vern,' Hoffmann pleaded. 'Just do as the detective says. I've got Mary to think about. The new church . . .'

'*Mary?* You weren't thinking about her when you were screwing Michaela Falke, were you? And you can forget the church. Elliott's known for years about your affair. He's been stringing you along. He has no intention of letting you take over when he retires.'

Hoffmann's face was a mass of confusion. 'You're lying.'

'You know I rarely lie, Tobias.' Reid raised the gun.

'Wait,' said Kirby. He had to buy some time, but he also wanted answers. 'There's something I need from Mr Hoffmann before you kill him.'

Hoffmann stared at Kirby, incredulous. 'You're going to let him kill me? You're a policeman, you're supposed to protect me!'

Kirby's eyes locked on Reid's and saw him nod once, giving Kirby the go-ahead. 'We know you called Will Stark on the night he was killed. You still haven't told me why. Given there's a gun pointed at your head I'd take the opportunity to unburden yourself if I were you.'

'DI Kirby is right,' said Alma, who'd fallen silent. 'You ought to tell us. I, for one, would love to know.' Sarcasm dripped from every word.

If Kirby had been in Hoffmann's shoes he didn't know who he'd be more scared of, Reid and the gun, or Alma. She oozed hostility like a wood burner radiated heat.

Hoffmann shuffled nervously on his feet. He was sweating profusely and not just from the heat of the fire, which had burned down to a pile of embers. 'We're waiting, Mr Hoffmann,' said Kirby, wondering how long it would take the firearms unit to arrive. Kobrak would have called Hamer as soon as he was in the stairwell. He couldn't allow himself to think about Connie, trapped in the well, as the distraction might cost him someone's life. Perhaps, even, his own.

'Yes, I did call Will that night now I think about it,' said Hoffmann, wiping his brow. He was trying to sound upbeat and failing miserably. It was like watching a bad comic dying on stage.

'Why didn't you mention it before?' asked Kirby.

'I forgot. I must have been in shock about Will and . . . I didn't think. I'm sorry.'

'And what did you talk about during this call?' Alma asked the question this time. 'Or have you forgotten that as well?'

'I . . . I don't know. This and that. Will and I talked all the time. I can't recall every conversation we—'

'We found a hair, Mr Hoffmann,' cut in Kirby. They were reaching crunch point. 'It was trapped under the rope around Will Stark's neck. We think it was left by whoever hung him from the scaffolding rig.'

'Then it can't be mine.' He ran a trembling hand over his bald head and smiled weakly. 'Can it?'

'But it could belong to your wife.' Kirby let the sentence hang in the air for a moment. 'She dyes her hair, doesn't she?'

'What's that got to do with it?' Hoffmann's forced jollity evaporated as quickly as he'd switched it on.

'Whoever it belongs to dyes their hair blond. I can only think of one person on the estate at the time the murder took place who dyes their hair, and that's your wife.'

'She hasn't done anything!' wailed Hoffmann.

'My officers are with her now. A DNA test will prove whether the hair belongs to her or not – we got lucky, the follicle was still attached. If it comes back as a match and with you dead she'll have to carry the can alone. That strikes me as rather unfair, wouldn't you agree, Vernon?' Kirby turned to Reid. A siren wailed somewhere nearby then cut out. The troops were arriving. Reid heard it too.

'Did you kill Will?' Reid asked Hoffmann, stepping nearer. 'The truth, Tobias.'

'He attacked me!' Hoffmann blurted. 'We were arguing . . .'

'About what?'

'Kevin Shires.' Hoffmann started to cry again. 'I'd seen Jason Roye earlier that day. He'd come back to the estate looking for Kevin's body. He was asking all sorts of questions. I was worried.'

'Worried about what?' asked Reid.

'That he'd find him!' shouted Hoffmann, wiping snot on the back of his hand.

'And why would that worry you, Mr Hoffmann?' asked Kirby.

'Oh God,' he sobbed. 'Because I helped Will hide the body. His car was out of action, I . . .' Hoffmann was now grabbing at imaginary hair and slapping the top of his head. '. . . I can't believe I did it. Hid a kid's body. God help me.'

'Why did you do it?'

'He knew about my affair with Kay – Michaela – and he said he'd tell Elliott.'

'So you and Will Stark hid Kevin's body in the disused well?'

Hoffmann nodded. 'We used my car to transport Kevin's body from the tin church on Traps Lane back to the estate. Will knew about the well from when he took the old church down. No one would think of looking there. It was perfect.'

Reid shook his head in disgust. 'How can you say that, Tobias? He was sixteen years old!'

'It was a holy well,' Hoffmann cried. 'Out of all the places we could have put him, it was the best we could do.'

'I can't believe I'm listening to this,' said Reid, glancing at Kirby, who knew he didn't have long before Reid did something stupid.

'Going back to Will Stark's death,' said Kirby. 'You admit to killing him?'

Hoffmann nodded. 'Yes,' he snivelled. 'I was worried what would happen if Jason found the body. He was so determined. He had this look on his face like he used to have as a kid when he wanted something, and I just knew that he'd never give up. Ever. So I arranged to meet Will in the church and told him he needed to sort the situation out.'

'How?' asked Kirby.

'By going to the police,' said Hoffmann. 'I told him he should confess but he wouldn't hear of it. I'd helped clear up his mess and now he wouldn't do the right thing.'

'And so you killed him.'

'I didn't intend to,' Hoffmann cried. 'I was angry. He was walking away from me so I pulled him back. He tried to shake me off and stumbled. He hit his head and then my hands were around his throat and . . .' Hoffmann shook his head. Silence hung in the smoky air as the four of them eyed each other. Alma looked like a coiled spring ready to explode.

'And Will Stark told you he killed Kevin,' said Kirby.

Hoffmann nodded. 'He said he found Kevin attacking Alma in the old tin church . . . Will pulled him off and he fell and . . .' He trailed off, snivelling. 'It's not true, is it?'

Reid shook his head. 'Will didn't kill Kevin, Tobias.' He pointed at Alma. 'She did.'

'Oh, God . . .' Hoffmann ground the heels of his hands into his eyes. 'No, you've got it wrong. You must have.' Doubt crept into his voice, and he looked to Alma for reassurance. 'Alma?'

With his focus on Reid's gun, Kirby hadn't seen Alma take something from her pocket, so when she lunged at Hoffmann it came as a total surprise. She knocked Hoffmann off balance, and they both fell to the ground. Hoffmann seemed to have lost his strength and Alma quickly managed to straddle him. Before Kirby knew what was happening, she'd stabbed Hoffmann in the neck. It was an accurate strike, arterial blood spurting across the roof as Hoffmann frantically grasped at his wound. Alma was screaming something Kirby couldn't make out.

Reid was now pointing the gun at Alma's head, shouting at her to stop.

Sensing his moment, Kirby unsnapped his ASP baton and flicked it open.

CHAPTER 59

'Can you walk?' asked Kobrak.

'I think so.' Connie was sitting in an old office chair in the vestry. The relief at hearing Kobrak's voice had given her the strength she'd needed, but it had been an agonising wait while he found a way to bring her to the surface. He'd called the dive unit, who'd normally rescue someone in her situation, but they were currently out on an emergency call on the Thames. A passenger boat had collided with a freight barge and several people were in the water. It was deemed a serious incident, and they couldn't guarantee when someone would be able to get to Grasmere. In the end Kobrak had improvised with a piece of scaffolding he'd found in the main church. He'd laid it across the top of the well and fashioned a makeshift pulley from the rest of the rope that had been used to string up Stark. Unable to pull her entire weight up to the top, he'd taken most of the burden, allowing her to slowly ease herself up the narrow shaft to the safety of terra firma.

Using the armrests, Connie pushed herself out of the chair. Every bone in her body ached. She leant on Kobrak as he guided her out of the church and to a car she recognised as Kirby's Corsa.

'Where's Kirby?' she asked, as Kobrak opened the passenger door for her. The young DS hadn't explained how he had come to be in the church or how he knew where she was. He slammed her door shut and went round to the driver's side and got in. He suddenly seemed in a hurry.

'He's on the roof of Coniston House,' said Kobrak, starting the car and taking off without bothering to put his seatbelt on. As the wheels screeched on the tarmac, Connie realised something was very wrong.

'What's going on, Steve?'

Kobrak kept his eyes on the road as he sped past the maisonettes and swung round towards Coniston House in a manoeuvre worthy of a scene from *Bullitt*. 'Vernon Reid's got a gun. I think he's going to shoot Tobias Hoffmann and Alma Stark. Kirby's on the roof with them now.'

Connie looked at him, half-expecting to see a smile creep over his lips, but his mouth was set firm, his knuckles white on the steering wheel. 'You're serious, aren't you?'

'I was up there with him, but he persuaded Reid to let me come and rescue you,' said Kobrak, glancing at her. 'Reid's not a bad man but he thinks the world is about to end and that makes him extremely dangerous.'

Connie tried to imagine Kirby negotiating with an armed Vernon Reid and couldn't. If anything happened to him . . . she couldn't bear to think about it. 'How did you know where I was though?'

'Reid heard Tobias Hoffmann telling Alma he'd met someone else in the church tonight. It didn't take much for him to confess what happened. He said it was an accident.'

'That's bollocks!' exclaimed Connie. 'It was a hundred per cent deliberate. He grabbed me from behind and deliberately pushed me.' They were nearing Coniston House now and she could see squad cars parked at either end. Several ambulances were just pulling into the estate from the Marshall Street entrance and a helicopter was circling overhead. A group of people stood a little way off, eyes trained on the roof. 'Jesus,' she muttered under her breath.

Kobrak brought the car to a screeching halt and leapt out. 'Stay here,' he ordered, slamming the door behind him.

Connie wound down the window for some air. A strange smell was emanating from her clothing, and she suddenly had to get out of the car. She frantically fumbled with the door handle and panic seized her when she thought Kobrak might have locked her in. Then the door suddenly opened and she stumbled out, collapsing on to all fours before throwing up. A paramedic came running over and she could hear Kobrak shouting in the background. She felt an arm around her shoulders and someone guiding her towards the ambulance. Then everything seemed to stop as a gunshot rang out from the roof of Coniston House.

CHAPTER 60

In a few quick steps, Kirby had got near enough to bring down the baton hard on Reid's gun hand, but Reid pre-empted the move and raised the gun, pulling the trigger at the same time. It went off with a deafening bang and Kirby felt the bullet graze the side of his arm.

Reid steadied himself and aimed the gun at Kirby's head. 'No further. Drop the baton. I don't want to hurt you, Kirby, but make one wrong move and as God is my witness, I will.' Kirby did as he was told, and Reid kicked the baton away before turning his attention to Alma, who was desperately trying to pull the scalpel from Hoffmann's neck in an attempt to retrieve her weapon. Her hands slick with blood, she couldn't grasp the handle.

'Get up,' ordered Reid, but Alma ignored him, still scrabbling at the scalpel. 'I said get up!' Reid grabbed her by the back of her overalls and hauled her off Hoffmann into a kneeling position.

'That bastard killed my father!' she screamed.

'And you killed Kevin!' countered Reid. 'And Jason! He guessed, didn't he? I don't know how you did it, but you made sure he was in the garage when you set it alight.'

'Prove it!' Alma spat.

'You won't need proof where you're going,' said Reid, raising the gun. 'Forgive me my sins, Father, I—'

'Don't do it, Vernon,' shouted Kirby. His arm was throbbing where the bullet had grazed him and there was blood on his jacket. The helicopter that had been circling the estate now hovered directly overhead. Armed police would be coming up the stairwells at either end of the roof at any moment. Reid would be a dead man. Alma, who had been kneeling next to Hoffmann, suddenly made a grab for the scalpel sticking out of his neck. This time she managed to pull it out, and in one swift motion swung around and stabbed Reid in the leg. Reid staggered for a moment, before aiming at her chest and pulling the trigger. She jerked backwards and collapsed on the ground, unmoving, blood spreading across her shoulder and chest.

The apocalyptic scene was now illuminated by the bright search light of the helicopter. Kirby could barely hear himself think, the noise was so loud.

He and Reid stared at each other for a long moment. Reid's lips began moving but Kirby couldn't hear anything over the noise of the helicopter. The backdraft spread sparks from the dying fire that had flared up again, the flames hungry for anything they hadn't consumed. Dust and ash stung Kirby's eyes as he waved to the pilot in a gesture of *back off*. When he turned back to Reid, he'd gone. Then Kirby saw him standing on the edge of the roof, looking out over the woods.

'Vernon!' Kirby yelled at the top of his voice. He had no idea whether Reid had heard him, but Reid turned towards Kirby and smiled, shouting something. Kirby waved at the helicopter again. 'Get back!' he yelled, more through frustration than any possibility of being heard. Eventually it retreated a little and he could now hear what Reid was saying. He was reciting a passage from the Bible:

'The time of my departure has come. I have fought the good fight, I have finished the course, I have kept the faith; in the future there is reserved for me the crown of righteousness, which the Lord, the

righteous Judge, will award to me on that day; and not only to me, but also to all who have loved His appearing.'

'What's the passage, Vernon?' Kirby asked, moving slowly towards Reid. He needed to keep him talking, get the gun off him, although Kirby suspected that wasn't what Reid had in mind for himself.

'It's the second letter of Paul to Timothy. He told Timothy to stand by the truth, something Tobias never learnt despite his faith.'

'Vernon, please, just give me the gun.' Only a few feet separated them now and Kirby came to a halt. 'They're not worth it. Please.' He held out his hand.

'Promise me one thing first.'

'I'll try,' said Kirby.

'There's enough money in my flat to take care of Kevin's funeral. I want Sally to have it.'

'If you give me the gun and come with me then you can tell her yourself.'

Reid shook his head. 'I'm not going back to prison. Not now, not ever. Besides, people are waiting for me. For you, too. It will be glorious, DI Kirby. You'll see your mother again.'

For a second, Kirby was caught off guard. How did Reid know Livia was dead? He didn't recall mentioning it to him in their conversations. 'How did you know?' he asked.

Reid shrugged. 'Intuition. Lucky guess? Call it what you will. I'm right though, aren't I?'

'Just give me the gun, Vernon.'

Reid held out what looked like a Baikal pistol. 'You'd be surprised what gets left behind in a place like this if you know where to look,' said Reid, dropping the weapon into Kirby's hand. 'Consider it my parting gift. You might even clear up a few unsolved crimes. But you'd better hurry.'

'Vernon, you don't have to do this—' Kirby took a step forward but Reid mirrored his move, taking a step back towards the edge of the roof. 'Okay, okay.' Kirby held up his hands.

'You will make sure Sally gets the money, won't you?'

'I promise.'

'There should be enough for Jason, too.'

Kirby nodded.

Reid smiled. 'It seems I owe you an apology. Behind that badge, you're a decent man. God could do with people like you on his side.' Reid opened his arms wide and looked up towards the sky. 'It's time, David. I am coming.'

Kirby watched as Reid closed his eyes, a look of serenity on his face he'd never seen on the Waco survivor until now, before letting himself fall gracefully off the roof and into the smoke-tinged air.

CHAPTER 61

Hoffmann was dead. Alma had struck him in the carotid artery and he hadn't stood a chance. He'd suffered catastrophic blood loss. But when the paramedics tending Alma started working on her, Kirby knew she must be still alive. He wondered whether Reid had deliberately only wounded her or whether he had genuinely missed after she'd stabbed him in the leg. Not that it made much difference to the outcome. Reid was dead. His unwavering belief in David Koresh meant he'd died believing he was about to be reunited with his friends and family, that the world as he knew it was about to end. Kirby, a non-believer, found it gloriously naive that a man could step off a roof with such conviction. Would he ever be reunited with Livia? With the colleagues and friends he'd lost over the years? He doubted it very much.

'Detective?' One of the paramedics had come over. 'If you come with me someone will take a look at your arm. There are ambulances waiting below.'

'In a minute,' Kirby replied. He'd deliberately been avoiding leaving the roof. He'd had no word from Kobrak and didn't know whether Connie was alive or dead. He thought if he stayed up here he could avoid finding out for a bit longer. Then he saw Hamer emerge on to the roof, his face grave as he approached.

'Lew.'

'Sir.'

'You okay? Your arm.'

'It's a graze, that's all.'

'What happened up here?' Hamer surveyed the scene.

If someone had told Kirby they were on the set of a horror film he wouldn't have argued. One bloody body. Another only just alive. And scattered all around the scorched remains of Reid's pigeons. Several birds were still half-alive. Someone needed to put them out of their misery, but Kirby didn't have the stomach for it.

'Hoffmann confessed to killing Will Stark and to hiding Kevin Shires' body. Then Alma stabbed him in the neck with a scalpel and Reid shot her before killing himself. That's the short version.'

'Where did she get a scalpel from?'

Kirby shook his head. 'It must have been in her pocket. I didn't see her carrying anything before the attack.' Kirby rubbed his eyes, wondering whether he could have prevented Hoffmann's death.

'Did Alma say anything about Kevin Shires?'

Kirby glanced over to where the paramedics were loading her on to a stretcher. 'No. But she's guilty alright.'

'Do you think she'll confess, if she survives?'

'I hope so, for Sally Shires' sake.'

'Hmm,' said Hamer. 'How in God's name did Reid get a gun?'

'He said he found it here, on the estate. You never know, we might be able to link it to some unsolved crimes.'

'It would be a very small silver lining if we could.'

'Have you seen Kobrak?' Kirby asked. He couldn't put it off any longer.

Hamer nodded. 'He's on the ground. There's a team at the church now. We won't be able to bring the lad's body up until the dive team can get here. They're busy dealing with an emergency on the Thames at the moment.'

A sudden panic gripped him. 'What about Connie?'

His boss looked at him. 'She's fine. Kobrak managed to get her out. She's made of strong stuff. But you already knew that.'

Kirby rubbed his face with relief.

'You're close, aren't you?'

'Pardon?'

'I know she's living in your mother's old place,' said Hamer. 'I recognised the address on her witness statement. You should have told me.'

Kirby said nothing, just stared at his boss.

'Detective?' It was the paramedic again. 'You really should get that arm seen to.'

'Okay, I'm coming.' He watched the paramedic walk towards the exit, where he stood waiting for him.

'Look, Connie living in Livia's old place hasn't compromised the case in any way. I hardly see her.'

'But you discussed Brian Kaplinsky with her.'

'Well, yes, but that's got nothing to do with this.'

'Technically, it has.' Hamer moved closer, lowering his voice even though no one could hear. 'I hope you weren't planning on telling her about Kaplinsky's phone call.'

'No,' said Kirby. 'But I'll make sure she doesn't harass him again. You have my word.'

'Good.' Hamer stepped away, his voice back to normal. 'Now get that arm seen to.'

Kirby left his superior on the roof and followed the paramedic down to ground level. When he emerged from the block of flats he saw Kobrak, who came jogging over.

'You okay, Lew?' he asked, looking at his bloodied arm.

'Yeah, just a graze. Hoffmann's dead but Alma's hanging in there. Where's Connie – is she okay?'

Kobrak nodded. 'She'll be fine. She's in one of the ambulances. She's pretty shaken up but she was lucky. Kevin broke her fall.' He shivered as he spoke.

Christ. 'Thanks, Steve. Good work.'

The paramedic steered Kirby towards two ambulances that were parked off to the left, where he saw a small figure huddled under a blanket sitting by the open door of one of them. Connie looked up as he approached. She tried to stand before collapsing back on to the seat. Tears stained her cheeks.

'No one would tell me anything,' she gabbled. 'When that body fell I—' She looked at his arm. 'You're bleeding. What happened?'

'It's nothing. How about you?'

'I won't be going draining any time soon, let's put it like that.'

Since he'd known her, Kirby had learned a lot about urban exploration and the phenomenon known as draining – exploring sewers and culverts – and knew it was possible she'd suffer in any confined space after what she'd been through. He took off his jacket and stab vest so the paramedic could take a look at his arm. His shirt sleeve was soaked in blood. 'Why did you go into the church?' he asked while the paramedic cut the sleeve off his top and began cleaning the wound. 'It was a reckless thing to do.'

'I was looking for the old healing well and saw someone leave – it must have been Reid from what Steve said – so I thought it was safe. I knew that's where Kevin's body had to be. Reid must have dropped his torch in the well, and I saw the light.' She paused. 'Are you angry with me?'

'Yes.' He winced as the paramedic worked. 'When Hoffmann said he'd pushed you down the well I thought you might be dead and . . .' Kirby didn't want to verbalise how he'd felt, because it troubled him. He'd felt it like a claw hammer to his heart when Hoffmann had said what he'd done. 'Pain in the arse finding another bloody tenant.'

341

Connie burst out laughing, tears now flowing freely down her face.

'Seriously though,' said Kirby. 'It must have been a terrifying ordeal. Even those of us who do this for a living would have had a hard time in such close proximity to a dead body.'

'It was.' Connie wiped away a tear and smiled. 'But you know what the worst part was?'

'No, what?'

'Being rescued in the Fucking Corsa.'

CHAPTER 62

Depending on how one looked at it, Alma Stark was a very lucky woman. Reid's bullet had hit her in the shoulder missing her heart by some margin. It had caused significant damage but she'd live. Kirby, however, wasn't feeling so lucky. He was back at the boat after a frustrating hour and a half with her in the hospital. He'd questioned her about her relationship with Kevin Shires and the circumstances surrounding his disappearance and death in 1992. He'd also questioned her about Jason Roye and the fire in the Shires' old garage. She'd refused to say anything more than 'no comment'.

Mary Hoffmann, however, had been a different matter. The hair found trapped between the rope and Stark's neck was a positive match. This, coupled with Mary's discovery of her husband's infidelity with her best friend, Michaela Falke, had prompted her to talk. She hadn't known about her husband's affair – had she done it was unlikely she would ever have helped him hang Will Stark from the scaffolding rig in order to cover up his murder. According to Mary, her husband had burst into their flat on the night of the murder in a blind panic. He'd told her there had been a terrible accident. That he'd strangled Will Stark in All Hallows. His explanation had been that Will had attacked him. The two men had fought, Tobias choking Will unintentionally. Tobias had then pleaded with his wife to help him make it look like suicide. Years of loyalty meant that Mary had agreed. It also meant she'd kept his other dark secret: that he'd helped Will Stark conceal the body of Kevin Shires. Not that Hoffmann had told his wife everything – she hadn't known where Kevin's body was hidden and had been horrified when Kirby told her. Also, when told it had been Alma who killed Kevin and not her father, as Hoffmann had believed, Mary had shown remarkably little surprise. Although she didn't say in so many words, Kirby sensed an admiration for Stark. According to Mary, Will Stark had told her husband he'd strangled Kevin, something that so far Jenks had found no evidence to support. That he'd killed to protect his own daughter hadn't surprised Mary at the time, but his attempt to evade justice had, and she'd retained her suspicions. It simply hadn't been in his character, she said, for Stark not to take responsibility for his actions. Stark had lied to Tobias Hoffmann about almost everything. Kirby felt as though he'd managed to join all the dots, but as yet they surrounded a large empty hole where the evidence should be.

Recovering Kevin's body from the well had been a painstaking job. Connie's fall had damaged the remains as well as compromised evidence. Her recollection of the positioning of the body before she was pushed was vague at best, but after examination Jenks concluded Kevin had been deposited in the well head first. Kevin's skull also showed he'd suffered blunt force trauma in several places, some of which was consistent with landing on his head when he was dumped. Other injuries, however, weren't. His eye sockets were fractured, his nose had been broken, as had his jaw and several front teeth. It reeked of a sustained attack by someone out of control. Or someone who was having a psychotic episode.

The tin chapel, where Kevin's murder had taken place, was now also a crime scene. The floor had been taken up and blood stains found on the hardstanding below. Evidence also suggested Jason had slept rough there for at least one night, as they'd found his prints on several items they'd retrieved. It had also transpired Connie had explored the church during the week and been knocked over by someone making an escape to avoid discovery. The likelihood was this had been Jason, who'd then returned to the Shires' garage only to be killed by Alma the following day.

Kirby opened a beer and stared out of the window. It was hammering down outside and the pattering of rain on the boat deck above was soothing as he watched the raindrops pit the surface of the river. The spring flowers on Isabel's deck would lose their petals in this downpour and he decided he'd go and clear them up in the morning. Isabel was due back in a few days' time – his worry about her not returning seemingly based on nothing but his own paranoia. She'd called earlier to tell him she wanted to keep the baby. He'd reacted enthusiastically, telling her it was the best news he'd heard in days. She'd also told him she was prepared to let the FFI gene testing go for the time being, despite her worry that the baby might be carrying the faulty gene. The decision had surprised him but he'd felt immense relief. Now *that* had been the best news, but he kept that nugget to himself. He was sipping his beer when a withheld number flashed on screen and he hesitated for a moment before picking up.

'Hello?'

'Is that Ludovico?' said a voice. There was something vaguely familiar about it. A hammy Italian accent.

'Who is this?' Kirby asked. A snort of laughter came down the line in response. 'Pete? Is that you?'

'It's the luck of the paw, Lew. I'm back from the dead!'

This news trumped everything – the gene test, the baby – and Kirby punched the air, spilling his beer. '*Shit.* You've made my beer go everywhere. Please don't ever do that again, Pete. I'm not sure my heart could stand it.'

'What, nearly die or spill your beer?'

'The beer, of course,' said Kirby, grinning from ear to ear. 'It's good to hear your voice. How're you feeling?'

'Neck still hurts like hell and I can't turn my head. And you wouldn't believe the amount of pills I've got – seems my blood is too thin or some nonsense like that.'

'So what's the prognosis? Daytime telly, bit of gentle taxidermy?' It was a delicate question, Kirby knew. No policeman liked being out of action.

There was a short silence on the other end of the line before Anderson replied. 'I've got to have physio. They're not sure yet whether there'll be any lasting damage but yeah, I've got to take it easy for the foreseeable. On the plus side, I won't be able to drive the frigging Astra. Every cloud and all that. Anyhow, enough about me. How's the case going? I heard it all went a bit *Die Hard* on the roof.'

'Hardly. But it was bad enough.'

'I'm sorry I wasn't there for you,' said Anderson, real regret in his voice. 'You and me 'n' the paw . . . maybe the outcome would have been different.'

'Reid was on a mission, Pete. He was armed with a Baikal pistol. The only way things would have been different was if Armed Response had shot Alma before she stabbed Hoffmann, or shot Reid before he pulled the trigger on Alma. Either way, Reid was a dead man. Nothing I could have done or said would have changed that.'

'I still wish I'd been there though.'

'Yeah, well, I'm glad you weren't. You'd have moaned like shit about climbing the stairs.'

'There is that,' said Anderson, laughing. 'So what's happening with crazy, um, what's her name? Is she cooperating?'

'Alma. Like hell she is,' said Kirby, taking a swig of beer.

'But you're sure she's guilty?'

'Positive.'

'So talk me through it. You wouldn't believe how fucking bored I've been.'

Kirby heard Eleanor's voice in the background and Anderson unsuccessfully trying to muffle the phone. He came back on after a few seconds. 'Eleanor's telling me not to swear while I'm a guest of the NHS. She's also worried I'll tire myself out talking to you. Good grief.'

God, he'd hate to have to look after Anderson at home. He'd be a terrible patient. 'You're going to have to listen to her once you're out, you know that don't you?'

'Yeah, yeah,' said Anderson, brushing the comment aside. 'Come on then, tell me about Will Starkey. Fill me in before the nurse does his round. He's actually worse than Eleanor,' he whispered.

Kirby didn't bother correcting his partner on Stark's name and began to explain as best he could what they thought had happened, finishing with the rooftop scene. 'When Reid started waving his gun around, Tobias Hoffmann confessed to the murder of Will Stark. They'd met in All Hallows on the estate and argued about Kevin's body. Stark tried to walk away, which enraged Hoffmann, so he pulled him back and they fought. Hoffmann says he "suddenly" found his hands around Stark's neck.'

'That old chestnut,' said Anderson. 'Some people behave as though murder just happens. That they're unaccountable.'

Kirby had heard that argument many times over the years too. 'When he realised Stark was dead he panicked and got his wife to help him string the body up to make it look like suicide.'

'And what about Kevin?'

'Stark told Hoffmann he'd found Kevin attacking his daughter in the old tin chapel and had strangled him. We now know Kevin had actually been badly beaten about the head. Stark must have wrapped the body up before enlisting Hoffmann's help to move it. Anyhow, Hoffmann thought it was time Stark confessed, but he refused.'

'Because it wasn't his crime to confess,' said Anderson.

'Partly. Stark was still protecting his daughter – which also might explain why he stayed on the estate for so long. As long as he was there he could keep an eye on the church. Maybe the professional integrity everyone talked about was a sham and he just stayed there to make sure no one ever found Kevin's body.'

'That and the money from that weird contract,' said Anderson.

'True. Hoffmann had no idea it was Alma who killed Kevin until he was on the roof.'

'Why did Stark lie to Hoffmann about killing Kevin? Hoffmann seems just as likely to have helped hide Kevin's body whether Alma was the killer or her father. I thought Stark and Hoffmann were close?'

'So we'd been led to believe. I can't help but wonder whether Stark had an inkling his beloved daughter was somehow involved in Angela Barton's death – she was one of Hoffmann's foster kids who died of an overdose – and if he told Hoffmann the truth that Alma had killed Kevin, Hoffmann might become suspicious.'

'Is there any evidence connecting Alma to Angela's death?'

'There's nothing in Angela's file to suggest a link. But someone gave Angela those drugs and the police never did find out who.'

'What baffles me is motive,' said Anderson. 'Angela was Alma's friend – so was Kevin.'

'True, but they were both leaving – or in her eyes, abandoning – her. This is only a theory, and unless she talks we'll never be sure, but my guess is she didn't want Kevin to run away with Jason or Angela to move back in with her birth mother. It's possible her deep-seated fear of abandonment triggered psychotic episodes, the psychosis triggered by the suicide of her mother.'

'And Jason?' Anderson asked through a yawn.

'Forensics found ketamine in his system. But that's not what killed him. That was down to hydrogen cyanide poisoning. The sofa he was on was an old eighties job – wouldn't pass fire regs these days. He was doped up first and then the sofa was set alight with firelighter cubes. They're quick and easy to ignite with a nice slow build giving her time to get away.'

'Poor bastard. Can you prove it was Alma who started the fire?'

Kirby sighed with frustration. 'Not yet. I don't think she knew Sally Shires had kept all her son's things. When Alma discovered Jason was going through the stuff she probably couldn't resist going to see if he'd found anything. We found a mug under the sofa. It's possible she'd taken him a hot drink and that's how she administered the ketamine. What actually happened between the two of them we'll never know.'

'Had Jason found anything?'

'Reid said they found a birthday card from an anonymous sender, which we later found out also contained an accomplished drawing of Kevin. They also discovered a set of fanzines Kevin had subscribed to called *High Rize*. Reid was convinced whoever sent the card with the drawing also drew one of the comic strips in the magazine called Lady Electra. Lady Electra lived on a rundown council estate and rode a beach cruiser.'

'Christ, you couldn't make this shit up,' said Anderson. 'Alma's psych evaluation will be interesting. Can you prove she drew it though? I mean, she'd have been how old?'

'Sixteen. I managed to track down the old editor, a guy called Alan Snape. He owns a memorabilia shop near the British Museum, but it used to sell comics and fanzines as well as science fiction and horror books in the late eighties and nineties. Bit like Forbidden Planet but privately owned. He remembered this geeky school-girl coming in one day and asking how someone would go about getting their work published. He'd just set up the *High Rize* fanzine and was looking for contributors and gave her his details. Never expected to hear from her, I don't think. Anyhow, a week later he received the first two instalments of the Lady Electra comic strip in the post. It was just the kind of thing he was after so he published it. Every couple of weeks he'd receive the next instalment. He never met her again in person and didn't know her name but I'm willing to bet it was Alma.'

'And Snape didn't make the connection? They were tantamount to a confession.'

Kirby had questioned the shop owner about this. 'He did and he didn't. He just thought the girl was using real-life events as inspiration. It never occurred to him she might know something, let alone be the killer.'

'That takes balls for a sixteen-year-old,' said Anderson, yawning again.

'Pete, I think we've talked for long enough. I'm going to have Eleanor on my back if we don't wrap this up. I can fill you in on the details once you're home.' He'd noticed his partner forget a couple of names as they'd spoken – no doubt a side effect of the blood clot.

'Yeah, and I can see the nurse coming. And believe me, you don't want to get on the wrong side of him.'

Kirby said goodnight to his partner and downed the rest of his beer as the rain continued to pummel the boat. He thought about Alma Stark. Would she ever talk? He'd do his damnedest to make her crack but she was anything but stupid. Perhaps Kevin was the key. Had she loved him? Lady Electra had certainly loved her doomed lover in the comic strip, so it seemed likely. Perhaps he could play on that. The comic strips also indicated a personality who believed themself to be cleverer than anyone else. Alma had taken an enormous risk by publishing them and yet she'd got away with it for almost thirty years. Her audacity was admirable.

Currently, she was being held in custody at the hospital and wasn't going anywhere for at least a few days until the doctors were sure she was stable. SOCOs were going over every inch of her flat looking for anything that could link her to the fire in the Shires' garage. Kirby desperately needed evidence if he was going to charge her with Jason's or Kevin's murder. He was halfway to the fridge for another beer when something occurred to him. He'd seen car keys in Alma's kitchen but where was her car? He smiled to himself. Perhaps she wasn't that clever after all.

CHAPTER 63

The area behind the electricity substation looked very different compared to the last time Connie had visited. A clear, wide path had been trampled by the police from the gate on Traps Lane to the tin chapel. The undergrowth lay broken and bruised, the smell of crushed stems mixed with moist earth a heady reminder of camping holidays and countryside explores. When she reached the chapel it looked bare and forlorn, its contents stacked outside with what remained of its floor. Kirby had told her that blood stains had been found on some of the floorboards and also beneath on the concrete base where it had dripped between the cracks. The same sadness she'd felt watching Windermere House being destroyed returned as she picked her way over the debris.

Someone had cleared one of the small Gothic windows of ivy, and inside she could see the concrete base on which the church had been laid exposed bare. The entrance still had police tape hanging from the handle and she took the key Irene had given her and unlocked the rough wooden door. A sudden breeze made her shiver as she pushed open the door and stood on the threshold of where Kevin Shires had been killed.

That morning, Connie had visited Kevin's mother in hospital. Sally had days to live. With Jason dead – and with Reid also gone – Connie had once again felt the need to connect with the deceased's nearest living relative. She hadn't spoken to Sally of her traumatic encounter with her son's body, only that she'd been with him when he was found. Sally didn't need to know Connie had broken his brittle bones and screamed in terror at his lifeless body. Connie had encountered death twice within the past few weeks and reaching out to the relatives was the only way she knew of dealing with it. To do what Brian Kaplinsky had done – albeit in different circumstances – was abhorrent to her. She'd been able to do nothing for either Will Stark or Kevin Shires but she hadn't simply walked away. Not that she could have walked away from Kevin – being trapped with his body in the confines of the well was something she'd never forget. Although horror and revulsion had been the overriding sensations at the time, they had quickly been followed by an immense sadness at the tragedy of his death. She needed to tell Sally how sorry she was; it was as simple as that.

Connie didn't go into the tin church, preferring to stand in the doorway, and after paying her respects to Kevin Shires, she locked up and made her way to the main house where Irene stood waiting on the back porch. Leaning heavily on her cane, Irene had visibly aged in the past week and for the first time Connie thought of her as frail.

'Are you alright?' asked Irene, as they went through the French doors and into the living room.

'I'm fine. I just wanted to see where it happened. What did the police say?' She handed the key back to Irene and sat down. Her limbs felt heavy, a dull ache still remaining from her time in the well. Bracing herself against its walls for so long had made every inch of her body sore. It was like the time she'd learned to ski and discovered muscles in places she never knew she had them, only ten times worse.

'Not much. Only that they'd finished.'

'What will you do with the church now?'

Irene sat down with a sigh. 'I'm going to have it removed and the land cleared.'

'Then what?'

'I haven't decided yet. I could sell the plot but if I do then I'd probably have a building site at the end of my garden for a few years. Whoever bought it would be bound to build on it.'

'Couldn't you incorporate it into your garden? Restore the apple trees?'

'You've probably noticed, but I now no longer have a gardener.'

'You'll find someone, Irene,' Connie said gently. Reid's death had hit the elderly actress hard.

'If I'm honest, I don't know that I have the appetite for it any more – I was very fond of Vernon, despite his bizarre religious convictions. And in any case, someone will only build on it when I die. There's no pretending otherwise.'

'Why don't you build on it then? Design your own place, more suited to your needs, then sell the main house. You'd have your own private entrance from Traps Lane. That way you have control over what goes up.'

Irene regarded her for a moment and smiled. 'That boss of yours would be missing a trick if he didn't give you the role of curator. I'll think about it. But never mind me. What about you? I can't imagine what it must have been like being trapped in that well.'

'I won't be getting in any confined spaces anytime soon, that's for sure. My legs are still hurting from where I tried climbing up the walls to get away. Kevin was right there and I couldn't bear to touch him.'

'I'm very sorry it happened to you,' said Irene. 'I feel partially responsible. If I hadn't told you what Vernon was up to you'd never have gone there in the first place. Alma's my god-daughter and I had no idea about any of this.'

'You didn't tell me to go looking for Vernon, Irene, I went of my own accord. That was nobody's fault but mine. As for Alma . . .' Connie shrugged. 'How could you possibly know what she'd done? Her father should have gone straight to the police. If he had none of this would have happened.'

'I've been thinking about that. Will was incredibly stubborn. If he gave his word on something, he kept it no matter what. I've little doubt that he stayed on the estate to protect his daughter, but I can't help speculate it was about Kevin, too. He must have suffered terribly knowing what his daughter had done to that poor boy. Perhaps he felt he couldn't leave him.'

Boo-bloody-hoo, thought Connie. She had zero sympathy for Will Stark – he'd caused the deaths of too many people.

'Regardless, it was utter misfortune Will met my father,' Irene went on. 'None of the other entrants in the competition to design Grasmere would have agreed to his terms and yet in Will my father found an unlikely ally.'

'Actually,' said Connie. 'It wasn't complete misfortune.'

'Oh?'

'Did you know Will's grandmother suffered from polio?'

'No, but that's hardly surprising; his grandparents were dead by the time we met. What of it?'

'I found this, look.' Connie took out her phone and brought up a photograph on screen before handing it to Irene. Quatremaine's comment about nepotism being the reason why Stark won the Grasmere contract had been bugging her.

'What's this?' she asked, taking it. 'It's a list of names.'

Connie nodded. 'I went to the National Archives and did some research into your father's church, the tin chapel. I was intrigued about the marking on the door – the cross inside an inverted triangle?'

'The triangle is a sign for water,' said Irene.

'Yes. The cross inside the triangle was used by a number of churches that believed in the healing power of water. Your church – or rather, your father's church – had its own supply of healing water from the well on Chalfont Street. That list is from 1905 and names some of those supposedly healed by water drawn from the well.'

Connie watched as Irene scrolled down the list. 'Oh my,' she said, looking up. 'Elizabeth Stark.'

'Will's grandmother.'

'So you think Will wanted the Grasmere contract so he could safeguard the well? But it was dry by then, of no use.'

'Honestly? I don't know. Money's the obvious motivator for him agreeing to your father's terms, but it's a coincidence, don't you think?'

'Do you have any evidence?' Irene handed the phone back to Connie. 'Why didn't he mention it?'

Connie laughed – that was exactly what Kirby had said when she'd told him. 'None. Then again, not all Will's personal effects have been gone through. Who knows what family records there might be.'

They lapsed into silence for a moment until Irene spoke. 'Putting the events of Grasmere to one side, there's something I've been meaning to ask you.'

'What's that?'

'When we spoke on the phone – the night all this happened and I told you about Vernon – I rather hijacked your call.'

'You were upset.'

'I was. But you called me, remember? You wanted to come and talk to me about something. It must have been important.'

Connie remembered only too clearly why she'd called Irene that night and felt her cheeks redden with embarrassment. Not only that, Art had called her the day before to confirm he would have to bail out his son. RADE was well and truly on the skids.

'Come on, spit it out.' Irene thumped her cane on the floor.

'This is awkward,' said Connie. 'But I wanted to talk to you about the archive. It's in trouble. Well, more than trouble – it's going to close.'

'Why?'

'The Blunt family can't afford to keep the place afloat.' Connie thought it best not to mention the reason why they couldn't. 'My boss, Art, doesn't want to sell but doesn't have much choice unless we can find some investors. He promised me the curatorship if I could find someone.'

'And you were going to ask me.'

Connie nodded. 'I was, yes. I'm sorry, this probably isn't the right time after all that's happened.'

Irene sat for a moment as though mulling something over, then with an effort hauled herself out of her chair. 'Wait here,' she ordered, and left the room.

Connie shifted in her seat, her legs uncomfortable from sitting down. She got up to stretch and wandered over to Alma's drawing of Irene. It really was remarkably good and had captured Irene's personality perfectly. She heard Irene returning and went back to the sofa, easing herself down gently.

Irene was carrying a sheet of A4 paper and held it out.

'What's this?' Connie took it and saw a solicitor's letterhead at the top of the page.

'It's confirmation of the sale of Pinder Wood to Paragon. As of yesterday, Pinder Wood has nothing to do with me.'

Connie skimmed the contents of the letter, her eyes widening as she saw the sum Irene had sold it for. 'Why are you showing me this?'

'It's a lot of money,' said Irene, sitting down.

'Um, yes, it is. I mean, it's an unimaginable sum to me.' She handed the letter back.

'What am I going to do with it all? I've no one to leave it to – Alma's the only one left and she's in the clink – so I may as well do something useful with it.'

Connie stared at Irene, not quite daring to believe. 'You mean . . . ?'

'Yes, Connie. I mean I'm prepared to help you out with the archive.'

Connie felt tears prick her eyes and blinked them away. 'I don't know what to say. I . . .' She'd given Irene nothing to look at – no business plan, no future projections. In fact, she'd given Irene no assurance she wouldn't be throwing her money into a big black hole. There was still one massive question that needed answering. 'How much did you have in mind?'

'That rather depends on what kind of trouble your boss Art is actually in. I'll need to talk to him, obviously. Set a few caveats.' Irene's eye twinkled mischievously. 'But nothing as draconian as my father, don't worry.'

'Thank God for that,' said Connie, feeling relief sweep over her.

'So, can you arrange a meeting between us then?'

Yes, of course she bloody could.

CHAPTER 64

At first the garage looked like any other garage. A small Fiat was parked in the middle. Down one side ran a wooden workbench covered in paint tins and old brushes. Beneath were boxes filled with Christmas decorations, a deep fat fryer, an old coffee machine, some framed pictures – the usual crap that ended up in the loft or, in this case, the garage. Kirby was searching it with Drayton, which had given him the opportunity to have a word with him about Masters. It turned out Drayton was miffed she'd made the murder team over a friend of his. Kirby had told him in no uncertain terms to get over it and they'd settled into an awkward silence as they worked.

'We've got firelighters here,' said Drayton, holding up a box in a gloved hand. 'Several are missing.'

'Check with the fire department and see if they can tell us whether they're the same make as the ones that started the fire which killed Jason Roye,' said Kirby, looking around the small space. 'Any sign of drugs?'

'Not yet,' replied Drayton. They'd found nothing in Alma's flat apart from a small amount of cannabis and the usual painkillers and cold remedies found in most households. Nothing strong enough to knock out Jason Roye.

Kirby let his eyes roam over the garage's interior. He'd scanned the space several times before his gaze was drawn upwards towards the ceiling and the garage door. It was like the one in Sally Shires' garage, an up and over type. The inside of the door was painted black but something in one of the corners caught his attention.

'Sorry,' he said to Drayton, as he pulled the door closed, leaving them with just the overhead single bulb for light. With the door shut, Kirby could see a small box, also black, taped to the metal door in the top right corner. He looked around for a step ladder and saw one propped up against the wall.

'What have you found?' asked Drayton, as he opened the ladder and climbed up for a better look.

'There's a box taped to the back of the door.' On closer inspection the box was clear Tupperware, taped to the metal door with black gaffer tape. Kirby photographed it before carefully peeling away the tape and taking it down. It felt empty as he set it on the work bench and lifted the four snap locks that sealed it.

'What's that on the top?' asked Drayton, peering into the opened box.

Kirby knew exactly what it was. 'It's a train ticket,' he said, taking it out and turning it over. 'InterCity West Coast London to Glasgow, 16 September 1992. One way.'

'That's the ticket Reid mentioned to Irene Fontaine?'

'Yes, the one he thought he saw Alma throw away.' He handed it to Drayton who bagged it. Underneath the ticket, however, was what Kirby had been hoping to find. The card had been folded in half and when he opened it he saw the drawing Reid had described of Kevin. 'Bingo,' he said. 'Alma's card to Kevin, the one Roye and Reid found in the garage.'

Drayton looked at him. 'So we've got her?'

Kirby carefully bagged the drawing and the card. 'If we can match the firelighters it might be enough.'

'Or if there are traces of ketamine on any of this,' said Drayton, as he did the same to the Tupperware box.

Kirby prayed this would be the case. He wanted to see Alma locked up for a very long time.

'Why'd she keep this stuff?' asked Drayton.

'They were precious to her. The card and the ticket reminded her of Kevin. When I visited Alma there was a broken picture frame in her kitchen, a montage of concert tickets and train tickets. I'll bet you anything there's a gap and this ticket will be a match. Reid must have seen it in her hallway and realised it was Kevin's ticket to freedom. No one else would have given it a second glance. Reid was the only person who knew they were going to Glasgow. When Alma made a show of throwing it into the wind she was bluffing.'

'Why?'

'She wanted Reid to know she knew he'd seen it. She'd also killed Jason by then so it could even have been a veiled threat.'

'We'll never be able to prove this was the ticket Kevin purchased,' said Drayton.

The ticket was nearly thirty years old and the boys would have paid in cash. Finding the cashier who sold the tickets would be virtually impossible. Even if Alma began talking, which Kirby didn't think she would, all she'd have to say was she'd planned to go to Glasgow for a gig and she didn't go. There was no one left to contradict her.

'Where'd the boys get the money? That ticket wasn't exactly cheap.'

'Reid said Jason knew all the hiding places on the estate. He could have stolen money from one of his father's stashes. Or perhaps they saved up – Kevin did have a paper round.'

'Or maybe someone helped them,' said Drayton. 'And why Glasgow? Where did Jason go when he got there? There's still a lot of unanswered questions.'

So far they'd managed to trace Jason Roye to some digs in Glasgow's Partick district where he'd rented a room under the name Jason McElroy. The last job they'd managed to link him to was at the Clair Ridge oil field west of Shetland, where his employers had told them he'd been an experienced rig worker who'd worked all over Scottish waters. Something Ted Harper said wormed its way into Kirby's mind. There was no signal in the garage, so he left Drayton going through the rest of Alma's things and went outside. He rounded the corner of Ullswater House and began walking towards the church where he finally got three bars on his phone.

'Ted, it's DI Lew Kirby.'

'What can I do for you? Only I'm about to go and pick up my daughter from the airport.'

'This will only take a minute. Walter Flynn. You said he did time up in Scotland?'

'Yeah – attempted abduction, indecent assault—'

'Okay, I get the picture. What job did he do?'

'He was a crane operator. Why?'

It had been a long shot but Kirby still felt disappointed. 'Nothing, it was just a hunch. I was wondering how Jason Roye managed when he arrived in Glasgow. How he survived, found work and so on.'

'Do you know what sort of work he did?' asked Harper.

'So far we've been able to connect him to work on the oil rigs. How he ended up there is anyone's guess. He didn't have a weekend job before he ran away so it'd be interesting to know where he got the money from to go. Stole it probably.'

Harper was silent for a moment. 'Not necessarily. Walter Flynn was an offshore crane operator, which meant he worked on the rigs, so he had a lot of connections in that world. Look, I've really got to go. If you need anything else I'll be home tonight.'

Kirby thanked Harper and hung up. So it was possible convicted paedophile Walter Flynn had helped Jason and Kevin with their plan to leave Grasmere. He'd have had contacts in Glasgow, some no doubt under the radar, who would have been only too happy to help two green sixteen-year-old boys on the run. The thought made his blood run cold. Maybe the vigilantes on the estate hadn't been entirely wrong about Flynn after all.

CHAPTER 65

Connie could hear her phone ringing from the main reading room – she must have left it in the kitchen after making coffee for Art and Irene. They were now both closeted in Bonaro's office, discussing money. Connie had been relieved when Irene said she wanted to talk to Art alone, although it had left her curious as to what Irene didn't want her to hear. By the time she retrieved the phone in the kitchen the call had gone to answerphone, leaving a missed call message on the screen. The caller's name made her look twice.

After he'd texted, Connie had saved Brian Kaplinsky's number just in case she ever decided to contact him again. She'd fully intended to, except Kirby had warned her off. He wouldn't give her a specific reason and had been vague, but he'd made it crystal clear that without some solid evidence approaching Kaplinsky again would land them both in deep shit. But now Kaplinsky had contacted her. What did he want – had he had a change of heart? She waited for a few moments hoping a voicemail alert would ping, but it didn't. '*Typical bloody arsehole,*' she mumbled to herself.

In the list of missed calls her finger hovered over Kaplinsky's number. Kirby had explicitly told her not to contact him, but all she was doing was returning his call – surely that couldn't do any harm? Without giving it any deeper thought she pressed 'call'.

The phone was answered almost immediately and an angry female voice crackled down the line. 'Are you having an affair with my husband?'

'*What?* Who is this?' asked Connie, taken aback.

'Are you, you filthy little bitch?'

'I don't know what you're talking about. You've made a mistake,' Connie replied firmly. 'I don't even know your husband.'

'You met him though, didn't you? In that sordid dump he was living in. I saw the text message so don't bother lying to me.'

Christ, she must have seen the message from Kaplinsky inviting her to the Ullswater House flat and assumed the worst. 'It's not what you think. If you let me explain I—'

'Explain? It's too late for that.' There was a pause on the other end of the line and Connie heard a noise she couldn't quite identify. 'Well, now you know I know. And you'll really wish I didn't.'

Was that a threat? 'If you'd just listen for a minute I can explain the text message. It's really not what you think.'

'That's what he always says,' said the woman, her initial anger dying down a little, revealing a brittle edge to her voice Connie liked even less. 'But you did meet him.'

Kirby had only threatened to tell Kaplinsky's wife about his suspicion that her husband had witnessed Sarah Darke's death at Blackwater but hadn't actually done it, and Connie wondered whether she had any idea about her husband's nocturnal visits to the derelict asylum with her sister. 'Yes, I did. He knew my sister. She died in an accident and I thought he might be able to shed some light on it.'

The woman was silent for a moment and Connie heard the door to Bonaro's office open a few feet away. Art's and Irene's voices drifted out.

'What was your sister's name?' asked Kaplinsky's wife.

'Sarah Darke. She died at the Blackwater Asylum – the derelict psychiatric hospital where your husband worked as a site manager.' The voices got louder as Art and Irene stepped into the corridor.

'What makes you think he knows anything about that?'

Connie took a deep breath. 'Because he was with her when the accident happened.' When the woman didn't say anything, Connie went on. 'He called an ambulance and left her there. I wanted to know why.'

There was a short pause. 'And what did he tell you?'

Art and Irene were now outside the kitchen door, stalled, thankfully, by Art telling Irene about a drawing hanging on the wall there. 'He told me someone else was there. That when Sarah fell from the water tower, someone had been up there with her—' The phone went dead just as Art and Irene entered the kitchen and she cursed silently.

'Connie!' said Art, who was beaming like a Cheshire cat. 'I think a celebration is in order.'

'Really?' Connie looked expectantly at Art and Irene. 'Have you come to an agreement?'

'We have,' said Irene. 'And I for one could do with a drink.' She banged her cane on the floor; a gesture Connie had learned over the last few weeks meant there was no argument to be had.

'There's a lovely trattoria just around the corner,' said Connie, the conversation with Kaplinsky's wife still buzzing in her head. Had she been deliberately cut off?

'The food's terribly good,' said Art, his eyes lighting up at the prospect of eating a meal without the watchful gaze of his wife telling him to mind the calories.

'Do they serve Fernet-Branca?' asked Irene.

'I'm sure they do,' said Connie, who had no idea whether they did or not, but the odds were good.

'In that case, let's go. Your coat, Irene?' Art led Irene out of the kitchen and back to the main reading room where she'd left it.

As soon as they'd gone, Connie called Kaplinsky's number back. '*The person you are calling is not available*,' said the automated voice. '*Please try again later*.' She tried again and the same thing happened. '*Shit!*' she said out loud.

'Everything alright?' Art had come back to the kitchen without Connie hearing and was watching her from the doorway.

'Yes, fine. Sorry.' Connie pocketed the phone, confused. What the hell had just happened?

'Come on then,' said Art. He was champing at the bit to go and eat. 'We have a lot to discuss.'

'Of course. Let's go.' As she followed him out of the kitchen Art paused, putting a hand on her arm.

'Where on earth did you find her?' he asked, referring to Irene. 'She's incredible, if not a little eccentric. And I'm saying that as a Blunt. We practically invented eccentricity.' He chuckled. 'But really, Connie,' he went on, the words barely registering. 'I owe you a huge debt of gratitude. Thanks to you the archive will be saved and secured for years to come . . .' His voice continued, but Connie was drifting in and out.

'Sorry, what?' Connie had missed the last part of what he'd said. All she could think about was the phone call and the gnawing sensation that Kaplinsky's wife knew something.

'The curatorship. It's yours if you want it.' He paused. 'You do want it, don't you?'

Connie could feel herself blushing. 'Of course I want it. Yes! There is one thing though.' She looked up to see Irene watching them from the doorway of the main reading room. 'Dan Quatremaine was keen on the job. I told him I'd talk to you about it.'

'Dan Quatremaine?' Art looked aghast. 'I wouldn't let that scoundrel run this place if my life depended on it. I could tell you

367

a thing or two about him, but now's not the time. The job is yours, Connie. End of story.'

'Thank you,' said Connie, smiling weakly. It wasn't that she wasn't pleased, she was over the moon, but a sickening thought had just occurred to her. What if Kaplinsky's wife had been the mysterious figure up the water tower? What if she—

Irene thumped her cane on the floor. 'Come on, or I'll be dead by the time we get there and you won't get your money!'

'So where did you find her?' whispered Art, as he and Connie went to join Irene.

'I . . . it's a long story, Art. A very long story.'

ACKNOWLEDGEMENTS

Thanks as ever to the fantastic team at Thomas & Mercer and Amazon Publishing, especially to Hannah Bond, whose editing skills are as enviable as they are terrifying, and Victoria Oundjian for running such a tight ship. Your patience has been laudable and all the pints in the world wouldn't be enough to express my gratitude adequately.

Thanks to the team at David Higham Associates, without whose support and encouragement I'd never have made it to the end. To Jane Gregory, agent past, who I appear to have driven to retirement, and agent present, Maddalena Cavaciuti, who I'll probably drive to drink. To super-editor Stephanie Glencross, who knows where the bodies are buried and who can locate weak plot points like a diviner can water. My thanks also to Jack Butler, without whom I wouldn't be writing this (you also have the patience of a saint).

At times – no, let's be honest, most of the time – writing *The Drowning Place* has lived up to its name. It's been a bumpy ride and I wouldn't have completed it without the support of friends and dogs, although the latter are adept obstacle throwers too, especially when they die unexpectedly (yes, I'm looking up at you, Pancho). As ever, special thanks must go to Nancy Candlin, who has kept me sane during the many (and I mean many) plot meltdowns I've had. You are my sounding board, for which I am ever grateful. Also, to her husband, the Reverend David Candlin for the Bible classes. Any mistakes on that front are mine and mine alone.

If the writing of this book has taught me one thing it's that if pushed you can achieve things you never thought possible. That if you go the extra mile, endure the sleepless nights and headfucks – you can do it.

ABOUT THE AUTHOR

Photo © Annie Peel Photography

S W Kane has a degree in History of Design and worked at the Royal Institute of British Architects before taking on a series of totally unrelated jobs in radio and the music industry. She has an MA in Creative (Crime) Writing from City University. She began reading crime fiction at an early age and developed an obsession with crime set in cold places. A chance encounter with a derelict fort in rural Pembrokeshire led to a fascination with urban exploration, which in turn became the inspiration for her crime novels. She lives in London.

Follow the Author on Amazon

If you enjoyed this book, follow S W Kane on Amazon to be notified when the author releases a new book!
To do this, please follow these instructions:

Desktop:

1) Search for the author's name on Amazon or in the Amazon App.
2) Click on the author's name to arrive on their Amazon page.
3) Click the 'Follow' button.

Mobile and Tablet:

1) Search for the author's name on Amazon or in the Amazon App.
2) Click on one of the author's books.
3) Click on the author's name to arrive on their Amazon page.
4) Click the 'Follow' button.

Kindle eReader and Kindle App:

If you enjoyed this book on a Kindle eReader or in the Kindle App, you will find the author 'Follow' button after the last page.